The
Time for Vengeance

The Displacers Series

Book 5

Simon Brading

First published 2017

This edition published 2025

Cover design by Andrėja Dikšaitytė

www.forgottenscriptorium.com

ISBN: 978-1-917470-54-4

For James.

PROLOGUE

Paris, 1830

The man and woman fled hand in hand through the dark Paris streets, slipping on cobblestones that were wet from the winter mists. They were out of breath, terrified, continually looking behind them while they staggered along, clutching at each other for comfort, trying to find somewhere safe. All they needed was a few seconds - a brief moment of peace and quiet would be enough for them to escape. There was none for them, though, because whenever they paused or showed signs of slowing the Beast would appear from the dark of the night. It didn't matter which way they went, which random corners they turned, it was there waiting for them every time.

It was stalking them.

Playing with them.

Less than an hour before *they* had been the predators, taking what they wanted and preying on the weak, but now they were running for their lives, that night's job abandoned and their underlings lying broken in the house a dozen streets back.

It was an easy target, ripe for the picking, a three-storey townhouse, whose owner, a disgustingly rich merchant, was away on business for a few months and had left it in the care of just an elderly gardener and a single maid. It was to be one last enjoyable night of looting and destruction before taking their accumulated wealth and delivering it to the man who had sent them there.

Expecting a large haul from such an opulent home, they had brought their entire gang, twenty of them in total, all of whom were perfectly capable of taking care of themselves and dealing with any eventuality that arose, including fighting their way out of trouble if the alarm was raised.

Or so they'd thought.

After disposing of the two guardians the gang had free rein of the house and split up to go through the place faster, quickly and expertly rounding up anything and everything of value.

And then someone, some *thing*, started taking them out one by one.

The men were brought down so silently that at first the others had no clue that anything untoward was happening, but that in no way satisfied the Beast; it wanted noise, it wanted chaos, so it dragged its fourth victim to the landing at the very top of the staircase and sent it screaming into the void.

Even before the unfortunate man had landed in a crumpled heap in the entrance hallway and fallen suddenly silent, the Beast had leapt up onto the thin wooden beam of the banisters at the top of the stairs. It balanced there, preternaturally still, ignoring the ten-metre drop only millimetres away, and spread its arms wide to welcome the man's companions when they came to investigate.

The thugs emerged at the run from all sides, only to come skidding to a halt as soon as they caught sight of the figure, glowing eerily in the shaft of moonlight coming through a large skylight directly over its head.

A few of their fellow thieves, muggers and murderers had gone missing over the last months and they'd heard rumours, gruesome tales of some creature stalking the night, of a *Beast* that killed anyone who meant harm to others. Nobody had ever glimpsed anything more than a shadow in the corner of an eye before it was gone, though and they hadn't given much credence to the rumours until that moment when they realised the significance of the twisted body at the bottom of the stairs. However, their shock lasted only a few seconds before they came to a sudden realisation: the so-called Beast, the thing from their nightmares that they'd been so afraid of, was not some supernatural demon, come to carry them all to hell; it was flesh and blood.

It was just a man.

And a man could be killed.

Their fear dissipated, replaced by the courage imparted by vastly outnumbering their adversary, and they rushed at the man, streaming up the stairs to come at him from all sides, knives and cudgels out, thirsting for the blood of the person who had killed so many of their own.

Weapons flashed in the moonlight, but missed their target as the man moved, flowing impossibly quickly through his attackers. The Beast was a thing of the darkness, an animal, and their blows had no effect on it as it swept through them like a gale, knocking them down one by one by one by one, until it was only the man and woman, the leaders of the gang, the biggest, toughest and strongest of all of them, left watching from the foot of the stairs.

It calmly jumped back up onto the banisters and gazed down at them.

Silent. Still. Menacing.

They ran from it.

The houses spread out and the streets opened up as the couple reached the river and there they spotted what could be their salvation: the huge, square-towered shape looming on the island just across the water - the cathedral, with the sanctuary, safety and, more importantly, time that a locked door and its fortifications might afford them.

They were spurred on by the sight and ran across the bridge, their heavy footsteps thundering on the stone, the sound dulled only slightly by the curling mists rising around them from the river that brought frightening phantasms with them.

The doors of the cathedral were wide open and inviting, warm light spilling out along with the angelic sounds of a choir at practice. A last effort on failing legs took them across the square and they spilled into the church, spinning to slam the doors shut behind them. A heavy bar was on the floor to one side, dusty from perhaps a decade of disuse, and they lifted it into place, slamming it into rusty brackets.

They backed away, fighting for breath and clutching at one another for comfort, their eyes not leaving the huge doors.

Behind them the choir had faltered at the noise of the doors and the priest now approached, his shoes clicking on the stone floor the only sound in the cavernous space. 'What is the meaning of this? Why have you barred the entrance?'

The man turned to him and gathered enough breath to force out a single word. 'Monster.'

The priest's scornful look was banished instantly as the door shook with the impact of a titanic blow.

The man spun back to the door and scrabbled for the hand that the woman offered.

Behind them, the priest fled, taking with him the choir of small boys and leaving through a door at the far end of the cathedral.

Too late the pair realised that there was another way out, that they could have gone with the priest, could have asked for the protection of the church, could have done anything except just stand waiting for the beast to come for them.

The thought occurred to them both at the same time and they linked hands, putting their heads down and squeezing their eyes shut as if in prayer, seizing at their last chance.

Their concentration was broken almost instantly as a stained glass window above them to one side of the small rose window exploded and the Beast tumbled to the floor next to them in a dark heap.

They backed away, retreating into the nave, knowing there was nowhere to go, but still mindlessly wanting to put distance between them and it, like animals confronted by a predator.

The dark form uncurled, revealing a surprisingly young man.

The Beast laughed at them; they had thought they were safe in the cathedral with the door barred behind them, but they didn't know that it had herded them here - this was its lair, a vantage point from which to watch them as they guided their little group in their criminal endeavours, expanding their influence over the Paris underworld.

The laughter swelled, filling the cavernous space, but then, as abruptly as it had begun, it stopped, and when the echoes had finally faded, the Beast spoke.

'You know, you could have just jumped into the river.' The words came out as a barely intelligible growl, full of menace, but it was the darkness and fury in the man's eyes which caused the pair to step back involuntarily.

The Beast saw the movement and grinned malevolently. 'Now, are you going to do as I say, or are we going to have some fun?'

Sam Vives had waited more than three months for "the Twins", a brother and sister pair of Illuminati agents, to make their move. The woman, Tessa, had needed that time to recover from a serious injury before Displacing, or Leaping, as the Illuminati called it. Finally, though, they had gone and he had followed.

However, as soon as he had arrived he had given himself over to the *Beast*, to let *it* do what needed to be done.

The Twins began by putting together a gang of the roughest men and women they could find in the Parisian underworld, the ones that didn't bat an eyelid at the brutal tactics they proposed. They dealt ruthlessly with any reluctance or challenges to their authority and very quickly consolidated their hold on all major criminal activity within the city.

As soon as that was done, they embarked on a wave of violence and thievery unprecedented in Paris since the Viking invasion. Any efforts on the part of the gendarmes to stop them were met with such merciless ferocity and reprisals that the authorities were cowed into submission and they soon had free rein of the night.

They revelled in the terror they engendered, turning a once peaceful city into a nervous wreck that barred its doors at night and pulled the bedclothes tight for fear of being noticed.

For three months the Beast did nothing to interfere with them. It just watched, trying to discern whether there was a wider plan behind their looting, some objective that wasn't simply the accumulation of wealth. He couldn't find one, though, so in the end he came to the conclusion that there wasn't, that they had been sent just to fill the coffers of the Illuminati and had decided to have as much fun as they could while they did so. It suspected that they liked making people afraid, that it was their idea of a holiday.

Finally it had run out of patience and decided that it was time to act - if they wanted fear, it was going to give it to them.

Unmindful of the spiritual nature of the place he'd chosen to confront them, the Beast pushed greasy hair, unwashed since it had been in Paris, out of its eyes and surveyed its prey - Tristan and Tessa, the Twins, brutish enforcers for the Illuminati.

There was history between them and Vives - two violent confrontations with vastly different outcomes. The first had been a beating inflicted while Vives had been their captive, but the most recent had been on a much more equal footing and had resulted in the recent injuries to Tessa and an ignominious retreat.

That day, driven by the loss of his uncle, murdered by the treachery of the Illuminati leader, the so-called Master, Vives had taken his first, most important, step towards releasing what had always been lurking inside him and harvesting his rage at will by giving himself over to the Beast.

Undoubtedly, the two thought that their defeat in South Africa had been because they'd been distracted and caught off-guard, but the Beast knew they were mistaken in that belief; Vives' victory over them had been fuelled by fury at what they'd done to the woman he loved and the outcome would have been the same no matter how much time they'd had to prepare.

The Twins were used to getting their own way and went through life enforcing their will with an iron fist and no mercy. Today, however, they had met something far more violent, more ruthless and more deadly than them and it could feel their fear pulsing from them in waves.

Would they turn out to be typical bullies and give in at the first sign of resistance?

The Beast hoped not; he was fully aware that control over its body had only been temporarily ceded to him by Sam Vives and hadn't had nearly enough fun yet.

The movement was subtle, a mere curling of the fingers of the brother, but the Beast caught it and knew that it signalled their intention to fight.

Vives would have waited for them to make their move, but it wasn't so noble. Or so stupid.

It sank into its rage and attacked. They fell back, cowed by its fury as it flew at them, lips curled into a snarl. Blow after blow came in retaliation, but it just took them and shrugged them off, ignoring the pain and paying it back on them tenfold.

It was a force of nature, a whirlwind, and they could do nothing to stop it.

Benches broke, candles fell, and statues toppled as they fought their way down the nave and, somewhat appropriately, it was at the altar that things ended.

The Twins broke and fell to their knees, bowing down, not before the figure gazing down in pity at them from the cross, but before the dark-eyed Beast, growling above them, not *just* a man after all, but something more - something worse.

Slowly, the murderous light faded from its eyes as the Beast retreated, its task complete, and Sam straightened slowly from his crouch.

'I can feel it when you come into the past, that's how I followed you here, and I will be waiting for you if you or any of your Illuminati friends ever do so again. This is the only warning that you or they are going to get so spread the word: if I catch *any* of you again I will kill you.'

He glared at them and they nodded in understanding, heads that were battered and bloody bobbing briefly, painfully.

'But tell John, tell your *Master...*' He spat the word with contempt, putting all of the hatred he felt into it. 'Tell him and Quentin that I don't care what they do; I'm coming for them and I am going to destroy them, no matter what. For them there will be no choice, no warning, and no mercy.'

Not long ago these two would have laughed his words off as an empty threat, and rightly so, but there was a hard look in his eyes that the Twins knew only too well - killing meant little to him now; he had changed and was no longer the soft boy they had picked on in Victorian London. The fact that most of the men back in the townhouse wouldn't get up until after he'd left attested to that.

They cowered from the death they saw in his eyes as he loomed over them and the Beast writhed within Sam, trying to wrest control and finish them, but he forced it back with an effort; he needed them alive. At least for a little longer.

'Go.'

The word was whispered, barely audible in that huge temple to an uncaring god, but it served as a pistol shot to the Twins and they bolted, following in the footsteps of the priest and choir.

Sam didn't watch them go, instead he stared up at the crucifix.

A shiver up his spine told him they had left and the tension finally drained from him. He slumped to his knees, finally allowing himself to acknowledge his pain, and threw his head back to howl out all his rage, fury and grief, filling the vast space with a primal sound, an out-letting of the emotions he'd denied himself.

He could feel the Beast's approval, but it remained quiescent, content with what had been given to it, knowing that its time would come again.

Eventually, his voice, barely used in months, faltered and his throat became raw. He fell silent and peace come flooding back into the vast space, chasing away the echoes of his anguish. Try as he might, though, he couldn't find it within himself.

He remained where he was, head bowed, staring at the blood covering his hands, but then, when a pounding on the door and the shouts of gendarmes filled the cathedral with noise once more, he closed his eyes and let the river of time carry him home.

Sam opened his eyes and looked up at the multitude of stars in a black sky that was only faintly polluted with orange. He hadn't bothered to put up a tent; July nights in Spain were warm enough to go without, even here in the north, near the Pyrenees, and besides, in Sparta he'd made do with much less than a sleeping bag.

He lay still, gazing at the beautiful sky and letting the sounds of the night surround him while he catalogued his aches and pains. He hadn't come through the Displacement anything like unscathed, but neither had he wanted to; this had been as much a purging of his own soul as it had been of the time-line and he welcomed the sensations from his battered body, feeling more alive than he had in months.

Usually he couldn't wait to Displace, especially with Rachel, and did so whenever he could, but this had only been his second trip into the past since John and Quentin had sprung their trap at Easter; after Andrew's death things had changed. *He* had changed.

He had cut his ties to Rachel and the other Displacers, even going so far as to ignore his duties to the Society, and had shut out everything except his desire for vengeance, becoming consumed with it. Even the lure of excitement and adventure hadn't been enough and had bided his time, remaining in the present, conserving his energy. Finally, after three long months of waiting patiently for his chance, it had come and he had followed the Twins to Paris.

He'd hoped that the time in Paris would help him to forget, would drive the images of that day from his mind. He'd also hoped that giving himself over to the *Beast* and allowing it to carry out mindless violence against the two Illuminati would cleanse him, would be a healing catharsis for the grief and shame within him, but it hadn't, and the memories came flooding back, unbidden and unwelcome.

CHAPTER 1
BAD MEMORIES

London, April

'Andrew is dead.'

Before the words were even out of his grandfather's mouth, Sam was off the sofa and running from the room. He didn't hear Rachel's cry of alarm, or see James drop his phone and clutch his chest; he was in too much of a hurry, his every thought focussed firmly on his uncle.

Displacer Headquarters was less than a mile away from the safe house and he made it there in a little over three minutes. The code on the door provided an unwelcome delay, but it was a slight one and only seconds later he flung the door open then sprinted across the hallway and up the stairs without even his customary glance at the wooden plaques on the wall. On the first floor landing he crashed into a man coming the other way and they both went flying, but he just rolled back to his feet and raced on without so much as apologising.

He came across a few more members on the stairs and landings of the second and third floor and a couple of them turned to him, demanding answers, but he dodged past them, ignoring their questions.

A group had gathered on the landing of the fourth floor and were peering through the open door of the bedroom where Andrew and John had shut themselves away to do their planning and Displacement. He forced his way through them and burst into the room, but then skidded to a halt in shock and stared, horrified, at what he found.

Philip was in an armchair to one side near the door. He was white as a sheet and gently shaking, his head cradled in his hands. Lisa was staring out of the window on the far side of the room, a phone held loosely and forgotten at her side, a tinny voice was coming from it, calling for her attention.

Sam barely noticed them, though, because it was the tragic tableau in the middle of the room that caught and held his attention.

Anne was sitting on the floor in the middle of a spreading pool of blood, rocking back and forth as tears poured down her cheeks and bawling inconsolably as she cradled Andrew's motionless form against her. A huge knife, almost a sword, was lying discarded next to them, almost submerged in the viscous liquid that was still seeping from a gash in his uncle's chest.

'No...'

At the sound of his voice, Anne seemed to come to herself and she peered up at him through watery eyes as red as the blood covering her. The sorrow fled her face, instantly replaced by a look of sheer hatred that had Sam rocking back on his heels. 'It was John,' she spat. 'He's the Master.'

Sam's eyes widened at the name. 'The Master? John? But...'

His brain caught up with his body in that moment and he realised who the man he'd knocked over on the first floor landing had been.

John.

He growled and spun on his heels, then pushed his way roughly back through the growing crowd outside the door. He careered down the stairs at a reckless pace, taking them four at a time, heedless of his own safety, then ran out of the front door and leapt up onto the wall separating the small front garden from the street. He stood there, balancing precariously, craning his neck to see over the heads of the civilians.

As always there was a fair amount of foot traffic so near central London and there were dozens of people wandering past - tourists, locals, businessmen and women, but there was no sign among them of an overweight and balding man in a royal blue t-shirt printed with a picture of the TARDIS from Doctor Who.

One direction was as good as any so he decided to head for the nearest Tube station at Hyde Park Corner.

Having to weave around the people was slowing him down too much, so he leapt off the pavement and ran along the gutter, ignoring the horns from the angry drivers. He was in no danger of being hit, though; he was going much faster than the afternoon traffic.

He got to the end of the road where it met the large roundabout and veered straight across without looking, causing more chaos as a car swerved to avoid him and came screeching to a halt. He weaved through a large crowd of Japanese tourists taking photos, then leapt onto the Royal Artillery Monument and climbed up next to the howitzer, clinging to its barrel as he scanned the open area around the Wellington Arch.

Nothing.

The tube station was nearby, though, perhaps he had gone there. If he hurried, maybe he could still catch him before the next train...

'Oi, you! Get down from there, you silly bugger!'

Sam glanced down to find a policeman, a sergeant in his late thirties, scowling up at him.

He took one last look around, then dropped the more than twenty feet down to land next to him, making him step back in alarm and fumble involuntarily at his belt for his baton before he stopped himself. Another policeman, a younger officer, came from around the side of the monument and joined him in staring at Sam, flanking him, trying to intimidate him.

The sergeant eyed Sam warily. 'Right, then, perhaps you'd like to explain...'

'Sorry, but I have no time for you right now.'

He turned and started to go, but the man reached out and grabbed him by the collar.

'No you don't sunshine, you're coming with us!'

Sam looked down at the hand holding him, then up at the policeman, giving the man a weak smile.

It was extremely easy to get out of the grip and even easier to avoid the flailing attempts that both men made to catch him and in seconds he was racing towards the tube station.

The policemen wouldn't give up, though, and shouted as they ran after him, calling the attention of the passers-by. Sam quickly realised that there was now no way he was going to get down to the platforms in time to find John, and even if he did there would likely be more police in the station and they would never stand idly by and let him deal with the man.

He slowed his steps, feigning tiredness, allowing the policemen to catch up with him, then, just as they dived at him, he reversed course abruptly and slipped between them.

If the circumstances hadn't been so tragic he would have smiled at the curses from the two men as they stumbled over each other in their attempts to catch him.

He easily outpaced them as he retraced his steps towards the Society, but now there were the sounds of sirens in the air and two motorcycles with flashing blue lights appeared around the roundabout, cutting through the traffic towards him.

'No!' He renewed his efforts, trying to watch his pursuers over his shoulder while simultaneously dodging around pedestrians. Headquarters was only a couple of hundred metres away and if he could get there someone would be able to explain why he was climbing on public property like some drunken football fan and resisting arrest, it wouldn't just be the word of a boy who probably looked guilty as hell and dishevelled after so much running.

He was only about fifty metres away from his objective when one the bikes cut across in front of him. He jerked to the side and managed to avoid it, but the second one was there to block him and its rider snatched at him, slowing him down just long enough for the first rider to dump his bike and leap athletically onto his back.

They went down in a heap and there was a brilliant burst of light as Sam's head hit the pavement, stunning him.

'Stay still, lad, don't make this worse on yourself.' The man's hot breath was right against his ear as his arms were pulled behind him.

Even at such a disadvantage, it would have been easy enough to get out of the lock, but the second biker now joined the first, placing a knee on the back of Sam's head, causing fresh lights to flash behind his eyes and a burning sensation in his cheek as it was ground into the road.

He tensed his muscles, ready to do what he could to break free, but then the realisation hit him that there was no point; he hadn't been able to save Andrew and John had gotten away - there was nothing more to be done and it wasn't worth calling any more attention to himself and the Society than he already had.

He relaxed, not making even a cursory effort to get free, and resigned himself to a trip to the local police station. He just hoped it wouldn't be too long before his grandfather could use his influence to get him released so he could start work on tracking down John.

'Constables! I'll take it from here, thank you!'

The thinly disguised order came from the direction of Headquarters and was accompanied by the sound of dress shoes clacking on the pavement as someone jogged up to them. Sam tried to turn his head to look at the source of the voice, but the policeman's knee kept him pinned to the pavement and prevented him from doing so.

'What? But...'

'I said, I'll take over. Thank you. Now, please let him up.'

The voice was quintessentially British; calm, but insistent, brooking no argument, and Sam was roughly dragged to his feet and spun in place to face a man in a black suit.

He was in his mid-thirties, well over six-foot, with light-brown hair and piercing blue eyes. He reminded Sam very much of Daniel Craig in the Bond films although he didn't have the permanent pout the actor seemed to have. He was holding a rather stereotypical ID badge in a small black wallet out for the motorbike policemen to read and when the two uniformed officers who had chased Sam finally stomped up he moved his arm without bothering to look at them so that they could see it too. The two men peered at the badge with dismay and stood panting, fighting for breath, obviously rather annoyed to have been denied their prize.

The agent put the badge away in his inside breast pocket, then beckoned to Sam. 'This way, please, Mr Vives. My companions can deal with these fine officers while I escort you to the scene.'

'Scene?' The word shook Sam out of his stupor somewhat and for the first time he noticed the commotion around Headquarters - there were multiple police cars blocking the road, but there was also an ambulance and a familiar SUV with blacked out windows drawn up on the pavement outside the building itself. 'Oh.'

'Indeed.'

The man said nothing more as he led Sam along the middle of the road, making sure that he stayed close to him to prevent questions and further misunderstandings as they went past gawking pedestrians who were in the process of being herded away by uniformed policemen. They were waved through a cordon that had already been put in place Headquarters and went up the stairs and into the house.

The man closed the door firmly behind them and made sure nobody was around before turning to Sam and finally speaking to him. 'Right, then, now we're alone we can get down to business. First things first - did you find him? Did you see which way he went?'

Sam shook his head, mutely.

'Damn, it would have been nice to get an idea of which way the bastard was heading and how.'

The agent looked genuinely annoyed and Sam found himself warming to him, despite his cool exterior. He struggled to find his voice. 'What are you going to do to find him?'

'Half of all MI5 agents have already been taken off whatever they were working on and mobilised into a taskforce for this. Surveillance is being set on all of the perpetrator's known properties in case he shows up at any of them and his British bank accounts have been frozen, although I doubt he'll be stupid enough to ever touch those again; he's probably got most of his assets stashed offshore in some tax haven. CCTV is working to locate him and we've also put an alert out for him in all ports and airports, but again it's unlikely anything will come from that because he probably had a plan in place for this eventuality and some other way of getting out of the country.' The agent shrugged. 'Honestly, I'm not hopeful and if we don't get him in the next hour or so, it's unlikely we ever will, sorry.'

Sam sighed without much real disappointment because he had already assumed as much, after all he and Rachel had learned from Jacques how easy it was to avoid the detection of the authorities without any resources, it was only going to be easier with the essentially infinite ones available to the Illuminati. If they were ever going to catch John, they were going to have to rely on someone making a mistake or on intel from Diana.

Sam was so caught up in his own thoughts that he was slow to notice that the man was peering around curiously, alternately taking in the name plaques, the various souvenirs on display from Displacements, and the crest above the front door that was a replica of the one outside. He wondered whether a man in his line of work should really be in Headquarters and free to look around. 'Um... How much do you know about, uh, well, *us?*'

'Your Society? The work you do here? Not much I'm afraid. As one of the agents on permanent standby to deal with you I have access only to some very sparse personnel files. All I know is that you do important work that has to be kept top secret. Oh, and that you hold one *hell* of a lot of clout.' He smiled and held out his hand. 'My name is Carter, by the way.'

Sam took the hand and shook it briefly, feeling the impressive strength of the man's grip, which almost equalled his own, but didn't come anywhere near Rachel's. 'Um, I was told by one of your colleagues in Barcelona that it would be better for me not to know any names...'

Carter chuckled briefly. 'That's S.O.P. for Six; they're a bit uptight like that sometimes. I'm Five and we play by slightly different rules. Besides, Carter isn't my real name - it's just the one I've been assigned for this operation.'

'Oh. OK.'

They looked up as another black-suited man came down the stairs. He was carrying the large knife that Andrew had been killed with in a clear plastic bag and held it up so that his companion could see it.

Sam looked at the bloody weapon and swallowed. He closed his eyes, feeling suddenly sick, as the memory of his uncle's body lying in the huge pool of viscous red liquid came rushing back to him.

'Poor fellow never had a chance; the blade went right through his...' The man stopped as he saw Sam's reaction.

Carter nodded towards the exit and spoke into the ensuing silence. 'I'll join you outside in a while, Agent Ross.'

'Yes, sir.' The man shot Sam an apologetic look, then went out the door.

'I should be going as well,' Agent Carter said, 'there's nothing I can do here and I'm better served coordinating the teams. Here,' he handed Sam a white card that was blank apart from a telephone number. 'If you turn up anything, or you need something, just call. Use the codeword "Society" and you'll be put through to someone on the taskforce.'

'Can I give you my number so you can ring me with what you find?'

The agent smiled. 'No need, we already have it. And don't worry; I'll make sure you're kept informed.'

'Thank you.'

'It's the least we can do.'

Carter held out his hand again and Sam took it. They shook, but the man didn't let him go, instead he held on as he leaned in to speak to Sam in a soft voice. 'We'll catch him, I'm sure of it.'

He gave Sam's hand a last reassuring squeeze then went out into the noise and chaos that was the street outside.

Sam watched the door close behind him, then just stood staring at it, unsure what he should do next. He turned, thinking to find the other members, but his eyes alighted on the name plaques and he noticed that John's name was still in place on the wall. He snarled and tore it off its peg, then hurled it down the hallway, putting all his anger into the throw. It clattered loudly against the dining room doors and shattered into several pieces, which flew off in all directions.

Something broke in him then and he staggered, his legs giving out under him as the exertions of the Displacement and the sprint across London finally caught up with him. He hit the wall hard and slid down, landing heavily on his knees. He bent over and put his forehead on the floor, wrapping his arms around himself as he began sobbing, unable to control himself for some reason.

'Hello?' The door on the other side of the hallway opened and he heard the tentative voice of a woman, investigating the source of the noise that the heavy wooden nameplate had made hitting the doors.

'Sam?'

He looked up through tear-clouded eyes and saw Julia poking her head out of the sitting room, looking down at him with an expression of surprise that quickly turned to sympathy.

Sam didn't know her very well; she wasn't often around because she was usually busy, working towards her doctorate in psychology at Oxford University. He had seen her online a few times, during the occasional conference call on Skype, but only ever met her in person once, at the Christmas dinner. She was in town for the Easter holidays and Sam had been looking forwards to finding out more about her and the other Displacers he hadn't met before at the dinner the Society was supposed to be having that evening.

She hesitantly came out of the sitting room, closing the door behind her and knelt down beside him, reaching out to put a hand on his shoulder.

Sam brought himself under control as best as he could. He wiped his eyes and looked up at her, forcing a smile. 'Sorry, I think I might have scratched the woodwork.'

'What?' She glanced in the direction that Sam was looking and saw the pieces of the wooden plaque on the floor. One of the bigger chunks had rebounded almost to where they were and the letters "ohn" could be clearly read on it. She smiled in understanding. 'Ah.'

The smile faded instantly as she looked into his red eyes, seeing the pain in them. 'Why don't you come into the sitting room? Everybody's there and you shouldn't be alone right now.'

Sam nodded and let her help him up then followed her into the sitting room.

There were more than a dozen members there, but instead of being spread out around the room they were gathered together near the door and as he came in, what quiet conversation there had been died out immediately.

He met their eyes one by one, seeing the confusion and doubt in their expressions, and realised that they almost certainly had no idea what was going on. He also saw that they were hoping that he could tell them something, anything and he opened his mouth to do so, but stopped when he realised that two people were missing.

'Where are James and Rachel? Didn't they follow me here?' It had been almost an hour since the Displacement, more than enough time for them to have arrived, even with the traffic and the police cordon.

'Maybe they're upstairs with Lisa and Philip.' Richard said softly from a nearby armchair.

'I have to find them...'

Sam turned to go, but Julia stopped him with a hand on his arm. 'Can you tell us what's going on first? Please? None of us know... Just that there was blood, and... Is Andrew really...?' She swallowed, unable to finish the sentence.

He looked around the room again, wondering how he could tell them, what he should say. In the end he decided that the best thing was to be straight with them. 'I'm sorry. He's dead.'

There were gasps from around the room and several of the members turned away or closed their eyes. To Sam's surprise a few of them even made religious gestures.

'It was John. He's the Master. He killed Andrew.'

All noise died off at the news and the sorrow on many of the faces was replaced by shock.

'I'm sorry, I can't say any more right now, I'm not... I can't...' Sam shook his head, not quite sure what else to say. 'I'm sorry.' His voice croaked as the tears threatened to come again and he hurried out before they could question him further; he needed Rachel, needed her comforting embrace.

Julia came after him and caught hold of his arm him just outside the door. 'Sam. If you ever need to talk...'

'Thank you.' He smiled at her briefly, then turned and ran up the stairs. He headed for the fourth floor, but was stopped on the landing of the third floor by a couple of policemen.

'Sorry, sir, but you can't go up there.'

'Please, I really need to speak to my friends.'

He tried to push past, but the men continued to block his way. They looked at him, not unkindly, obviously quite aware of what was going on and seeing how it was affecting him. 'Sorry, son, it's nothing personal; it's a crime scene now. We can't let you go up until we get the all clear from forensics.'

'Can one of you at least go and ask...' Sam stopped when he saw Lisa coming down the stairs. She was wearing some kind of boiler suit instead of her own clothes; they had been blood-stained so they were probably in the possession of the police already.

'Lisa! Can you ask Rachel to come down and see me?'

Lisa frowned. 'I thought you knew; Rachel said she'd sent you a message.'

Sam patted his pockets, but his phone wasn't there; he'd left it back in the safe house. 'I didn't get it.'

She reached out to put her hand on his arm.

'What is it? What else has happened?' He thought back to when he'd ran out of the safe house, replaying the events in his mind, pulling them out of his unconscious, using observation techniques taught him by Master Hamato. He heard, as if for the first time, the cry of alarm from Rachel and saw James collapsing back into his chair, his hand over his heart.

'Grandad?' He could feel the tears welling up again. 'Is he...?

'He's going to be fine, Sam. Rachel got him an ambulance and they took him to Chelsea and Westminster Hospital. It was just an angina attack. They don't think it's anything serious, but they're going to be holding him under observation for a while.'

Sam couldn't believe it; the day was just getting worse, the nightmare never ending.

His legs were trembling again and there was a strange new tingling sensation in his chest. He turned to clutch at the banisters, leaning on them as a darkness closed in on him from all sides and he felt himself slipping.

'Steady there!' He felt strong hands grab him and help him gently to the floor and he looked up into the kind face of one of the policemen.

'Deep breaths, son, it's only a little panic attack. You've had a big day by all accounts - maybe you should lie down for a while.'

'I can't, I need to get to the hospital. My grandfather...'

'You're in no state to go anywhere. Why don't you give it a couple of hours, have a lie down?'

Sam shook his head and tried to stand, but his limbs wouldn't obey him and he flopped back onto his arse.

The policeman looked down at him. He searched Sam's face, then shook his head and sighed before turning to his companion. 'We got a stubborn one here, you alright on yer tod for a while, Bill?'

The other man nodded. 'All covered, Ian.'

The policeman, Ian, turned back to Sam and pulled him bodily to his feet with a hand under each of his arms, then supported him as they went down the stairs.

'Come on then. There's a couple of cars still outside, one of them'll give us a lift.'

'Thank you.'

Sam felt stronger with each step he took and by the time they reached the ground floor he was walking almost unaided.

Ian stopped them in the hallway. 'Wait here; I'll see what I can get for us.' He went out of the door.

Sam turned to Lisa. 'Everyone's in there,' he pointed at the sitting room. 'I told them about Andrew and John, but apart from that they have no idea what's going on. I couldn't tell them... I didn't know how to explain... would you...?'

'Of course, Sam. Leave it to me. Give my love to James, please, tell him we're thinking of him.'

'I will and I'll be back as soon as I can.'

'No rush; everything's taken care of. You be with your family.'

'You're all my family.'

She smiled at him. 'We know, Sam.'

Ian shielded Sam from the dozens of TV cameras and journalists which were now clustered outside Headquarters and bundled him into the back of a police car to go tearing headlong through the evening traffic, sirens blaring. In only a matter of minutes they were pulling up outside the entrance of the hospital and the policeman accompanied Sam inside. He flagged down a nurse and had a quiet word with her while Sam shifted from foot to foot, wanting nothing more than to go running through the corridors, shouting Rachel's name. He knew it wouldn't be the best of ideas, though; he'd already pushed his luck far enough with the authorities for one day.

Thankfully, Sam's patience wasn't tested too far, because Ian soon finished and turned back to him. 'I have to be getting back, but I'll leave you in the capable hands of Miss Peters here. I hope your grandfather is alright.'

Sam wasn't in so much of a hurry that he couldn't appreciate the lengths that the man had gone for him and he stuck out his hand. 'Thank you. For everything.'

'You're welcome.' The man gave him a warm smile, nodded to the hovering nurse, then left.

The nurse, a dark-haired woman who looked only a couple of years older than Sam, took him through to the emergency department and showed him into a small room where he found his grandfather lying in bed in a darkened room, hooked up to several machines.

In the dim light James looked so fragile and grey that for a second he thought the worst, but when the old man turned at the sound of the door and smiled in welcome his eyes were as clear and bright as ever. Then, when those eyes flicked to the side and he scowled at the nurse, any remaining doubts Sam had were completely dispelled. 'Have you come to get me out of this hellhole, sister? I've got better things to do than lie around all day and believe me, I'm not considering dying any time soon.'

'You'll be released as soon as we've got some fluids in you and are sure you're stable, Mr Hudson.'

James grumbled something inaudible in reply and the nurse smiled at him amiably, but then turned serious when she looked at Sam. 'And you. Mr Vives is it? The nice policeman said you'd had a bit of a turn, so we're going to do a few tests on you too. That's also a nasty graze you've got on your cheek - we'll have to get that cleaned up for you.'

Sam reached up to touch his face. He hadn't even realised that he'd been hurt when the motorcycle police had knocked him to the ground. 'I'm fine, it was just...'

The nurse tutted and shook her head. 'No arguments. Sit down and someone will be in as soon as possible.'

Her expression brooked no arguments, so he nodded. 'Yes, ma'am.'

She grunted in satisfaction and gave him a big grin. 'Good. I was beginning to think that stubbornness ran in your family...'

Sam shot a bemused look at James as the nurse left, but before he could say anything, a heavy weight hit him in the side, almost knocking him off his feet. He'd been so focussed on his grandfather that he hadn't noticed Rachel standing behind the door and when it had closed she'd hurled herself on him, wrapping her arms around him.

She broke down into tears and Sam lasted only seconds before joining her.

A different nurse came in to take Sam's pressure and clean up what turned out to be only a tiny scratch on his cheek. Then, all that was left to do was wait for James' results to come back. Thankfully, he was declared to be fine, but they still kept him for a few hours, despite his steadily worsening temper, before releasing him.

The three of them took a taxi back to Headquarters where Sam immediately fell into a deep sleep on a sofa in the sitting room and didn't wake until a full twenty-four hours later, despite Society life going on around him and a recurring nightmare of blood and flashing blades, which had him tossing and turning every few hours.

CHAPTER 2
GOING THROUGH THE MOTIONS

The funeral took place three days after Andrew's death. A coach, rented for the day, took the entire Society up to the little church in the village near the Price estate in the morning, then brought them back to Headquarters after a subdued lunch for a traditional Displacer wake - with some ceremony, his photo was hung up on the wall in the sitting room next to Susan's portrait, then everybody gathered around it to tell stories about him and read from his mission reports before they were sent to the archive.

When they filed into the dining room for dinner afterwards, Sam had been presented to the new member, a weedy fourteen-year-old with glasses and messy black hair called Dylan Lloyd, who hadn't been able to come to the funeral because of school. He was a descendant of the Everett Lloyd whose diaries Sam had been reading, but there hadn't been any other Displacers in his family since, which meant that his parents had no idea of his talents and they had to be kept from them. The boy was shorter even than Sam and had looked up at him in wide-eyed awe as he'd shook his hand, which had drawn hastily-stifled sniggers from Rachel and made Sam wonder if he himself had ever been so young and innocent - he was almost positive that Rachel hadn't.

Anne had been placed next to Sam at the table. She was still completely in shock and conversation with her had been difficult, but half-way through the meal she had turned to him and actually tried to apologise for not having done more to save Andrew.

Sam had shaken his head, unable to meet her eyes as the tears had come. 'You brought him back. That's enough.' He'd only just managed to get the words out before he pushed his chair back and left the room to run upstairs and lock himself in a second floor bathroom where he had bawled his eyes out. Again.

Andrew's will was read in the dining room the next day, after the plates had been cleared from dinner. It was done by the Society's lawyer, Hamish Craig, one of the Elders that Sam had never met until the funeral. He was a direct descendant of the Hamish that Rachel and he had befriended at Symposium - apparently the name Hamish had been given to the male heir of the Craig family since the times of Robert the Bruce and he was something like the twenty-fifth Hamish Craig, although only the fifth to be a member. It was hard to see any familial resemblance with the giant Scotsman, though; the man was short and quite rotund, in his fifties, with thinning red hair and small round glasses, the picture of an office-bound lawyer.

Once the legal formalities were over and the smaller bequests had been dealt with - keepsakes for Anne, James, a few other Displacers and Sam's family - the rest of Andrew's belongings were divided up.

Despite the fact that he had left everything he'd gained during official missions to the Society, such as the goldmine shares in South Africa (as was expected of all members), there was still a hell of a lot left over and, to Sam's shock, it was to be shared equally between him and Rachel. Rachel had also been left Andrew's London flat and contents, while Sam got the one in Barcelona, along with a key to the mysterious locked room and a letter to be opened after he'd used it.

So, not only did Sam now have more money than he could spend in a lifetime, but he also had a place of his own which, would certainly make it a lot easier to keep his Displacing a secret from his family. It was just a shame it had come about in such tragic circumstances.

After the business had concluded, the members drifted away to the sitting room, but Sam stayed in his seat, then, when everybody had gone, he approached the lawyer, who was still clearing away his papers.

'I want to make a will.'

The Elder stopped what he was doing and smiled up at him. 'Well, we'll just have to sit down sometime, then, won't we, laddie? And may I say what a pleasure it is to finally meet you ...'

Sam shook his head, interrupting him. 'I'm going back to Barcelona in a few days. Can you draw something up for me before then?'

'I suppose I could slap together a temporary will and draw up an official one later. Depends how complicated it is. After all you're a rich man now and...'

'It'll be simple,' Sam said, interrupting him again. 'All the stuff I inherited from Andrew and everything Displacer-related goes to Rachel. Everything else to my family.'

The man nodded slowly. 'Och aye, that's simple enough. But you do know that you have to give a verbal will as well, right?'

'A what?'

'A verbal will. You have to state the main points of your will in front of three witnesses because a physical will just disappears if you die in the past.'

Sam blinked; it had never occurred to him that something as mundane as paperwork would disappear if someone ceased to exist. 'Oh, of course. Um. Can we just do the physical one now and the verbal one later? Maybe on Skype?'

'Of course laddie, I'll get right on it.'

'Thank you.'

'But do you really think you're going to need one so soon? You're still young...' The Elder trailed off and frowned, seeming to see something in Sam. 'What are you planning, laddie?'

'Nothing!' Sam forced a smile and shrugged. 'But I'm not young, I'm a Displacer and I just think it's about time I had a will.' Not wanting to have to answer any more all-too-insightful questions, he gave the Elder a respectful nod, then hurried out to join the other Displacers in the sitting room.

With Andrew gone, the Society no longer had a leader and, according to the rules, they couldn't be without one for more than four days. That grace period was now up, so that evening a new leader had to be elected and nobody was allowed to leave Headquarters until it was done, no matter how long it took.

Ralph, of course, had immediately put himself forward. He had tried to become the leader before, running against Andrew and only narrowly losing, so he obviously fancied his chances and had stared around the room, as if daring anyone else to oppose him. For a moment it looked like nobody would and Sam shared a worried glance with Rachel; even if Ralph wasn't the spy in the end, his feelings for Sam were clear and his being elected leader would mean big changes for them both.

What happened next was one of the most satisfying things that Sam had ever witnessed, even though at the time he hadn't been able to fully enjoy it.

James told Ralph to stand in the centre of the circle of armchairs, where they could all see him and the man did so reluctantly, suspecting some kind of trick.

The old man stared at him for a few seconds, seeming to look right through him, then grunted in something that was almost amusement and turned to the Elders sitting closest to him. 'Philip, Richard, Hamish, are you seeing what I'm seeing?'

'Yes.'

'I am.'

'Aye.'

James nodded at the expected responses. 'Sorry, Ralph, but you are not a candidate for leadership of the Displacers.'

Ralph put his hands on his hips and stared down at James angrily. 'I know you don't think I'm worthy. None of you have ever respected...'

James just waved his hand and cut him off. 'Worth and respect have nothing to do with it, Mr Price, your status, however, is another matter. Leadership of the Honourable Society of Displacers is only open to active Displacers and I am sorry to say that you have gone through the Transition; the trauma must have been too much for your body. It happens sometimes.' He smiled a hint of satisfaction in his expression that he couldn't quite hide. 'Welcome to the council of Elders, Mr Price.'

Ralph spluttered, blinking at James in disbelief and not a little resentment. 'That's absolute claptrap! Of course I can still Displace!'

'Very well, then show us. Displace. Any time-line will do.'

'What? Now?'

'You're recovered sufficiently from your injuries to be able to Displace?'

'I have.'

'Then yes, now please. And don't forget to bring me back a nice souvenir.' James smiled at Ralph and settled back in his chair, folding his arms across his chest to wait.

Ralph glared at him for a long moment, then huffed and stalked over to the nearest empty chair where he closed his eyes and settled in comfortably.

An expectant hush fell as the members stared at him, the only sound the soft ticking of the grandfather clock in the hallway outside.

A minute went by, then two, and nothing happened except for Ralph's cheeks getting steadily redder and the lines on his forehead getting steadily deeper.

'Would you like me to run you a bath?'

Rachel's comment drew disapproving looks from a few members, but they were Ralph's cronies and it was expected of them. The rest were amused, although most had the decency to try to hide their grins behind their hands or in their drinks. There were, however, at least a few unkind sniggers from those who had been on the wrong end of Ralph's snide remarks and holier-than-thou behaviour and were enjoying his difficulties.

Ralph coughed and shifted in his seat, but otherwise ignored what was going on and persevered, but after almost five minutes had gone by, far longer than even the worst current Displacers needed to Calm themselves, he swore under his breath. He opened his eyes and glared resentfully at James then, saying nothing, got up and stomped back to his original armchair near the back of the group.

With Ralph disqualified from taking over the leadership the choice was simple; Lisa had stepped into the gap left by Andrew's death, handling the authorities and the Society with ease. The members were unanimous in voting for her, but before she accepted she stood and moved across the room.

She stopped in front of the armchair that Sam and Rachel were squeezed onto and reached out to take Sam's hand.

'It should be you, Sam, you should be our leader.' Her voice was quiet, but the silence in the room was such that her words, meant just for him, nevertheless reached everybody.

Sam shook his head. 'I'm not a leader. I'm just a soldier.'

'I think you underestimate yourself.'

'Whether I do or don't doesn't matter; you're the best of us now, Lisa, not me. We need you to lead and you've more than proven that you can do so in the last few days.'

'Thank you, Sam.' She squeezed his hand before turning to address the room. 'I humbly accept.'

There was a roar of approval and the members surged from their seats to congratulate her, but she only let the mayhem go on for a few short minutes before issuing her first orders, which had them scrambling to obey and made them forget their troubles, at least for a while.

One of the first things she had them to do was turn off all the computers and switch off their Internet connection.

With so much going on nobody had thought to stop using the computers, but it was essential that they do so; John was a programmer and had set up all of the computers, writing their software and keeping them updated, but he was also a hacker and would have undoubtedly installed his own pieces of malware on them. Lisa ordered them to be kept off until new ones could be brought in. In addition she told everyone to stop using any personal computers and laptops that John had had any contact with.

That was all understandable, acceptable and easy to deal with, but there was one much further reaching consequence of John being the Master than the Illuminati having a window into their activities that nobody had taken into consideration - he had written the program used to search for new members.

The implications were huge and not just for their future, but for the past as well; they had lost many potential new members over the last ten or fifteen years, poached by the Illuminati before they could get to them, and now they knew why.

Early the next day counter-espionage experts from MI5 arrived to sweep the house for bugs and they took the computers away for analysis, hoping that John had left something behind to track him with. Because it was a Saturday, Dylan had permission from his parents to be at the Society and he demanded to be allowed to accompany the computers to the MI5 labs; he'd been learning hacking and programming from John and insisted that he had the best chance of anyone to spot one of his tricks. Even though she didn't think it would do much, Lisa didn't have the heart to refuse him; not only was he was desperate to do something to help, but he also seemed to think he had to prove that he hadn't been corrupted by John's influence.

It wasn't just Dylan who was kept busy, though, because there was a lot that had to be done around Headquarters before it could be considered secure again. A team led by Julia changed the locks and keypad codes on the front and back doors and the attic, issued new access codes for the Internet and online services to all the members, and even replaced everybody's phones with new secure ones provided by MI5.

While Headquarters was in an uproar, James retreated to the quiet of the safe house and threw himself back into his research. He hadn't made much leeway in the past, but now they knew who the Master was, it make things somewhat simpler and he set about cross-referencing the intelligence fed to them by Diana with John's family tree - information that was readily available seeing as there was a whole department of the Society, run by the Craigs for centuries, dedicated to tracing the ancestors of Displacers. In a matter of days he had made various connections, but while none of them provided ways of attacking the Illuminati, it was encouraging and far more of an advancement than he'd made in the previous months.

One piece of information he turned up was useless in itself, but interesting nonetheless, as it shed some light on the real reason behind Sam's first Displacement to Port Royal and the importance of his defeat of Quentin.

He came across an entry in the log of a Royal Navy captain sent to hunt pirates in the Caribbean from November 1718, only a few months after Sam's visit to the time-line. It spoke of the capture of a group of pirates, among them the first mate of the Queen Anne's Revenge, Bill Jones, who was described as an "over-sized and overly-belligerent oaf with a scarred face" who had "done much injury to the four marines set to subdue him." That man, the same one who had stood by Quentin during Blackbeard's competition, was John's ancestor.

With this new information it became clear that Quentin's objective hadn't been to get his hands on the diamond as they'd assumed, but rather that he'd had his eyes on the bigger prize all along - to ensure that John's ancestor became the pirate's heir. The more aggressive nature of the man when compared with the gentler Smithy, who'd actually won the competition, might well have changed the whole balance of power on the east coast of the United States and could have placed John's family in a favourable position to become major powers in the nearly-formed nation after the revolutionary war, just over fifty years later.

Sam didn't want to let James out of his sight so he joined him at the safe house and began doing research of his own. He wanted to know how things had gone so horribly wrong and how John had manipulated things without them knowing, but above all he *needed* to know whether he could have done anything to prevent it.

He took over a room in the safe house and began laying out all the material that John and Andrew had put together while shut away in their room; dozens of books and hundreds of papers detailing their plans and research which had been bagged up as evidence, some of them bloodstained. To that he added Anne's tragic mission report, then slowly began putting together a picture.

He had finished before the weekend was over.

The inescapable conclusion was that Andrew was never supposed to have made it back from the Holy Land. He was supposed to have died in the past and quietly disappeared from history, while John came back alone with a story of woe and continued as one of the Society, his identity as the Master safely hidden.

Instead of using the Displacement he'd made the month before to pave the way for the mission, he had obviously set an ambush. They had arrived in an opulent courtyard in the Temple Mount complex in Jerusalem and immediately been surrounded by hostile Templars. Andrew was supposed to have been killed right then and there, but Anne had set about the soldiers with a fury and a skill born of far more years of fencing than Sam and driven them back long enough to grab Andrew and pull him towards the fountain in the middle of the courtyard.

Seeing his well laid plans going awry, John had been forced to improvise and had thrust the knife into Andrew's chest himself, however, he'd been too late to stop them from diving into the water and returning home.

Anne had continued her aggression when they got back, clawing at John and dragging him down as he tried to escape. She had been succeeding, but then Lisa and Philip came, drawn by the commotion and pulled her off him. They had not understood what was happening, had only seen the blood, thought she was hysterical and sought to calm her down. Unfortunately, their act of compassion had allowed John to make good his escape.

The rest he knew and Sam could almost hear John's high-pitched laughter in his ears when he remembered his encounter with him on the stairs. He could have ended everything in that second if he had only been quicker witted, if he'd only put two and two together. Instead he'd gone charging around, like he always did, but without Rachel there to clean up his mistakes.

He thought he'd feel better when he had everything worked out and saw that there was nothing he could have done, but he didn't, if anything he felt worse and even more determined to catch the murderer.

The search for the fugitive wasn't going well, though.

MI5 had sent agents to his house in North London as soon as they'd got the call from Lisa notifying them of Andrew's death but, as expected, he hadn't gone there. Not only that, but the house had apparently not been lived in for years - the neighbours said that they had never seen anyone go in or out and had assumed that it was owned by foreign investors. After a brief investigation MI5 and the Elders came to the inescapable conclusion that John had known that he would be discovered at some point and had given the Society a fake address. There had been no sightings of him on CCTV or at the borders either - it was like he'd dropped off the face of the Earth, or at least the British Isles. MI5 were going to continue looking, but they had as good as admitted that it was hopeless.

It was then that he realised that he might have a way to find John - if he could track Quentin's movements just by concentrating on him, maybe he could do the same for other Displacers.

It was easy enough to find out if it was possible - Julia was scheduled to go on a mission that very afternoon and, when she did, Sam was in his room at the safe house, waiting, trying to sense it.

It worked, and not only did he feel it when she went, but he knew it was her. He would be able to tell when John went into the past, just as he could when Quentin did, and, by extension, the Twins as well. Unfortunately he had never met any of the other Illuminati, so they would be free to come and go as they pleased, but they were the least of his worries.

That just left the question of how best to use this new information.

His first instinct was to go downstairs and tell his grandfather, but he stifled it before he was even out of his chair and settled back down to think things through properly.

He very quickly realised that he didn't want the Society involved.

Despite appearances, John wasn't an idiot, and if Sam had worked out that he could track him into the past like Quentin, he would as well. Following him into the past would be the most dangerous Displacement he ever went on; John would no doubt be waiting for him with an overwhelming force, ready to spring a trap worse than the one that had so nearly succeeded in South Africa and Sam knew he couldn't take anyone else into that, especially not Rachel.

Besides, wasn't everyone always telling him that it was *his* job, his *destiny* to safeguard the time-line? Then it should be him who risked everything, not anyone else.

It wasn't just the danger stopping him from speaking to James, though; any mission to find John in the past would be open to debate as to what to do when they caught him and killing just wasn't the Displacer way.

But that was exactly what Sam intended to do. If the man couldn't be brought to justice in the present, he would hunt him down in the past - it would be far more satisfying to do to him what he had planned for Andrew anyway.

He just hoped he'd be able to go through with it when the time came; he had never liked killing, even when he knew that his victims would be fine once he'd left the time-line. He wasn't sure if he'd actually be able to kill John, especially knowing that it would erase him from existence.

So, much as he hated it, he was going to have to lie to Rachel, his grandfather and the men and women who he had come to see as his family. He had to hide what he was doing from them in order to keep it secret. The trouble was, the only way to do that and ensure that none of them insisted on going with him was to cut himself off from them.

He was going to have to push them away to keep them safe.

All too soon the Easter holidays were over and it was time for Sam to go back to Barcelona.

Rachel drove him to the airport in Andrew's Mini - hers now and accompanied him all the way to passport control. They kissed and held hands, staring into each other's eyes, delaying their goodbyes as much as possible, but Sam had to go through sooner or later or he would miss his flight. He turned to go, but stopped after only a couple of paces and hurried back to fold her into one last, long hug.

When he finally released her she pulled back and frowned at him. 'What's wrong?'

He smiled and shook his head. 'Nothing. Just.... you know; Andrew.'

Rachel nodded. 'I know.'

They kissed one last time and then he walked away.

The day after he got back to Barcelona he went to Andrew's flat.

The instructions he'd received in the will were clear and very simple: before doing anything else, he was to go to the locked room, then read the letter from Andrew.

He opened the door as instructed, but when he saw the contents of the room he could only stand there, envelope forgotten, staring dumbstruck at the incredible artworks on display around the room. There were four of them - a magnificent white marble bust and three paintings. They were of widely different styles, though, which was why it took him a while to work out that they were all of the same subject; Susan, the wife Andrew had lost. She was Sam's aunt, sister to his mother, the reason why he called Andrew "uncle" even though nobody who wasn't a Displacer knew why.

This was why he never spoke about her; she was locked up in this room, both metaphorically and physically.

When he was finally able to tear his eyes from them and he sat down against the wall next to the door to read the letter.

It was a handwritten note on Society stationery in his uncle's untidy scrawl, dated the day before he had died and Sam had to take a deep breath and fight back tears as he realised just how naive he had been about everything.

Sam

Do not mourn for me.

As a good friend of mine once wrote "I have been half in love with easeful Death" these long years since Susan was killed. That doesn't mean I've been wishing for it, or gone looking for it, though, just that it is not something I am afraid of and, quite frankly, it is more than welcome. I just hope that it serves in some way to help you and the Society.

For these last few years the only thing that has kept me going has been you and I thank you for that. Watching you grow and learn has been remarkable and, when I see how you have changed and what you have become this last year, I know that I leave matters in hands that are far more capable than my own.

However, you must *learn to believe in yourself; you are the only one of us who knows for sure what needs to be done - you have shown that time after time.*

So, yes, seek advice from people like James and trust in Rachel, but make sure that the final decision is yours and yours alone; if you listen to what your heart tells you and have confidence in your own sense of what is right and just, you will never go wrong.

As for the pieces in this room.

I spent entire lifetimes learning from various masters, trying to reproduce my memory of Susan as faithfully as I could. It wasn't healthy, I know, but it was my penance, and these crude works are nothing more than the by-products of that.

My purpose in showing them to you, and my sincerest hope, is that they may serve as a lesson - that whatever happens, no matter what losses you take, there is always a way to continue the fight and be true to yourself and your family.

Beyond that, they are useless. Do with them what you will.

Once last time I say to you - do not mourn for me; I am certain that whatever gave us our powers has Susan in its warm embrace and I will finally be reunited with her, just as I am sure that I'll see you around some time!

Andrew

Sam folded the letter back into the envelope and carefully put it back in his pocket, then stood and moved further into the room.

For several hours he gazed at the artworks, each a masterpiece in its own right, likenesses of an aunt he had once known but didn't remember. Representations of a love and a loss that his uncle had kept hidden, but which must have scarred his soul just as much as his body.

School started up again the following day. He was just as determined to leave at the end of the year, but his heart was no longer in it and he only did the bare minimum in order to pass. He even gave up fencing and instead spent the majority of his time poring over John's mission reports and reading anything MI5 or Diana turned up. His grades began to suffer accordingly, but luckily he was far enough ahead for it not to matter too much.

He spent an entire month moping around, just waiting for news of John or sign of the Illuminati travelling.

By that time he had managed to almost completely cut himself off from the Society. He had started the process in London as soon as he'd made the decision to tackle the Illuminati on his own. While the other members had come together to face the threat and as a means of comfort, he'd isolated himself, shutting himself away with his grandfather. When he did go to Headquarters, for meals and such, he barely needed to play up his sadness at his uncle's passing to be left alone and was able to use James' health as the perfect excuse to leave again as quickly as possible.

In Barcelona it was even easier because of the sheer distance involved, but he also stopped taking part in the discussions on WhatsApp and the Skype conference calls. He did accept the regular calls that came from James and Lisa, but he refused their requests for him to go on missions, variously pleading schoolwork or not being ready to Displace again so soon after Andrew's death and hung up as quickly as he could.

It was painful to push away the men and women he'd come to see as his family, but doing the same to Rachel hurt much more. It was just as easy, though; because of her martial training and past Displacements which gave her knowledge of how the British secret services worked, she had been appointed as the Society's liaison with MI5. The job kept her extremely busy, running back and forth, evaluating leads and advising the teams they had around the country. She even flew to Germany to follow up on a possible sighting by MI6 agents, but they were all dead ends and she felt that they were no closer to catching

John than they had been the day of the Displacement. She was so dejected about it, thinking that she was somehow failing the Society and Sam in particular, that he was sorely tempted to tell her what he was doing, just to make her feel better. It killed him to see her that way, but it was the price he had to pay.

He felt it when she went into the past on a mission he'd refused to go on and the temptation had been there to reach out and join her. It would have been easy enough to do so, but he wouldn't let himself; he had to hold himself ready to Displace and chase down the Illuminati at a moment's notice.

Another month went by without him sensing John, Quentin, or the Twins. Diana had given them intelligence that Tessa was still recovering from the injury Sam had given her in South Africa, but she had no idea where either John or Quentin was and couldn't explain why they hadn't made a move.

Sam was beginning to doubt his course of action. It would be so easy just to give up, to beg Rachel to come and visit him, to tell Lisa he was ready to go on any missions she had, but then everything changed.

Along with everything else he'd given up, he'd stopped eating lunch with Rafa. Instead he'd been taking a packed lunch so that he could eat alone. However, for some reason, that day he'd forgotten to bring one and had gone to the dining room where he'd overheard Rafa and another boy discussing the computer game they were currently playing - the latest instalment in the Assassin's Creed franchise. Seemingly out of nowhere an idea sprang to life his mind and the more he thought about it the more *right* it felt.

It was almost as if he'd been placed there at exactly the right time to overhear their conversation.

He Displaced in the evening, after his last full day at school before the exams started. He didn't tell anybody that he was going to do it, nor did he call anyone on Skype to watch over him like regulations stipulated, instead he just told his parents he was staying with a friend, went to Andrew's flat, laid down on the sofa and closed his eyes.

He went to a mountain in early twelfth century Persia, placed himself at the mercy of Hassan al-Sabbāh, the founder and master of the original assassins, and begged to be taught. He was inducted into the order and stayed for more than twenty years.

He didn't tell the Displacers where he had gone or what he had done; they wouldn't have understood that he'd needed to round off his martial arts education with one last thing - he had finally overcome his squeamishness about killing and now wouldn't hesitate when he met the men responsible for his uncle's death.

The only thing stopping him was the continued inactivity of the Illuminati.

Two weeks later, the day after his exams finished, he got up in the morning and told his parents that he needed some time to find himself and wanted to get to know Spain a little more.

They didn't argue; they knew how much Andrew's death had affected him and had seen the profound change in him. Instead they wished him well and told him to keep in touch.

After a last lunch with them he packed his camping rucksack, said his goodbyes and left. He didn't have a destination in mind so he just started walking, heading north over Collserola, where he and Rachel had trained so many times, trying to put as much distance between him and everyone that he cared about as he possibly could, deliberately walking away from the Displacers, his family and Rachel.

Since then he'd merely hiked aimlessly, taking his time to go nowhere in particular. He'd used cash withdrawn before leaving Barcelona to buy food, slept outside whenever he could and stayed in hostels when he couldn't. All the while he kept contact with his loved ones to a minimum, only sending starkly cold messages when he had to, not giving them any clue as to exactly where he was.

He hit the barrier of the Pyrenees in the north of Catalonia, somewhere near Andorra, and turned west, staying in the foothills. He wandered through various beautiful natural parks until eventually the mountains had ended, giving way to the sea, and still he had continued. He followed the coastline all the way across the Basque region, past San Sebastian and Bilbao, and it was there, more than five hundred miles later, somewhere near the city of Santander that he had finally got the opportunity that he'd been waiting for.

It didn't surprise him one bit that it was the Twins who were sent back to test the waters.

CHAPTER 3
HOMECOMING

Spain, Present Day

Sam shifted in his sleeping bag, trying to find a position that was remotely comfortable with all the cuts and bruises he'd sustained in the fight against the Twins. He eventually gave it up as impossible, but he didn't really mind the pain, he had grown accustomed to it in Sparta and it was a reminder of what he'd achieved.

He pulled his new MI5 phone out of his rucksack and switched it on; it was time for his daily check-in with his parents.

The new phones had come with a suite of apps, written by MI5 programmers, which replaced the ones to be found in the usual app stores. They worked just as well as the more common ones, if not better and were supposed to be unhackable, but for some reason they had all been given cringeworthy names. For example, "Mi5sive" was the email app, "Mi5sal" was the directory of contacts within the agency and "Mi5spelt" was the rather tongue in cheek name for the app that replaced WhatsApp. There were a few games on the phone as well, including "Mi5 Pacman" and "Mi5sile", a copy of the thermonuclear war game from the film *War Games*. There was even "Mi5tletoe", a dating app for agents, which the Society members were only moderately sure was just a joke.

Sam opened "Mi5sive" and wrote a quick email to his parents, telling them that he was enjoying "backpacking" around Spain and was meeting interesting people - little white lies that would put their minds at ease. A slightly longer and less serious email went to Violeta, accompanied by a couple of photos he'd taken of the views and a silly selfie with a cow he'd gone past that morning and knew she would laugh at.

Next he opened "Mi5spelt" and wrote a quick message to Diana to thank her for the heads-up about the possibility of the Twins travelling that day. After the death of Grant Davis in South Africa, she had been promoted to team leader and had taken over his old group with three young Illuminati who she hadn't met before and whose names she immediately gave to the Society to add to their list of known agents. She kept in contact with the Twins, though, because they were her friends, which was why she had been able to alert Sam of their plans.

Sam didn't know any of her new team so he wouldn't be able feel them when they Displaced, but it didn't matter, he would always be able to focus on Diana if they were ever sent on a mission. He didn't particularly care about them, though; he just wanted John, and he was hoping that her raised position and the direct line of communication she now had with him would deliver him into their hands. He had kept in contact with her purely because of that, not because of their romantic involvement; he felt that he had to keep his distance from her, just the same as he was doing with Rachel. Initially she had gotten the wrong idea, though, and had sent him messages of a more intimate nature. He had stoically ignored them and stayed strong to his convictions and, after a couple weeks, she had reluctantly begun to limit herself to just sending him information about the Illuminati.

He always turned his phone off as quickly as possible after sending the emails to his family because he didn't want to have to receive phone calls and have to answer questions from the Society, and he was about to do so this time as well but, after much consideration, he decided that it would probably be best to write a short message in the Society's group chat to inform them of his Displacement for their records.

Displacement to Paris, 1830, April to July. Full report to follow.

The message sent, he was about to exit the app and turn off his phone, but his attention was caught by something unusual and he hesitated.

There were always dozens of unread messages in the group chat and that day was no exception, but bizarrely every message he could see was identical, despite having been sent by more than a dozen different people -

Sam, James is sick. Come home.

He went cold as he read it and hastily typed a reply -

I'm on my way.

He switched off the phone and struggled out of his sleeping bag to begin packing. He soon finished, but when he swung his rucksack onto his back he swayed dizzily, almost overcome with tiredness, the Displacement taking its usual toll. He ran through a quick breathing exercise he'd learnt in Tibet to clear his head, then dug a cereal bar out of a pocket and wolfed it down. Feeling slightly better, he started towards the orange glow on the horizon that marked the city.

After only a few steps he broke into a run.

Sam reached the tiny airport on the outskirts of Santander in the early hours of the morning, after jogging through the Spanish countryside for six hours straight. In one of his brief breaks for food and water he'd used his mobile to book a seat on the first available flight to London, but it wasn't until eleven in the morning, so he curled up on the seats in Departures to wait for check-in to start and closed his eyes. He was too anxious to sleep, though, so he soon sat up again and watched the airport waking up around him.

He was so tired that it took him a while to notice that he was getting ever increasing attention from the security guards. There were very few people in the terminal with him but they were all cleaners or airline workers preparing for the day; he was the only "civilian", as it were. Even so, he had no idea why he warranted such vigilance, until he saw how their noses wrinkled imperceptibly every time they walked past and realised how he must look and smell; he hadn't stayed in a hostel for almost a week so both he and his clothes were filthy. The last thing he wanted was to be mistaken for a vagabond and thrown out of the airport or in some other way prevented from taking his flight, so he got up, groaning at the protests of muscles which had stiffened once they'd cooled, then hobbled to the toilets.

The reflexion in the bathroom mirror showed just why he had been getting so many looks from the guards. It hadn't been just his scruffy appearance that had made them suspicious, but also the bruised and battered mess that was his face; the cuts and welts liberally covering it were clear signs that he had been fighting recently. There were also clear signs of his exhaustion in the bags under his eyes and he had an untidy scraggly beard, dark to match his hair. He didn't need to shave more than once a week, but it had been a couple of months since he'd bothered and it had grown fairly long. It was awful and it would have to go as soon as possible, but he had more important things to worry about at that moment.

He looked around to make sure there was nobody else in there with him, then stripped off his soiled t-shirt.

He couldn't help but chuckle at the vision before him; while his arms, face and neck were dark brown from the sun, the rest of his body was a pure white - it was a disgraceful appearance for a Spaniard from a beach city. However, he was also painfully thin from constant walking with the bare minimum of food, his ribs standing out and his muscles sharply defined. His mother would probably make him sit at the dinner table and eat solidly for a day or two if she saw him, but he quite liked how he looked - a bit like Brad Pitt in *Fight Club* (although he was under no illusions that he was anywhere near as good looking).

After washing as best he could and scrubbing his armpits twice with hand soap from the dispensers, he put a dark blue long-sleeved shirt. It was far too hot for it, but it was the only thing he had that was remotely close to being clean, having sat at the bottom of his rucksack the whole journey, put there just in case by his mother so that he had "something presentable" to wear. There was nothing he could do about his torn and dirty jeans, though, unless he wanted to travel in his swimming shorts and he still smelled, having run out of deodorant more than a week before, but he no longer stood out like a sore thumb.

When he finished he smoothed down his unruly hair and inspected himself one last time in the mirror.

The man that looked back at him was less frightening than before, less the Beast and more the child he'd left behind.

Thankfully the flight was almost empty and Sam was able to stretch out in some semblance of comfort. He finally managed to fall asleep and before he knew it they were landing at Stansted airport. The train ride to Liverpool Street Station was only three-quarters of an hour, but he still found himself dozing off again so, instead of risking a tube journey and possibly overshooting his stop by half a city, he decided to take a taxi for the short ride across Central London.

Just before lunchtime he was standing on the pavement outside Headquarters and frowning up at the building.

Now that he was there he finally realised just how much he didn't want to be; he had cut himself off from the Society for a reason.

But, if his grandfather was ill, then he couldn't ignore that. He couldn't stay away.

James would be at home, or in hospital if he was really sick, but Sam had decided to come to the Society; he wanted to have a shower, put on some clean clothes and hopefully find some answers to what exactly was wrong with his grandfather before going to see him.

Sighing, he trudged up the stairs, patting the coat of arms on the column for luck as he went by, and let himself in.

He stumbled to a halt in the hallway as he caught sight of the wall and stared in shock, his rucksack sliding unnoticed off his shoulder to thud heavily on the floor.

There were dozens of name plates hanging from the pegs - almost all of the members were there. Including James.

He spun around as the door to the sitting room opened and Lisa appeared.

'Sam...'

The sharply intelligent Indian woman looked him up and down, taking in his dishevelled appearance before contemplating his abused face with obvious concern. She made no comment, though, and he offered no explanation. Instead he just gritted his teeth and resigned himself to the coming ordeal.

'Where is he?'

In reply she just stood to one side and motioned for him to go past her into the room.

Sam set his shoulders and went in.

His eyes flicked to Andrew's photograph in its place on the wall, but then settled on James. The old man was sitting across the room in his armchair, which had been pushed close to the fireplace where there was a fire roaring merrily despite it being summer. Rachel was in the chair next to him and there were a couple of Elders opposite them.

The rest of the room was filled to the brim with Society members.

All conversation stopped as Sam came in, and there were a few murmured comments and gasps at his condition in the ensuing silence.

He looked around coldly, ignoring the tentative smiles and attempts at greetings that came his way. The trap he had suspected on seeing the nameplates in the hallway was now confirmed; there was absolutely no reason for the entire Society to be here at this time on a weekday except to ambush him.

He would have turned and walked out straight away if it hadn't been for the shocking sight of his grandfather.

Despite his proximity to the fire, James was wrapped in a blanket and he looked truly old and ill, much more so than he had after Andrew's death. The hands that clutched the arms of the chair looked skeletal and there was a sallow tinge to his skin that Sam had never seen before, but he was relieved to see the same vitality in his eyes as ever.

Sam walked across the room towards him, ignored everyone, including Rachel, who had stood to greet him, to kneel in front of James. He took one of his grandfather's hands and felt the bones moving beneath the skin as James gripped him back.

'Hello, Sam.'

'Grandad. How are you?'

'I've been better, but I'll be fine now you're here.' James' grasp on Sam's hand turned suddenly and unexpectedly strong, as if he were afraid he would leave. His voice lost its tremulous weakness and he leaned forward in his chair to lock Sam's gaze with his. 'We need to talk.'

Sam fell silent, transfixed by the sheer power he felt radiating from his grandfather. It was something he'd never felt in the gentle old man before and for the first time he fully understood how he could manage the Society so effortlessly.

With a supreme effort he managed to drag his eyes away from his grandfather's long enough to survey the room, taking in all of the people watching them intently.

He turned back to James and gave him a pointed look.

The old man nodded in understanding and lifted his voice slightly to address the room. 'Could everyone leave us, please?'

Without a word, everybody stood up and went through into the dining room. The doors closed behind them and then suddenly it was just James, Lisa and Rachel in the room with him.

Sam sighed as his hand was finally released. He got to his feet then slid into one of the chairs facing James that the two Elders had just vacated. He kept his face expressionless, emotionless, letting them know how upset he was as he waited for Rachel and Lisa to take their seats.

His gaze finally settled back onto his grandfather. 'You lied to me, you all did.' *You're not ill.*

James smiled. 'No. Unfortunately that's true; I'm dying.'

He held up his hand to stop Sam from asking any questions. 'Let me finish. I'm dying, just slower than we made you think. I have six months, maybe a year if I'm lucky, but two at the most, and there's nothing that anyone can do about it.'

'I'm sorry.'

James shrugged. 'I've had a good innings and to be honest it's about bloody time.'

Sam looked around the small group.

Lisa's concern was plain to see, but Rachel's face was as expressionless and cold as his. She refused to meet his eyes and just stared into the fire.

'So if you're not ill, then what is this? An intervention?'

James laughed hoarsely. 'Good grief, no! We're not Americans! Well, most of us aren't, anyway. No, this is a cry for help and a plea for reason.'

'So it is an ambush.'

The old man gave him a crooked smile. 'Not quite.' He waved his hand vaguely in the direction of the dining room. 'All those people in there, every member who could come at such short notice, did so to show their support for you. We're not idiots, Sam, we know what you're doing and why you're doing it, but we want you to know you don't have to go through this alone. We want you to come home so we can help you.'

Sam took a deep breath while he considered what to do. He was still convinced that it was best if he handled the Illuminati on his own, but it would be nice not to have to be alone while he waited and now that his secret was apparently out of the bag there was no reason why he couldn't see if they would accept his terms. He could always walk out and disappear again if they didn't. He'd always wanted to visit Brazil and there were plenty of places to get lost there, along with some pretty spectacular beaches...

He pushed the thought of enjoyment out of his mind and hardened his expression; it was time to make his demands perfectly clear. 'If I come back I'm not going to do any missions unless I deem it necessary in order to stop the Illuminati; I have to keep myself ready for if John Displaces.'

James immediately nodded. 'Alright.'

'And I'm going to kill him. Quentin too. No more civilised behaviour, this ends for good. Can you accept that?'

James' eyes widened and he exchanged a shocked glance with Lisa. After a few seconds her face fell and she gave him a reluctant nod then looked away to stare at the fire. He sighed, his dismay plain, then slowly turned back to Sam.

'Good.' Sam had seen the exchange and spoke before James could say anything, not wanting to face the old man's disapproval. 'Lastly, I don't want anyone coming with me. When I go, I go alone.'

Rachel immediately opened her mouth to protest, but James beat her to it.

'No, that's completely unacceptable.' James shook his head emphatically, but then his voice dropped until it was barely audible over the crackling of the fire. 'Are you forgetting what I told you about the Prophecy? About Rachel? We can handle the day to day business without you, but you *cannot* handle the Illuminati without her.'

For the first time Rachel showed some signs of interest. Her head lifted and she frowned at James. 'What does that mean? What about the Prophecy?'

Sam stared at her. He couldn't believe that she didn't know what they were talking about, but finally he had to admit that it looked like she genuinely didn't and he glared at his grandfather. 'She doesn't know? You *really* haven't told her yet?'

'Know what?' Rachel insisted, looking at Sam now.

'That you're supposed to die for me.'

'Nah! Give over!' She laughed, but then stopped when she realised he was serious. 'James? Is this true?'

'Not now, Rachel. We'll talk about it later.' James dismissed her firmly, using his authority as an Elder with her for the first time ever, and thrust a thin finger at Sam. 'We talked about this, boy; there's no getting away from your destiny. Or hers.'

'I refuse to believe that.'

The old man shook his head sadly. 'You don't have a choice.'

'Yes I do; I can be alone. None of you need to be in danger. I can take care of the Illuminati easily enough on my own.'

'You can't, that's just it. You will die if you try to do this alone; the Prophecy is very, *very* clear on that point.'

Sam tutted and shook his head. 'Every time something doesn't go your way you just pull a new bit of the prophecy out of your hat to suit your needs. When are you going to tell me the whole thing so I can bloody see for myself what it says?'

'Let me know when you have fifty years to study it and I'll show it to you,' James snapped sarcastically. 'There are over ten thousand fragments in more than a hundred different languages, some of which are so dead even we haven't been able to decipher them fully. Over the last two centuries dozens of members have spent their entire careers as Displacers chasing rumours and hunting down prophets. The Society as a whole has spent, quite literally, *thousands* of years on trying to understand the prophecy, and we're not even close to seeing it as a whole yet. We understand more about it than ever, thanks to that tiny fragment you brought back, though; it showed us that what we'd thought were conflicting elements were actually referring to two different ideas, but we are still a long way from the prophecy being a useful tool.' He stabbed his finger at Sam again. 'You may be smart, boy, you may be the most powerful Displacer there's ever been, but you are a mere *pebble* in this avalanche and if you don't heed our warnings you will be buried. And then we'll be powerless against the Illuminati again.'

He was panting for breath and red in the face when he finally finished and he turned away, coughing uncontrollably and wheezing.

Rachel handed him a glass of water and he gulped at it eagerly.

James' eyes were bloodshot when they met Sam's again, but they were still sharply focused. 'Philip was wrong when he said that you weren't the one that the prophecy talked about, He has never been a particularly avid student of it and his knowledge is sorely lacking, but the dual, or rather triple nature of the Prophecy became perfectly clear to me as soon as he read his translation. I did nothing to correct him, though, and I advised the council and Andrew not to tell you differently, thinking that it would take the pressure off you if you believed that we weren't completely dependent on you. I was wrong, though, and, if anything, I've made things worse.'

He paused and sipped at the water, wetting his throat before continuing.

'The fragment of Prophecy you brought back speaks of the Diviner, that is to say you, merely paving the way for the Changer, as if the role were not particularly important. It implies that it is the Changer who is the "one" as everyone insists on saying. That just isn't true, though; while the two figures have their own destinies and purpose, they are irrevocably linked and equally important - the Changer cannot exist without the Diviner and vice versa.'

'And what does any of that have to do with the Protector? With Rachel?'

James glanced at Rachel then closed his eyes and sighed. 'That is the one thing that is unequivocal. Without the Protector you will fail and die. Then, without you there to guide them, the same will happen to the Changer.'

'But if I'm with her *she* will die.'

'There is a chance that she won't.'

Sam laughed. 'A chance? Come on, James, don't be coy. How much of a chance?'

James didn't miss Sam's use of his name and he took a deep breath before replying, his eyes clouding in sorrow. 'Barely anything. Perhaps one in a hundred fragments talk of the Protector surviving.'

Sam looked at Rachel in triumph. 'You see? *That's* why I don't want you with me.'

He fully expected her to agree with him, but instead her blue eyes flashed ice at him.

He faltered in his conviction for the first time.

James' anger, his pain, and finally his sorrow, none of that had made him even consider that his chosen course wasn't the correct one, but in the face of Rachel's disapproval something in him shifted. He should have been glad to be able to play on those negative feelings to force her further away, but he found that he couldn't; the bond he shared with her tugged at him and his heart responded.

'I...' He blinked and stammered to a halt, suddenly unsure what to say. He glanced from Rachel to Lisa and then finally to James, looking for help, for support, but found none. Even Lisa, who had always been so supportive of him, was just watching him sternly, but then again she was the leader of the Society now and she could no longer treat with him on a personal level, she had to put the good of all first.

He looked down at the floor and took a deep breath while he tried to sort out his feelings.

Even in the face of this new information, Rachel was still determined to stay beside him. It made him proud, made him love her more, but at the same time it terrified him; just like Andrew had never been able to get over Susan's loss, he knew he wouldn't be able to either. He couldn't risk losing her and if that meant he died, then so be it; she would be safe. Damn the consequences *and* the Prophecy.

'I'm sorry, I just can't.' Sam thrust himself to his feet and began making his way quickly through the scattered armchairs and sofas towards the door.

'Sam, please...!'

There was clear desperation in James' hoarse cry, but Sam ignored him and went out into the corridor - he couldn't look back, because he wasn't sure if he could stand seeing the expressions on Rachel's and his grandfather's faces, whatever they were. He grabbed his rucksack from where he'd dropped it and swung it onto his back as he raced for the door, hoping to get as far away as possible before they tried to stop him or he gave in to the little voice in the back of his head, insisting that he change his mind.

The doorbell rang just as he got to it.

He pulled it open and stopped dead in his tracks.

Standing on the doorstep was a small oriental man in Buddhist robes.

He bowed and held it as he extended his hands, offering Sam a scroll, sealed with a huge red wax seal, as if it were a holy relic. Which it was.

Sam automatically returned the man's bow before reaching out to take the roll of paper with shaking hands.

The monk straightened, smiled widely, then walked away without saying a word.

Sam shut the door quietly and dropped his rucksack. It knocked into the hall table making it rattle, but he barely registered the noise as he stared at the name on the scroll under the seal.

His own.

'Sam? What's going on?' Lisa had come out into the hallway at the sound of the doorbell and her voice was full of hope at seeing him still there, but at the same time concern as to why the supposedly secret Headquarters had received an unexpected visitor.

He didn't answer, but just walked past her, as if in a trance, back into the sitting room. He picked his way slowly across the room back to James and Rachel, only vaguely aware that the double doors leading to the dining room were now open and the other members were crowded around the opening, watching him.

He met James' eyes and saw the sorrow in them. 'I can't escape it, can I, Grandad?'

The old man shook his head gently, tears welling. 'No, boy, you can't.'

Sam sighed, nodding reluctantly, then turned to Rachel. He flopped into the chair next to her and passed her the scroll.

She rotated it in her hands before blinking at the perfectly circular lump of wax. 'This is the seal of the Dalai Lama...'

She made to give it back to him, but he shook his head and looked away into the fire. 'You read it, please.' He said, his voice cracking.

Rachel broke the seal carefully, then took her time to examine the piece of paper. It was thick parchment, about A4 size and there were a few lines of beautiful handwriting on it. She cleared her throat, swallowing the lump that had welled up in it, then read it loud enough so that all the members could hear.

When Rachel finished reading and fell silent, Sam turned his head to look at her.

There was murmuring from the members, who had started to slink back into the room, but Sam didn't hear them as he stared into Rachel's eyes, seeing the pain accumulated in them and the loneliness that was mirrored in his own soul. There was also a healthy amount of rage that made him quail slightly; when Rachel was annoyed she didn't calm down until the reason for her anger was resolved and Sam knew that, in this case, that resolution probably wouldn't come through reasoned discussion. Even so he knew he had to say something in order to start the healing process. It had to be him that made the first move; her pride wouldn't let her do it, especially when it wasn't her that was in the wrong.

He swallowed his own not inconsiderable pride and wet his lips before speaking. 'I'm sorry.'

She didn't answer, she just thrust the scroll at James and stood up, holding her hand out to Sam.

He took it and she pulled him roughly to his feet and led him out of the room.

He stumbled after her, mutely.

She dragged him down the stairs to the kitchen.

'Rachel, I...'

She didn't let him say anything more.

She spun and slapped him across the face, sending him stumbling into the wall by the door.

He recovered his balance quickly and turned back. He had just enough time to take in the fury that was twisting her expression before he was sent reeling again by the fist that slammed into his nose. He felt something crack, but disregarded it and just stood facing her, taking the blows as they came, faster and faster, over and over.

Several times he almost lost his feet as she kicked his legs, striking at his thighs and the sides of his knees, but he grasped the door frame for support and held firm, always turning back to face her.

Eventually she began to run out of steam and her blows became less forceful and less damaging, even though they were just as painful. Then, as tears started to pour down her cheeks, he reached out and caught hold of her.

He held her, ignoring the blood that was streaming down his face from his nose, eyebrows and numerous other cuts, ignoring the fresh bruises on top of the ones that he already had, ignoring the pain from the rib that he'd felt crack, joining the three on the other side that had been broken by a kick from Tessa. He let go of his hold on the emotions seething inside him for the first time since Andrew's death and felt his own sobs coming to match hers. They slid down the wall until they were on the floor with her sitting on his lap and together they howled out their anger, their frustration and their sorrow.

'I love you.' He hadn't said the words since he'd started pushing Rachel away, but he meant them as much or more than he ever had.

Rachel laughed. It wasn't the response he'd expected, but it was good enough. She looked up at him with red eyes, mascara streaks down her cheeks and his blood smearing her hair and forehead. 'Wait until you see what a mess I've made of your face before you say that.'

'It's nothing more than I deserve.'

'Got that right.' Rachel nodded. 'Hold still.'

'What...?'

She reached up and in one quick motion pulled his nose, putting it back into place.

He barely flinched; all he felt was one of his many agonies lessening slightly.

She inspected her handiwork, turning his head from side to side. 'That will do for now until we can get it looked at by a doctor.'

'You broke my nose on purpose, didn't you? So that I'll look as bad as you.'

'Might've...' She grinned, but then her brow creased in a frown and she blinked as she looked into his eyes. He felt the bond that he shared with her tugging at him again as she gazed into his soul. 'You're different...' Her eyes widened in alarm suddenly. 'My god, what have you done, Sam? What is this?'

He reached out to stroke her cheek, leaving a smear of blood. 'Not now. Later. I promise I'll tell you everything, but right now I want to speak to the Society while they're still here.'

'Looking like that?'

'It'll add drama to the situation.' He grinned at her, showing his blood-stained teeth.

Rachel got off him and helped Sam struggle to his feet. His legs were unsteady underneath him and he leaned against the wall as his head swam.

When his vision cleared he looked down at the kitchen floor.

'Wow, that's a lot of blood.'

'Why do you think I brought you down here where there are tiles, instead of one of the rooms upstairs with a carpet?'

'Good thinking. I'll have to remember that when it comes time for me to get vengeance.'

'Keep dreaming, boy; you still can't beat me.'

That had been true a few months ago, but now Sam knew differently. He said nothing, though.

'Are you sure you want to do this now? We could get the doctor here to look at you first. It won't take too long, I'm sure the members won't mind waiting.'

'No, I'm fine, I just want to get this over and done with.'

'OK, hang on a minute then.' She ran across the room grabbed a roll of paper towels from the counter and brought it back to him.

She grinned. 'Don't want you dripping everywhere.'

'Thanks.'

Sam began to go, but she reached out and grabbed him, pulling him back around to face her.

'This discussion isn't over by a long shot; I'm still angry and you owe me one hell of an explanation, but just so you know - if you ever try to leave me out of things again I'll do a lot worse than this... I might even start cutting things off.' She grinned, then slapped his face again. It wasn't nearly as hard as before but it still made his head ring. 'Now come on, we've got some old people to shock.'

The Society members were waiting for them in the sitting room, but the only one sitting was James, the rest were milling around nervously, uncertain as to what was going on.

The hushed and uncomfortable conversations that were going on faded and died completely as Sam and Rachel walked in and more than one expression turned queasy as they took in the two blood-soaked figures standing in the doorway.

Before Sam could say anything, James burst out laughing.

Everybody turned to look at the old man with mixed expressions of shock and surprise and Sam was certain that not a few of them were wondering if James had finally lost his marbles.

When the Elder finally calmed down he met the gaze of the people around him and smiled wryly.

'Today is probably one of the most important days in Displacer history and I'm wondering how the hell we write the report so that future generations don't think it's a prank.'

James looked around the room, meeting the eyes of the members one by one. Some of them were chuckling, sharing his humour, but quite a few were still upset at the sight of Sam.

He tutted and rolled his eyes. 'Oh, come on everyone, lighten up. We've all seen worse in the middle-ages!'

That finally brought smiles from most of the rest of the people and James nodded in satisfaction. 'Lisa, would you get someone to call Asclepius and have him standing by for after Sam has said his piece; we don't want the sight of *that*,' he waved his hand in Sam's general direction, 'putting us off our food.'

Lisa nodded. 'Julia, would you do that please? The rest of you sit down.'

While the members took seats, Julia pulled out her phone and wrote a quick message. She had become something of an assistant to Lisa over the last month, having finally finished her doctorate and come back to London on a more permanent basis, hoping to set up a practice. In the meantime she had become a kind of counsellor to the Society, helping them with any personal problems that they might have. Sam had felt her watching him since the moment that he had come in and wondered how long it would be before she tried to psychoanalyse him.

The reply from the doctor came quickly and Julia read it out. 'He'll be here in twenty minutes.'

'Thank you.' James nodded at her, then turned to Sam. 'Well, boy, what's on your mind?'

Sam looked down at the faces turned up towards him in expectation and suddenly found that his mouth was dry. In spite of all his experience, the conversations he'd had with royalty and celebrities in the past, he was still nervous speaking in front of this group in the present.

His gaze eventually settled on James, who sported a wide grin. He was obviously amused at Sam's hesitation, but there was no judgement in his eyes, just love, and Sam took comfort in knowing that, despite all the changes he had gone through, he could always find forgiveness and support from the man who had rocked him back to sleep when he'd been woken by nightmares, held his hand on walks in Brockwell Park, and taught him the rudiments of cricket during the long summer months that he had spent in London with his family as a child.

He gave his grandfather a grateful smile, then took a deep breath and began to address the room at large. 'That day, I had a chance to save Andrew. I reached out for him, just as I do for Quentin, and managed to find him. I had enough energy to Displace again and that's what I tried to do.' He looked at James and saw the realisation and horror in his eyes, the already pale skin turning bone white. 'I wasn't able to save Andrew, though, because the past got set for me before I could go.'

James moaned softly as he put his head in his hands and Sam felt tears coming to his eyes again. He called out to the old man. 'It wasn't your fault, Grandad! You weren't to know!'

James looked up, his eyes shining. 'I should have realised something was wrong when I saw how confused Rachel was. I should have seen what you were trying to do and held off on answering the phone.'

Sam shook his head. 'Don't even think those kinds of thoughts. This is why I didn't put this in my report - the only person to blame for what happened to Andrew is John and I have no idea whether I would have been able to save him even if I *had* managed to Displace.'

He held James' gaze, willing him to see things his way and, after a moment's hesitation, James nodded his acceptance.

Sam looked around the room and saw mostly attentive, but blank faces - only a couple of them had realised the true implications of what he was saying, so he was going to have to spell it out for the rest.

'I believe that I can feel it when anyone that I know Displaces, I just have to be receptive to it. I felt it when Rachel made her Displacements the last couple of months and I felt it when Lisa made hers.' He smiled, pausing for effect. 'And last night I felt it when

Tristan and Tessa Displaced and followed them to nineteenth century Paris.'

'That's why you were so beat up when you came in earlier… well, before Rachel…' Lisa waved her hand at the fresh blood covering Sam. 'I assume they didn't take very kindly to you spying on them?'

Sam grinned. 'They didn't like it one bit, especially when I beat the crap out of them.'

'You beat them? Both of them?'

Sam turned to find Rachel staring at him in disbelief and nodded. 'Yes. Both of them. At the same time. In a fair fight.' He grinned. 'Still think you can take me?'

He winked at her, then turned back to the room. 'My plan is simple. I'm going to shut down the Illuminati. I'm going to stop them from carrying out any kind of mission in the past. I gave the Twins a message to take back to John and all of the Illuminati - I told them that if I ever catch any of them in the past ever again I will kill them. And I fully intend to follow through on my promise.'

There was universal shock and disquiet at his announcement, but he'd expected as much and would have been more worried if they hadn't had any qualms about it, after all, it was the kind of behaviour that was more in keeping with the opposition. He ignored their disapproval for the moment, though, and continued.

'So, I can sense it when five Illuminati Displace - Quentin, John, the Twins and Diana Birch. As for any Illuminati members that we are not aware of, I am confident that if they try to change something big then the time-line itself will alert me or in some way guide me to them and I should be able to counter them.'

'They're not going to like that.' Sam didn't see who made the comment but he was glad when it brought a fair few laughs; it seemed that the members, while not exactly warming to the idea of killing people who, if it weren't for the acts of a single man, could have been sitting with them, were at least willing to consider it as an unfortunate necessity.

He took a deep breath, fighting back the exhaustion that was steadily creeping up on him again and surreptitiously put his hand on the door frame to steady himself, trying to gather his strength; he couldn't rest yet, he needed to say everything now, all at once, while everyone was there. They could joke and debate to their heart's content later, right now he had to tell them what he was going to do. Whether they liked it or not. With their approval or not.

'No, they really aren't going to like it, and I'm counting on that. Eventually I will back them so far into a corner that they will have no choice but to retaliate. When they get to that point, which I suspect will be sooner rather than later, then I fully expect them to set a trap for me... Which I am going to walk into it and destroy them all. This is why I wanted to stay away, though; so that they wouldn't know where I was and couldn't come for me in the present.'

The silence that greeted his statement was absolute and he smiled inwardly; the Society were nothing if not predictable in their reactions.

'This is my purpose, this is why I exist. I can feel that, even without understanding the Prophecy.'

He looked at James for confirmation and received a sorrowful nod in return.

'So, I will follow my destiny.'

He felt Rachel's hand slip into his and turned his head to look at her.

'Count me in,' she whispered, smiling at him.

'I didn't want to speak for you; it might be suicide.' He tried to smile back at her, but his face was completely numb.

'It's my destiny too and it's *my* choice to face it.'

Sam squeezed her hand. 'Thank you.'

Lisa spoke up. 'You're going to need more than just the two of you to take on all of the Illuminati.'

Sam frowned. 'James, does the Prophecy say anything about us getting reinforcements?'

'Sometimes, but it's never very specific about it. Several passages insist that you need to have the full support of the Society in order to succeed, but never actually say how that support should manifest itself.'

'Then I don't think it would be a good idea to take anyone else with us. I would, however, suggest that any members who are willing spend a Displacement or two getting some martial arts training as soon as they can, just in case.'

Lisa nodded. 'I'll start rotating people through a training schedule. Could you help me with that, please, Rachel?'

Rachel grinned happily. 'I'd love to.'

'Um.' Ralph spoke into a momentary silence. The newest Elder was sitting unobtrusively at the back of the group, near the dining room doors and Sam wondered why it had taken him so long to voice his dissent. He was looking very subdued, though, quite unlike his usual arrogant self, and Sam was pleasantly surprised when Andrew's old rival posed a normal question rather than making a snide comment or disparaging remark. 'What can the rest of us do? I assume you have something planned for us.'

'I do indeed. If you don't mind, Lisa?'

Lisa chuckled. 'Why would we mind? None of us have much of a clue as to what to do next, at least as far as the Illuminati are concerned.'

'In that case, I believe we should be concentrating on taking away what the Illuminati have gained. I can stop them from making any more advances, but we still need to take away what they've already got - money, power, political influence, it all has to go.'

One by one he met the eyes of everyone there, seeing the determination and the resolve in each of them and, more importantly, the renewed hope. 'I know that we still have the day to day work of preventing the time-line wandering to do, and obviously that must continue, but I would ask that every Elder put aside their own personal research and followed the leads that I'm sure James has on John's ancestors and the origins of the Illuminati's power.'

He searched the audience until he found the face he was looking for. 'Anne, I'm sorry to have to ask, but is there any way to salvage the operation to the Holy Land? Or find another date we can go and still get the same result?'

'I will look into it.'

'Thank you.'

'Next, I would like every Displacer not involved with the martial arts training to put aside their own personal ambitions and trips for now and place themselves at the disposal of the Elders, in case they need any Displacements made for research purposes.'

There were nods of agreement from most Displacers.

'Thank you.' He nodded, but then blinked as the slight movement caused a dark wave to crash over him - the activities of the last twenty-four hours and several months were catching up with him and he needed to wrap things up quickly. 'Well, that's about all I've got. Um, does anyone else have any ideas? Grandad?'

James waved the scroll in the air. 'Well, for a start, I think we should send an emissary to the Dalai Lama, both the current one *and* his predecessors; he seems to know a lot more than he should. Maybe he'll have some information we can use.'

Sam staggered slightly and clutched at the door frame again, blinking to clear his eyes. Only Rachel noticed, though, because the members had plunged straight into a discussion on how best to proceed with Sam's suggestions, many of them raising their voices to be heard, and were otherwise occupied.

'Are you alright?' Rachel whispered in his ear.

'I need to rest, find me somewhere private please. And close.'

'OK, let's go.'

Sam let Rachel pull him away.

They had barely left the room before the blackness that had been threatening to overwhelm him for some time finally did.

CHAPTER 4
A UNITED FRONT

Sam woke up only moments later, but that was long enough for Rachel to have dragged him down the hall and into the dining room.

Lisa had seen him go down and had come to help, bringing Julia with her, but had left the room discretely, closing the dining room doors after them so, thankfully, none of the other members had any idea that anything had happened and weren't fussing around.

Sam found himself on the floor with Julia taking his pulse, her fingers at his neck and when she pulled back he saw the blood on them.

'I hope you put newspaper down, otherwise the carpet's going to need cleaning.'

Lisa smiled. 'Don't worry, I'll send you the bill.'

'Actually, it's Rachel's fault, so...'

'Don't even think about it!' Rachel was kneeling on his other side and she slapped him on the arm.

Sam took a deep breath and closed his eyes, then started to sit up.

Julia put her hand on Sam's chest to stop him. 'What are you doing? Stay there, the doctor will be here soon!'

'I...'

She cut him off with a glare. 'Sam, you and I are going to have a nice little chat when you've rested.'

'I don't need...'

'Yes you do.' She looked up at Lisa for support. 'Sam is in no fit state to be going on missions, physically or mentally, either he talks to me or you ban him from Displacing.'

Sam laughed. 'She can't do that. None of you can.'

'*I* can.' Rachel put her hand next to Julia's on Sam's chest. She barely put any pressure on him, but he found himself unable to resist, his muscles refusing to obey his commands, and he collapsed back down with a groan. Rachel smiled in satisfaction, then leaned forwards until her face was inches from Sam's and glared at him. 'I will be by your side, night and day, and if I ever get even a *hint* of you trying to Prepare I will slap you silly until you stop.'

He grinned at her and gave her a suggestive smile. 'Promise?'

'Shut it, or I'll start now.'

'Wow, in public as well! Kinky!'

Rachel laughed, but Julia scowled. 'Don't change the subject Sam. I want at least an hour of your time. Just you and me. As soon as possible.'

'Please, Sam, do as she asks.' Lisa added.

'Alright then, but it won't do any good; ask James - he'll tell you you'll be lucky to find a brain at all.'

The front doorbell rang before Rachel could agree with him and Lisa hurried off to answer it. She came back a few seconds later with the doctor, a short and very bald man in his late sixties wearing a tweed suit and with round glasses, carrying an old-fashioned black leather medical bag, the same one that Rachel had gone to with Diana when she'd come back from Sparta. He tutted when he saw Sam.

'Well, I won't bother asking who the patient is. Can we get him into a chair, please? My knees won't stand treating him down there.'

Between them, Rachel and Julia helped Sam to perch on the edge of one of the dining room chairs.

'Shirt off please.'

Rachel reached out to help, but Sam waved her away. 'I may be mad, but I'm not feeble.' There was a numbness in his fingers that almost put a lie to his words, but eventually he'd managed to get all the buttons undone and shrugged out of it.

There were horrified gasps from the women in the room, even from Rachel, who had seen more than her fair share of injuries.

Sam's body was a mess. His arms and both sides of his chest were almost completely black from bruises, but it was the scars that were most shocking, especially as, apart from the one from his duel with Quentin, they were all new, even though they looked like he'd had them for years: his forearms were a web of hundreds of thin, almost perfectly straight, white lines; a long and jagged purple line went across the ribs on his left side under his arm; and there were extensive burn marks on the right side of his chest and upper arm. There were also dozens of other minor scars scattered haphazardly about his torso and back.

The women were appalled and Lisa turned away, looking queasy, but the doctor just took it all in with a professional gaze. 'Those have all healed quite well. Any tightness across the chest from those burns?'

'No.'

'Good. You've been lucky.' He took a stethoscope from his bag and used it to listen to Sam's lungs and heart, making him breathe in and out. He frowned and made some notes on a pad then started prodding Sam's ribs.

Sam sat and took it, feeling the broken ribs grating slightly.

The doctor tutted. 'You know, a normal person would probably scream in pain, or at least flinch, groan or say "ow" when I prod them like that. It would be rather nice to get *some* kind of reaction from you; it would certainly help my diagnosis.'

'Sorry.'

The doctor grumbled and started prodding him again.

Every time Sam felt a bone shift he nodded and flatly said "ow" until the man told him to stop in exasperation.

'Right then, four cracked ribs in total, three on the left, one on the right. Now let's have a look at that nose.'

He took some alcohol wipes from his bag. 'This might sting a bit.'

Sam sat unmoving as the doctor cleaned his face. The cuts on his already broken lips had been opened up again and were bleeding and there was a new cut on the bridge of his nose. Most of the blood had come from his nostrils, though.

When the doctor was satisfied that the wounds were only superficial he used a pen light to look into Sam's eyes. He grunted, but didn't say anything.

Next he put a hand on either side of Sam's face and turned it backwards and forwards, looking at the broken nose. 'Yes. Yes. Very nice. Whoever straightened this did a good job, of course it does help when the owner of the nose is impervious to pain and doesn't flinch.' He stepped back. 'Right then, trousers off.'

Sam was uncertain for the first time and the doctor raised an eyebrow. 'Shy, Mr Vives?'

'No... It's just I didn't have time to put on a clean pair of pants today and I've run about thirty miles in these.'

The doctor sighed exasperated. 'Well, I'm sure we've all seen worse, but we can send the ladies out of the room to spare your blushes and their sensibilities if you'd like.'

Sam sighed. 'No... It's alright. I doubt if they'll let me out of their sight even if did ask them to go.'

'You got that right; I'm not missing this for the world!' Rachel grinned at him, but it was painfully obvious that she was just putting on a brave face; her eyes were just a bit too bright and her mouth gave a slight twitch at the corner, as if protesting being forced to do something against their will.

Sam gave her a crooked smile, then stood and dropped his trousers, stepping out of them and kicking them to one side.

His legs were fairly free of injuries. There were bruises on his thighs from kicks that he'd got from both Rachel and the Twins, and his shins were a mess where he had used them to block, but there weren't many scars, except for one large one just above his right knee from a deep cut.

'Sexy boxers, Sam.' Lisa sniggered.

Sam looked down and groaned. He had dressed in the dark and hadn't realised which ones he'd put on. They were pink with red hearts - a joke gift from Rachel for Valentine's Day and he'd only taken them with him when he'd left home for sentimental reasons, not to actually wear.

He flopped back into the chair and looked up at the doctor. 'Please tell me I'm going to die within the next few minutes.'

A smile managed to break through the doctor's professional demeanour. 'No such luck, I'm afraid.'

The man knelt down with a groan and began manipulating Sam's legs, but was finished quickly. 'All done. You can put your trousers back on now, but I'd suggest a clean shirt.'

While Sam stood and began dressing, moving stiffly, the doctor gave the three women a look and together they moved out of Sam's earshot to the far side of the room.

'What's the verdict, Doctor?' asked Lisa.

'The injuries aren't a problem, they'll all heal fine, but there are several things I don't like...' The man bit his lip as he looked back at Sam.

'What?'

'Well, he's far too thin for a start. If he keeps pushing himself as hard as he obviously is without rest or proper nourishment then his organs will start failing.'

'So, he just needs food.'

'To solve *that*, yes. - there's nothing in his notes to indicate any kind of eating disorder, despite his symptoms, so it should just be temporary. However, that's the least of my worries - it's the lack of a reaction to pain that concerns me most. That might speak to some kind of nerve damage or perhaps an underlying psychological issue.'

Julia nodded. 'My thoughts exactly.'

They looked up as Sam joined them.

He grinned weakly. 'Well then, Doc, give it to me straight. How long have I got?'

The doctor ignored the attempt at humour and peered up at him over the top of his glasses. 'Mr Vives, you don't seem to have suffered any permanent damage from your exploits, although if you don't eat more and get some rest that may well change. As for your injuries, it is only your ribs that concern me, so for heaven's sake stop fighting and look after them. For now they're just cracked, but if they take any more punishment they may well break and that will lengthen your recovery time considerably. Now, if I give you some painkillers, are you going to take them?'

He raised an eyebrow at Sam, who shrugged noncommittally.

The doctor huffed. 'Thought not. I'll leave you in the capable hands of your friends, then.' He offered his hand and Sam shook it. 'Talk to someone, Mr Vives, please. Get off your road to self-destruction while you still can. I don't want to have to read your obituary any time soon.'

He picked up his bag quickly and efficiently and left, waving away their thanks.

There was silence for some time after he'd gone, none of them quite knowing what to say. In the end it was Lisa who took charge. 'Right, let's get some food in you, Sam. Julia, go and ask Richard to organise lunch, please.'

'He'll have to look out for the mess we left on the kitchen floor...' Rachel said, sheepishly.

Lisa rolled her eyes. 'Right. Of course. I'll go and take care of that. You stay here and make sure that Sam sits down and doesn't pass out.' She went to the door, then turned to grin at them. 'Try not to kill each other while I'm gone.'

The two women went out together and finally they were alone.

Sam sat heavily in the nearest chair. 'Can't I just go to sleep?'

Rachel sighed. 'Food first. Sleep later. You heard the doctor, you need food so your body can recover. You'll be no use to us as weak as Quentin.'

Sam chuckled softly - all he could do with his ribs in the state they were. 'That's the most convincing argument I've heard so far! Bring on the food!'

Dinner was enjoyable and, despite almost falling asleep in his plate several times, served to drive home exactly how much Sam had missed both the company of his colleagues and Richard's superb cooking.

Sam knew perfectly well that his body needed food, he hadn't really need Asclepius to tell him that. It wasn't as if he had been starving himself, he just hadn't eaten as much as usual and that, as well as all the walking, had burned all the excess fat off him. If you added to that the fact he had just Displaced then it was no wonder he was starving. However, at that moment he needed sleep just as much as food, if not more, so he ate as much as he could as quickly as possible, then excused himself.

When he got up from the table, the room went silent and everybody looked at him as if expecting him to make a speech.

'Um.' Sam clutched at the back of his chair to steady himself and looked around in panic, searching for words to say to the people, the *family*, that had brought him back from the brink of destruction.

'Thank you, it's good to be back. Uh, bona nit.'

It was totally inadequate, but all he could get out in the face of welling emotions.

It seemed to serve, though, because there were smiles all around and a chorus of good nights, including a surprising number of replies in Catalan as, followed closely by Rachel, he rushed from the room, not wanting to break down in front of them.

Lisa had allocated them a room on the fourth floor for the night and Rachel helped Sam up the stairs to it, at times almost carrying him bodily as his legs gave way.

His energy, what little he'd had left, was fading fast, but Rachel insisted that he clean himself up before getting into bed; he hadn't had the energy to do anything more than wash his hands and face before dinner and he was still liberally covered in blood and filthy from his hiking.

They got into the shower together and Rachel washed him down while he supported himself against the walls with both hands. He could feel her taking in every one of the new scars on his body and he could sense her distress as she traced the three larger ones with her fingertips: the burn, the one across his ribs and the one on his leg. All three spoke of life-threatening injuries that she hadn't been around to witness or prevent.

She said nothing, though, knowing that he would tell her about them in due course.

Once finished she dried him off, then together they tumbled into bed. She wrapped her arms around him, pulling him tight against her chest, and for the first time in months he fell instantly into a deep sleep.

When he woke he was alone. He stretched, luxuriating in the feel of a real bed and not hard ground or a lumpy mattress in a cheap hostel.

He could have stayed there for hours, watching the colourful reflections of the sun off the cars passing by in the street outside swimming dreamily across the ceiling, but there was a particularly pressing need he had to deal with. He slid out of bed and grabbed the bath robe that had been put out for him, one of the deep blue Society ones with the crest on the breast pocket, then padded across the room and flung open the door.

He immediately came stumbling to a halt in the face of the strange sight that greeted him, all thoughts of the urgency of his situation temporarily banished.

For some reason the name plates from the entrance had been placed neatly on the carpet of the landing to create a new wooden floor that almost entirely covered it.

Completely baffled, he peered down at them and unconsciously began reading them one by one. It was only when he'd got to the tenth or twelfth that he realised that he'd had no idea of the surnames of most of his colleagues; the first time he'd come to Headquarters, Andrew had introduced him to everyone using only their given names. He'd never really taken the time to read the plaques since, either, only ever glancing at them in passing to see who was in and he now found out that Lisa was Lisa Curran, that Julia's surname was Weaver, and that Anne was Anne Barclay.

Before he could read them all, Rachel came bounding up the stairs. 'Afternoon, lazy! I thought I heard you moving around.'

He frowned at her. 'How?'

'I was in the computer room underneath the bedroom and you can hear the squeaky floorboards.'

'Ah.' He nodded, then waved at the beautifully carved wooden plaques. 'What's all this?'

Rachel leaned on the banisters and looked down at the plaques. 'It's an old Displacer tradition, apparently, a bit like those bets we made in Symposium, you know, with our time. These are pledges. To you.'

He looked at them, trying to count them and eventually gave up; he was still too tired. 'Is this everyone's?'

'I think so. When people started doing this last night, the word spread, and the members who weren't here rang in and gave instructions for their plaques to be placed here. Traditionally they were supposed to hand them over in person, but Lisa wouldn't let anyone disturb you. Apparently there was quite the discussion after we left the table yesterday and this is the result.'

'What does it mean, though?'

'It means they have put their lives in your hands.' They both looked up as James came hobbling up the stairs. He stood at the top, with his hand on Rachel's shoulder, fighting to get his breath back while he surveyed the wooden tiles on the floor. He was looking slightly better than he had the day before, as if Sam's return had taken a weight off of him.

'They are saying that they will follow you wherever you might lead them and to whatever consequences, trusting that you will do the right thing. They are saying that they are fully aware that any sacrifices they might be asked to make will be absolutely necessary and telling you that they are willing to make them.'

Sam shook his head in alarm. 'I can't take that responsibility!'

James shrugged. 'It's not your decision anymore; whether you like it or not our fate and that of the world is in your hands now. So, while Lisa is still our leader, her job has essentially become to make sure your plans are carried out as effectively as possible with the resources at our disposal. And yes, the decision to follow your lead was unanimous: every member's plaque is here.'

The old man frowned, reconsidering. 'Actually, I tell a lie, there's one missing: young Dylan's. Being under eighteen in experience disqualified him, I'm afraid, although he was very vocal in trying to convince us to allow him to give you his plaque anyway. He told us all in no uncertain terms that he will make up the years in his next Displacement, so that he can give you it in person.' James chuckled. 'There's a healthy bit of hero worship going on there, I think.'

Sam wasn't happy with that, either, but he said nothing. 'What am I supposed do with them?'

'Well, it would probably be rude to tread all over them, so I would pick them up and put them back downstairs!'

'Don't I need to say something to them? I don't know, thank them, or tell them I accept?'

'No, there's no need to do anything like that. You just let your actions speak for you from now on.' James smiled and nodded. 'You'll be fine, boy. You just wait and see.' He turned on his heels and disappeared back down the stairs.

Sam watched him go, then turned to Rachel. 'Can you help me pick these up so I can get past? I *really* need the toilet!'

Sam dressed in the clothes that Rachel, not wanting to go anywhere near the filthy ones in his rucksack, had bought for him that morning while he'd been sleeping. At Rachel's insistence, he brushed his teeth for about ten minutes, then they made their way downstairs together.

They dropped the plaques off in the hallway. The only one that had been left hanging was Sam's and they placed Rachel and James' ones next to it; unusually it was just the three of them in the house - none of the other Elders were there and the Displacers were all at work or school.

They found James in the sitting room, reading in his armchair in front of the fireplace.

'We're going to get some food, do you want a cup of tea or anything, Grandad?'

'No thanks, Sam, I'm fine.' He waved at them, vaguely, without looking up from his book.

Sam and Rachel grinned at each other as they went down to the kitchen; obviously whatever James was reading was far more interesting than them. They didn't mind, though, they needed the time alone to catch up - there was a lot that needed to be said.

Sam made them both sandwiches using the morning's fresh crusty bread and leftovers from the previous night and they sat down at the table.

He glanced at the floor next to the door. The tiles were as spotless as ever. 'Remind me to apologise to Lisa for not cleaning up my own mess.'

'I think that's the least of Lisa's worries right now.'

'Do you think she's upset that I've kind of come in and usurped her position? Especially after I told her I was fine with her taking over from Andrew.'

'I don't think she minds at all, in fact she's probably quite glad; the last few months have been hard for her, because she's finally coming to see exactly how bad things are for us. As a normal Displacer she was never really told all the details, but as the leader she got the bigger picture dumped on her all of a sudden, and you and I both know that Andrew was barely keeping us afloat, even with your help.'

They fell silent as they ate, the only sounds the soft ticking of the clock on the wall above the sink and the characteristic creaks and groans of the old house.

Sam ripped huge chunks off his thick sandwich, which he barely chewed before swallowing and taking another, but Rachel barely touched hers; she'd already had breakfast and lunch and wasn't particularly hungry so she had only a couple of mouthfuls then passed her unfinished sandwich to him to polish off, which he did eagerly, while she went to make tea for them both.

Finally, Sam wiped his mouth, pushed both empty plates away, grabbed his tea, then leaned back in his chair and grinned at her contentedly. 'So, are you going to take everybody to train with Master Hamato?'

'Maybe later, but not right now. He has to see something in someone to accept them and would never take any of them as students as they are.'

'Does that mean that he might not have agreed to train me?'

Rachel nodded. 'He might have refused, yes.'

'And what then? Does that mean I would never have been able to train with him? With you?'

'Correct. You only get one chance, but I knew that he would see the same thing in you that I did and it was a risk I was willing to take.'

'I'm very glad that you did, a lot of my best memories come from that Displacement.'

Rachel winked and leered at him. 'I bet they do.'

Sam shook his head in mock exasperation. 'Not *just* that!'

They laughed, comfortable together once more, almost as if the last three months hadn't happened, and Rachel shifted her chair slightly so that her leg was pressed against his under the table.

'What are you going to do with everyone, then?' asked Sam. 'You agreed readily enough when Lisa put you in charge, so you must have some ideas.'

'I was thinking you and I might take them on a kind of boot camp together. We could spend a couple of years in the wilderness somewhere teaching them the basics.'

'Why don't we just send them all to Sparta? See what happens.'

The thought of that gave them another good laugh.

'Seriously, though,' said Sam, 'how many of the Displacers is it really worth trying to train? I have a feeling Dylan would be keen, and I seem to remember Julia did some rowing at university, so she'll have a good base of fitness, but who else? Lisa?'

Rachel shook her head. 'Julia and Dylan are on my list, but Lisa is out. It doesn't look like it, but she's in her late thirties and has never done anything remotely physical. We'd never be able to train her to a level where the Twins wouldn't just kill her in one exchange. Hamish Junior would be a good option, though.'

'The lawyer's son?'

'Yeah. He's in the army so he's already fit and has a good technical basis.'

'I've never met him, but I hope he's as big as the Hamish we met at Symposium. Now *he* would certainly give the Twins something to think about...'

Rachel frowned. 'Is that why you want people trained? To fight the Twins and the rest of the Illuminati?'

'Of course.' Sam shrugged. 'Why else?'

Rachel sighed. 'With the possible exception of Hamish, none of the other Displacers would be able to stand up to either of the Twins for more than a few seconds.'

'*We* can. And with enough training...'

'*No*, Sam!' She cut him off irritably. 'If it was just about training hard enough then anyone could be heavyweight champion of the world, but you need more than that - you need an aptitude for it, a gift, an instinct. We have it, but the rest of the Displacers... Assess them like you would a potential rival. Can you honestly tell me you have seen *anything* in them that would indicate they could get anywhere near the level we or the Twins have? Even after decades of training?'

Sam thought about it for a while then shook his head. 'No, I suppose not.'

'I thought you wanted them trained to give them a bit of self-confidence, to give them some chance to survive long enough to escape if they were ever attacked, I didn't know you wanted an army. You can't just teach people a few tricks and expect them to have a chance against men and women who have dedicated their lives to fighting. This isn't bloody Hogwarts and I refuse to provide you with cannon fodder!'

'Hogwarts? What...?'

Sam didn't get the reference, but Rachel didn't stop to enlighten them, she just barrelled on. 'What has made you so bloodthirsty, Sam? How did you beat the Twins? And those scars... What did you do? I need to know.'

Sam stared down into the dregs of his tea while he considered what he should say. He was afraid that, after only just getting her back, telling her the truth would just push her away again, that she'd be appalled by what he'd done. The day before he'd half decided to give her an abridged version of his secret Displacement to Alamut in Persia that kept the worst parts from her, but he realised then that he couldn't do that. He had to be honest with her, not only because the air had to be clear between them if they were to have any kind of chance at continuing their relationship. He could never tell her exactly *what* he'd become, though, could never tell her about the Beast.

He looked up at her and nodded determinedly. 'You're right, I owe you that explanation.' He pushed his chair back from the table and stood up. 'Come on, let's go back up to the room; I don't want anyone interrupting us.'

CHAPTER 5
NECESSARY EVILS?

'I killed my first man the day I arrived. He was the first of many, of dozens, hundreds of men and women that I killed while I was there, enough to make his death seem almost insignificant, but I remember him the clearest.

'He was a few years older than me, with dusky skin, a full beard and the darkest eyes I've ever seen. I remember the confident look he had, thinking that he had me exactly where he wanted and I remember how that look changed to one of surprise as I threw him off a cliff. I remember the scream that was cut off long before the echoes faded and I remember the approval on the master's face when I turned and found him standing behind me.'

Sam perched on the edge of the bed facing Rachel, who sat on the floor against the wall. He leaned his elbows on his knees and looked down at this feet, not meeting her eyes as he spoke; he didn't want to see the disappointment or the disapproval that would inevitably be in her eyes when she heard what he had to say. He wasn't ashamed of what he had done; it had been necessary, but it had been a complete betrayal of the principles of the Displacers, as well as Sam's own, and he knew that she wouldn't be able to help herself.

'When I arrived in the time-line I found myself chained to six young men, standing at the bottom of the mountain, in the driving snow, dressed just in simple tunics and trousers. They were shivering, shaking the chains, making them clink, but after Sparta I barely noticed the cold.

'There was a man standing on a rock above us. He was alone, but I had the sense that there were others with him, just out of sight. He was dressed like us, but he didn't seem to feel the cold either. He was old and had a white beard that had been shaped into a point, but he stood steady on that rock in the driving wind as if attached to it.

'He looked at us for long minutes and I could feel the men around me weakening, quailing beneath his gaze. I must admit that I felt slightly intimidated myself, but I forced myself to meet his eyes and not look away.

'Eventually he spoke. He thanked us for being there and said we were all worthy candidates. He said that the rewards of heaven were waiting for the person who made it to the castle at the top of the mountain. For *one* person only. He threw a key at us and while we were watching it bounce on the rocks at our feet he disappeared.

'Naturally, a fight broke out. One of the men was killed straight away, strangled by his two neighbours with their chains, but while they were occupied, the other three managed to get themselves loose. I was furthest from the key when it landed so I decided to just wait for the rest to release themselves. The last one tried to throw the key away when he was done, but I stopped him with a single punch, knocking him out, then unlocked myself and ran after the five men who were left.'

Sam let out a shuddering sigh. 'Sometimes I think back and wonder why I didn't just knock all six of the men out and make my way up the mountain alone. It would have been easy enough; none of them had my training and that way I wouldn't have had to kill that man. Then again, without that first easy kill, I might not have been able to pass the tests the old man put me through later and it would have all been for nothing. Or maybe the old man wouldn't have been satisfied with how I had triumphed and wouldn't have accepted me. I really don't know and I never will.

'We started up the mountain, following a steep road that wound around it. It was easy going at first, but after only a couple of minutes our way was blocked by hard-faced men in turbans. They told us to leave the road and go into the rocks, brandishing long hooked knives to emphasise the only other choice we had. Apparently this wasn't going to be a simple endurance race up the mountain, we were to take the shorter, but far more dangerous route.

'One of the men fell before we'd gone more than twenty metres up that first sheer rock face, almost taking another with him, but Jacques' training served me well and I caught and passed several of them until it was only one man in front of me. He climbed strongly, obviously born in the mountains and I thought I was going to have to take some risks if I wanted to catch him, but I was wrong because he was lying in wait for me at the first plateau, about fifty metres up.

'He sprang out at me from behind a boulder as I pulled myself onto the ledge, aiming to send me tumbling back over the edge. Perhaps he saw me as his only rival, perhaps he intended to do the same to all the men as they arrived, whatever the case, I sidestepped him easily, tripping him as he went past. He fell and I realised that I had killed my first man, without even really meaning to. I don't know how long I stood there, staring at the point where he had disappeared over the ledge, but it couldn't have been very long because the others still hadn't reached me. When I finally turned, the old man was there, only a few feet behind me. I saw the amusement in his eyes and knew then what we were to him: nothing more than playthings that might one day prove useful. He had knowledge that I wanted, though, so I forced myself to give him a respectful bow and forged on.

'In the end I might as well have killed all of the men, because that was the result of me reaching the top first - I was forced to watch as those that hadn't already fallen to their deaths were thrown off the precipice. Only then was I taken inside the fortress which was to be my home for the next twenty-four years.'

Rachel leaned forwards, interrupting him with an alarmed look. 'Twenty-four years?'

Sam nodded.

'Damn it, Sam!'

Sam just nodded again.

She stared at him angrily and Sam waited patiently for her to say more, but she had no words and in the end she just sat back against the wall and waved irritably for him to continue.

'That race up the mountain was by far the easiest of the trials that I was to face.

'I learned how to kill with blade, hands, feet and missile, I learned the use of drugs and poisons, I learned to resist torture... And behind it all was the old man, working at my mind, trying to instil a blind obedience, the same that I saw in the rest of the assassins that he trained - a religious fervour and a willingness to obey his every order. I played along, feigning compliance, knowing that to do any less would have cost me my life.

'I won't bore you with the details, but suffice it to say I served faithfully, carrying death to whoever my master deemed worthy, and with each success I was rewarded with a higher place in the pecking order and more training. I eventually worked my way up to the master's right hand, becoming his most effective killer. I was not a friend, even then; I was never anything more than a tool to be discarded when no longer useful, but I wasn't bothered about that, because I was too busy gobbling up the titbits of secret techniques and knowledge that my position won me. And even twenty-four years and almost a hundred successful missions later there was still so much he still had to teach me.

'The end came suddenly and the very day the master died his sons came for me. They wanted no competition for his throne and couldn't believe that I didn't want it.

'I killed them without a thought and while their blood was still warm on my hands I came home.'

Sam stared down at his hands, remembering how simple it had been to take those last two lives - a quick thrust with a knife between the correct ribs for the young one, but for the other, the cruel one, a swift slash at the neck and then the slow draining of life as he watched, savouring the play of emotions as the man faced his end... He'd grown accustomed to killing over the years he'd been there and it had become easy. Seductively easy.

Rachel had barely kept her emotions in check as Sam just glossed over the two decades that he had spent in the past without her, barely giving any details. It didn't matter, though; she knew him too well and could easily read between the lines. She could see in his eyes his horror at the things he'd done, even if he didn't actually tell her about them and could feel the scars on his soul, mirroring those on his body.

To her surprise, though, she found that she didn't care nearly as much about the lives Sam had taken as she did the risks he had taken with his own. If he'd died the Displacers would have been left defenceless against the Illuminati and, worse, she would never have known what had happened to him.

Half of her was screaming in rage and wanted to beat him up again for that.

The other half wanted to hold him tight and never let him go.

The best part of her won, as she'd known it would.

She got up and went to sit next to him on the bed, then put a finger under his chin to lift his face towards her. 'Was it worth it? Was it worth...' she grimaced at what she saw in his eyes. 'This?'

'Yes. I have what I need.'

'And you felt that it was the right thing to do? You were sure?'

'Oh, yes.'

'Then I guess that's all I really need to know. You can tell me the rest when you're ready.' She gave him a weak smile, which was all that she could manage at that moment, then began fumbling at his t-shirt, pulling it up over his head.

'What are you...?'

'Don't go getting any ideas, I just want to see your body.'

With his t-shirt off, she started on his trousers.

When he was sitting in his underwear - decent cotton boxers she'd gotten him from Marks and Sparks - she sat back and turned to face him. 'Tell me about your scars.' She reached out to grasp his forearms and turned them so that his hands were facing down, exposing the webs of thin white lines on them. 'These are from knife fights, right?'

He nodded slowly. 'Yes, an essential skill for assassins and the traditional method of meeting challenges for honour or supremacy.'

Rachel wet her lips and took a shuddering breath; there were more than a hundred small scars on Sam's arms that spoke of dozens of duels.

She wasn't sure she really wanted to hear any more, but she forced herself to go on. 'The burn?'

'A mission that went awry. It was one of my first and I was just an apprentice, part of a team that was sent to destroy an entire family in Venice. One of my companions was particularly inept - he woke his target and a lantern fell over in the resulting chaos. I was the only one to escape the flames by diving into the canal with my clothes on fire. I returned to finish the mission later.'

'The knee?'

'A sword wound from a guard in Egypt, whose master I was killing. I was lucky not to lose my leg.'

Rachel waited for him to say more, but it seemed that that was it. She nodded and then traced his ribs where the longest and thickest scar was. 'And this?'

'A lesson. From the master himself. I grew too bold and said something that I shouldn't have. He challenged me, a seventy year-old man, and he beat me. Easily. He knocked me to the floor and then held me down while he used my own dagger to slowly slice me, twisting the blade so that it would leave this scar. He told me that it was a reminder of my place and promised that the next time I forgot it he would cut a little bit deeper and take my heart.'

Sam grinned humourlessly. 'He died soon after, so I never got to test that promise.'

Rachel was feeling sick, but not just because of what he was telling her - while he'd been speaking she had been gazing into his eyes, trying to find some sign of the sweet and comically innocent boy she'd met just over a year ago, but there wasn't any. Instead his eyes were cold, with no emotion in them. She had only seen eyes like those once before - when Master Hamato had been extremely drunk and started remembering a past he had tried to forget.

They were the eyes of a killer.

It was not that the Sam she knew was lost forever, though; Master Hamato had been able to put his past behind him and live his life joyfully, so there was no reason that Sam wouldn't be able to do the same, at least after the Illuminati were no longer a threat. He would only be able to do that if he didn't go too far down the dark path he was on, though; killing people in the past who would return to life after he'd gone was one thing, killing Illuminati and wiping them from history was quite another - he might not be able to come back from that.

'Sam, I don't think the prophecy says anything about you having to kill the Illuminati. I think you only need to stop them in order to protect the time-line.'

He huffed, the sarcasm from his British half making itself felt. 'If you can think of another way to make sure that they *never* threaten the time-line again except by killing them, then please tell me; I've been working on the problem for months and this is the only solution I have.'

Sam thought back to the time between Andrew's death and the journey to Alamut to study with the assassins. He remembered the sleepless nights he'd spent, with his mind going round and round in circles, trying in vain to come up with some way of defeating the Illuminati once and for all. He remembered his own resignation when the solution finally appeared and recalled with shame the excitement and eagerness he'd felt to finally be doing something, despite knowing that what he had resolved to do was against everything that he believed in. The fact that it wasn't his fault, that he had been placed onto that path, had become a mantra to him and he repeated it now to Rachel, using it in an attempt to justify his actions to her, just as he did to himself every day.

'I am what they made me. They have forced my hand. This is *their* doing, not mine, and I'm merely going to finish what they started.'

'OK.' Rachel sighed, not liking it one bit, but seeing the reasoning and the twisted logic behind it. 'What's your plan?'

'I do have one play that we could make...' He smiled at her, but it wasn't his usual smile, the one that she loved so much, it was a new one, to go with the look in his eyes, one that seemed to promise suffering, and she had to suppress a shudder. 'I want to go back to Symposium and get answers out of the Quentin there. However I can.'

It was late evening when they finally made their way back downstairs. James was in his chair, right where they'd left him and if it weren't for the tea pot and cup on the table next to him they would have thought that he hadn't moved in the hours they'd been upstairs.

He glanced up from his book as they came in and looked back and forth from one of them to the other. 'Hrumph,' he grunted, shaking his head. 'I didn't think it would take so long for you two to make up.'

Sam said nothing, but Rachel answered James with a grin and no sign of shame. 'Making up only took an hour, then there were... other things to do.'

Both Rachel and the Elder burst out laughing, but Sam just groaned and slid onto a sofa opposite his grandfather.

Rachel sat next to him and moulded herself against him.

James nodded and looked at them in approval. He placed his book to one side and folded his arms across his stomach. 'Well? You two look like you have something to say.'

Sam smiled at his grandfather. 'I might have a way to find out more about the Illuminati.'

James' face lit up in delight. 'Wonderful! How?'

'Well, we know that Quentin has gone back to Symposium at least once since I've encountered him...'

'Stop right there, Sam.' The Elder growled, his face suddenly cold. 'I can see where this is going and no, you can't do that.'

'But I can get answers easily enough...'

'No, Sam! I forbid it!'

James' shout filled the room and Sam felt Rachel stiffen in his arms as they both stared at the Elder in shock. It was the first time they had ever heard him raise his voice in anger, even under extreme provocation, and they were both at a complete loss for how to reply.

The anger faded quickly from the old man's face, though, and was replaced once again with tiredness.

'I'm sorry, that was uncalled for.' He ran his hand over his bald head as he sighed. 'I shouldn't have expected you to understand after only an establishing visit, but Symposium is *sacrosanct*. Using it in that way will taint your presence there, possibly beyond repair. Quentin has defiled it already, but you *will not*.'

James gave each of them a stern look and they nodded to show their understanding.

'Thank you.' The Elder gave them a smile. 'There will be other opportunities; you'll come up with something better, Sam, I know you will.'

He slapped his hands on the arms of his chair. 'Now, come on, I'm starving. Let's go and have a nice dinner as a family while we still can.' He stood with surprising energy. 'Oh, and, now you're rolling in it one of you can pay.'

CHAPTER 6
CHANGED CIRCUMSTANCES

Diana read the messages from Rachel slowly, carefully, savouring them and committing them to memory before deleting them for safety.

Sam was back.

She could sense that there was something that Rachel wasn't telling her, something very wrong, but the news was still the best thing that she had heard in months.

The world had seemed so bright, the future so perfect after that night they had shared in the hotel in London, but then, just two days later, everything had fallen apart. The heart had been ripped from Sam and he hadn't been the same again.

She had spied on them whenever she could over the following days, wanting to be close to them, even if she couldn't be with them, and had been watching as they had buried Andrew. She had studied Sam with her binoculars as he stood amongst the gravestones on his own and had seen the precise moment when his sorrow had turned to rage. She had known then that he would plan something terrible, something that would ultimately be self-destructive, but she had been powerless to stop it; all of her messages to Rachel had been ignored and Sam hadn't answered except with cold requests for information on the Illuminati. She had tried to find an opportunity to see him in person, but he had gone back to Barcelona before she had a chance and then she couldn't follow him without provoking too many questions.

Now he was back and something bad had obviously happened. Just as she had predicted.

She wanted to meet up with them to find out what was wrong and what she could do to help, but it was impossible; after being made leader of Grant Davis' team the Master was undoubtedly keeping a close watch on her and it would be extremely dangerous for her to attempt to do so.

Leadership of the team had its upside, including an astronomical increase in the amount of money she was being paid and a few other perks, such as shares in Illuminati corporations and access to the private jets. However, it mostly meant a lot more stress, not only because of the closer scrutiny, but also because her new team really did not like her; they were of the opinion that one of them should have taken over from Davis, not her. The Master hadn't done anything to disabuse them of that opinion or cement her position with them, he had just given her their personal details and contact information then told her to get on with it, saying that if she couldn't keep them under control then she didn't deserve to lead them.

In an effort to get to know them and try to win them over she invited them to her flat for dinner. She took the precaution of hiding cameras in all her rooms first, though, not only because she didn't trust them in her home, but also because the videos would give the Displacers faces and personalities to go with the names she'd already provided them with.

Illuminati always worked in groups of four, so there were three of them, two women and one man, and they turned up as a group. Almost an hour late. Diana said nothing to reproach them, she just smiled coldly then led the way through to the living room where she served them drinks. She watched them closely, trying to get a read on them, as they helped themselves to the nibbles that she had laid out, while wandering around to peer at her various souvenirs and decorations.

According to his file, the man, Jason Tuttle, was twenty-five. He was very nervous and kept shifting and twitching in his seat, looking around as if expecting an attack and constantly playing with a switchblade knife, flicking it out and pushing it back into its handle. Whenever his eyes met hers she could see the hostility written plainly in them and every time his knuckles whitened on the knife as if imagining plunging it into her heart. His black hair was greased and slicked back and he was dressed in tight black jeans, a white t-shirt and a tatty leather jacket that he refused to take off. He reminded Diana of the rockabilly dancers she had seen in Yoyogi Park in Tokyo a few years back; a group of men who dressed up and did bad dance routines every Saturday. In their case, they'd probably just seen a few too many bad movies, whereas Tuttle had most likely been to the fifties in order to perfect his look. Diana wasn't quite sure what his role in a team would be, besides providing something to ridicule with his strange getup - he certainly wasn't a fighter, if his inexpert manipulation of the knife and his scrawniness was anything to go by.

The younger of the two women, Laura Matthews, was sixteen and looked like she hadn't had a decent meal or a good night's sleep in years. She was tall and thin, pale, with lank brown hair and heavy, dark eye makeup. She was dressed all in black in a hoodie and cargo trousers and had a heavy-looking messenger bag over her shoulder that she was never out of contact with, which undoubtedly contained a laptop. Her nails were chewed ragged and she seemed to always be wanting to do something with her hands but, when there wasn't anything, she unconsciously stuck a finger in her mouth and started biting. During the meal she barely looked at anyone, instead just seeming to stare into nothing, mumbling to herself under her breath. Despite never giving any sign that she was following the conversation around her, she nevertheless always had an answer when addressed that was invariably short, intelligent and to the point. Diana thought it was more than likely that she was a computer expert and again she despaired slightly; a hacker wasn't the most use when most of their missions would take them back to before computers were even conceived of.

The third and last member of the team was Emily Clarkwell, twenty years old and she couldn't have been more different to the other two. She was short, just over five feet tall, beautiful, with long black hair and startlingly clear blue-grey eyes. She was dressed in a stylish and impeccable white summer dress that clung to her upper body and then flared out from her hips, making her seem almost childish despite her wiry arms and deep cleavage. Of the three, she was the one who scared Diana the most. The man was overtly, almost laughably aggressive, but this woman had a way of *flowing* rather than moving and a quiet menace to her that reminded Diana very much of Rachel. The similarity went no further than that, though, because Diana could tell that there was something inherently wrong about her; the intensity in her eyes was tinged by a madness and a feeling of sheer *age*, which made Diana wonder what the woman had gone through - even as their leader, the Master hadn't given her access to the Leap reports of her team.

All in all, she wasn't particularly impressed with them. They weren't a team, they were the kind of ragtag group of misfits that would save the day in a movie, but who in real life wouldn't get beyond arguing about what the plan should be. They had very obviously been left to their own devices and not taken under the wing of someone more experienced and she wondered, not for the first time and probably not the last, what they could have become if only the Displacers had gotten to them before the Illuminati.

Despite their obvious disrespect of her, Diana was still determined to win them over. She hadn't been sure how to proceed, though. She had immediately discarded trying to turn them with kindness; they would probably see it as weakness, and she was sure that they wouldn't respond very well to her trying to assert her dominance by force. Besides, if it got down to fighting, Diana was now certain she would lose; she had a bit of training, mostly thanks to Tessa, which would be enough to defeat Laura and probably Tuttle, but it was nothing compared to what the small woman, Clarkwell, must have.

So, she had decided to work around the problem and approach it from an unexpected angle; she was going to try some good old childish fun. She wanted to make them see that things didn't have to be so serious and that if they worked for her they might actually enjoy it.

Instead of cooking, she ordered takeaway from the local Indian restaurant that she went to at least a couple of times a month, getting in a vast array of different dishes with varying degrees of spiciness, and was pleased when her guests tucked in enthusiastically - they obviously enjoyed Indian food just the same as most English people of university age.

At first they ate mostly in silence, the three of them on one side of the table and her on the other, but then she made her move.

She had warned them about a few of the dishes, but one in particular, a vindaloo dish that was the speciality of the restaurant, was almost suicidally spicy. Usually a single mouthful was enough to cause eyes and noses to water and more than one spoonful made most people want to almost drown themselves to take away the burning sensation. It was a favourite with the students at the local university and had become a kind of rite of passage, but even the most foolish or drunk of them never managed to eat more than a couple of spoonfuls.

She divided the reddish brown mush into four equal parts, then pointedly looked at her guests, catching and holding their attention, as she spooned one of the portions onto her plate, issuing a challenge.

The three looked at each other, puzzled, but shrugged and started putting the food onto their own plates. She left them to it and went to the fridge to grab some milk; the alkalinity would counter the acidity from the spicy food and serve as an antidote. She came back and poured four glasses from the six pint bottle bought specially for the purpose, putting them deliberately in the middle of the table, just out of reach of everyone, then stood opposite them.

'Last one to drink their milk wins.'

The rockabilly wannabe paused in the flicking of his switchblade. 'Wins what?'

Diana smiled; she had their attention. She went to a cupboard at the side of the room and lifted out a golden mask which she brought back and placed on the table next to the milk.

'Is that real?' Jason's voice was breathless as he gazed greedily at the golden face, which shone invitingly in the overhead lights. It was incredibly detailed and lifelike, encrusted with jewels and painted with makeup around the eyes.

'Nope.'

It took a second for them to register what Diana had just said, but then her three guests turned to stare at her in confusion.

Diana laughed at the look on their faces. 'Well, it *is* a genuine Egyptian relic, but it's not worth as much as, say, Tutankhamen's mask, either in real value or archaeological value. It was actually made less than two hundred years ago and is only gold leaf over a lead base.'

Tuttle growled, his annoyance plain on his face, his knife open and clenched ready in his hand. 'Then why insult us by offering it as a prize?'

'Well, while it might not be worth much money, relatively speaking, it does have quite a lot of sentimental value and not a little bit of history behind it. Quentin Price brought that back from what was supposed to be a simple mission to Egypt that the Master had sent the two of us on. He thought that it was his great prize for having outwitted the Displacers and Sam Vives in particular. He gave it to me to give to the Master and while it was in my possession I noticed the scratches on the back here.'

She showed them the inside of the mask where some of the gold had been scraped away, exposing the dull grey metal underneath.

'The Master told me to get it tested anyway, just in case, but the results just confirmed what I already knew; that it is a cheap replica made to fool a fool like Quentin. That was the first of three times that I have personally witnessed Quentin get his pride massacred by Sam Vives and subsequently be punished by the Master for his idiocy. '

Diana grinned and for the first time the others smiled with her.

'The Master didn't think that the mask was worth keeping and told me to dispose of it as I wished. I decided to keep it and it has become one of my favourite souvenirs - a reminder of the failures of Mr Quentin Price.'

Her story surprised and delighted them in equal measures and their faces now lit up as they looked at the mask, glinting in the light, each of them smiling at the possibility of owning something with such a meaning. Even if they hadn't been personally witnesses to Quentin's disgraces, they all knew of him because the Master had always held him up as an example for them to follow, rubbing his successes in their faces. At least until recently.

'Count me in!' Clarkwell laughed gaily.

Diana shuddered; somehow was so wrong about the sweet sound coming from the terrifying woman.

'Good.' She forced a smile and nodded, then looked questioningly at the others. 'How about you two?'

'Quentin recruited me and I've never met a bigger asshole before or since.' Tuttle leaned back in his chair, grinning widely as he looked around the group. 'I'm going to put it on a pedestal with a plaque and I think I'll call it, "Price's Shame", or something like that.' He ran a hand over his hair, even though it was still perfect and there was nothing to smooth back into place.

'You'll have to beat me first,' said Laura, staring fiercely at him.

Diana was somewhat surprised at the strength in the young girl's voice and her sudden determination. Even though she wasn't looking at the mask greedily like the other two and didn't seem to particularly covet it, she was resolved to fight for it just the same. Diana made a mental note: Laura wasn't the pushover that she appeared to be at first glance.

'OK, then, one spoonful at a time, all together.' Diana picked up her teaspoon and waved it at them. There was already one in front of everyone in preparation for her little game.

She dug it into the food and presented it to them. She waited for everyone else to do the same.

She smiled inside as the three made a fuss over making sure they all had the same amount.

'Ready? On three. One, two... three!'

All four simultaneously put the curry into their mouths. Diana held up her spoon to show that it was all gone followed by the others.

She watched them closely waiting for them to react. It would take a few seconds, but...

'Holy crap!' Jason gasped. His mouth opened and he sucked in huge gulps of air, trying to cool his tongue as he broke out into a sweat and his eyes started streaming. Diana watched as his hand involuntarily twitched and his eyes flicked unconsciously towards the milk. More information to note: Jason was somewhat lacking in self-control.

The Hacker, Laura, was more subtle about it, but was feeling the effects just the same. She passed her hand across her forehead, smearing her heavy black eyeliner, then wiped her nose on the sleeve of her hoodie before looking around the group and grinning. 'Wow! That stuff's amazing!'

Clarkwell shrugged. 'It's not bad, it's hot enough, but I'd like it to have a bit more taste to go with it.'

She was barely even sweating and Diana wondered if she had somehow performed some sleight of hand and gotten rid of her mouthful. She discarded the theory immediately when a runnel of mucus ran from the woman's nostril.

Clarkwell's eyes widened in alarm and she scrabbled for her handbag and produced a lacy pink handkerchief with which she genteelly wiped her nose. 'Oh! That was very rude, you'll have to excuse me!'

That was interesting; it seemed that appearances mattered to the girl. Diana made another mental note, but in this case wasn't sure how she could use the information. She smiled sweetly and looked around the group. 'Anybody want to chicken out yet?'

They all shook their heads, although she could tell Jason wasn't entirely convinced, but his masculine pride wasn't going to let him back out before the rest of his entirely female company.

The second round produced more spectacular results.

Jason yelped in a very unmanly way and leapt for the milk. Laura was too busy fighting her own battle to take much notice, but Clarkwell laughed at him, dabbing her now running eyes with her handkerchief.

Diana wasn't exactly immune to the effects either and could feel the sweat beading at her hairline and the moisture welling up at the sides of her eyes. She loved spicy food and regularly used chili peppers or piri piri sauce when she cooked at home, but she never ordered the "Volcano Vindaloo" as the restaurant had dubbed it.

She cleared her throat and swallowed several times before attempting to speak. 'Well, that's one down, three to go. Looks like the girls come out on top.'

'As it should be.'

It was Clarkwell that had spoken, but both young women turned to grin at Jason's discomfort.

He didn't take it badly, but just laughed. 'All it proves is that I'm not stupid enough to carry on.' He refilled his glass with milk and toasted them with it before knocking it back.

He already looked much better and Diana saw Laura eyeing the glass enviously as she wiped her hand across her forehead again. Her mascara was now smeared halfway down her cheeks and her normally pale face was a bright pink colour that closely matched Clarkwell's handkerchief.

'Right then, third round?' asked Diana. 'I hope neither of you have ulcers...'

The women didn't answer, but just filled their spoons.

They ate simultaneously.

Laura had had enough, but she had enough control to reach out for her milk calmly and take sips instead of just gulping it, holding it in her mouth to cool her tongue before swallowing it.

'Well!' she said when she'd finished the entire glass. 'That was certainly a unique experience.'

Diana turned to look at Clarkwell and found the strange woman staring at her with a disconcerting smile on her face.

She was toying with her spoon, twirling it between her fingers and Diana eyed it warily, recalling Sam's story of how Rachel had impaled a target dummy with a wooden chopstick from a distance of several metres the first day of their trip to Okinawa. She wondered what damage could be done with a metal spoon in the right hands.

She forced herself to smile, forcing back a queasiness that was not only due to the curry. 'Shall we continue?'

Clarkwell nodded, but laid aside her teaspoon and picked up a desert spoon. 'How about we speed things up a bit?'

Diana's eyes widened. She wasn't sure if she could take another teaspoonful of the curry, let alone a whole desert spoon, more than three times as much. She had to continue, though; the fun wasn't over yet and she had to play it through to the end if it was going to serve its purpose.

She answered the woman's smirk with a shrug and what she hoped was a friendly smile. 'Of course.'

She changed her spoon and they dug into the food, taking most of what was left. They didn't bother with a countdown or any other ceremony, but just stuck the food straight into their mouths and started chewing.

Diana held her opponent's steel-grey eyes, watching as they slowly turned red and began to water, her own prickling at the same time, her vision blurring. There was a raging fire in her belly now, where before there had only been hot coals and she breathed rapidly through her mouth, fighting against the burning sensations, fighting against the sudden urge to run from her flat and dive into the river that ran past just outside, the filth be damned.

Clarkwell was trying hard not to show signs of her own discomfort, keeping her expression impassive, but it wasn't just her eyes betraying the fact that she was suffering: her face was almost bright red beneath the black curtains of her hair and her knuckles had whitened as she clutched the spoon, threatening to bend it.

Diana took comfort from the sight. If she could only hang on just a little longer...

She couldn't stand it any longer, though. She broke and lunged for the milk, gulping it down, but it wasn't nearly enough and she refilled and emptied the glass over and over. Five glasses later she collapsed back into her chair, gasping for breath.

Only when Diana had finished did Clarkwell calmly reach for her own glass. Her control only lasted for the first few sips, though, and soon she was gulping glass after glass of milk down just as greedily as Diana had.

When she finally slammed her glass down she laughed. The other members of the team laughed with her and Diana herself smiled and applauded.

She wasn't upset with the result; she had been meaning to let one of the other three win all along, although with the amount of spicy food she ate she hadn't really expected to lose. It was better that way, though; she had been able to take the game much further than she'd thought she would, making it all the more fun for everyone involved.

She stood and picked up the heavy golden mask and presented it to her. 'Your prize, madam.'

'Thank you.' Clarkwell took it in both hands and put it in place over her face. 'Do you think it suits me?'

That brought fresh laughter and Diana joined in with genuine delight.

Diana thought that the evening had gone well, that she had managed to break the ice with her new team and at least make some inroads into gaining their respect, but then she reviewed the videos of what they'd done when she hadn't been around to see. It was only a few minutes of footage, but first she saw Laura, the hacker, going into her laptop, left on the coffee table in the living room, and insert a pen drive for a few seconds, then she saw Jason searching her bedroom, looking through her drawers and cupboards, and lastly she saw Clarkwell touring the entire flat, looking at the latches on the windows and making an impression of the keys that Diana had left hanging from the front door.

She didn't know if it was the initiative of the team, or whether they were doing it at the Master's orders - another sign of his paranoia - but she knew then that she would never be able to trust any of them. She was going to have to keep her distance and treat them as the subordinates they were. Nothing more.

She had no idea what had been done to her laptop so, instead of trying to get rid of whatever malware had been installed, she decided to buy a new one, which she kept in her safe for personal use, and left the old one for official Illuminati business as a decoy. In addition she bought a new telephone to use for the sole purpose of contacting the Displacers and changed all the locks.

Lastly, she went about secretly buying some new properties.

At some point she was going to have to make a clean break from the Illuminati; either they were going to be destroyed by the Displacers, in which case she would be free, or they were going to destroy them in turn, in which case her betrayals might become known and she would have to disappear. She doubted she would be able to hide for long if the latter happened because she'd already helped them gain influence in enough governments - without any opposition, the Illuminati would only expand all the more rapidly and the whole world would be theirs. She refused to be a part of a world run by the Illuminati, though, especially since it necessarily meant that her friends and lovers had been killed, so she had decided that she would live what remained of her life in whatever freedom she could.

With the money she'd been hiding away in an offshore account for years, supplemented by the substantial sum she had been given by the Displacers as one of their employees, she bought three properties. One in the outskirts of London that she could use in secret for the next few years if she ever managed to meet up with Rachel and Sam again, one in a remote part of Australia that she could disappear to if the Illuminati won the war, and lastly one in Catalunya so that she could be close to Sam.

A week after the dinner, the Master contacted her. An email told her to be on Skype at nine in the evening and at nine on the dot the call came.

'Good evening, Miss Birch.'

The voice was distorted and the screen black as always and she had to remind herself that John had no idea that she knew that he was the Master. As far as he was concerned the only people who knew his identity were his former colleagues, the Displacers.

'Sir.'

'How are you settling in with your new team?'

'Not bad. It will take some time for them to get used to me after the loss of Davis and there has been some reticence on their part, but it's nothing I can't handle.'

'Well, you will have a chance to show me what you can do next month; I'm sending your team on a mission.'

Diana frowned, playing up her reluctance. She was walking a fine line; she needed to show just enough hesitation to let the Master think that she was scared of Sam, like she should be, but not so much that he thought she wasn't up to the job of leading the team. 'Really, sir? Is that wise? Sam Vives knows who I am and if he was able to track the Twins...'

'The Twins were too obvious in their activities, they caused too much of a stir in the time-line, and that is what attracted the attention of Vives and the Society's Elders. You will be going on a far more simple mission, just to collect a few funds, and shouldn't make more than a ripple.'

She nodded as if accepting his explanation, even though she knew he was lying. 'Very well, sir, I will make sure that my team is ready for when you give the word.'

'Good. I will be in contact soon. The Leap will take place in the second week of August, I will contact you with more details before then.'

The connection broke and Diana closed the lid of her laptop. She kept the computer shut down most of the time since the dinner party; she had no idea if Laura had been able to take control of her camera and didn't particularly fancy anyone watching her walking around. She'd even taken to wearing underwear and a top in bed instead of sleeping naked, just in case there was some other surveillance that she hadn't caught.

She sighed. Sometimes she wished she hadn't agreed to help the Displacers; things had certainly been a lot simpler when she'd just been an Illuminati foot soldier, but then she remembered Sam and Rachel and the night they had spent together and knew that it was worth it, if only for that one memory and the chance of a life with them in the future.

John logged out of Skype and unplugged the webcam from the USB port, then ran an antivirus check on his laptop while he turned off the router and disconnected the telephone wire from the wall.

Ever since the day his luck had finally run out he'd been taking extreme precautions with his cyber presence. It was the easiest way for the Society and their MI5 lackeys to track him so he never remained connected to the Internet for very long and had completely abandoned all of his social media and email accounts, He had even thrown away all his old electronic devices, no matter whether the Society knew of their existence or not, bought new ones, then formatted them and reinstalled the operating systems himself.

And he'd moved around. A lot.

While the virus check, an extremely thorough one which he had written himself, was running, he stood up and went to the window of the luxuriously-appointed penthouse flat. It was one of many, dozens, that he had bought over the years, but had never actually been to. One of many such safe houses around the world with nothing to connect them to him except a torturous route through blind companies and subsidiaries of minor concerns that he owned, usually through fake identities. This was one of his more salubrious ones, situated near the botanical gardens in Kuala Lumpur, and it had a very impressive view of the Petronas Twin Towers that he was growing to love, but would have to leave behind in a couple of days at the most.

After fleeing Displacer Headquarters and making his way out of the country using a secret private yacht, he hadn't stayed in the same place for more than a week at a time, following a plan that he'd had in place for just such an eventuality. He hadn't just been fleeing, though, and he certainly hadn't been idle - plans were coming together, information was being gathered and resources were being put into place to give the Displacers a very nasty shock indeed.

At the same time he would see if Sam Vives truly had the stranglehold over the past that he claimed to have, and to that end he would send Diana Birch and her team, all eminently expendable, to carry out some lucrative, but ultimately unnecessary task. If it wasn't true, then there would be no need for the drastic measures that he had in mind and he would be able to go back to doing what he had always done - letting others take the risks and do his dirty work for him. If it was, then it wouldn't be too hard to take care of him; in the present he was just another little boy with nothing remarkable about him.

John was fully aware that he should never have become personally involved, but at least now he didn't have to pretend to be someone he wasn't and could enjoy a bit of the empire he'd built up over the last couple of decades. And, finally, Andrew Berry, the man who had stolen the love of his life, then let her be killed, was dead.

He smiled.

There was certainly a pretty thick silver lining to this cloud.

CHAPTER 7
ABILITIES

'This girl, Emily Clarkwell, is someone that John's program flagged, but by the time we got to her she had gone. The other two I don't recognise.'

James was hunched over, watching the videos of the dinner party on Rachel's laptop. Diana had sent the files to Rachel and she had in turn passed them on to Sam and the rest of the Displacers so that they could familiarise themselves with the newly identified Illuminati.

The Elder was with Lisa, Sam, Julia and Rachel in one of the libraries on the first floor of Displacer Headquarters. The four of them had already seen the videos, but James had been at home ill and hadn't had a chance to do so.

He looked up at them questioningly. 'This is the team that Diana is taking with her on her next Displacement?'

Lisa nodded. 'They are ostensibly going back to secure more funds, but she is under the impression that they are actually being sent back as a test to see if it's safe.'

'Well, that's patently obvious.' James huffed. 'So, perhaps we should consider ignoring them in order to lure bigger game into the past for Sam to hunt.'

Sam shook his head. 'I already thought of that and it doesn't matter whether I confront these three or not, John still won't go into the past; he won't take the risk. He'll send Quentin and frankly he has dropped on my list of priorities - I'll kill him for what he's done to us, but it's John I really want. So, we're going to take care of these three and make damn sure he knows that he can't do *anything* in the past any more. I want him backed into a corner and desperate enough to make a mistake, and when he does MI5 will be waiting.'

The Elder still wasn't convinced. 'This could be another distraction, another bit of sleight of hand to have us looking one way while Quentin does something else a lot more important. Why endanger four people otherwise?'

'Even if it is, I would know if Quentin Displaced and would head him off instead. They won't fool me again.'

James nodded. 'Yes, I'm sure of that, my boy.'

'Diana said that her team wasn't exactly top shelf material, she actually said that they were "even less inspiring than Quentin" in her message to me, which is saying something.' Rachel's comment brought much needed laughs.

All too soon they fell silent again, though, and James gave a sigh. 'Well, I suppose the Elders would feel it if something truly important was in the works, so this may well be as simple as it looks. It will, of course, be a trap, so please be careful.'

'Of course, Grandad, I always am.' Sam smiled indulgently.

James growled mockingly. 'Don't patronise me, boy! I'm going to be worried about you as long as you keep doing stupid stuff all the time. I just hope Rachel can keep you on a tighter leash from now on.'

To Sam's shame, Lisa and Rachel laughed delightedly at that.

James grinned as he glanced around the little group, noting the renewed confidence that Sam's return had brought to them and to Lisa in particular; she needed it the most if she was going to lead them through this difficult time.

It had been several weeks since Sam had rejoined the Displacers and, while the Society as a whole had begun to believe in themselves again, they had only been making slow progress on plans to counter the Illuminati.

Anne believed that she was closing in on a possible date to carry out the Templar mission. Obviously they couldn't go back to the same time they had gone before because the Illuminati would have already fixed that date, so they were trying to find similar circumstances at another point in the time-line where the same result could be achieved.

The other Society members had mostly been helping him track John's ancestors back through time, working on linking him to banks and corporations. They'd found he'd made his largest gains in many of the more turbulent times, using unrest and war to further his interests and there was evidence to suggest that the Illuminati had provoked many of those events themselves, including the First World War and the Great Depression. They had the same problem trying to affect most of those events as they did the Templars; the time-lines around them were so active that most had already been fixed and it was impossible to find a way in. It was frustrating in the extreme, but they weren't letting that stop them and at weekends the second and third floors were taken over in their entireties as "war rooms" for the various groups assigned to different time periods to plot and plan.

Ultimately, they were hoping it wouldn't matter too much; if Sam could confront John in the past then the whole house of cards would tumble into ruins, the empire that he had painstakingly built would fragment and fall apart with nobody left to run it - they were at war and, much as he didn't like it, one of the best ways to win a war was to kill the leaders.

James pushed aside thoughts of his grandson killing and waved at the laptop which displayed a grainy image pulled from the videos of Tuttle and Laura. 'Tell me about the others.'

Rachel consulted a notebook where she had jotted down the information Diana had sent. 'Jason Tuttle and Laura Matthews, twenty-five and sixteen years old respectively. Diana doesn't have very much information on them beyond the tiny amount of information that was in the files she was given and the impressions that she got of them from this one meeting. She says that Tuttle is probably a make-weight; he didn't seem to display any particular talents beyond vanity. Matthews, on the other hand, is a hacker and installed something on Diana's computer while she was in the flat.'

James grunted. 'Well, that's not going to be much use to them in the past.'

Rachel nodded. 'That was Diana's assessment as well.'

'Did someone say "hacker"?'

They looked up as Dylan Lloyd walked in.

James looked at Julia. 'I thought you locked the door?'

Julia looked mortified. 'I thought I did, sorry!'

Dylan didn't seem to hear them, he was too focussed on the laptop on the table. He pointed at it and looked quizzically at James. 'May I?'

The Elder turned the screen of the laptop towards him so that the boy couldn't see it. 'You shouldn't be in here, this is supposed to be secret.'

Again the boy didn't really listen, he just plucked the computer from James' grasp and sat down with it on his lap.

James laughed and shared an amused look with the others. 'Please, be my guest.'

Dylan didn't take any notice; he was too busy with the computer. He tutted and shook his head. 'You really shouldn't be using this program for videos; it's rubbish, I'll install a better one.'

He started typing furiously and swiping the touchpad with rapid movements of his finger, starting several downloads. The fan on the laptop began to whine as the processor was pushed to the limit.

Rachel frowned. 'I hope you're not going to get a virus on my laptop.'

Dylan just snorted in reply without even looking up.

About a minute later he nodded in satisfaction. 'You said that this girl did something to a computer? Which video file is it on and what's the timecode?'

Rachel consulted her notepad. 'Um, towards the end of the feed from camera one, near the end... Three oh six-ish.'

Dylan clicked a few times. 'OK, got it.'

He made a few adjustments, typed in a few things, then nodded. 'Yeah, she's a hacker alright and fairly competent by the looks of things.'

James raised an eyebrow. 'How can you tell?'

In response Dylan turned the laptop around so they could see the screen. 'These are crappy cameras, but MI5 taught me a few tricks for image enhancement when I was helping them go through our old computers.'

He had frozen the video and zoomed in on Diana's laptop. Somehow he had cleaned up the image enough so that they could see there were lines of indistinct green code on the black screen.

James squinted at the enlargement. 'Do you know what she's doing?'

'No. I'm a genius, not a miracle worker.' He grinned.

'Thank you, Dylan,' said Lisa, giving him a pointed look. 'We can take it from here.'

Dylan's face fell when he realised that he'd been ordered to leave. He stood up reluctantly, putting the laptop back in place on the table in front of James, then started to walk away.

He stopped and turned around. 'Oh, I almost forgot in all the excitement.' He reached into his jacket pocket and pulled out a wooden plaque. He held it out towards Sam with a grin. 'I just got back from a three year Displacement so there's nothing stopping me from giving this to you now.'

Sam shot a questioning glance at James and received a shrug in reply, then took the nameplate from the boy. 'Thank you, Dylan, I appreciate it.'

The boy looked around the group before looking back at Sam. He shifted his weight nervously and looked down at his feet. 'Uh...'

Sam stifled a laugh. 'Was there something else you'd like to say?'

The boy lifted his head and Sam was surprised at the determination in his eyes. 'Please take me with you when you go to fight them.'

'Why do you think we're going to do that?'

Dylan grinned, shamefacedly. 'I've kinda been listening for a bit longer than I might have let on.'

Sam had to laugh as the older Displacers all rolled their eyes, almost in unison. He shook his head, still grinning wryly. 'Not this time. Maybe next time after Rachel and I have had a chance to train you.'

'But...'

'No, Dylan, I'm sorry. It's too dangerous.'

The boy nodded reluctantly and left.

Sam turned back to the group. 'Three years? Where did he go?'

Lisa shrugged. 'I don't know, I haven't had a chance to read his report yet. He came to me a week ago and told me that he wanted to do some research for a history project at school, that it was perfectly safe and that the dates weren't on the reserve list. So I let him go.'

'OK...' Sam paused. 'The what list?'

James put his face into his hands.

Rachel spoke to Sam gently, as if to an idiot - she seemed to have taken over that job from Andrew. 'There's a list of dates to reserve if possible because they are the ones that most commonly go astray.'

'Oh, OK... How come I've never seen it? Where is it? '

'It was on the private website before we had to take it down. It's among the printouts that we gave everybody until we get a new computer system up and running.'

Sam gave her a blank look. 'Private website?'

'Oh, god.' She put her head in her hands, mirroring James.

'Hey! It's not my fault if nobody told me any of this stuff when I joined!' Sam threw his arms up in the air in frustration and turned to leave. 'I'm going to go for a run; I need to blow off some steam. Coming, Rachel?'

'Of course.' Rachel grinned at her fellow Displacers and followed Sam from the room.

They made their way up the stairs. Rachel had long since moved into the flat that she had inherited from Andrew, but Sam was reluctant to go there and was still using the bedroom on the fourth floor they'd been allocated when he'd returned. The flat in Barcelona had only ever been a temporary home for his uncle and Sam had been there often enough that he didn't feel bad moving in, but the one in London had been Andrew's real home - he was afraid that going there would reawaken feelings that he didn't have time to handle.

'You want to go for a run or do you fancy doing some sparring at the dojo?' Rachel had found a Karate dojo nearby that was like a gym. It was open all day and late into the night so that people could drop by and use the mats and equipment whenever they wanted.

Sam considered briefly. 'Actually a spar would be good, but let's get a run in first, I don't want to fight with my mind like this.'

Rachel grinned. 'You still don't like it when we tease you, do you?'

'Of course not! Would you?'

'Probably not, but I'd make sure I did something about it, whereas you seem to revel in your role as the resident fool.'

'Well, I have to do *something* so as not to look so damn *perfect* all the time, don't I?'

'Don't look now, but we're being followed.'

They had just passed Speaker's Corner and were running alongside Park Lane back towards Hyde Park Corner, about to finish the first of the three circuits of the park they wanted to make before heading towards the dojo.

Sam had been staring at the ground in front of him, lost in his thoughts, so he hadn't noticed that anything was amiss. He didn't break his stride, just lifted his head a fraction and prepared himself. 'Who is it? Illuminati?'

She glanced sideways at him and pouted. 'You didn't look to see who it was!'

'You told me not to.'

'I know, but people always... oh, never mind, it's just Dylan.'

'Has he been following us for long?'

'Since we started. I didn't say anything before because you looked like you needed time to think, but now I'm bored and I'm using him as an excuse to interrupt you. Besides, he's starting to look a bit ragged.'

Sam chuckled. 'I'm surprised he managed to keep up with us this long. Perhaps there's more to him than I thought.'

He slowed to a walk.

Rachel pulled up at his side. 'Are you going to say something to him?'

'No, let's see if he is brave enough to make the first move. Sensei mode?'

Rachel laughed and nodded. 'Sensei mode.'

He reached out to take Rachel's hand and they walked, not looking behind them, just enjoying the scenery.

In less than a minute they heard the steady footsteps of someone jogging up behind them.

Sam waited to the last possible second then put a subtle pressure on Rachel's hand. She knew exactly what he wanted and they spun in place to face the boy.

He was so close that he barely had time to react and yelped, throwing his hands up in surprise, automatically taking up a defensive position, even as he stumbled to a halt on legs that were shaky from half an hour of running at the fast pace the two incredibly fit Displacers had been setting.

Sam stood with his hands behind his back and inspected him, taking in the stance and the fists that the boy's hands had curled into, doing his best impression of the way Master Hamato looked appraisingly at his students. To his credit Dylan didn't flinch, but that might have been less because of his spirit and more because Sam wasn't coming close to possessing the same menacing stare as Master Hamato, despite his experience.

'It looks like you've been hiding something from us, Mr Lloyd.'

The boy straightened from his stance and smiled. 'Actually, I think you've been underestimating me.'

'Perhaps.' Sam nodded in acceptance. 'I apologise. Enlighten me.'

'I've been training and working on my fitness since I joined the Displacers and learned about you two, but my latest Displacement was the first opportunity I've had to go into the past and actually learn something. I studied with the Hwarang and learned a lot of technique, but as you can see my body hasn't caught up yet.'

Sam didn't know who the Hwarang were, so he looked to Rachel for an answers and, as always when it came to anything to do with fighting, she had them.

'The Hwarang were like social clubs for young men in ancient Korea. To start with they just educated their members in culture, the arts and Buddhism and at one point they were mostly known for wearing make-up and fine clothes and being a bit feminine. But in the sixth and seventh centuries they became more martially focussed as the three kingdoms of Korea started fighting amongst themselves.' She grinned at Dylan. 'And I'm really hoping *that's* when you chose to go.'

Dylan nodded. 'Late seventh century.'

'Good choice.'

'My teachers were mostly Buddhist monks. I learnt horse riding, archery, throwing techniques, as well as empty hand fighting and sword fighting.'

Sam grinned. 'Fun, isn't it.'

Dylan grinned back at him. 'Oh, yes! Better than any computer game.'

Sam looked at Rachel. 'Are the Hwarang on your list for a visit?'

She shook her head. 'After some of the other stuff I've done, well, *both* of us have done, they're a bit soft.'

Dylan was indignant at that. 'They are not! Please, just give me a chance to prove it!' He put his hands up again and gave them a determined look. 'I'll fight you both if I have to!'

Sam laughed. 'Not here!' He called over his shoulder as he turned and started jogging away. 'Come on and this time feel free to run with us.'

They arrived at the dojo ten minutes later. While Sam took Dylan into the training hall, Rachel signed them in at the front desk, chatting with the receptionist, a young woman who was studying for her second Dan in Wado Ryu karate while she scanned their membership cards.

Sam bowed to the flags and shrines that were set up on the other side of the room. There were Japanese, Korean and Chinese flags, as well as a row of pictures of the founding masters of martial arts such as Aikido, Karate and Iaido: every martial art that had been practised in the dojo was represented and honoured in some way.

Dylan followed Sam's lead, bowing with only a moment's hesitation, then followed him to the changing room.

Sam pulled out a key and opened his locker. He pulled out two plain white uniforms and handed the spare one to Dylan, then started getting changed without a word.

The boy hurriedly stripped off his tracksuit and started putting on the uniform, but stopped with one leg in the trousers when he saw what Sam was wrapping around himself.

'A white belt? I understand why I have to wear one, but why do you?'

Sam paused and looked at him. 'I've never taken an exam so I've never earned a belt in anything and I don't presume to know more than anyone else.'

Sam went back to changing, stacking his street clothes in the locker before putting Dylan's clothes on top. He gave the boy a quick look. The uniform was a bit big for him, but he had long legs and the trousers weren't dragging, it would do for the day. He smiled. 'Ready?'

Dylan nodded determinedly and they went back out to the training area where Rachel was stretching on the mats while she waited for them, lying on her front in full splits. In contrast to Sam she was wearing a white ITF Taekwondo uniform, with a black belt and black stripes on the seams of her trousers and jacket. She was the only one in the room; the dojo only really started to get busy in the afternoons when schools got out and people started leaving work.

Sam paused to wink at the boy. 'Rachel, on the other hand, *has* done a few exams.'

Sam almost laughed as the boy swallowed, counting the number of stripes on Rachel's belt.

'Don't worry about it, kid; she started training well before she became one of us and she'll be the first to tell you that the belt means nothing.'

'Nothing?' Dylan was uncertain. If a black belt meant so little, then why did people revere it so much?

Rachel propped herself up on her elbows and looked up at him. 'Nothing. I've seen yellow belts beat black belts, I've also seen white belts breaking bricks because they knew they could. It's the heart and the soul behind the belt that really counts.'

Sam laughed. 'Of course, having technique doesn't hurt. Come on, let's see yours.' He smirked. 'Do you need to warm up?'

The boy laughed and shook his head, but didn't reply.

Sam exchanged a nod with Rachel - it was a good sign that the boy was relaxed enough to keep hold of his sense of humour at a time like this.

He led the boy over to the side of the room where Rachel had left a small holdall.

Dylan's eyes widened when Sam pulled out several knives and held one out to him.

'Here, let's see what you can do while you get your breath back from the run.'

Dylan took the knife from him and looked at it. 'Are you sure they won't mind?'

Sam pointed across the room at a target on the wall. 'No, they have a few people here who play at using shurikens and stuff. They're not particularly good at it so don't worry; they're used to patching up holes in the wall if you miss.'

Sam smiled, then spun and threw one of the knives at Rachel.

She didn't even move from her splits, she just plucked the knife out of the air inches from her face, then sent it flying across the room without looking. It thudded into the target and stuck there, quivering.

'Not bad.' Dylan nodded grudgingly.

Sam raised an eyebrow. 'Not bad?'

'Well, she didn't hit the centre, did she? It was a good effort from where she was and the position she was in, though.'

Sam glanced at Rachel and grinned at her cross expression. *Good effort*, he mouthed at her, making her screw up her eyes at him in a promise of pain to come.

The dark-haired boy hefted the knife that Sam had given him. He pushed his glasses back on his nose with his left hand then whipped his right out. The knife flew across the room and embedded itself in the target inches from Rachel's, but still not quite in the exact centre.

'Oops, I guess I didn't get the balance exactly right.'

'Good enough!' Sam chuckled and bent down to dump the remaining knives back into the bag. 'I guess we don't really need these.'

As he straightened he threw a lazy punch at Dylan's face.

The boy sidestepped it with ease, so Sam followed it up with a kick to the side of his leg, stepping after the boy as he dodged back. He threw attack after attack, gradually accelerating, and each time the boy blocked or dodged.

'Hang on! Hang on!'

Dylan threw his hands out and Sam instinctively stopped. He watched, bemused as the boy reached up and took his glasses off, folding them closed and laying them carefully on top of the weapons bag.

'I've got some contacts on order, but I don't want to break these; my Mum'll kill me.'

The boy smiled then leapt to attack.

He moved fast, much quicker than Sam had been expecting, and much quicker than Sam had been moving before. Three years of training had served him well even though his technique was rather limited having only come from one source and not multiple ones like his own and Rachel's.

Rachel had to stop stretching and scramble out of the way as Dylan pressed Sam across the room with a flurry of blows and she moved to the side of the room and knelt to watch.

It was an impressive display, but unfortunately the boy's stamina left much to be desired and he slowed considerably after only slightly more than a minute. Sam took pity on him and finished it quickly, sweeping his legs out from under him, putting him on his back.

Sam nodded in appreciation. 'Not bad,' he said with a grin. 'But you've got a lot to work on; your body knows what it should be doing, but doesn't understand why it can't because it doesn't know its limitations yet. You need to do a lot more sparring and keep up with your fitness.'

Dylan groaned in disappointment and looked up at him from the floor. 'I get it, I still have a lot to learn and until I do you won't be able to use me. Story of my life.'

'I never said that.' Sam offered Dylan his hand and pulled him up. He took a couple of steps back and bowed, a gesture that Dylan repeated readily. 'We can certainly use you and if you work hard enough over the next few weeks you can come with us when we go to face that team.'

Dylan's face lit up and he almost jumped for joy. 'Thank you! Thank you!' he started to leap forwards to hug Sam, but Sam stepped away from him and gave him a stern look.

'Dylan, this isn't a definite yes. When I say you have to work hard, I mean it. If we take you into the past as you are now and we face someone who is even as remotely capable as some of the people we know then you will die. Very quickly.'

'But you've seen I can handle myself! Yes, my stamina and strength aren't what they were at the end of three years in the past, but that doesn't matter if I can lay someone out quickly enough, surely...'

He stopped when Sam held up a hand. 'Go sit at the side of the dojo and watch. Rachel? Would you mind?'

'I thought you'd never ask.'

'Full speed from the start, OK?'

'Good for me, as long as you give me a massage later; my back's still hurting from the last time.'

Sam grinned. 'You're on!'

Dylan grouchily went to kneel where Rachel had been. He wondered what they could show him that his teachers hadn't, or that he hadn't mastered himself as one of the top Hwarang. After all, he had proven his worth in war when it had mattered and been chosen as leader of one of the groups after only a couple of years of training. How much better than him could they possibly be?

The answer was much, much better and he soon felt very ashamed at how arrogant he'd been.

He watched, mouth hanging open as his fellow Displacers put on a display such as he'd never seen, even in the action movies he devoured whenever he could.

His astonishment turned into dismay after the first thirty seconds as he realised just how little he knew, but after less than thirty seconds more that dismay faded and was replaced by a fire in his gut; a desire to learn, to work and to one day be able to move just like they did.

His eyes flickered back and forth, trying to follow movements that were almost too fast for the eye to register, trying in vain to figure out what stimulus each of the fighters could be reacting to in order to block or dodge a blow that they couldn't possibly have seen coming.

They used techniques that he had never seen before, that he had never even dreamed a body could carry out, but techniques could be taught and learnt - what really interested him was the spirit behind the movements. His teachers, the Buddhist monks, insisted that a *body* could only do so much, but a *mind* could do anything.

He had never been a very physical person, preferring to spend his time behind a computer rather than in the mud like most of the other boys his age. He had only really gone to Korea so that he could prove to Sam that he could be useful and help him to save the world, but now he realised that he would do anything to gain even a fraction of what these two had.

The gesture that he had made with his wooden nameplate, only an hour before, suddenly took on new meaning for him.

'Are we really going to take him?' asked Rachel.

She was lying face down on the bed in their room in Headquarters with Sam sitting on her upper legs. He was leaning forward to massage her lower back, where she had recurring problems after taking a beating at the Twins' hands in South Africa months before.

'Of course.'

'Why? We can handle Diana's team on our own.'

'I know, which is precisely why we're going to take him. It'll be a relatively easy first mission to break him in with.'

Rachel grunted in reply, then groaned in pleasure as Sam's strong hands dug into her muscles.

'We could even do some training once we've dealt with the Illuminati. Depending on where we are, obviously.'

Rachel wasn't entirely convinced. 'I suppose. I just hope we're not leading a fifteen-year-old to his death.'

'I was fifteen when I faced Quentin for the first time and I coped alright. And I was *truly* fifteen, not like Dylan.'

'I know you were. And you almost died. Several times if I remember correctly.'

'*Almost* doesn't count.'

'I know, but it only has to not be "almost" just once for it to be game over.'

'If there's any sign of anything unexpected we'll send him home, alright?'

'OK.'

'Now shut up and relax, it's my turn in a minute.'

Rachel laughed. 'I don't think you get a turn today, it's your bloody fault my back's hurting, wanting to impress the boy like that.'

'I didn't do it to impress him.' Sam spoke quietly, seriously. 'I wanted to show him how dangerous it could be.'

'He didn't run away in terror at your incredible prowess, so maybe there's hope for him.'

She chuckled, but Sam couldn't quite see the humour, or shake the feeling that he was making a mistake taking anybody into the past with him. 'We'll see.'

CHAPTER 8
WALKING INTO THE TRAP

They arrived on a narrow plateau, high in the Nepalese Himalayas. For Sam and Rachel the mountains looming overhead were a familiar sight, having spent years in the Tibetan Himalayas and they all but ignored them as they immediately crouched to limit how visible they were to the enemy and began scanning their surroundings, but Dylan just stood where he was, gawping like a tourist.

'Wow...'

'Dylan! Wake up!' Sam snapped at the boy.

'Sorry, sir.' Dylan sheepishly squatted down beside Sam and Rachel.

Sam gazed around assessed the situation. There was no sign of life, but appearances could be deceiving and definitely were in this case since he knew that the Illuminati were there somewhere; he could feel them.

The plateau was fairly small, only about a hundred metres wide and two hundred deep. On either side there were almost vertical cliffs, rising hundreds of metres up and there was a precipitous drop only a few metres behind them. The only way out, except for a fairly dangerous climb either up or down, was a boulder strewn slope to their front.

It was the perfect setting for a trap and Sam idly wondered which of the Illuminati had known of the existence of this tucked-away piece of tranquillity and why.

At the base of the slope at the far side of the plateau was a squat building. It was a Buddhist temple and was fairly small as such things went; the front of it only about fifty metres across. A short flight of steps ran around the whole building and served as a pedestal on which it sat and it had a gold roof sitting above painted doors and walls that had once been red, but had faded to pink with the weather. A lot of effort had been put into its construction, despite its isolation and the obvious difficulty in getting to it, but it was suffering in its exposed perch on the side of a mountain.

'What is it with the Illuminati and raiding temples and tombs?' Sam muttered under his breath.

Rachel chuckled and spoke equally quietly. 'Their leader is John, and we know how much he likes Lara Croft.'

Sam grunted, but didn't otherwise let her comment distract him. He finished his visual sweep. 'Anyone see anything?'

Rachel reported first. 'All clear to the right.'

'Nothing to the left, or to our rear either, sir' said Dylan, 'except for a pretty big drop. Unless they brought a helicopter with them I think we're safe from there.'

Sam straightened from his crouch as he finally allowed himself to relax slightly. He grinned and shook his head, amused despite himself. 'Yes, thank you, Dylan. Let's go.' He glanced sideways at the boy. 'Just like we rehearsed, please.'

'Yes, sir.'

They began spreading out as they moved towards the temple, but before they had gone more than a few paces, the large wooden doors of the building swung open. Four people came out and descended the few steps to the rock plateau and began walking towards them.

Sam immediately called a halt, but the Illuminati kept advancing, staying close together as if for comfort, and he took the opportunity to assess them.

He was amused to see that Diana had slipped back into the "femme fatale" persona which had had so much of an effect on him when he'd first laid eyes on her outside a cave in Egypt but, despite not having seen her in more than twenty years, he didn't let his eyes linger on her for long; it was the others he needed to worry about at that moment.

The man, Tuttle, was frowning as he flicked the blade of a switchblade knife, which certainly didn't belong in the time, in and out over and over. Sweat was beading his forehead, despite the cold of the mountain air, and his eyes were darting back and forth between the Displacers - he was not anything to worry about.

The gangly hacker, Laura Matthews, was biting her lip as she came forwards. She was lagging ever so slightly behind the others, as if supremely reluctant. Of everyone there, she was the one with the least training and it showed - as she walked forwards, she kept her hands clenched at her sides, her knuckles white, almost as if she'd been taught how to make a proper fist only moments before and didn't want to open them in case she didn't know how to close them again.

He dismissed both Tuttle and Matthews as threats in moments, but there was no way he could do the same for the third member of Diana's team.

Emily Clarkwell didn't so much walk across the plateau as *prowl*. While most martial artists seemed to glide across the floor while barely touching it, there was a weight to her steps that was completely at odds with her small size - she was about the same height as Master Hamato. She looked like a lioness, searching for food for its children, but the hunger in her eyes was tinged with madness and the way she was staring greedily at him spoke of a desire, a *need*, for violence which was nothing to do with survival. But it wasn't her physical presence that was bothering him the most; he sensed something wrong in her that went beyond any mental problems, something that scratched at his senses like fingernails on a chalkboard, setting his teeth on edge, while at the same time pulsing with a power that he had never felt before.

It was a puzzle for some other time, though, and he tore his gaze away from her with some difficulty and looked to Diana; the fun would begin with her.

The Illuminati finally stopped when they were about five metres away and there was complete stillness as the two groups sized each other up.

It would have been like a scene from a cowboy film, with the good guys facing the bad guys, if it weren't for the bright orange robes that both Sam and Rachel were wearing or the colourful local dress that the others had on.

However, the standoff was broken after only a few seconds when Diana laughed, making both Tuttle and the hacker start. 'I see you've brought a pet with you this time, Vives. He's cute. What's your name, sweetie?'

Dylan snarled at her. 'Dylan Lloyd. And I'm not your "sweetie", Miss Birch.'

Diana tilted her head and smiled at Sam. 'Ooh, I like him, Sam, he's got a temper.' She looked back at the boy. 'It's not too late to leave these losers and join us. I'm sure we can find a place for you.'

'Not going to happen, sorry.'

Diana shook her head and again looked at Sam. 'Well, he doesn't exactly have much in the way of witty repartee does he? I'm quite disappointed. What *do* you teach your new recruits?'

Sam gave her a twisted smile. 'Manners.'

Diana laughed, but stopped abruptly in alarm when he slowly sank into a crouch, curling his hands into claws.

'I gave you fair warning. I told you never to come into the past again.'

'Yes, but...'

He cut her off with a growl. 'Enough! You had your chance to put a stop to your greed and you didn't. Now it's time to face the consequences.'

Sam had barely finished talking before he burst into a sprint, taking everyone by surprise, including his own companions.

He closed the gap between the two groups in less than a second and leapt at Diana, bearing her to the ground under his weight.

She hit heavily, her head striking the rock with a sickening crunch, and immediately fell still.

Sam stood slowly, leaving Diana crumpled on the ground. Blood was spreading in a puddle from her head and he glanced briefly at the red liquid on his hands before lifting his head and looking up at the other three Illuminati, a killing light in his eyes. 'You're all going to die.'

Laura and Tuttle immediately turned and ran in panic, the girl towards the temple and the man off into the rocks of the mountainside.

'Rachel! Dylan! Go!'

They barely needed telling; they knew what their job was and they immediately sprinted after their prey. Sam had assigned them their targets already, so Rachel went after Tuttle while Dylan pursued the hacker, which left Sam with Clarkwell.

Sam turned his head towards her and beckoned with a bloody hand. 'Come on then.'

He spoke softly, but it was enough to spur the girl into action and, with a surprisingly melodious laugh, she ran at him.

Rachel gave Sam a worried glance as she leapt after Tuttle, but he was too focussed on the fight ahead to spare her a thought.

Emily Clarkwell was by far the most dangerous of the three Illuminati, just as Diana had said and, for an instant, she considered letting her quarry go and staying to fight alongside Sam. He had been explicit in his instructions, though, and she trusted his abilities, so she continued to run, shutting out the sounds of the ferocious fight breaking out behind her as she tried to catch up with Tuttle, who had already disappeared from sight in the rocky terrain of the slope.

Her distraction almost cost her everything. She rounded a huge boulder at speed without even considering the possibility that it might conceal an assailant and saw the flash of light from the blade as it came slashing at her far too late. She swerved desperately and managed to avoid it plunging into her chest, but it still sliced through the sleeve of her robes and bit deeply into her left bicep.

She staggered to a halt, gritting her teeth at the sudden pain, but otherwise ignoring it, and spun to face the man.

However, instead of pressing his advantage he was just standing there grinning at her, weaving his switchblade from side to side, gleefully displaying the fresh blood dripping from it as if it would intimidate her into submission.

He obviously hadn't done his homework.

The look of surprise on his face when her foot broke his nose with a crunch and knocked him unconscious was extremely satisfying.

Dylan jumped up the steps and raced into the temple, but immediately slid to a halt, stunned, as he took in the incredible sight beyond the doors.

The large room was filled with hundreds of figurines, representations of Buddha, lined up in neat rows against the walls, all gold and shining yellow in the light from the ornate lamps hanging overhead.

It was beautiful, but in the silence at the top of the mountain it was somehow eerie at the same time; it felt like all the tiny fat men were staring at him, and he wondered where everyone was: there should be worshippers, monks, caretakers, someone to bear witness to this wondrous spectacle.

He only realised that he'd completely forgotten his mission when the sound of something heavy crashing to the floor further into the temple woke him from his stupor. He cursed himself for a fool and sprinted across the room, past row after row of red cushions, towards a heavy-looking curtain that was still gently rippling after having been disturbed recently.

He burst through into a larger, but much plainer room; a simple dining area with two long wooden tables lined by benches. He ran past them without slowing, heading for the wooden door at the far side which was the only exit.

The door led to the kitchen and he found his quarry scrabbling at another door across the room that most likely led to the mountainside. It was barred and locked and she'd tried to use a frying pan to break it open, but it had proved inadequate for the job and the sound of her discarding it in frustration had been what had called his attention back to his task.

When she realised she couldn't escape through the door she turned to search for another way, but froze when she saw him.

On the mountainside Dylan had been so preoccupied with answering Diana that he hadn't really taken in her companions and he got his first good look at Laura in that moment.

Far from being the evil Illuminati agent he'd assumed she would be, he found himself confronted by a girl about his own age.

Tears were streaming down her face and she was obviously terrified.

'Please don't hurt me!' She slid down the door to the floor where she buried her head in her hands and sobbed uncontrollably.

The initial exchange took Sam by surprise.

The woman's technique was unconventional to say the least. There was no defence, no avoidance or prevention of his attacks, instead she used them to magnify her own, using the impetus she received from Sam's blows to add to the force of her own, deflecting it back at him like an aikido master and at the same time converting the pain from them into a cold fury that frightened him with its intensity.

She was unrelenting and Sam found himself on the back foot, forced to retreat over and over, almost immediately reduced to just trying to block her attacks in the face of her frenzied onslaught.

And all the while her grin just grew wider.

Sam had a trick up his sleeve, though, and he reached deep inside himself, down to where he had buried the Beast. It responded with an eager roar and he gave himself over to it.

The Beast never defended; it didn't see the point, so it immediately went on the offensive.

A touch of uncertainty crept into the woman's eyes as her advance was stalled and they widened in alarm when she began to be pressed backwards. The ferocity of her attack and total disregard for the damage that she was taking, which usually ended with her opponent cowed and beaten, was being matched and even surpassed, something that had never happened before.

The momentary worry disappeared quickly, though, and she smiled in delight. Apparently excited at the prospect of a challenge she laughed and dug her toes in, standing head to head with the Beast as they began trading blows.

For the first time ever the Beast found itself impressed and it growled its glee as they battered each other without regard for the consequences, each stoically shrugging off blows that would have sent lesser fighters staggering back.

For a while it seemed that they were evenly matched; the woman had the advantage of speed and was landing more hits, but the Beast had more weight behind its strikes which more than made up for it.

The deciding factor in the end was the way they dealt with the damage they were taking. The Beast shrugged off any injury it sustained, knowing that it could leave them for its host to concern himself with later, but the woman didn't have that luxury and the damage began to tell. She weakened and slowed, until finally she was unable to effectively absorb the Beast's blows. She stumbled, going down to one knee, an eye closing, a rib snapped and blood streaming from the nostrils of a broken nose. Even so she didn't give up and leapt forwards, keeping her body low to go under the Beast's guard and grappled with it, throwing it off balance.

They fell, pummelling each other again and again as they rolled across the sharp stones of the mountain plateau.

Neither of them noticed the cliff face coming ever closer.

It was the Beast's instincts that saved them. Somehow it sensed the emptiness yawning behind it moments before they got to it. It was too late to halt, but there was time enough to scrabble and find itself something to grab as the two of them went over.

The Beast fled instantly. It knew that its job was done, but it also realised that this was a failure it couldn't deal with.

Sam gasped as he came up short, the jolt threatening to tear his arm from its socket.

He flailed with his feet, searching desperately for a foothold in the rocks before his grip gave way. Thankfully he found one and seated his right foot, taking some of the strain off his supporting arm, but he knew that he still wouldn't be able to hold on for very long.

He craned his head to look down.

The woman was just hanging there. Motionless. Clasping onto the voluminous sleeve of his robe and gazing up at him with grey eyes that were suddenly clear of all fury, clear of all madness.

'What are you waiting for? Climb! Climb up me! Come on, damn you!'

He shouted at her, but all she did was smile in return.

Rachel got back to the plateau just as Sam went off the side of the mountain.

For long seconds she stood there, unbelieving, but then the sound of Sam's desperate shouts spurred her into motion. She dropped Tuttle's unconscious form from her shoulder and ran towards where she'd last seen him.

She threw herself to her belly on the edge of the cliff and looked over, taking in the scene, horrified.

Sam's hand was just below her and she grabbed it with one of hers, using the other to find a handhold so that she had something to pull against. Agony washed through her body, threatening to drag a scream from her, as the effort tore something already weakened by the knife wound in her arm, but she just blinked away the pain along with the stars that flared in her vision and held on.

'Please! Climb up!'

Sam pleaded with the woman, trying to get her to start moving, to do something to save herself, but she wouldn't or couldn't and just hung there.

He felt Rachel's hand wrap around his, taking more of the pressure off and giving him enough confidence to search and find another indent in the rock face that he could just about dig his other toe into. With three points of contact he could hold on without any problem and with Rachel's strength added to his they would be able to pull the unresponsive woman up easily enough.

He started to tilt his head up to speak to Rachel so as to coordinate their efforts, but was halted by a soft voice.

'Please don't turn away. Keep looking at me.'

'Why?'

'It's important that you see me die.'

'No! You don't have to die! I've got you, you can climb over me.'

She shook her head. 'No, I don't want to. I've had enough. My life has been too long already. I've seen too much and lived through too much.'

'You're still young, you can...'

'I'm eight hundred years old.'

Sam's mouth gaped open in shock. He had no idea what to say; even the most experience Elders typically only reached three hundred years of age, four or five hundred in the most extreme cases, but this girl, who Diana had said was just twenty years old, had already lived so much longer than that. It was almost impossible to believe, but it would explain the mad glint that was still in her eyes despite her current serenity. It would also explain why his powers reacted the way they did to her.

With death only inches and a slip of her hand away, the woman calmly started talking, never looking away from him, and Sam found himself transfixed by her eyes and the hypnotic sound of her voice.

'A lot of girls go through a phase where they romanticise death and suffering. They dream of being a tragic heroine in some story, hell, you just have to watch something like Snow White or Sleeping Beauty to see the fantasies some of us have of being woken up from a death-like sleep by a handsome prince. Or princess.' Her eyes flickered briefly to Rachel, then fixed once again on Sam. 'Just around puberty they start thinking that they are misunderstood, that their problems are special, that they're going through something that nobody else has ever been through before. In the past that would have meant reading sorrowful poetry about lost loves, or something equally dull, nowadays it means dressing in black while putting on heavy make-up and painting their fingernails to match. Poor innocent little Laura has never really grown out of the phase, although I must admit the aesthetic suits her.'

She smiled faintly, but it was gone as soon as it had appeared as she continued.

'Of course, most girls grow out of the phase fairly quickly, but "most girls" don't have our talents, do they?'

She took a deep breath as if she had to steel herself for the revelations to come.

'I was forced to *live* that phase for eighty years in my first trip to the past.'

She paused to let the number sink in and nodded in satisfaction when Sam's eyes widened; such a long Displacement was almost unheard of and, if someone did come back from one, they invariably weren't the same person.

'That day I'd been reading about some of the cults in places like India, South America and Egypt - ancient civilisations who revered gods of death. Just for fun, you know? I got in the bath one evening, candles lit and bubbles popping, daydreaming and lamenting my oh-so-terrible life, and opened my eyes as a priestess in Mexico, my knife poised above the heart of an unwilling victim.'

A shadow passed across the woman's eyes as she thought back to that day, so many lifetimes before.

'I had no idea what was going on, of course, and when I got over the initial shock I found it all very romantic, and quite a bit of fun, even though I was obviously just having some kind of breakdown.'

She smiled faintly and Sam nodded his understanding, thinking back to his own first Displacement and how long it had taken him to realise that he wasn't just dreaming.

'The first day I was there I killed twenty or thirty people, I don't know exactly how many because I lost count after a couple of hours, and it was the same every day after that. Day after day, month after month, year after year, over and over I cut the hearts out of men and women so that the sun would go on shining and my people would remain dominant.

'After sixty years my body gave out and I no longer had the strength to perform the sacrifices well enough myself. My shaking hands were no longer capable of inflicting the painless death that my victims deserved, so I stepped back and allowed others to take over.

'Then, one day, when I was about ninety-five, while my dying body was being bathed, my senile brain had a flash of something dimly remembered - a childhood that had been forced aside by blood and death, a girl, a family. I closed my eyes, ready to take my last breath...

'And opened them back in my bathroom, screaming.'

She squeezed her eyes shut and shuddered, gritting her teeth, and Sam panicked as her hand slipped a few millimetres on his sleeve. The woman showed no sign of having noticed how close she had been to falling, though.

'I screamed until ambulance men arrived and they gave me something to knock me out. I screamed again when I woke up in the hospital and kept screaming until the doctors took pity on me and sedated me again. Every time I came awake it was with a scream as I struggled to understand what was going on and my mind tried to convince my body that it should be so very much older. Eventually, after weeks, I stopped screaming, but all I could do was sit and stare at the walls in the cell they put me in, endlessly scrubbing at hands that I thought were covered in blood, until my nails tore and they had to put me in padded gloves.

'I convinced myself that what I had gone through hadn't been real, that I was mad and all of the doctors I spoke to agreed. It wasn't until

Quentin Price turned up and explained what had really happened that I began to heal; my mind finally had the information it needed to bridge the gap between who I was, who I had been, and who I could be.

'After I convinced the doctors I was sane, they released me and I went to work for the Illuminati, carrying out the missions that they wanted me to, becoming the killer they convinced me I was, but my mind craved something more - it needed to find its way back to that old, dying woman that I had been, because for some reason it was only in those final few years that I truly felt whole again.' She sighed wistfully. 'I have lived whole lives, even going back to times before recorded history, just so that I could grow old and finally find those fleeting moments of peace at the end of my life.'

The woman paused and looked away. The brilliant blue sky was reflected in her pale eyes as she gazed up at the mountains towering on every side around them, taking them in emotionlessly.

'I studied for entire lifetimes, while at the same time conditioning myself to feel nothing, trying to make myself the perfect assassin that the Illuminati wanted me to be and I thought that I had done exactly that and become the best at what I do, but you are so much more. Even after just one fight I know that.'

Her eyes abandoned the spectacular view and once again caught and held Sam's in their grasp.

'*You* are the death that I wanted to be, but somehow you still have life in you, you have *love* in you. You have exposed the lie in everything that I am and made a mockery of my very existence, but you have also shown me what I could have been if I'd had another path to walk and I thank you for that.

'So now you understand why I've had enough and I hope you also understand why it's better for everyone this way, especially my parents; they'll forget about all me and all the trouble I gave them.'

She smiled sadly and a single solitary tear rolled down her cheek. 'It was very nice to meet you, Sam Vives.'

She opened her hands.

Sam snatched at her, but it was too late. He watched, aghast, as she fell silently, only looking away after long seconds when she struck an outcrop and started tumbling wildly.

He squeezed his eyes tight shut and pulled in ragged breaths, fighting the flaring panic and the feelings of hopelessness and shame welling up in him as he returned to that mountain in Persia and relived his first kill. However, it wasn't the young man he saw now, his mouth open in a scream, limbs flailing, his panic clear; his place had been taken by the calm-faced woman with steel in her eyes who he had failed...

'Sam!'

Rachel's voice finally broke through to him and his eyes shot open, only then remembering where he was and that he was still dangling from the edge of a cliff.

It was a matter of a few seconds for him to scramble up and onto the plateau. It would have been so easy to do the same for Clarkwell if only she'd tried.

With an effort, he pushed the dark thoughts out of his mind; there would be time for regrets later, for now there was a mission to finish. 'Where's Dylan?'

He struggled to his feet, his strained muscles protesting, feeling the fresh injuries that the woman had inflicted and revelling in the pain that told him that he was still alive. 'Go tell Diana it's alright to wake up now. I'll see where the boy is.'

Sam started jogging towards the temple, accelerating as the stiffness slowly left him.

He ran through the doors and skidded to a halt, just as Dylan had but, unlike him, it wasn't at the sight of the Buddhas, but rather because of the two people sitting on cushions at the front of the room.

Dylan was cradling the Illuminati girl in his arms and rocking her back and forth as she sobbed, her head buried in his chest.

The boy looked up at Sam and there was a flash of aggressiveness that surprised him, like a mother animal defending its young.

He decided to leave them be for the moment and went back outside.

Diana was up and already tending to the deep cut in Rachel's arm, the still-unmoving form of Jason Tuttle at their feet and Sam hurried over to them in concern. 'Is she OK?'

'She'll be fine,' Diana answered grumpily. 'More than I'll be; you banged me on the head pretty badly and I passed out for real for a while there. If that was your idea of putting on a show for the kids then I hate to think what would happen to someone if you did it for real.' She paused in patching up Rachel only long enough to poke a finger in his chest. 'I'm probably going to be washing this bloody fake blood of yours out of my hair for weeks and those eggs you told me to strap to my back for the "authentic head cracking sound" as you *so* delightfully put it, they're dripping into places I really don't want to discuss in such a holy place.'

'It worked didn't it?' He grinned. 'It won't matter if the blood doesn't wash out because you can barely see it; it matches your hair colour almost perfectly.'

'Oh, ha ha.'

'And as for the eggs: well, I think you have a couple of volunteers to help you clean those up.'

Diana snorted. 'As if I'd let you come anywhere near me after treating me like that.' She sniffed and pouted, playing at being upset, but then shot him a lascivious look that shot hot sparks through his body.

He cleared his throat and tried to think about something else before he embarrassed himself; the robes were quite loose and the way they fell wouldn't exactly hide much. Thankfully, the body on the floor gave him a good excuse to change the subject. 'What about Tuttle?'

'Rachel did a number on his face, but he'll be fine. He'll probably be out for a good while yet. Although, I have no idea why you don't just chuck him off the cliff, the little sh...'

'Diana!' Sam interrupted.

'What? I'm just saying - we'd probably be better off without him.'

Sam shook his head. 'No. Enough people have died for today.'

He glanced at the cliff edge and winced.

Diana finished with Rachel, then went to Sam. She looked his extensive injuries over quickly then shrugged and just wrapped her arms around him.

Rachel joined them, enveloping both in a hug.

'I hate this. I hate having to be apart from you.' Diana's voice was muffled, her face pressed into Sam's shoulder.

Rachel's voice cracked with emotion as she replied. 'So do we.'

They stood there for a long while, drawing comfort from each other, but then Sam sighed. 'We've got a problem with Dylan. See if you can find something to tie Tuttle up with and let's go inside.'

Sam and Rachel went up the steps and into the temple, leaving Diana outside in case Tuttle woke and they needed to keep up the pretence of her being seriously injured.

Dylan and the girl, Laura, were sitting where Sam had left them, but they were no longer in each other's arms. Instead they had their heads together and were speaking in hushed voices.

They looked up as the two Displacers walked towards them down the rows of cushions and Laura cringed back at the sight of the blood covering them.

Dylan leaped to his feet and placed himself between the girl and his two colleagues. His hands unconsciously curled into fists and he took up a vaguely defensive position.

'I won't let you hurt her.'

Sam looked at him sadly and took a deep breath. He reached out a hand and put it on Dylan's shoulder. 'That was never the plan. I'm sorry, but we hid a few things from you.'

'Tuttle is out for the count, but Emily Clarkwell is dead.'

There was a gasp from the girl and Sam glanced in her direction. 'I'm sorry, there was nothing I could do; she made a choice and took her own life.'

He watched her, wondering how he would take the information, whether she would believe him or not and was surprised when the fear slowly faded from her face and was replaced by understanding.

'Oh...' Her voice was barely audible, even in the silence. 'She finally did it, then.'

'You were expecting it?'

She nodded minutely. 'Every mission we went on she would deliberately put herself in harm's way, as if she was trying to get herself killed, then seemed disappointed when she didn't die, even annoyed sometimes. More than once I wondered why she didn't just end it herself and one day I actually got up the courage to ask her. She said "where would the fun be in that?" She didn't want to say any more, but I pressed her about it and in the end she told me that she was "giving death a sporting chance to come for her". She also said that she was waiting for something, but when I asked her what, she said she had no idea, but would know when it happened.' She shook her head. 'She was so alone and so *damaged*. I felt really sorry for her. I had no idea Leaping could do that to someone.'

Rachel gave Sam a meaningful look as she answered. 'It's actually a really common side effect of being in the past for too many years at a time and that's why we tell our agents not to be away longer than ten years or so; you never know what they'll come back like.'

After the sixteen-year trip they had taken to Tibet earlier that year, James had warned them of the dangers to their minds of such long Displacements. He had shown them a few of the dozens of papers that had been written on the subject and which included actual case studies of Displacers who had stayed too long in the past. Sam had been surprised to find out that the way he could just slip back into his normal life as if he hadn't been away for months or years was something all Displacers experienced and that the experts said it was a kind of defence mechanism for the brain, to prevent trouble with things like split personalities. The papers theorised that the safe limit for a traumatic Displacement, like to a war zone or similar, was only five years, but under normal circumstance, where the Displacer lived a life in similar conditions to their own, they could be up to fifteen years in the past until the effects became tangible. Anything longer than that and there were no guarantees.

Sam and Rachel had been able to go to Tibet for so long without any side effects not only had they been themselves, but precisely because of the nature of the work they'd done with the Dalai Lama. However, it was not surprising that Clarkwell, who had gone on multiple *eighty-year* trips and been completely different people each time, had been so mentally scarred.

The same should have been true of Sam's Displacement to Persia, but it had just felt *right* to him and as such it was a risk he'd been more than willing to take and besides, if he hadn't gone then he wouldn't have the Beast, which meant he wouldn't have beaten the Twins and would have lost to Clarkwell and the Illuminati would be free to continue their rampaging through time. He met Rachel's gaze unwaveringly and nodded to show he understood her concerns, but then looked back to the girl.

Laura was much calmer now and she sniffed and wiped her eyes on her sleeve, smearing the heavy black makeup which didn't really match her simple, unbleached linen clothing. 'I'll miss her, she was good to me, but in the end it was what she wanted and it's probably for the best.'

Sam was startled by the way that the girl's words echoed the ones that Clarkwell had spoken to him just before the end, but he said nothing as the girl accepted a handkerchief from Dylan and blew her nose noisily.

When she had finished she bit her lip and worriedly looked back and forth from Sam to Rachel. 'And what about me? What are you going to do to me?'

Rachel stepped forwards, pushing Dylan gently aside when he tried to block her. 'We're not going to do anything to you. But we would like you to leave the Illuminati and join us.'

The girl's fear swiftly turned to indignation at the suggestion and her angry glare revealed some of her true character. 'No way! I'm not going to join you! You're evil, all of you; you killed Grant Davis, you threatened to kill all of us as well and you just attacked and killed Diana with no provocation! I'd rather die!'

'None of that is actually true, darling.' Diana stepped out from around the door where she had been listening and Laura stared at her.

'But you're...'

'Unconscious, with a potentially fatal head wound, tragically leaving behind a beautiful corpse, taken before my time?' She grinned. 'Not quite.'

Sam held up his red-stained hand and waved it at Laura. 'Blood pack. I slipped it behind Diana's head before she hit the ground. It cushioned her fall and made an impressive mess.'

Laura blinked at him, then looked back at Diana. 'Does that mean you planned this? With them?' She put her head in her hands and groaned. 'Of course you did. I've been such a fool...'

When the girl looked up again, she was smiling wryly. 'I knew something was up when Dylan turned out to be so nice. But I just thought he was a prisoner or something, being forced to work for the Displacers against his will.'

Dylan shook his head. 'They aren't like that.'

'I've always been told they were, that they're the bad guys - the evil Displacers who are trying to control time for their own ends - and we're rebels, fighting for freedom. You know, all Star Warsy and stuff. And then when we heard that Sam Vives had threatened to kill us it just seemed to confirm it.'

'You haven't been on the kinds of missions for the Illuminati that I have, so you haven't had a chance to see the truth.' Diana said. 'I'm guessing that your team has never been trusted with anything important and all you've been doing is running around after treasure. You haven't been doing anything truly world changing, so you haven't drawn the attention of the Displacers. Which means you haven't met the delectable Sam here, or you would know who the good guys really are. Like I did from the first time I met him.'

The girl frowned, still sceptical, and it was easy to see why, when Sam was still covered in blood that wasn't all his own. 'But the look on his face when he attacked you, it was...' She shuddered and looked at Sam. 'Does this mean that the death threat was all just part of the act?'

Sam briefly considered what he should tell her. Finally he decided that she had to know the truth if she was ever going to consider joining the Displacers, no matter how it made him look. 'No, it wasn't. Not entirely anyway. I *will* confront the Illuminati and stop them wherever and whenever I find them, but I wasn't serious about killing any of you unless I really have to - as Rachel said, we'd rather you join us. The

Master and Quentin are a different matter, though; they *are* going to die for what they've done.'

Rachel gave him an exasperated look, but Sam just shrugged. 'Laura, Believe me, I hate killing, but we've tried stopping the Illuminati in other ways and it doesn't work. Some of us have even died in the attempt.'

He swallowed the lump that appeared in his throat suddenly and took a deep breath before continuing. 'So, I've resigned myself to fighting fire with fire and killing them before they kill any more of us, or irreparably damage the time-line. But please, don't think that I am a typical Displacer, because I'm not; most of them are actually quite sweet.'

Sam looked from the girl to Dylan, who had gone back to stand beside her and was hovering protectively. 'Take Mr Lloyd, for example.'

The girl nodded reluctantly. 'I think I understand, but what was that you said about the time-line? We were told that time just sorted itself out when we came home, that it didn't matter what we did or took, we would never change anything.' Laura looked up at Sam in confusion.

Rachel interrupted Sam before he could answer, knowing that his understanding was still sketchy at best and he would probably just make a mess of it if he tried to explain. 'Never mind that for now, I'm sure Diana can fill in the blanks for you later.'

Diana walked over sat down next to the girl. She wrapped an arm around her shoulders and shook her gently. 'You and I are going to have a nice long chat when we get back. It's time you heard the truth about the Master and his lies.'

Rachel smiled at Diana. 'Thank you. Now, do you think we can leave the subject of killing behind now, please, because I still want to know why someone like you is working for the Illuminati. You don't seem greedy for power like Quentin and the Master, or bonkers like certain other Illuminati we know.' She widened her eyes comically and tilted her head towards Diana.

'Hey!' Diana gave Rachel a scowl and stuck her tongue out, crossing her eyes, provoking laughter from the Displacers.

The girl didn't join in, though, and Sam saw how confused she was. He didn't blame her; she had gone from fearing for her life and learning of the death of a colleague to kidding around in just a few minutes. He sighed and grinned apologetically at her. 'Take no notice of them, they're *both* crazy.' He ignored the looks that came from both of the women and continued. 'So, why *did* you join the Illuminati?'

Laura took a moment to think before answering, as if she wasn't quite sure of her reasons. 'I guess it was because I was bored. School has never been much of a challenge for me and the life of an average teenage girl is horrifyingly dull. To cap it all off my parents were poor. They couldn't afford to send me to a decent school so I ended up in the local state school and you try being a hacker without enough money to buy your own computer - I had to make do with the ones at school which were laughable. When Quentin turned up he promised me fun and adventure, but above all he promised me all the computer equipment I could possibly want. It wasn't a hard choice.'

Sam sighed. 'I'm sorry to say that is becoming a fairly familiar story for us; we're finding out that the Illuminati prey on those in need, promising them a better life through riches.'

Laura's forehead creased in annoyance. 'So? Doesn't everyone in the world work for money? Don't you?'

'Of course we get paid, and well, but that's not *why* we do it and besides, there is a *vast* difference between what we do in the past and what the Illuminati do.'

Sam saw that she still wasn't convinced and he gazed around the hall of the temple, searching for inspiration, allowing himself to properly take in the sight of the Buddhas for the first time. It was truly a peaceful place, despite the recent violence outside.

He smiled. Perhaps the Illuminati had done him a favour in bringing them there; what better place to try to sort through the turbulence in his mind, and perhaps make another convert, than a Buddhist temple?

'Actually, you know what? Forget about waiting for Diana to explain how things really are until you're back home where you might be under surveillance, why don't we stay here and talk for a while? It's safe, it's beautiful, it's peaceful and I'm in no hurry to get home. Also this is as good a place as any to spend a few years training with Dylan, if the monks will let us.' He looked at Diana and Rachel, seeking and receiving approval.

He turned back to Laura. 'How about it? Do you feel like being here with us for a little while?'

Laura looked up at Dylan and smiled coyly. 'I wouldn't mind that actually.'

The boy's eyes widened in surprise and then he coloured in embarrassment as she reached up and took his hand.

Rachel laughed at his reaction, but then frowned as something occurred to her. 'OK, but what are we going to do with Tuttle? We certainly don't want him seeing us all chummy like this.'

Diana smiled evilly. 'Oh, I think I might have an idea.'

Half an hour later they sat out of sight on the plateau, sniggering quietly as Tuttle regained consciousness.

Rachel had used a technique she'd learnt from Master Hamato to hang him over the drop by one leg and once he'd finished screaming in panic they felt him building his energy. It took him several attempts, but eventually, in spite of his precarious situation, he managed to Calm himself enough to go home.

When the Illuminati had invaded the monastery they had only found a caretaker and a couple of old monks who were too fragile to travel around with their colleagues to preach in the neighbouring villages or go on pilgrimages. The Illuminati had locked them up, getting them out of the way so they could loot without being bothered and Laura led the Displacers to them as soon as they were alone, so that they could make sure they were alright.

The two old monks thought that Sam and Rachel were monks as well because of the robes they were wearing and readily agreed to let them stay. Both of them had been ordained as monks by the Eighth Dalai Lama himself, but Sam felt a bit of a fraud pretending to be one, even though Rachel insisted that he wasn't and threatened to slap him about if he didn't stop being silly - an attitude which he pointed out wasn't very Buddhist, earning himself a kick in the arse when next he turned his back on her.

The guest quarters at the monastery consisted of several run down huts hidden away amongst the boulders of the slope, which were hardly ever used. The monks let them have them in return for restoring them to some semblance of habitability and Sam, Rachel and Diana took the larger of them while Dylan and Laura took one of the smaller ones each.

In addition to repairing the huts, they made themselves busy around the monastery, doing odd jobs like cooking and cleaning. They also occasionally joined the monks in the temple when it was time to meditate, but spent the majority of their time training on the plateau and in the mountains and going for long hikes.

Nightmares woke Sam up every night during the first month. They were the same ones that had kept him sleepless since his Displacement to learn from the assassins, but now it wasn't just a young man he threw off the mountain, but a diminutive woman as well. When he came awake screaming, unable to recognise anyone or anything around him, Diana and Rachel were there to calm him and bring him back to himself. Over the days and weeks, the two women worked at making him to realise that neither of the deaths had been his fault and, thanks to the talks, the surroundings, the constant training, and the meditation with the monks, the dreams gradually faded in intensity. While they never left him completely, they no longer dominated his sleep and he was free to rest for the first time since his first kill.

It took Laura a week to make her decision and she approached Sam and Rachel after a meditation session, bringing Dylan with her for support. She could see that they were who and what they said they were; the way they treated and were treated in return by the monks was enough proof of that, even if Diana hadn't explained to her the difference between the two time travelling factions. She told them that she wanted to join them and Sam and Rachel immediately accepted. The tears of joy that ran down her face as she was hugged by each of them in turn were proof enough that her life had changed.

Right from the start Laura joined them for meditation and trained with them under the watchful eye of Dylan. She never quite managed to make the same kind of progress as everyone else, though, because she just wasn't the physical type. There was no shame in that; some people just weren't, but it was unfortunate in the violent world they worked in. Even so, she easily managed to get to a level that would put most black belts to shame, solely through perseverance and hard work on a daily basis. Then, when training was over each day, she spent the time until bed in conversation with Dylan, thoroughly exploring their geek side, talking about computers, programming and everything science fiction.

The five of them lived and worked in the monastery on the mountain plateau for three years. Rachel, Sam and Diana got to know each other again and, with the help of the monks, the peaceful surroundings and his two lovers, Sam managed to find some of the peace that had been taken from him with Andrew's death.

Dylan and Laura got closer as they started to grow into their adult bodies. They both filled out, but the change in Laura was especially remarkable - she ate well, exercised and, with no computer to keep her occupied, slept at night. She quickly lost the unhealthy look she'd seemed to be deliberately cultivating as a hacker and turned into a beautiful young woman. They moved into the same hut and often went for walks together on the mountainside, taking supplies with them and camping out so that they could be alone, and eventually fell in love. They were inseparable, never straying far from each other's side, and the monks became very protective of them, perhaps recognising the innocence in their young souls.

Eventually, though, they all came to the realisation that they had to return home; there was only so much training, meditation, and enjoying themselves that they could do before they had to go and face up to their problems. Before they left, though, Laura had a surprise for them. Now that thoughts of the present day had intruded on the paradise of the past she admitted that she had certain things in place that would help the Displacers in their fight against the Master. They barely needed the excuse to stay and delightedly postponed their return so as to spend one last week discussing her ideas.

Apparently, because he was on the run, John couldn't cope with all the computer work that needed doing. He had enlisted Laura's help and every week she was given access codes and instructions for the financial transactions and payments that needed to be made. Out of natural hacker curiosity she had done her own investigations, installed her own backdoors, and plenty of other things that none of them except Dylan really understood. In short, she could all but shut down a not inconsiderable part of John's financial empire at the push of a button and in the meantime the Displacers could use the account details to trace more of his assets. It wasn't going to be enough to take down the Illuminati's financial empire once and for all, but it was a big step in the right direction.

Unfortunately, to be able to do all that when the time was right she was going to have to stay in the Illuminati, like Diana.

Dylan wasn't at all happy about that, but he saw that it made sense and he knew that it would be easy enough for him and Laura to keep in contact, certainly easier than it was for Diana, Sam and Rachel; there was no need for them to physically meet up if they didn't want to, they could meet virtually whenever they wanted using secure connections.

When Sam and Rachel were finally satisfied that Laura had given them all the information she could, they went home, more than satisfied with how springing the Illuminati's trap had turned out.

When Diana opened her eyes she gasped in pain, putting her hand to her head and bringing it away covered in blood; to make it look like she'd left just after the fight, Rachel had opened a wound in her scalp that bled impressively, but wasn't at all life threatening. However, it wasn't only physical pain she was feeling; the absence of the woman that had been sitting to her left, whose hand she had been holding when they'd gone into the past, was a sudden and wrenching emptiness. She had almost been able to put Clarkwell out of her mind whilst at the temple, but she still occasionally recalled the woman's words, overheard from a distance while she had lain on the plateau, feigning unconsciousness. She again remembered the sad tale that she had told, and thanked any god that was listening that she hadn't had the same experience with her own first Leap into the past.

'Well, Miss Birch?'

She looked into the camera of the laptop and prepared to launch herself into the act that she had rehearsed with Laura. She wasn't sure that her acting skills were going to be up to the task of convincing the Master how traumatic and brief the Leap had been, but Tuttle surprised them all and drew all attention away from her.

He stood, throwing over his chair, and shouted into the screen. 'This isn't worth it! Get someone else to do your dirty business, I'm out!' With a last rude gesture he ran from the room.

Laura cried out in shock at the drama and huddled up in her chair, doing her job of pretending to be traumatised.

Diana pretended to force a smile while blinking her eyes rapidly, trying to show classic symptoms of dizziness from her head wound while at the same time attempting to be strong for the Master

'Somehow they were waiting for us, sir. Vives incapacitated me immediately and the only reason I survived is because of Matthews here; she managed to drag me away while their attention was on Tuttle and Clarkwell. Vives killed Clarkwell and I think he may well have tortured Tuttle. The details are a bit hazy because of my head, I'm afraid.'

'Can you add anything, Miss Matthews?'

Laura looked up at the screen through tear-filled eyes and shook her head, quite obviously in shock.

Diana was astounded at the girl's acting skills and resolved to take a course at the earliest opportunity, or perhaps go on a Leap to Hollywood in the twenties and see if she could wangle her way into a movie or two. She bowed her head, trying to appear contrite. 'I'm sorry, sir. We failed. Please give us another chance. We won't fail you again.'

Laura sniffed and wiped away her tears then gave the camera a fierce look, nodding in eager agreement with Diana. 'Please, sir! Next time I'll be ready, I promise!'

'I am sorely disappointed in you both and normally I wouldn't put up with such incompetence... However, I am feeling magnanimous today - I will give you one last chance.'

Diana stifled a smirk; the Master was trying to sound reluctant, but he wasn't nearly as good an actor as Laura. 'And Tuttle, sir?'

'He will be dealt with; I can't use someone that weak. You will receive replacements for your team as soon as they become available, but until then consider yourselves at leisure. Without pay.'

The connection broke and Diana turned to glare at Laura; they had agreed to keep up their act just in case they were under surveillance.

'Think yourself lucky that I didn't throw you off that cliff for your failure! Get out of my house!'

Laura burst into tears and ran away, wailing.

Diana shook her head and growled in anger as she turned off her laptop, still playing a part for possible watchers. She selected some music on her phone and sent it to the sound system, then went to make herself a cup of tea, humming along with one of her favourite Placebo songs as she began replaying the memory of an entire three years spent with the two people she loved most in the world.

CHAPTER 9
FAMILY

Violeta's ninth birthday was on August 18th, shortly after the Displacement, and Sam didn't want to miss it.

He'd been away for too long, put his parents through enough grief, and it was time to go home, but not for too long. Sam felt that he could only really take a couple of weeks off from the fight; the rest of the Displacers were working hard and he could do no less, but he needed a break as much as he needed to be there for his sister.

He and Rachel wandered along Oxford Street and bought a ton of presents for Violeta before hopping onto a plane to Barcelona the day before her birthday.

It was a tearful reunion and Rachel was feeling a bit awkward watching the four of them hugging and crying until Sam's mother beckoned to her and pulled her in to join them.

'You're family now, Rachel, you should be here with us.' She gave Rachel a kiss on the cheek and whispered in her ear. 'Thank you for taking care of my son.'

Despite herself, Rachel felt her own eyes welling up.

When they finally broke apart, Sam's mother frowned and ran her hands through his hair, tugging gently. 'Are you letting this grow? I can cut it for you if you like.'

'Aw, Mum!' Sam glanced at Rachel in embarrassment; for the first time in more than forty years he once again felt like the boy he'd been only a year or so ago.

Rachel just laughed through her tears.

Even though she didn't approve of his hair, his mother liked the way Sam was dressed: he had got into the habit of wearing long-sleeved shirts in public to cover the scars on his arms and if anything he looked like his father, the lawyer. Rachel would never admit it, but she quite liked the change too.

The five of them spent the entire afternoon together as a family, catching up. Everything was so comfortable and natural that it was almost as if Sam had never been away.

After dinner that evening, when Violeta had gone to bed, Sam and Rachel left; Andrew's flat was nearby and Sam wanted to start making it into a home for the two of them.

They dragged their luggage the few streets to the flat and Sam opened the door for them.

They stood in the doorway looking at the trinkets and the memorabilia scattered around the hallway and they realised that they would probably never know where most of them had come from or the stories behind them. In that moment the full weight of Andrew's loss returned to them, hitting them hard. They reached out unconsciously to hold hands and clung to each other for comfort as, for the second time that day, their emotions threatened to overcome them.

Sam had only come to the flat a couple of times before he'd left Barcelona so everything was exactly as Andrew had left it, although there was a fine layer of dust on everything and the air was stale and smelt of must.

Something caught Sam's eye and he smiled involuntarily as a happy memory pushed back the pain. He reached out with his free hand and flipped open the wooden box on the shelf near the door and pulled out a large gold coin. Rachel chuckled as he showed her the indentations from Violeta's teeth and told her how they had got there.

Sam had never gotten up the courage to tell Andrew about the marks and now it was too late.

He put the coin back and sighed, then, leaving their suitcases where they were, he led her to the room with Andrew's artworks.

He waited by the door while Rachel wandered around, studying them. 'These are all in a different style. He must have spent lifetimes studying with different masters to be able to produce these! I thought he didn't like art; he never went to galleries or anything.'

Sam could only shrug in reply.

Rachel turned in place, counting the works. 'There's five of them...'

'Six if you count the portrait at Headquarters.'

Rachel nodded. 'Six. Six lifetimes spent learning how to paint, how to sculpt... I don't remember seeing anything in his reports about any of this.'

'There's nothing, no. He never told you about what was in this room?'

'No.'

'He never told James either - I asked. He kept this a secret from everyone, even those of us who were closest to him.'

Rachel stopped besides a bust and ran her fingers gently over the marble, taking in the exquisite detail of the carving. She drew in a ragged breath and moisture glistened in her eyes. 'This is love...'

Sam smiled. He had known that Rachel would see it the same way he did. He went to her and wrapped his arms around her from behind, then bent forward to whisper in her ear. 'I know we're kind of married already, *Lady Vives*, but will you marry me? Properly, I mean.'

He felt her stiffen slightly and he wondered if he had made a mistake, but it was a fleeting doubt as she spun around in his arms and locked her lips to his.

When they eventually came up for breath, she pulled back and there were tears of joy streaming down her face, the melancholy of before all but forgotten. 'Yes! Of course, yes! Hell yes!'

She grinned, wiping her eyes and sniffing away the very unladylike snot that had bubbled up.

He reached for her again, but she turned suddenly serious and stopped him with a hand on his chest. 'But not until this is all over, OK?'

Sam nodded. He was disappointed, but he understood. 'That's fair enough.' He gave her a cheeky grin. 'I suppose you want a ring anyway, right?'

'Of course! But I'm not going to wear it; it's not good for martial arts, it gets in the way.'

Sam laughed. 'OK, we'll go shopping for it when we get back to London, but I'm just going to get you a cheap one if you're not going to wear it.'

Rachel kissed him. 'I don't care; it's what it means that is important. And no way are you getting away with buying me a cheap one, Buster; you're rich enough to buy me something good! But I don't want a diamond, they're just tacky, get me something good, like platinum or something. Oh, and you're going to get two, so that you can have one too. OK?'

'Fine. Whatever you say, Mrs Vives.'

'*Lady* Vives.'

She grinned and they kissed again, briefly, but then just held each other, feeling how perfectly they fit together, each thinking about the future that awaited them if they survived to see it.

They finally separated and looked around the room again.

'What are you going to do with all this, Sam?'

'I have no idea. I thought of taking it to London and putting it in Headquarters, but I'm not sure that's fair on all the other people who only have one portrait there. Then again, nobody will see it if I just leave it locked away here, which is a shame.'

'I think maybe you should give one piece to your mother.'

Sam looked at her in surprise. 'But she won't know that it's her sister.'

Rachel shook her head. 'It doesn't matter. We'll just tell her that it's something that Andrew left her in the will or something, but I think she should have something, even if she doesn't know what it means.'

'I think that would be lovely. We'll decide what to do with the rest, later.'

'Worst comes to the worst we'll just take it with us to wherever we end up living and any guests we have will get to see them.'

'OK.'

They turned and left the room and Sam sighed when he saw the dirt everywhere. 'I'm going to open all the windows to get some air in, then sweep and mop, can you look to see if there are any clean sheets for the bed, please?'

'I don't mind a bit of dirt; we've had worse.' Rachel shrugged, but nevertheless went off to the main bedroom, lugging their suitcases behind her.

There was a party for Violeta in the afternoon the next day and Sam's parents had invited all of her friends from school. Unfortunately, being the middle of summer, a lot of them were on holiday and only half a dozen showed up.

To begin with, Sam's sister had fun, opening her presents and laughing as she always did during her birthday parties, but then, when they'd had cake, chocolate, Violeta's favourite, and settled down to play games she went quiet. She didn't join in when Sam's parents brought out paints and everybody started to make a mess in the room that had been covered in plastic for the day, instead she sat in an armchair with one of the books that Sam had brought for her from England as a present.

Sam pulled his mother aside and asked her about it.

'She hasn't been the same since Andrew died and when you started moping around feeling sorry for yourself that didn't help either. I'm not saying that it's your fault, not one bit, but I guess with first one thing, then the other...' She shook her head and looked at Violeta. 'She's been spending more and more time in her room lately. She hardly draws anymore and she's a lot quieter, but she has been reading a lot. I hope you don't mind, but I gave her your laptop to use; she seems to be having a bit of a love affair with Wikipedia right now and she's always online when she hasn't got her nose in a book.'

As if she knew they were talking about her, Violeta glanced up from her reading. She grinned happily at them and for a second she seemed like the energetic little scamp that she had always been, but the smile disappeared as soon as she looked back at the back and was replaced by a serious look that was almost a frown.

'Apparently she's changed at school as well - her teachers all say she's made vast improvements in her work, but they're worried because she's become much less sociable. They've been keeping an eye on her, just in case there's some bullying going on or something, but haven't seen anything.' She sighed. 'I don't know, sometimes I think we should take her to see someone, but she's only nine, she'll get over it. Right?'

She gave Sam a hopeful look and he realised that she was actually seeking reassurance from him. It was the first time in his life that she was truly treating him as an adult and it surprised him. At the same time he was shocked by the insecurity that he saw in her; his mother had always been so sure, so certain, much more so than his father, who always seemed to be worrying about something. Like him, she had more worry lines now and he saw bags under her eyes from lack of sleep - one more thing to blame the Illuminati for.

'I'm sure she'll be fine, but I'll have a talk with her, anyway. Hey, how about she stays with me and Rachel tonight and I'll bring her back tomorrow evening? You and Dad can go out and have dinner or take in a movie or something - whatever it is the young people do nowadays.' He grinned at her, trying to lighten the mood.

His efforts were rewarded with a smile and a few of the lines on his mother's forehead smoothed out slightly. 'Actually, that would be nice, thank you, Sam.' She reached out to caress his cheek fondly. 'When did you get so grown up?'

Sam didn't answer, he just smiled.

They turned to watch as his father hurried up to them, covered in paint. 'We're running out of pink already... why doesn't Violeta have any boys as friends? I can do airplanes and cars no problem, but bloody unicorns?!?'

They couldn't help laughing at the panic on his face, but when he got even more upset Sam took pity on him. 'I think Rachel is pretty good at drawing, I'll see if she feels like taking over for a while, if you want?'

'Yes! Please! Anything but this!' He lifted his foot and showed them where someone had painted something that vaguely resembled a pink horse on his favourite slippers.

Violeta went with them to Andrew's flat after all of the guests had gone. The other children had barely noticed that the birthday girl hadn't really been playing with them; they were all friends from school so it had just been another play-date for them, only with more cake and balloons than usual and they'd had a good time.

Sam asked Violeta what she wanted to do, whether she was tired and wanted to go to bed or not, and she told them that she wanted to watch a film. Neither Sam nor Rachel minded; watching a movie was an easy way of keeping Sam's sister entertained and it would give them a chance to snuggle that they hadn't had during the afternoon.

Sam set up Rachel's laptop in the sitting room and connected it to the television while Rachel went with Violeta to wash up and put their pyjamas on.

When they came back Sam pointed to the TV screen where he'd brought up a few options. 'What do you want to watch, Vee? You fancy some Disney? Pixar? Look, here's *Monsters Inc.*, you like that one, don't you, Boo?'

He grinned at her and ruffled her hair, remembering when she'd been just like the little girl in the film, but Violeta shook her head and pushed him to one side. She seized the mouse and started clicking rapidly through the menus of the streaming service.

Sam watched her, impressed with how proficient she was. He idly wondered whether they had a budding hacker on their hands and whether it was too early to introduce her to Dylan.

'This one. I want to watch this one.' Violeta clicked on a film and Sam saw that she hadn't chosen a Disney film, hadn't even chosen a cartoon; she'd chosen *Shakespeare in Love*.

'Really, Violeta? It might be a bit old for you...'

'No! I want to see this one. Now shush, Sammy, it's starting!'

She jumped backwards onto the sofa and wriggled around until she was curled up against Sam. He put an arm around her and as Rachel leaned against his other side, he said a quiet thank-you to Andrew for installing air-conditioning, otherwise it would have gotten very cosy very quickly in the Spanish summer heat.

They watched the film in English, something that Violeta had no problem with; Sam's mother had made more of an effort to make sure that Violeta spoke English than she had with Sam and she was far more fluent than Sam had been before he'd met Rachel and spent so much time in England.

Sam had seen the film before with Rachel, so he had no need to watch it to know what was going on and he spent most of the time, except for the good bits, watching Violeta. Despite it being meant for adults she seemed to understand it all and she surprised him by laughing at some of the references that Rachel had needed to explain to him the first time around.

It was astounding how much she'd changed in the months that he'd been away and he wondered if it really had been Andrew's death and his leaving that had changed her, or whether she'd just grown up and he'd missed it.

She hadn't grown up so much that she could stay awake much past her bedtime, though, and her eyes started to droop in the middle of the film. She came fully awake for the play at the end, which she enjoyed immensely, but then they closed fully during the end credits and by the time the music had finished she was snoring gently.

Sam smiled and gently picked her up. He carried her down the hall to the spare bedroom and put her in bed. He kissed her on the forehead and stroked her hair fondly before going out, leaving the door slightly ajar, just in case.

By that time Rachel had turned everything off in the sitting room and she met him at the door to their own room, smiling, leaning against the door jamb.

'You're good with her.'

Sam shrugged. 'She's my sister.'

'Even so, I know a lot of brothers and sisters who can't stand the sight of each other, whereas you treat her with respect, almost like an adult sometimes.'

'I guess I've just never been able to do baby-talk or speak to her like someone her age; it doesn't feel right to me.'

Rachel smiled and pushed herself away from the wall. She stood on tiptoes to kiss him, stroking his hair. 'Well, maybe one day, after we're married, we'll have a kid of our own and you'll learn.'

She grabbed his hand and pulled him into their room, closing the door firmly behind them.

Sam woke in the middle of the night and for a second he just stared up at the ceiling, wondering why, but then he heard a noise coming from outside the bedroom. It wasn't Rachel because she was still fast asleep at his side, snoring loudly, and for a second he thought that the Illuminati had come for them. He was about to wake her and tell her that there was an intruder in the flat, but remembered just in time that they had a guest.

He rolled out of bed, using every ounce of stealth he could so as not to wake Rachel.

'What's wrong?'

He groaned. No matter how many times he tried to sneak around her, Rachel always knew he was there and exactly what he was doing. 'Violeta's moving around. I'm going to see if she's alright.'

'OK, but don't you dare put your cold feet on me when you come back.' She rolled over and her snoring immediately started up again.

Sam shook his head and slipped out of the door. He looked towards the spare bedroom, but quickly realised that the light he could see wasn't coming from Violeta's room, but from the other end of the flat where the front door was.

He moved quicker, wondering if for some reason Violeta had got it into her head to go outside. He had a sudden vision of her missing their parents and deciding to go wandering in the night looking for them. They would kill him.

The light wasn't coming from the hallway, though, it was coming from the room with Andrew's artworks.

He pushed the door open and found Violeta sitting on the floor, gazing up at one of the paintings. It was one of the more classical ones, depicting a smiling Susan as a romantic figure in a long white dress, reclining on a couch with her head propped up in one hand. It was one of Sam's favourites, and by the expression on her face it seemed that Violeta liked it too.

He sat down next to her and she climbed onto his lap and snuggled up against him. He wrapped his arms around her, feeling her shivering gently because of the chilly tiled floor.

'She's beautiful.' Violeta's voice was almost a whisper.

'Yes, she is.'

They sat in silence for long minutes, looking up at the painting, but then Sam started when he felt something touch his arm and he looked down to find her small fingers tracing his scars. In his haste to see if his sister was alright he had forgotten to put on a shirt to cover them and was just dressed in a pair of boxers. She didn't seem disturbed by them and was running her fingertip along them as if they were nothing more than lines on a piece of paper, though, and after a few minutes he felt her relax against him and heard her breathing settle. He sat for a little longer, gazing at the painting, but then stood up, with her still in his arms, and took her back to bed.

Despite having gotten up and wandered around during the night, Violeta still woke them up early by bursting into their room and crawling into their bed. She laughed at their groans and wriggled between them.

'Wake up, Sammy! I'm hungry!'

'What time is it?'

'Late.'

Sam looked at the clock on the bedside table and groaned; it was six.

Rachel's voice was muffled as she buried her head in her pillow and turned her back on them. 'She's your sister. Your problem. See you in an hour.'

Sam groaned for a third time as Violeta started pushing at him, rolling him back and forth. 'Va! Vamos!'

He let her push him around for a while, then he growled and sprang at her. She giggled as he grabbed her and slung her over his shoulder as he stood up.

'Come on then, let's go feed the monster!'

True to her word Rachel joined them in the sitting room almost exactly an hour later. Sam was watching the news, sipping at a cup of tea, while Violeta was lying on the floor reading something on the laptop and neither of them noticed her when she sneaked in and stood behind Sam's armchair to watch them fondly.

She couldn't believe how different things had become in such a short time. Being a Displacer was fun and all and she loved time travelling with Sam, but it was her day to day life that had changed the most and now, thanks to him, for the first time ever, she felt that she was part of a proper family.

Sam finally realised she was there and craned his neck to smile up at her. 'Morning!'

'Morning.' She bent over to give him a kiss, then poked her tongue out at Violeta, who giggled and waved, but immediately looked back at the laptop. 'Have you two decided what we're going to do today?'

'Not yet.' Sam looked down at Violeta. 'What do you think, monster? Do you want to go to the beach? The zoo?'

Violeta rolled onto her side and looked up at them. 'Can we take a picnic and go for a walk?'

Sam was slightly surprised, but pleasantly so. 'Of course. We can go up towards *Tibidabo*, or we can go to the pool at *Crueta del Coll*, or we could even go to the *Labyrint d'Horta* if you wanted. Have you been there yet?'

Violeta shook her head.

'Why don't we do that then? We can get you lost in the maze and leave you there forever.'

Violeta laughed at the idea. 'Silly Sam!'

They got to the maze around eleven and Violeta spent a whole two hours running around, looking like the child she'd been before Sam had left. He and Rachel chased her around the small maze until she knew it back to front, but she never got tired of it and every time Sam or Rachel begged for a break she would drag them back in, laughing.

They sat in the shade next to the big house for lunch, munching on sandwiches. There were some other children there and Violeta got talking to some of them and to their relief she spent the afternoon with them, kicking a football and playing hide and seek in the maze under the watchful eyes of about a dozen equally relieved parents.

They took Violeta back to Sam's parents in the late evening. She was so tired that she was falling asleep on the metro and Sam had to carry her up the stairs to the flat. He laid her in bed and kissed her on the forehead before quietly sneaking away.

They stayed to have a drink with his parents. They were cheerful and rested; even just a single day on their own together had done them good. Rachel saw this, and before Sam could say anything she offered to take Violeta again. They leapt at the chance and swiftly arranged to have her stay with them the following weekend.

It was Sunday so that left Sam and Rachel with the whole week on their own.

The first thing they decided to do was learn more about each other's Displacements. As a rule Displacers refused to discuss anything when they were in the past except for the mission, preferring to live "in the moment", and they'd been so busy in the present that Sam had never really had a chance to find out much about what she'd done before he'd met her.

Rachel gave Sam her book of personal reports, which was a large diary, much like a girl's personal one. And pink. When Sam gave her an amused look she shrugged. 'I was a lot younger once.'

In return, Sam gave her his secret pen drive. She had been on most of his Displacements with him, but she'd never read the whole story of his first one to Port Royal, and she also wanted to read about his two most recent ones without her - the ones to Iran and Paris, which had caused such a change in him.

They read things about each other that made them uncomfortable, but it was mostly stuff that they'd known about to some extent already, for example Sam read how Rachel had lost her heart and her virginity to an Austro-Hungarian count and Rachel read about how he'd slaughtered an entire family of nobles in Romania on the orders of his assassin master.

However, there was nothing about the Beast in Sam's notes; that was too private, too shameful to put into writing and she remained in ignorance about the full extent to which his soul had been tarnished.

When they'd finished, they put aside the notes and moved on, putting what was past in the past, as was the way with the Displacers, although Sam couldn't help but feel guilty that he now knew everything about Rachel, while he still had his secret.

The weekend with Violeta was fun and far more tiring than the single day had been, but afterwards it was time to meet with Diana at her new, secret property a few miles up the coast from Barcelona. They had arranged to be with her for the last four days before they had to go back to London - that was all they could risk having her with them - and she had been flying around the world for almost a week, throwing off any surveillance and leaving a false trail, just in case. For the last leg she flew into Marseilles and took a train from there and they met her at the small local train station in the village where she'd bought her house.

The first thing they did was sit her down and tell her about Sam's marriage proposal. They could see how hurt she was by the news, but she had still kissed them and said she was happy for them. She told them she knew what the two of them had was special and that she would be glad just to be with them for as long as they would have her.

They had known she would feel somewhat left out and had discussed what to do about it - they made a promise to her then that, even though she couldn't be part of the marriage in the eyes of the law, she would never be any less to them than they were to each other.

Diana's house was on a gated estate up on a hill looking out over the Mediterranean and was completely isolated from the rest of the properties on the estate by high fences, bushes, and a large gate. She'd had a security system installed, complete with cameras covering every approach, so even Diana felt safe enough to relax her guard completely. It was a little taste of paradise and they lazed around her swimming pool, dining together, sleeping late and wearing very little in the way of clothing for the whole time. While being together in the past was fantastic, it was so much better in the present, so much more *real*, no doubt because of the nature of Displacing and the fact that you left the past behind when you returned.

All too soon, their four days with Diana were up and so were the two weeks that Sam had allowed himself.

They left her in the morning and took the train back to Barcelona where they had one last meal with Sam's family, said their goodbyes, and that very evening were on a plane back to London and an uncertain future.

CHAPTER 10
FIRST STRIKE

Anne was waiting for them when they got back to London and they barely got in the door of Headquarters that night before she all but jumped on them.

'We've done it! We've got a plan!'

They stood in the hallway, their bags on the floor at their feet, bleary eyed from the long day they'd had and stared at her.

'Anne, it's ten o'clock, why are you even still here? Can't this wait until tomorrow?' Rachel was feeling a bit grumpy; the underground had been full of drunken young men, celebrating a rare win by the England football team. Their singing had been very loud in the confined space, which had been bad enough, but then a couple of them had started leering at her and making rude comments and Sam hadn't let her beat them up, which was worse.

Anne looked abashed and she visibly cringed away from her. 'Oh. Sorry, Rachel.'

Sam, however gave Anne an encouraging smile. 'Actually, I'd really like to hear it. Would you mind putting the kettle on while Rachel and I put our luggage upstairs? We'll be down in a few minutes.'

The smile instantly came back to Anne's face. 'OK!'

She skipped off and disappeared down the stairs.

Rachel snarled at him when he turned to her, but he pulled her into a kiss anyway and soon felt her relaxing in his arms.

He pulled back and rested his forehead against hers. 'Come on, this is why we've come back, we might as well get to it.'

'I know, I just expected to have a night's sleep first.'

'There'll be plenty of time to sleep once we've destroyed the Illuminati.'

He picked up both of their suitcases and started up the stairs with them, leaving Rachel to plod after him with their hand luggage.

They came back down five minutes later and found Anna sitting at the table in the kitchen. She was sipping from a glass while she was waiting for them, a bottle of Jack Daniels by her elbow.

Rachel sneered at the liquor and went to the cupboard. She filled a glass with some expensive vodka and went to sit opposite the American woman.

Sam shook his head at them both and poured some tea from the pot that Anne had prepared. He was over sixty years old now and still didn't understand humanity's obsession with alcohol and other ways of blurring the mind; he just saw them as a waste of time - what use was having a good time under their effects if you didn't remember what you'd done afterwards?

Anne waited just long enough for him to sit down before she started talking rapidly, almost babbling in her excitement. As she spoke she leaned forwards on her arms and looked from Rachel to Sam and back and Sam frowned slightly; she looked tired and frazzled and not a little bit crazy.

'As you know, we were looking at dates around the time when the Templars were at their strongest. It was Andrew's idea originally to take advantage of a couple of his ancestors being high up in the order and make as much of the Illuminati's riches as we could our own. With me so far?'

She looked at them expectantly and they nodded.

'That possibility was effectively closed when we failed last time and I assume that the Illuminati have since done what they can to set the time-line, so I've decided to approach the same problem from a different angle. I thought of looking instead at when the religious order fell and became the basis for the banking system that we have today. When they were destroyed in 1307 the monarchs of the various countries that the Templars were based in tried to seize their assets, especially France where the king was bankrupt. The pope, however, decreed that their wealth should go to the Hospitallers. Most historians say that is what happened, and a lot of their wealth did indeed transfer across. However, there is a huge discrepancy in what the Hospitallers and others received from the dissolution of the Templars and what the

Templars were reported to have before their downfall - a *lot* of their riches are unaccounted for.'

'The Illuminati has it,' said Sam.

'Precisely!' she nodded enthusiastically. 'Now, we've discovered that one of John's ancestors was a commander in the Order at the time of its destruction but, while most of the Order and even the Grand Master himself were burnt at the stake or murdered, there are no records of what happened to him - he effectively disappeared from the face of the planet.'

'Ah...' Sam could see where Anne was going but decided to let her finish; she deserved the chance to give them her full reasoning.

'Well, we know where he was assigned at the time, we found a reference to him being in a small church in Malta.'

'And?'

Anne's eyes sparkled and her words came out in a rush. '*And...* What the hell was a high-ranking Templar, the descendant of a Grand Master, doing in a small church on an unimportant island in the middle of the Mediterranean when most of the Templars at the time were in Paris, Rome, or London? What on *earth* would be so important to warrant him being there?'

'He had the money, of course.'

Rachel wasn't feeling as patient as Sam; she got grumpy when she was tired, but Anne didn't notice and smiled at her in delight. 'Exactly!'

The American turned back to Sam, thankfully missing it when Rachel rolled her eyes. 'So, what do you do when you see trouble ahead? When you see the tides of public opinion turning against you. When monarchs all across Europe start to look at your wealth with greedy eyes?'

'You hide it.'

'Exactly, and you pick somewhere that is out of the reach of those greedy monarchs, like a little island in the middle of the sea.'

Rachel frowned. 'Alright then, so the money is there. What are we supposed to do about it? Go back and say to whoever owns the island, "look there's a lot of money hidden here, why don't you go and take it?"'

Anne laughed. 'That's one idea I suppose, but I found a better one when I continued to look into things. I don't know how much you know of the history of your country, Sam, but Malta was under Spanish rule at the time, more precisely the rule of the kingdom of Aragon.'

Sam shrugged. He'd always been more interested in the history of places that weren't Spain.

'Well, in 1530 the island was taken over as a vassal state of Sicily and, funnily enough, when they took a closer look at their new property there was no sign of the money.'

Sam nodded. 'OK, so it got moved sometime between, uh, 1307 and 1530.'

'Right! And I know exactly when and how!' She grinned. 'I have everything I need to be able to send their treasure straight to the bottom of the Med!'

Sam laughed and clapped his hands. 'Excellent! Rachel and I will go when she's recovered.'

'No.' Anne shook her head. 'I'm going next week and I'm taking Hamish Junior and Julia with me. Lisa's orders.'

Sam automatically began to protest, but then stopped himself, or rather something stopped him.

There was nothing preventing Rachel from speaking her mind, though. 'Anne, this is no time to...'

'Rachel.' Sam put his hand on her arm and she instantly went silent and blinked at him.

'You're not actually going to let them...'

'Yes.' Again he stopped her with a word. 'This is the right move. I can feel it.'

'Oh, OK...' Rachel didn't look particularly convinced, but she knew enough to trust Sam's feelings and didn't pursue the matter.

Anne leaned forwards, looking slightly concerned and tense. 'Sam, there is one thing that I wanted to talk to you about, one slight drawback in the plan. We're going to be sinking the three ships with the treasure on board, which means we won't get our hands on any of it... Is that...?'

'I don't care, as long as it's out of Illuminati hands.'

'Good.' The American woman smiled. 'Everyone always seems so keen on getting their hands on as much money as possible, but Lisa said you'd say that. We could always keep looking for other alternatives, ones that gave us a chance to get something out of this, but I think this is our best shot at hurting our enemies.'

'Then go with it.' Sam smiled at her. 'It's the right thing to do.'

'Thank you.' Anne nodded and downed the rest of her Jack, then pushed herself back from the table and stood up. 'Well, I've kept you from bed too long and I need to get some sleep myself!'

She took her glass and the bottle to the sink, then made her way towards the stairs, but Sam called out to her before she could disappear.

'Anne?'

She turned back. 'Yes, Sam?'

'Are you alright?'

'Yes, of course I am!'

She smiled, but Sam just held her gaze, knowing that she wasn't and eventually she sagged. 'No, of course I'm not, Sam! How can I be?' Her eyes were starting to glisten, but she didn't cry, she just became angrier as she spoke. 'And I know you're not either, but this will be a step in the right direction. We'll take that bastard's world apart piece by piece until he's got nothing left and no place to hide and then we'll kill him!'

She spat out the last words, then stood there panting, fists clenched, glaring at him, daring him to contradict her or tell her to calm down.

He didn't, though, he just nodded reassuringly. 'Don't worry, he'll die soon enough, I promise you that, but we're going to make him suffer first.'

Anne seemed satisfied with his answer and relaxed, nodding her gratitude. 'Thank you.' She smiled briefly then left.

Rachel watched her go, a troubled look on her face, but she waited until the sound of her footsteps on the stairs faded before turning to Sam. 'Are you really happy with them going without us? You know you could always just go with them yourself, I don't mind too much.'

Sam shook his head and grinned. 'Maybe the time-line wants them to gain a bit of confidence, or is saving us for something else, who knows, but as I said - this feels right. Besides, you and I have gotten too used to doing everything around here. We need to let someone else have a bit of fun for a change.'

Three days later, Anne, Julia, and Hamish were ready to go on their mission and Sam, Rachel and Lisa joined them in the sitting room to witness it.

They sat on one of the larger sofas, with Anne in the middle leading them, and when they were ready they linked hands and closed their eyes.

Sam leaned forwards and watched them as closely as he could while at the same time reaching out with his senses. He had never actually been present when another person had Displaced without him and he wondered if he would see something that other people couldn't because of his "special" nature.

He didn't.

He felt their energy building up gradually, then the sudden flare of power as they Displaced, but then it immediately vanished, leaving the world exactly as it had been before. He saw a couple of scratches appear on Julia's hand and a bruise suddenly blacken Anne's cheek, but beyond that there was nothing - no fanfares, explosions of colours, lingering sparks, or spinning number plates.

He was actually quite disappointed.

The three Displacers opened their eyes and slow smiles spread across their faces. They burst out laughing and hugged each other, joyfully celebrating.

Sam looked at Rachel and raised his voice over the noise. 'I'm guessing they were successful...'

She grinned back at him. 'How can you tell?'

It took a while for them to calm down, but eventually they separated.

'You still got them, Hamish?'

'Here you go.'

Hamish handed something to Anne and she stood and came over to them. She held her hand out. On her palm were three large golden coins. 'We brought a souvenir back for you. Mission accomplished, Sam.'

She handed a coin to each of them, then went back to be with her teammates.

Sam flipped his coin, then looked at Lisa. 'How do we know if it worked?'

Lisa grinned. 'I think if we listen carefully enough we'll be able to hear the sound of John screaming in pain as he sees his bank statements.'

The celebrations for the Maltese mission, or "Strike One" as Anna, a baseball fan, had dubbed it, started shortly after and went on well into the night. The party was rather more enthusiastic than the ones thrown after Sam's successes, but that was to be understood and he didn't take any offence; the Society had gotten its first ever proper win against the Illuminati - his victories had only prevented them from making further gains.

After an impromptu dinner, courtesy of Richard as per usual, the party migrated to the first floor library where there was more room to move around. Dylan set up his laptop and started acting as a DJ and, despite the music not being to everybody's taste, nobody seemed to care; they were in the mood to dance and have fun and most of them had drunk too much by then to really notice.

Near midnight, Sam's good mood slowly left him as he became tired and the music and drunken people began to irritate him. The others seemed to be able to forget how much there still was to do, but he couldn't, not even for one second.

He went downstairs, heading for the kitchen where he knew Rachel was in conversation with some of the elders, intending to grab her and persuade her to go to bed, but when he reached the entrance hallway he heard soft noises coming from the dimly lit sitting room and went to investigate.

Anne was standing in front of Andrew's photo, crying into a glass of bourbon, the fingers of her free hand resting lightly against it, caressing his smiling face.

She started slightly when he appeared by her side and snatched her hand away from the photo.

'Sorry if I startled you.' Sam apologised; sometimes moving silently wasn't entirely necessary.

'It's alright, I was just...' She gesture at the photo, but then tutted and leaned forward unsteadily to peer myopically at it; she'd left marks on the glass over the photo. She tried to clean them with the sleeve of her jumper, but just managed to smear them even more. 'Bugger.'

Sam reached out to pull back her hand. 'I'll clean it tomorrow, Anne, don't worry.'

Rather than resisting him she surprised him by turning sharply and flinging her arms around his neck, throwing her full weight against him in her drunkenness and almost knocking him over.

She was a good two inches taller than him in her heels and Sam found himself leaning back slightly as she bawled on his shoulder. He wondered for an instant how girls could put up with the uncomfortable position before putting the thought out of his mind and wrapping his arms around her. Not sure what else to do, he tried to comfort her by stroking her back and making calming noises.

He looked past her at Andrew's photo and at the portrait of Susan hanging next to it which showed Susan laughing and relaxing in an armchair in that very room.

James and Andrew had told him enough stories about Susan that he knew how remarkable she had been and the fact that the American woman had been able to plan and carry out a mission so closely related to the one that her lover had been killed on said a lot about her determination and drive, not to mention how capable she was. So, in a way his uncle had been very lucky to find the love of two incredible women, but that didn't take away from the fact that he had been robbed of a future with both of them.

After about a minute Anne pulled back from him and wiped her eyes. 'I'm sorry, Sam, I don't know what came over me.' She staggered a couple of steps and flopped into an armchair.

She pulled a tissue from her sleeve and dabbed ineffectually at her eyes before squinting at him with bleary eyes. 'You know, you remind me of him sometimes.'

'Really?' Sam shifted another chair around so that he could sit facing her.

'Yes. There's a quiet strength that you both have, had, uh, have...?' She snorted, laughing, and filled her glass from the bottle sitting on the small table next to her, upending it and shaking it roughly to get the last drops.

She took a big gulp and exhaled noisily before continuing. 'You do what you have to do, both of you. Without complaining, without any fuss, oh so English-lily, Englily, Eng... ah, whatever...!' She cut herself off, motioning angrily with her hand and spilling whisky on the floor next to her.

'And you know what the worst thing is? You don't do it because you're being told to or because you're getting paid or anything so... so... ordinary. You do it because it's your *duty*.' The last word came out harshly and for the first time ever he saw something approaching resentment in her, but it was gone in an instant, replaced by sorrow as she sighed. 'Don't let your duty kill you, Sam. Life is worth more than some damn time-line.' She downed the rest of her glass, then stood up on unstable legs, waving the bottle.

'I'm empty.' She tottered out of the room, leaving Sam alone with his thoughts, troubled, his bed forgotten.

The laptop smashed into the mirror of the hotel room, shattering it and scattering sharp splinters of glass everywhere.

John threw back his chair and stood up. 'You fu... owww!!!' He kicked at the table and his words turned into a howl of pain; he was in a Japanese hotel room, which was a mix between modern and traditional with western furniture and tatami mats, and he wasn't wearing shoes.

He hopped around for a few seconds, swearing, before eventually tumbling onto the futon bed and clutching his toe. Knowing his luck he'd probably broken it.

The toe was the least of his worries at that moment, though; it was what he'd seen on his laptop that had him really furious - a full quarter of his hard-earned wealth had vanished into thin air in front of his eyes, the accounts disappearing as if they'd never existed while he'd been logged into them. At first he'd thought it was some kind of error, but he soon found that others had gone as well and when he'd finally put two and two together he'd exploded and lashed out.

The laptop was easy enough to replace but he regretted the kick; it wasn't easy to get medical treatment in Japan at the best of times, but being on the run made everything so much harder and riskier.

He limped back to the table and downed the rest of his Suntory whiskey then picked the ice out of the glass and rubbed it on his foot.

'Ah...' The pain faded, but he kept at it as he gazed out of the window at the temples of Kyoto, dotted here and there below him, scattered seemingly at random amid the modern buildings.

This was no way to live - constantly on the move while the damn Displacers chipped away at all he'd worked towards for the last couple of decades. They had taken a fair amount from him over the last couple of weeks, somehow tracking the transactions he'd been making online and closing down some of his smaller accounts, but those losses, while they stung, were inconsequential compared to this one.

Enough was enough, it was time to stop running, he was done with it. It was time to turn the tables.

They had hurt him and in return he would destroy them.

He reached into his laptop bag and pulled out the small black notebook where he kept his list of possible missions for his minions. Most of them were mundane: lists of artworks and treasures that would be nice additions to his collections, or small adjustments that could be made to the time-line to marginally turn things in his favour, however, at the back, there were a few things that were altogether more *special*. That was where he kept his ideas for missions that would cause wide-sweeping changes in the present, missions that were too dangerous to carry out or too unpredictable in their results, but had the potential to make him the owner of entire countries or even a king.

He flicked through them, rereading them for perhaps the thousandth time and smiled as he found the perfect one. However, before he sent his minions out to make him the most powerful man on the planet, he was going to get some revenge and make sure his bridges were well and truly burnt.

CHAPTER 11
GRANDFATHER

Sam and Rachel got up late the next day, had a quick breakfast, then hopped on a bus to go and see James, who had unfortunately missed all the excitement. Since his angina attack, Sam's grandfather had been ill quite a lot and he'd been bedridden for the last few days, but he had plenty of books and regular visitors from the Society, so he wasn't as unhappy about being confined to his home as he was embarrassed; he'd caught a cold. In summer.

Rachel had keys to his house and she let them in. They found James in the sitting room, wrapped in blankets, reading, and Sam was heartbroken to see that he was looking so much worse than the day he'd got back from Spain.

James took one look at the pity on Sam's face and snarled. 'Piss off and come back when you learn how to smile, boy.'

Predictably, that put a smile on Sam's face and made Rachel laugh.

'That's better.' He put his book to one side and looked up at them. 'You've got something to say and it's not about the mission yesterday that I've heard so much about.' He jerked a thumb at his phone sitting on a table next to him and it buzzed as he received a message, making James groan. 'I'm really thinking about leaving the group message thingy; it's been non-stop since yesterday afternoon. And since when do Displacers use smiley faces when they discuss a successful mission?' He looked back and forth from one of them to the other, but he obviously didn't expect an answer and after a few seconds his mock frown disappeared, replaced by his usual jovial expression. 'Well? Spit it out then!'

Sam took Rachel's hand and together they smiled down at the Elder. 'We haven't told anyone else yet because we wanted you to be the first to know, but we're going to get married.'

'About bloody time!' Far from being surprised James shook his head in exasperation. 'How long have you two been together? Twenty, thirty years? It only took Andrew about five to propose to Susan.'

Sam looked at Rachel. 'Um, well, we've been a bit busy...'

'Excuses, excuses.' He waved a hand at them. 'If there's a will there's a way. Always. Just look at me and Jess - there was a bloody war on and we managed well enough!' He grinned at them. 'So, when's the big day? Soon I hope.'

Sam shook his head. 'No, not until this is all over,'

James' face fell a bit at that. 'We have no idea when that will be, Sam, and I'm not getting any younger - I'd quite like to be there.'

Rather than becoming morbid at the reminder that his beloved grandfather was dying, Sam smiled at him. 'Oh, this will be finished long before you kick the bucket, Grandad, don't worry.'

'Will it?' James blinked at him in surprise.

'It will.' Sam nodded confidently.

James leaned forwards suddenly and squinted up at him sceptically. 'Are you just saying that, boy, or do you know something?'

'I know it.' The words were out before he realised that he did - for some reason he was certain that, one way or other, the war was fast reaching its conclusion.

James held his gaze for a thoroughly uncomfortable length of time, his Elder hat firmly on, before finally nodding, apparently satisfied, and looking at Rachel, who had been following the whole exchange in silence, a faint smile on her lips as she watched them fondly. 'Go up to my room, wouldya? There's a black box in the top drawer of my bedside table, about this big.' He held his hands about eight inches apart. 'Fetch it down for me, please.'

Rachel squeezed Sam's hand then released it to run upstairs.

Sam slipped onto the sofa next to James' armchair. 'How are you feeling, Grandad?'

James grumbled. 'I'll survive. What about you? You done anything stupid recently?'

'I let a girl slip out of my hand and fall to her death.'

The old man frowned. 'I still haven't gotten around to reading your last report fully, but I'm sure I would remember something like that if I'd heard about it.'

Sam shook his head. 'I didn't put the details in my report, I just said that the girl, Clarkwell, died. We fought and she went over the edge of the cliff. I tried to save her, but she didn't want me to. There's not much more beyond that. Besides, it was three years ago and I've done a lot of meditating on it since then.'

James didn't look convinced, but at that moment Rachel returned from her mission and he smiled at her. 'That's the one, bring it here.'

He took the box from her and opened it. He fished around inside, pushing aside medals and jewellery until he found what he wanted. He pulled out something wrapped in tissue paper, which he unfolded to reveal a ring. He held it out to Rachel. 'Here, grab a hold of that.'

She took it from him and shook her head. 'James...'

'Hang on, I'm not finished.' He put aside the box, then pulled at his hand, taking off his own ring and handing it to Sam. 'Here. And that one's for you, lad.'

They looked down at the rings in their hands. They were both simple gold bands, but Sam's one was thicker while Rachel's was delicate. Both were engraved on the inside with the same initials and a date.

Sam shook his head. 'Grandad, I... we can't!'

'Of course you bloody can, boy! I'm just glad I found a good home for them before I popped my clogs. They're not much; we didn't have a lot of money back at the start, your grandmother, sorry your great-grandmother, and I.'

Sam frowned. 'Great-grandmother...? Oh right, Mum's parents died when she was really young.' He blinked, puzzled. He kept forgetting that James wasn't really his grandfather, but rather his mother's grandfather. He felt sure that he should know what had happened to his actual grandparents, but for some reason the details were hazy and his mind kept slithering back and telling him that James was really his grandfather. 'They died, right? Why can't I remember?'

James sighed. 'Because your mind keeps slipping over them. They died on a Displacement together.'

'They were Displacers?'

James spoke patiently. 'Yes, lad. They have gravestones next to Susan in the cemetery and their portraits are on the wall above hers and Andrew's.'

'No they're not, I would have remembered.'

'No, you wouldn't. I've told you about them at least half a dozen times over the years, but the time-line is protecting itself; it's making their family forget them. I only remember them because I did drawings and put them everywhere.'

Sam looked around the room, seeing as if for the first time the pictures, mostly pencil sketches, of a smiling man and a woman on every wall. He concentrated, thinking hard, trying to recall something about them.

'I know that you're my great-grandfather, I know that I *have* to have grandparents, but I can't seem to hold on to that fact.'

Sam looked at the drawing on the wall above James. There was something familiar about the two people in it, but he didn't know if it was because they resembled his mother or if he could actually recall having known them.

'OK, so how is it that I have no problem remembering that Susan existed, but they keep disappearing from my mind?'

James sighed. 'Because with Susan it creates no problem with the time-line if you remember her, she can just be... dead... and it doesn't create a paradox. Although, I bet you had problems remembering why Andrew was your Uncle, right?'

Sam nodded.

'Well, your grandparents are a different matter; they can't just be removed from the time-line so it has to do a bit of work to heal itself, which is why I'm now your grandfather for all intents and purposes.'

'Oh... I see.'

James saw that Sam didn't really and laughed. 'It was a good question, lad, but it is still something you should have been able to work out for yourself by now!'

Sam chuckled and shrugged. 'Well, you know me.'

He smiled at James, but then blinked and frowned. He looked around at Rachel. 'Er... What was I saying?'

'I have no idea...' She shrugged, puzzled, and shook her head, then grinned cheekily. 'Maybe you're going mad in your old age.'

Sam laughed. 'I'm only ten years older than you!' His gaze alighted on the rings in their hands. 'Oh, yes, the rings! Only if you're sure, Grandad.'

'Of course I'm sure, you bloody idiot! I wouldn't have offered otherwise.'

Sam frowned. A shadow had passed across the old man's face, but it had been instantly replaced by a smile so he said nothing and just turned to face Rachel. He took the ring from her hand and slipped off the sofa to kneel at her feet.

'Oh, don't be daft.' Rachel pushed him, sending him sprawling onto the sofa, then flopped down beside him. She grabbed his ring from him and they began trying to put them on each other. Rachel's was too small and didn't go on her ring finger so Sam ended up putting it on her little finger, while his was far too big and Rachel laughed as she put it on his thumb.

'Feel free to get them altered...' James shook his head in exasperation as he watched them fool around.

Rachel went over to him and bent down to kiss him on the cheek. 'Thank you, James, they're *just* what we wanted.'

There were tears shining in James' eyes when he looked up at her. 'You're welcome, luv. Now, why don't you sit down while that lazy, good for nothing boyfriend of yours puts the kettle on? You have managed to teach him how to make a decent cup of tea by now, right?'

'He's Spanish. I don't think he's ever going to be able to.'

'Well, his mother's English and he has my genes in there somewhere, so keep working on it.'

'I will, even if it takes another century.'

Sam rolled his eyes and pushed himself off the sofa. He made his way across the room to the door, but paused to glance back at them before going out. Rachel had perched on the sofa next to the old man and he was already chuckling as she launched into some story - probably something embarrassing about him if he knew her.

He smiled; his grandfather looked much better already.

After tea they went for a walk. James was fed up with being stuck indoors and wanted to get some fresh air, so Sam took him upstairs to help him get dressed, while Rachel took the food they had brought with them, a "care package" from Richard, to the kitchen and started organising it for later.

They wandered down the street, crossed the main road and went through the council flats to Brockwell Park, then turned right onto the perimeter path.

Sam had so many memories of the park, of kicking a ball around with his father, of flying kites, riding bikes, and of James teaching him to hold a cricket bat. It had a much more decrepit look about it now, though, but it still felt good to be there with James again and he wondered if he and Rachel would ever take a son or daughter of their own there.

James wasn't feeling up to going all the way around, so they just went as far as the Herne Hill station exit, before turning towards home, going past the house in the middle of the park that had once had a restaurant. James told a laughing Rachel that Sam hadn't been able to pronounce the word "restaurant"; his less than two year-old Spanish tongue not quite making its way around the English word. He had tried valiantly, though, because he knew that that was where ice cream was to be had, and had come up with "rinkronk" to say whenever they were in the park and he wanted a treat.

James was huffing by the time they crested the small rise back to the gate where they had come in and they paused and sat on a bench so he could get his breath back.

He laughed. 'Never get old...'

Rachel laughed with him, but it took Sam a second before he got the joke; James wasn't looking bad for being several hundred years old and the same went for him and Rachel - she was almost sixty, while he himself was now closing in on seventy.

A sudden cold wave passed through him as his mind couldn't help but go back to Emily Clarkwell and her claim of being eight hundred years old, but his dark thoughts were forced back when Rachel squeezed his hand reassuringly, picking up on his distress, and he smiled at her gratefully.

After ten minutes, James had rested enough and he slapped his thighs before standing up. 'Come on then, I'm hungry and I haven't had Richard's food in at least a week. That's far too long.'

Sam and Rachel heated the food while James hovered, watching hungrily, and when it was ready, they took it to the dining room. They didn't talk shop during the meal; James had forbidden it, instead he asked them to tell him about their trip to Barcelona.

They had him in stitches describing Violeta's birthday party, but he got very quiet when Sam told him about her strange behaviour. He shook his head and tutted. 'She must have been closer to Andrew than we thought, I should have known she'd take it hard too.'

They were just finishing up when Rachel received a message. She shot a glance at Sam when they heard the ring tone; the first bars of "Protect Me From What I Want" by Placebo, the ringtone that Diana had chosen for herself as a joke.

She pulled her phone out of her pocket and unlocked it.

Sam leaned towards her, craning his head to try to read the message. 'What does she say?'

'Who?' asked James.

'Diana, that's her ringtone.'

'She...' Rachel blinked, rereading the message. 'She's been put on alert for a new mission and because she lost most of her team in the Himalayas she's going to be rejoining Quentin's. She doesn't have any specific details, but says that the Master told her it's going to be dangerous, but potentially change the entire world.'

She looked up at Sam and he gave her a smile, even as he felt a knot in his stomach; this was what they had been waiting for, but now the time had finally come he found that he was scared.

James perked up considerably after the message and Sam began to wonder if the old man had really been ill or just bored because now that there was the prospect of research on the horizon - not just perusing history to try to find some small way to hurt the Illuminati, but an actual mission to counter their efforts - he seemed to return to his old self. He could barely sit still whilst they finished their meal and he spoke excitedly to them, listing points in the time-line that the Illuminati could attack to "change the world" as Diana had put it.

Rachel got up after about half an hour and took the dirty plates to the kitchen, saying that she would put the kettle on. She was there for more than twenty minutes and when she came back she was tucking her phone into her pocket.

She sat down next to Sam and he took advantage of James pausing for breath to lean across to her, raising an eyebrow and smirking. 'I think you forgot something.'

'What?'

'Where's the tea?'

She coloured and immediately stood up again.

James didn't seem to notice and, frankly, Sam didn't mind. Anyone else, Rachel included apparently, would be bored by James' monologue, but Sam was fascinated. History had always been a favourite subject of his and would probably have been what he would have liked to study at university if he'd been able to have a normal life. It was of course unnecessary to study it now; he had so many people to talk to who had experienced huge parts of it that books and studying were rendered pointless.

James wasn't just reciting dates and events, though - the study of history for Displacers was not limited to what happened where and when, in fact that was of relatively little importance to their work; what mattered most was what led up to something - what tiny discoveries had led to huge leaps forwards sometimes centuries later, what seemingly meaningless event would spark fires in people's imagination and later become religions that were followed by millions.

The depth of knowledge that the Elder was showing, reciting everything off the top of his head, was staggering. Sam knew that this was his speciality, but even so it was amazing and he suddenly realised how easy it must have been for John to build such an empire with such information. Thankfully, though, most of the events had been fixed by the Displacers and could no longer be changed and James was ticking many of those off his mental list as he went.

Ultimately, though, as the old man went on and on, it was clear that the Illuminati had far too many options for the Displacers to be able to prepare effectively on their own - they would have to wait for Diana to send them more information or, more likely, Sam would have to play it by ear on the actual Displacement, just as he'd done before.

Rachel came back in with tea and biscuits for everyone and soon after, to her obvious relief, James tailed off into silence.

He seemed to come back to the world at large and grinned sheepishly at his audience. 'I guess I went off on one a bit there, didn't I?'

Rachel laughed, but Sam just shook his head in admiration. 'Wow, Grandad.'

James raised an eyebrow. 'Was that "wow, you should be in a mental institution", or "wow, you're the most impressive human being I've ever had the immense honour to meet"?'

This time Sam laughed. 'A bit of both I guess, but mostly the second. I think I speak for Rachel as well when I say feel free to "go off on one" whenever you want.'

Rachel punched him hard on the leg under the table and he turned and smiled sweetly at her. 'Yes, darling? Did you want to say something?'

She gave him a dark look that promised punishment in their next sparring session, but then grinned. 'I don't think James will take it badly if I say that history is not my thing and that I'll bring a book next time we are invited to lunch.'

James laughed and saluted her with his tea. 'Not at all, my dear, each to their own!'

Sam and Rachel had planned to stay until evening, keeping James company until the group of Elders he'd arranged to have dinner with arrived, but one of the things Rachel had done in the kitchen, when she should have been making tea, was inform Lisa of Diana's message. She had naturally asked to see them that at Headquarters to discuss their options, which put paid to their plans and meant leaving not long after they'd finished the tea.

He said goodbye to them on the doorstep, standing in the last of the sunshine coming over the tops of the row of houses across the street.

Rachel kissed him on the cheek before holding up her hand and showing him the ring that was still on her little finger. 'Thank you, James.'

'I'm sorry they're just plain bands.'

She shook her head. 'Don't be; they truly are what we were going to get anyway.'

Sam stepped forwards and gripped his grandfather's hand. 'Is there anything we can get for you before we go? Do you need any shopping? Any milk or bread or anything?'

'Thank you, but no; I have someone for that already: the council sends a nice little girl round every couple of days. It's one of the perks of being an old fogey!' He winked. 'Go on, get on with you! I have to call the boys and get them to work.'

Sam gave his hand one last squeeze. 'Thank you for everything, Grandad.'

James smiled warmly. 'You're welcome, Sam.'

The old man watched them as they went down the short garden path to the road and all the way to the corner, where they waved to him before disappearing.

He slapped his hands together and rubbed them gleefully. 'Right! To work!'

CHAPTER 12
PACKAGE

'I'll get it!' Dylan called out as the front doorbell rang. He was already heading to the kitchen from the dining room and he was more or less going past the door anyway.

It was Sunday and the members who were in town and didn't have anything else to do were at Headquarters for the lunch that Richard served every week. Dylan was busy running up and down the stairs, bringing food up from the kitchen where the chef himself was serving it up. Usually he had someone else serving with him - both Sam and Rachel were junior enough, despite their talents, to be roped into helping out, but they were off having lunch with James again so it was just him.

He didn't mind helping out; everyone was very grateful and treated him well, especially the older members who couldn't move so well. Everyone except Ralph, that was, whose grumpiness, in Dylan's opinion, didn't suit his new status as an Elder, and who didn't seem to like how friendly he was with Sam.

He opened the door to find a courier standing on the doorstep. He wasn't a Royal Mail employee, they wouldn't work on a Sunday, instead he was one of those ones that flew packages around the world with next day delivery. He was dressed in brown and had a matching baseball cap pulled down low over his head and smiled when he saw Dylan, then glanced at the white box in his hands to read the label.

'Delivery for a, uh, Mr, J. J. Hudson?'

The man had a bit of an accent, German, maybe, or Austrian, and, with the curly hair poking out from under the cap, the blue eyes, and strong jaw, he reminded Dylan a bit of David Hasselhoff - he and Laura had watched a few episodes of Knight Rider together at a distance, connected by an encrypted chat, mainly to laugh at the ridiculous technology on display.

He nodded. 'This is the address. Can I sign for it?'

'Of course.'

Dylan took the PDA the man offered and signed his name with the stylus.

'Here you go.' The man handed over the package. It was small, about the size of a shoe box, but surprisingly heavy. James' name was written on the label next to an "URGENT" stamp, but there was no return address.

'Thank you.'

The man gave him another smile, then jogged down the steps to where a big brown van was parked, warning lights flashing and two wheels up on the pavement.

Dylan closed the door and put the package on the table under the name plates; that was where mail was left to be picked up by the members. He'd text James and ask him what he wanted done with the parcel later, but first he had to get to the kitchen, otherwise there would be some hungry mouths berating him for being too slow.

He ran down the stairs and was just turning the corner into the kitchen when something like a huge hand slapped him in the back and threw him through the air to crash into the table.

He lay still, stunned, a ringing in his ears and the room filling with smoke around him.

Richard shouted something at him from across the kitchen, but he couldn't quite make out the words. He pushed himself up into a sitting position, wincing at the pain in his ribs and fighting to focus on the man, but his head swam and he found his attention wandering.

The smoke that he'd thought was from burning food was actually streaming down the stairwell and spilling into the room. It was beautiful, mesmerising, the patterns swirling in the overhead lighting...

'Dylan!'

The ringing receded just enough for him to be able to hear his name being called and it brought him back to himself. 'I'm alright, what happened?'

'I don't know. Do you have a phone?'

Dylan fumbled at his pocket and drew out a Society smartphone - the MI5 supplied ones were tougher than they looked. 'Yes!'

'Ring the incident number, then stay here and rest, I'll go and find out what's happened.'

Richard soaked a dishcloth under the tap and wrapped it around his mouth before going to the stairway. He ran up the stairs and out of sight. He was extremely sprightly, despite being in his sixties, a common trait among the Elders until they reached truly advanced age.

Dylan leaned against a table leg to steady himself as he pulled up one of the special numbers that was programmed into every Society phone. As he did so he tried to think of what to say. Obviously there had been some kind of explosion, but it was impossible to know if it was deliberate or... *Oh god, the delivery driver...*

He went cold as he waited for the phone to connect. As ever there was a single ring and then only a beep as an indicator to speak. 'Roost is under attack, repeat, Roost is under attack.'

'Confirmed. Help is on the way.'

The connection went dead and he put the phone back in his pocket.

All he wanted to do was to lie back down and wait for his head to stop spinning nauseatingly, but he knew that wasn't what Sam or Rachel would do.

Clutching at a nearby chair he used it to pull himself to his feet. He coughed in the rising smoke and staggered to the sink. He wet another cloth, following Richard's example, and turned to leave, but remembered that there was a small extinguisher under the sink for kitchen fires. It wouldn't do much to a real fire but it was better than nothing. He grabbed it and plunged into the stairwell.

Sam, Rachel and James knew that something had happened when they all received text messages at the same time. They instantly stopped eating and grabbed their phones; messages, real SMS messages and not WhatsApp type messages, were extremely rare, and for all of them to receive one at the same time meant bad news.

The message was an automatic alert that advised of an incident and requested a reply as confirmation of life.

Sam went white. He had been given a manual when he'd received his Society phone, but rather than telling him how to use it, the thick booklet had been a long list of dos and don'ts and had included the protocols for incidents and medical emergencies. He had read it carefully, but had never expected to receive this particular message; it was only ever sent under extreme circumstances.

They sent their messages and almost immediately James received a call. Sam and Rachel sat silently on the edge of their seats as he listened for a few seconds, his lips pursing and his frown increasing until it almost covered the entirety of his hairless head with wrinkles.

'Understood.' He hung up the phone and looked at them.

'There's been a bombing at Headquarters. Go, please, be my eyes and ears.'

They leapt to their feet. Sam ran straight for the door, but Rachel took a second to kiss James on the cheek and whisper in his ear. 'Don't worry, I'm sure everybody's fine.'

'I dearly hope so.'

She smiled, then joined Sam as he sprinted out of the house.

It was too far to run all the way to Headquarters and even on a Sunday a taxi would get stuck in traffic, but the nearest Tube station was only a couple of miles away in Brixton and the direct line to Green Park was the fastest way to get there.

They sprinted the whole way to the station with only a brief stop as Sam stopped to vomit up his lunch in a waste basket, to the disgust of a passing old lady.

Rachel rubbed his back. 'This takes me back...'

'Urgh... I don't know how you do it; you don't even look queasy.'

'I didn't pig out on chips, darling.'

'Hey, I'm a growing boy, I need the calories.'

She was far too tense to laugh and barely smiled at his joke. 'Come on, we need to get going.'

Less than half an hour after they had left James' house they sprinted past Wellington Arch and turned into Grosvenor Place for the final stretch, but they found their way blocked and were unable to go any further.

A barrier had been thrown up across the entire width of the street, blocking all access to pedestrians or vehicles and the road beyond was packed full of police cars and fire engines, all with their lights flashing. About a dozen uniformed policemen were manning the barrier, holding back the army of journalists and onlookers, and they didn't look like they would be in the mood to go easy on someone trying to sneak past them.

'How are we going to get through?' Sam asked in frustration. 'We could try to go around the back, although that's probably blocked off too... How about going over the wall into the palace gardens and climbing back over past the barrier.'

Rachel rolled her eyes. 'Why don't we just try asking a policeman?' The time on the tube, unable to do anything except wait for the train to make its way across London had allowed them time to recover from their mad dash, but is had also given them a chance to calm their panic and recover a little of their humour; they knew they were going to need every ounce of it to get through the next few hours.

Sam laughed. 'What are you going to do? Bat your eyes at them?'

'Watch and learn, boy.'

They slipped through the crowd and Rachel singled out the one policeman who had a flat hat on and was obviously in charge and beckoned to him. He frowned at her, but nonetheless bent down so that she could talk in his ear. After a few seconds he straightened and gave her a surprised look before backing away a couple of steps and speaking into his radio.

Sam couldn't believe his eyes when he waved them through.

He fell in at her side as they jogged through the emergency vehicles. 'What did you say to him?'

She sighed and Sam chuckled inwardly. Sighing was really difficult to do when running, but Rachel was an expert, especially when it came to sighing at him. 'Oh, Sam, how can you be so spectacularly good at what you do in the past and yet have no clue about anything in the present? I just gave him our names. James will have rung ahead to tell MI5 we were coming and they would have given our names to whoever is coordinating this army.'

As they drew closer to the house they slowed down, not wanting to believe what they were seeing.

There was a gaping hole around where the front door had been, exposing the corridor and some of the sitting room. The door itself had been blown outwards and was embedded in the side of a car, which had swerved into the path of an oncoming lorry. The destruction wasn't limited to the ground floor, though, and the black streaks on the white stone above the cracked windows of the ground and first floors showed that there had been a fire, although it looked like it had been put out already, so it couldn't have been too serious.

A couple of policemen appeared and stopped them before they could get more than just a general idea, but they were immediately called off by a man wearing a familiar black suit who came running towards them from a black SUV parked on the pavement outside the building.

'Mr Vives? Miss Evans?'

He didn't look like he really needed the confirmation, but they nodded anyway.

Rachel immediately jumped in and took charge, getting down to business, and Sam felt relieved; he hadn't had a clue what to do or say, but Rachel, as ever, did.

'Casualties?'

'One dead so far and five seriously injured, two of which are critical. Twelve others with minor injuries. Despite the force of the blast and the number of people present, casualties are relatively light, mostly because everybody was gathered in the dining room at the back of the building for lunch and were protected by the heavy wooden door and thick walls.'

Rachel swallowed before continuing; it was a hefty butcher's bill, but it could have been far worse, and by the look of the building it probably should have been. 'Do you have a name for the fatality?'

The man consulted his smartphone, identical to the ones that the Displacers had. 'Julian Reddick, American national, aged seventy-eight. We believe he was crushed by the dining room door when it was blown off its hinges by the explosion.'

Sam sighed. Julian was one of the more experienced and fun Elders. In his youth he had been a baseball player and had a lot of anecdotes - actual interesting ones, unlike most of the usual Elder fare - about his life on the road in the United States in the fifties. He'd immigrated to England in the sixties after getting a job in the city and was Anne's great uncle.

'And the nature of the other casualties?'

Again the agent consulted his phone. 'The serious injuries include two major head-wounds and several crushing injuries from falling debris. The minor injuries are mostly from falls and smoke inhalation - one gentleman has a broken arm and another a few broken fingers, but nothing remotely life-threatening.'

Rachel frowned, puzzled and looked at the black stains on the building from the smoke. 'No burns?'

'Only superficial ones. Things would have been different if it weren't for...' he consulted the phone again. 'Dylan Lloyd and Richard Peterson, who dragged most of the unconscious and injured out of the back door before the flames could spread. If it hadn't been for them, things would have been a lot worse. Witnesses say they managed to get at least eight people clear on their own.'

'Does Mr Hudson have this information?'

'It has been sent to him.'

'Thank you. Now, what about the cause of the explosion? Accident or design?'

'Design, without a doubt - a parcel bomb. Mr Lloyd reports a package being delivered moments before the explosion and placing it on the table near the entrance where the blast originated. We've already contacted the delivery company involved and they insist that there was no delivery scheduled for today, so we're certain that is the source and we're looking at CCTV footage to try to identify the driver.'

'It'll be John, he's behind it.'

The agent nodded. 'Most likely, yes.'

'Where are our members now?'

'The more critical casualties have been evacuated to a secure hospital already, but the rest are waiting a couple of doors down for more transport to become available.'

'Can we go and see them, please?'

'Of course. This way.'

He took them to the small, paved-over front garden of the building two doors down, where they found the injured members being treated and their statements being taken by several more MI5 agents. Dylan and Richard were wrapped in blankets, sitting on the steps of the building watching the activities. They were both blackened with smoke and wheezing slightly, taking sips from water bottles, but neither of them showed any sign of injury except for some singed hair on one side of Dylan's head.

Dylan looked up as they approached. He smiled weakly and his voice croaked as he spoke. 'How the hell am I going to explain all this to my parents?'

The agent chuckled. 'Don't worry Mr Lloyd, we'll take care of that for you - they won't ever know that anything has happened.'

The boy blinked up at him in surprise. 'You can do that? But what about my hair?'

'We have very talented hairdressers, haven't you heard of extensions? Or you could just tell them you had a haircut. That might be a bit easier...'

Dylan grimaced. 'I hadn't thought of that.'

Sam nodded. 'They're amazing. Trust me, your parents won't notice a thing.'

The agent smiled, then turned to Rachel. 'I have a few things to do, Miss Evans. If you have any questions just ask one of the others to come and get me. And of course Mr Hudson will be appraised of anything new as soon as we have it.'

'Thank you.'

The agent nodded at Sam. 'Mr Vives.'

Sam nodded back. 'Thank you, Agent...' He smiled apologetically. 'Uh, sorry, we didn't ask your name, did we?'

'No matter, Mr Vives, and it's Black. Agent Black.'

Sam laughed, remembering his conversations with two other such agents.

The man smiled, then went to speak to the black-suited man coordinating a group of uniformed policemen in the road in front of Headquarters.

Rachel surveyed the members scattered around the small space, cataloguing who was there and making sure they were comfortable, before turning back to Dylan and Richard.

'Do either of you have anything to add to what you told him? Something that would be just for our ears?' She looked at them pointedly.

Dylan just shook his head mutely, but Richard took a deep breath and sighed. 'The portraits are gone and by the looks of things the contents of at least the first floor library, if not more, were destroyed. There are documents in those libraries that are irreplaceable, even if we do have digital copies.'

Sam had a sudden horrible thought. 'Do either of you know if the fire spread as far as the attic?'

They shrugged.

Rachel broke back in. 'We'll find out, but before that, is there anything else you can think of?'

The two dishevelled heroes shook their heads again, reluctant to say more than was necessary through abused throats.

Rachel nodded. 'Then let them take you to a hospital, both of you. Leave this to us. And well done. Very well done.'

She met both of their eyes one by one and Sam was surprised to see the gratitude and pleasure on their faces at her praise, even from the Elder.

They left them and walked a couple of doors down to Headquarters, where Agent Black was still trying to bring order to the chaos. While they waited for him to have a moment for them, they gazed up at the house in dismay.

It was in a very sorry state. As Agent Black had said, the explosion had been somewhat contained by the heavy wooden doors of the dining room, but that meant that it had needed a release. It had apparently found it not only through the sitting room, which had been reduced to a debris-filled black hole, but up the stairs as well. So, even though the explosion had taken place on the ground floor, the destruction was almost as bad on the first floor. The second floor looked a little blackened, but didn't seem too bad and the third floor seemed relatively intact as well, although most of the windows on both floors had been shattered. Thankfully, the attic was well protected and appeared to be completely untouched, but they wouldn't know for sure until somebody checked.

Unconsciously, they reached out and clasped hands; Headquarters had always been a stable point in their existence, somewhere that every member of the Society could come for comfort and be surrounded by friends and colleagues. To see it brought low was upsetting in the extreme, and the loss of the portraits in particular was devastating.

Finally, Agent Black finished what he was doing and came over to them. 'Was there something you needed?'

Once again Rachel took charge. 'Tell me about the structure and the contents, please, especially the attic; there is some very sensitive material up there.'

The agent frowned. 'Anything dangerous we should know about?'

'No, nothing like that, just extremely valuable and of a very sensitive nature.'

He nodded, evidently understanding what she meant, and pulled out his phone again. He brought up blueprints of the building on it and used them to point out the damage. 'At least one load-bearing wall at the front of the house was destroyed and the shared wall with the building on the right was damaged as well. They have since been shored up and we're fairly confident that, if the entire building hasn't already collapsed, then it's not going to right now, however it is still in danger of doing so and will need major repairs quickly. The ceiling of the sitting room fell in as well, but that's not a threat to the integrity of the building. As for the floors above - there is extensive fire and structural damage to the first floor, the second floor caught fire only briefly but was waterlogged from the extinction efforts. A couple of the rooms and the hallway of the third floor suffered a little water damage as well from preventative action, but nothing beyond that. Lastly, according to my information, the attic is untouched.'

'Could you have someone verify that, please, and send the information to Mr Hudson?'

'Of course. Anything else?'

'Our members, the ones in the hospital and here, do they have proper security in case of another attack?'

'Yes, all non-essential Five and Six operations have been suspended and top priority has been given to this. There are security details in and around the hospital and a special secure ward has been allocated to the Society. We will transport the last of the members there shortly, even if they are not injured, for a complete checkup, and they will be kept there until the all-clear is given.'

'Excellent, and security on our building?'

'The Met are going to take care of that,' the man smiled. 'We have to give them something to do otherwise they tend to get their noses out of joint.'

They all laughed at that and it was a relief to ease some of the tension.

'Anything else, ma'am?'

'For now no. Thank you, Agent Black.' Rachel smiled and nodded. The man nodded in reply and went back to work.

When he was gone Rachel put her hands on her hips and surveyed the building with narrowed eyes. 'I guess there's nothing much else we can do here, and MI5 seem to have everything well under control. I'm going to go to the hospital to speak to everyone there, can you go back and make sure that James is alright please and that he knows about the attic. Find out what he wants to do - whether we need to move anything, or if he thinks we can rely on the police to handle security.'

Sam nodded. 'OK, no problem.' They both had a thought at the same time and they looked up at the house - their things were all in the third floor bedroom where they'd been staying.

He sighed, knowing what was coming. 'Well, even if the fire didn't spread throughout the whole building I doubt we're going to be able to stay here. Where shall I meet you?'

Rachel grinned despite herself. 'It's a real pity, but it looks like you're finally going to have to come to my flat... Unless you want to stay with James.'

To his shame, he actually had to think twice about which to choose. While his heart leapt at the thought of having a second home with Rachel in London, he still wasn't sure if he was completely ready. There was also the fact that James would likely be more than happy to have him stay and that being near to the old gentleman was probably a good idea while the Elder was ill.

'I'll...' He coughed as his voice caught in his throat and he grimaced at his own cowardice. 'I'll stay with you.'

'About bloody time! Well, while you're going to see James I should have time to get home and do some tidying up before you arrive; there are dirty dishes everywhere and I know I haven't run the washing machine in more than a month!'

Sam chuckled. 'OK, I'll see you there later tonight.'

Rachel looked around. Dylan and Richard, the last two casualties left on the scene, were being taken away by ambulance men. 'I'll ride with them. Tell Agent Black where we're going before you leave, please.' She leaned in to kiss him, but it was perfunctory, almost automatic, her mind on other things and she hurried away before he had time to return it. Sam didn't mind that she was distracted; there were more important things to concern themselves with at that moment than making sure to kiss properly.

He put her out of his mind and went to do as she'd instructed.

As soon as the fire had been declared extinguished the police had opened a single lane of the road to traffic and the press and onlookers had taken advantage of this to move into position on the pavement opposite the house, against the wall of the palace gardens.

A man with dark curly hair and mirrored aviator sunglasses covering his cruel blue eyes stood among them.

He watched as screaming ambulances took five seriously injured victims of the bombing away one by one, immediately followed by a dark van carrying the single body bag, which made its exit silently, with far more dignity. Then, when the sirens had faded, he turned his attention to the building a couple of doors down, where the medics were treating the rest of the men and women who'd been in the building, all alive and well apart from a few knocks and bruises and scorches.

And all the while he fought to keep the rage and frustration from showing on his face and giving him away to the security agents swarming around for some reason, as if he'd attacked a government building or something.

One! He'd only managed to kill *one* of the targets. And just an optional one at that, for which he wouldn't even get paid unless he took down the main targets as well.

He was furious at the failure. Not that it was any consolation, but the fault didn't entirely lie with him; the operation had been a shambles from the beginning because his employer had insisted on micro-managing the whole thing. The man had planned the whole thing himself, completely ignoring all suggestions on how to professionally and effectively carry out the mission and absurdly insisting on a bomb because he'd wanted to do damage to the building for some reason. He had almost refused the contract then and there, but he was being paid an obscene amount of money, far more than his usual fee, and he needed it; security measures were becoming tighter and tighter every year and it was time to retire. It wasn't that it had become any harder to carry out the jobs themselves, because it wasn't, it was more that it was almost impossible to get away with them safely now. Especially in cities like London with so much CCTV coverage and the advances in facial recognition software which would very soon render his disguises useless.

The injured members of the so-called Displacers were taken away in groups as vehicles became available for them until finally there were only two left and he watched as the girl clambered into an ambulance with them and sat at the back of the vehicle by the door. There was clear concern on her face, but also calm composure; she was in charge and knew what she was doing.

No wonder she was one of his secondary targets.

The man couldn't help but snarl at the reminder of how badly everything had gone wrong, but when the woman next to him glanced up at him in fright he hastily covered his slip with a cough and moved away from her.

It wasn't just the bomb that had been imprecise, but the information he'd been given as well - *none* of his main targets had been in the building like they were supposed to, not the principal target, nor either of the secondary targets. He should have checked, but his employer had assured him of the accuracy of the information and refused to give him time to gather his own intelligence.

He would be having stern words with the man after the job was done and perhaps he would even do one last job before retiring, the first ever for himself. For fun...

The ambulance doors slammed shut, cutting off his train of thought and his view of the girl. The vehicle sped away and he almost followed, not wanting to lose her, but the principal target was still on the scene, speaking to one of the plain-clothed security service agents, so he stayed, wanting to get a better look at him, curious as to why he warranted the distinction of his, extremely expensive, personal attention.

Five minutes later he followed at a discreet distance as the target walked towards Hyde Park Corner. He couldn't help but be impressed; despite the youth evident in his face he had a confidence about the way he moved that spoke of many, many years of training and experience, the kind of assurance that he had only ever seen on fellow mercenaries who, like he, had Special Forces training. He knew instinctively that this boy had killed and had done so often; it was in his eyes and in every turn of his head as he slid through the pedestrian traffic, unconsciously taking in everything around him.

This, at last, was a worthy challenge, one he would savour and it was one that he would handle his own way. First, though, he had to remove the girl; he'd seen how they were with each other, how they had moved in concert even when just standing on the street - they would be impossible to kill together unless it was with a sniper rifle. That was something he kept as a last resort, though; he liked to be able to see the look in his target's eyes as they died.

And his clients liked it when he could tell them exactly how surprised and terrified their enemies had been at having their lives cut short abruptly and painfully.

CHAPTER 13
THE BUTCHER'S BILL

The ambulance pulled up at a side door of the hospital and Rachel stood by, checking out the security arrangements, while Richard and Dylan were put into wheelchairs, grumbling the whole time and handed over to a team of medical personnel who came out to collect them.

There were several big men scattered around the entrance, most likely armed police, trained to protect things like the Houses of Parliament or Whitehall. They were intimidating-looking, like nightclub bouncers and had obviously been chosen as much as a deterrent as a solution. While they didn't have the same subtle cat-like surety about them as the more athletic MI5 agents, Rachel could tell that they were well-trained: taking in everything around them without getting fixed on a single thing: not leaning or slouching or otherwise putting themselves off balance; keeping their hands free and clear of obstructions so they could pull weapons as quickly as possible - all things she'd had drummed into her over and over during her own training.

There was a smaller man with them, who wasn't quite so scary-looking, but who had an air of confidence and command about him that told Rachel that he was an officer, but one who was used to being in the field and not behind a desk. He pulled a thick sheaf of papers out of his pocket as he watched them get out of the ambulance.

As he flipped through them Rachel saw that they were passport photos of the members, blown up to A5 size. She grimaced when she remembered her own photo; taken almost five years ago. She had been wearing braces at the time and her mother had made her wear her best dress, a horrible royal blue thing with white lace that had gone into the bin as soon as she was old enough to decide what clothes to wear for herself. She grinned briefly as she remembered Sam's reaction when he'd seen her passport for the first time; he'd spent several days laughing on and off. He had kept laughing, in fact, until she'd demanded to see his, which turned out to be no better - he'd had a very unflattering bowl cut that his mother had given him. They had quickly come to an agreement not to mention the photos ever again.

The man gave the surrounding goons a discrete signal before making marks on three of the pages, once each for her, Dylan and Richard, then waved them through.

An MI5 agent was waiting for them inside and he reported to Rachel while Dylan and Richard were wheeled past.

'Miss Evans, I'm Agent Brown.'

Rachel shook hands with him. 'Are we secure? I saw the Bobbies outside, but I assume they're just the window dressing.'

The man grinned. 'Yes, ma'am. We have snipers covering every side of the building, our own cameras running face recognition software at every access point of the main hospital building and we're running the plates of every vehicle in a mile radius. We even have a drone on standby to give covering fire if need be, but that won't be called in unless we come under full attack.'

Rachel nodded. 'That's not likely, but appreciated. What about dogs? I assume you have something sniffing for explosives, given the nature of the attack.'

His eyes widened in surprise at her competence in security matters. 'Indeed! We have sniffer dogs searching for explosives at every entrance point as well.'

Rachel grinned. 'Have I left anything out?'

'No ma'am, except the information on who trained you so well; that little detail is not in your file.'

Rachel shook her head and chuckled. 'You wouldn't believe me if I told you.'

The man nodded, accepting her words, but there was obvious disappointment in his eyes when he motioned for her to follow him.

They walked down a corridor, following in the footsteps of Dylan and Richard and came to a double door, guarded by uniformed policemen armed with stubby automatic weapons. Their eyes flickered over Agent Brown before coming to rest on Rachel and she got the impression that they were memorising her face at the same time as they were assessing whether she was a threat.

The agent pulled a card from his pocket and pressed it against a sensor on the wall and in response the doors swung open. Rachel narrowed her eyes at them; they moved heavily, with more inertia than normal doors and there had also been a slight hiss as they'd started moving.

'Gas and bullet proof?'

The agent saw the direction of her gaze and shook his head with a wry smile. '*Bomb* proof.'

The doors closed behind them with a soft clunk and they moved down a short corridor, like an airlock, with more double doors at the end. 'This facility is one of several secure wards in various hospitals around the city. The walls are reinforced, there are no windows, it has its own generator, kitchen, food storage and waste management system, and there is an escape hatch that I'm not going to reveal the location of unless we have to use it. This ward is one of three such for the exclusive use of the Royal Family - it is here that we would bring them if the Palace, which has its own underground ward, is deemed not to be secure.' The man looked at her, again searching for information. 'Perhaps you can tell me how we received permission from Her Majesty to use this ward today?'

In reply Rachel just gave him a cheeky grin and shook her head.

The agent sighed wistfully. 'Oh well, in this line of work you get used to not knowing everything, but I must admit to being rather curious about your organisation and so are a lot of my colleagues.'

Rachel frowned. 'That's not going to be a problem, is it?'

'Oh, heavens no! We all know what happens when we poke our noses in where they don't belong.'

'Good. Thank you.'

'Don't mention it.'

While they'd been talking they'd gone through the doors at the end of the corridor, the agent again using his card to open them, and were now in a reception area. However, instead of a nurse behind the desk, there was another stern, uniformed policeman.

They nodded to him and went through a pair of double doors.

Here at last they found the Society members.

The room was obviously the main patient ward. It was large and rectangular, with white-walls, filled with beds and there were nurses and doctors everywhere.

The similarity with a normal hospital ward ended there.

Aside from the lack of windows to the outside world, the room was also sectioned by a maze of panels that went from floor to ceiling. They were several inches thick, about three metres wide, metallic silver up to just above waist height, then transparent above that so as not to block vision or make the space claustrophobic. They were set up seemingly at random, but to Rachel's eye their purpose was immediately obvious: they acted both as firing positions and cover for patients.

Rachel realised that the agent had been watching her, waiting for her reaction and for her professional assessment.

'Where's the surgery?'

'At the far end.' He pointed to some doors at the very end of the room.

Rachel grunted. 'What happens if you need a clear lane to rush emergency patients there?'

'The panels drop into the floor, individually controlled by remotes given to the room controllers.' He pointed to three men standing around the room, each held a remote at the ready in their left hands, leaving their right free for weapons.

'Dead man switches? Thumbprint controlled?'

'Biometric. They only work for whoever they have been assigned to.'

It was Rachel's turn to shake her head in admiration; this was all far more impressive than anything she'd ever come across in any of the Displacements she'd been on to learn from the best security providers in history. Unfortunately, being limited to Displacing outside of her lifetime meant that she wasn't quite as up to date as she wanted to be.

'Is there a course I can go on so that I can learn about all of this?'

The agent laughed. 'Yes, but do you really need to?'

'Oh yes, my experience is... dated.'

He gave her a puzzled look, but didn't press, so she went back to business.

'Where do the medical personnel come from?'

'Good catch, ma'am - they are highly-experienced doctors and nurses from the hospital who are on call twenty-four hours a day, three hundred and sixty-five days a year. They have been previously screened and have signed the official secrets act. They are continually monitored, with their knowledge and consent, to make sure they remain secure and aren't contacted by outside elements and, believe me, they are paid *very* well to compensate for that lack of privacy. They are trustworthy and will say nothing when they leave here.'

'That's good to know.' Rachel looked around the room, but there were so many people rushing about that she couldn't get a clear view of the patients.

'Status update on the casualties, please.'

The agent pulled up the relevant information on his smartphone.

'All eighteen of the people who were involved in the incident have now arrived and are in care. The one fatality is in the morgue awaiting autopsy. The five serious injuries are in surgery already, and of the two who were critical one is reacting well to the surgery...' He swallowed and Rachel tensed, knowing what was coming. 'The other passed five minutes ago. I'm sorry.'

She took a deep breath, composing herself before she spoke. 'Name?'

'Anne Barclay. American national, aged thirty-four.'

Rachel closed her eyes and fought back the tears, but even so one managed to squeeze its way out from between her eyelids and roll slowly down her cheek.

Anne had been desperately unhappy since Andrew had died, but had been recovering slowly, working hard to be cheerful and gradually becoming herself again. Her mission to Malta had been the first ray of light to break through the dark cloud that had been suffocating the Society since the death of Andrew and had opened the way for the new wave of optimism that had hit the Displacers. They had all been feeling so much better recently because of her and the thought of her life being snuffed out so suddenly was heartbreaking and would be to everybody.

She forced herself to take a shuddering breath. 'Does Mr Hudson have this information?'

Her voice came out weaker than she'd wanted it to and she coughed, clearing her throat, before opening her eyes to look at the agent.

His gaze was full of pity, but he hid it in an instant. 'He does.' He spoke quietly in a warm voice.

'What about everyone else, do the people here know?'

'No, not yet. And, uh, it's probably better if it came from you, ma'am.'

Rachel nodded. She took a deep breath and suppressed her emotions; she couldn't afford to have them at that moment, she had to present a strong front, if only for the injured Displacers and Elders scattered about the room.

'Where is Lisa Curran? Is she here?'

He consulted his phone briefly. 'Yes. She's at the back. She was knocked unconscious by a blow to the head and is still out. By all accounts she is one of the injured who Mr Lloyd and Mr Peterson dragged clear of the building.'

'Prognosis?'

'Good. Possible concussion, but no internal bleeding or permanent injury. She'll wake up on her own sometime soon.'

'She should be in charge here, not me.' She muttered it under her breath, but he heard her just the same.

'Well, unfortunately she is incapable of being in charge and in all likelihood won't be until the morning, so in the meantime you are it, Miss Evans, and from what I've seen, you're more than capable.'

She gave him a curt nod of thanks. 'Is there anything else I should know?'

'Not right now, ma'am.'

'OK, I'm going to wander around and talk to people. Please give me updates on the people in surgery as soon as you get them.'

'Yes, ma'am.'

The agent smiled, then left her alone.

She stood in the middle of the room and gazed around, taking in the bodies in neat rows and the busy medical personnel.

The more she stood there, the more she realised that all she really wanted to do was find a corner to curl up in and cry, preferably with Sam. That wasn't an option, though; she had work to do.

She forced herself into action, plastering a confident but sombre look on her face and went to give care and comfort to some of the people she loved most in the world.

Over the next three hours, Rachel spoke with most of the members, making sure that each of them was comfortable and had what they needed, and got first-hand reports on their conditions from the doctors. She was utterly exhausted and getting more and more upset by the minute, making it harder and harder to maintain her optimistic mask, so it was a relief when Agent Brown appeared. Matters were only made worse, though, when she caught sight of his concerned frown.

She started to ask him what was the matter, but he gave her a warning look and motioned for her to join him, then led her out to the reception area where they wouldn't be overheard.

'We've identified the bomber and it's worse than we thought, he is *very* well known to us and very professional. We have various aliases on file for him, none of which is probably real, so I won't bother with a name. What's strange is that this isn't his usual modus operandi; he has used bombs only once or twice in the past, mostly on cars, but his preferred methods are rather more personal.'

'Then why are you so sure that it's him?'

'We've analysed the CCTV footage of the man who gave the package to Mr Lloyd. It's him alright. You're all very lucky to have survived.'

'I don't feel particularly lucky.'

The agent took a deep breath before continuing, as if gathering his strength. 'The man in question is a professional assassin for hire, German, trained with the KSK, and this is the first known instance of him missing a target, so yes, you have been lucky.'

'I assume he'll try again.'

'We're not sure. He has a reputation for not ever giving up on a contract once he accepts it, but he's completely dropped off the radar and it's possible that he's left the country already.'

'What kind of possibility?'

He shrugged. 'Fifty-fifty, maybe?'

'Those aren't good odds. How are you going to keep us safe if he hasn't given up?'

'This is one of the securest locations available in the country and it has the added advantage that we've already got most of you here, so everybody who's already here will stay and we'll bring the rest of your members in - we've already contacted them and arranged an escort. You'll stay here for as long as it takes to apprehend the assassin. Shouldn't be more than a few weeks, if that.'

'That sounds fine.'

'It does, doesn't it? Unfortunately at least one of your members is refusing to come in.'

Rachel chuckled. 'Let me guess. Mr Hudson?'

The agent laughed. 'Tough old fart, isn't he?'

'You don't know the half of it... Have you met him?'

'A couple of times, yes.'

'Well wait until you've been drinking with him... Anyway, what are you going to do about him?'

'We're not going to force him to come in, if that's what you mean; we don't have the authority to do that, even if it is in his best interest.'

Rachel was astounded. 'Really? You don't have the authority? Why not? You're MI5, aren't you?'

The agent grinned. 'We are, indeed, MI5. How very astute of you, Miss Evans.'

Rachel pouted and gave him an evil look and he hurriedly continued.

'We don't have the authority because there is only one person in the country who does, apparently.'

'Who? Please don't tell me it's me right now, because even I'm not stupid enough to order him in.'

Agent Brown laughed. 'Don't worry you're safe! No, that "person" is, in fact, Her Majesty.'

'Seriously? And does that apply to just him or all of us?'

'It applies to all members registered officially with the Palace. We, the other security forces, and the police can only really ask you politely to do things.'

Rachel rubbed her hands in mock glee. 'Nice! No more speeding tickets for me then! I'm gonna get that Ducati I always wanted!'

The agent laughed and shook his head. 'It doesn't work like that; you still have to obey the law or you'll be arrested, you just can't be held and one phone call will have the Bobbies sweating in their boots.'

'Dammit!' She chuckled, not really disappointed; she wouldn't willingly break the law, even if she could get away with it; it just wasn't something she would enjoy doing. 'So what do we do about James, uh, Mr Hudson?'

'We've already set up around the clock surveillance on his property, but it's pretty hard to throw an effective cordon around him in that area.'

Rachel nodded. James lived in a purely residential area. Not only were there multiple approaches from the front, but the back garden bordered onto four or five others and the fences weren't exactly high - it was an assailant's wet dream. 'What assets are in place?'

'There are checkpoints at both ends of the street as well as the house opposite and we've put a two man team in the back garden, but Mr Hudson is refusing to have any agents in the house, not wanting, and I quote "people traipsing in and out". He has, however, agreed to have Mr Vives stay with him and the two of them are there now.'

'Oh. Alright.' Rachel was disappointed, she had been looking forward to finally having Sam in her flat, but she quickly realised that the circumstances weren't exactly the most romantic and him being with James was for the best. In fact... 'I think I'll go there as well and help out with security. You don't need me here anymore, and as soon as Miss Curran is able to I'm sure she'll take over anyway.'

The agent nodded. 'Very well, I'll arrange transport and inform the team of your arrival.'

'I'm going to swing past my home first, though.'

He frowned. 'That's not a good idea.'

'I'm assuming the clothes I left in the building are waterlogged, stinking of smoke or burnt to a crisp, and I sprinted a few miles in the ones I'm currently wearing, so I'm surprised you can stand so close to me. I need something clean and I damn well want my own underwear!'

The agent chuckled. 'Very well. But I'm still going to get someone to drive you.'

'That would be appreciated, thank you, but they're not going to go in with me; I don't want them seeing the state of my flat or have them watch me rummaging around in my underwear drawer, even Sam hasn't had that "pleasure" yet.'

'As long as they can at least check the corridor and your door for tampering.'

'That's fine.'

'Very well then, I'll set it up. Do you want time to say goodbye?'

Rachel looked around. There was no point going around the room and disturbing people just to say "goodbye", but there was someone she wanted to speak to before she left. 'Give me five minutes.'

Agent Brown nodded. 'Of course. But first - can I have your phone, please?'

Rachel pulled it out of her pocket and was just about to hand it over when she had a thought. 'You're not going to stomp on it and tell me the bomber can track me with it, are you? I quite like this phone.'

The agent shook his head. 'No, the only people who can track your phone are us.'

He smiled at her shocked expression, then gently pulled her phone from her limp grasp.

'Shall I put the code...?' Rachel started.

'No need.' The agent was already in her phone and downloading something.

'You have a backdoor to my phone?' Rachel suddenly went pale. 'Um, the photos I take with it... Are they private?'

The agent just looked up at her from under his eyebrows and smirked ambiguously.

Rachel groaned. 'Jeez, sometimes I wish Polaroids were still in fashion, at least you only had to be worried about losing them...'

The man frowned, slightly puzzled at her comment, but said nothing and after about a minute he handed the phone back to her.

'We've been ordered to install a panic button on your phones. We'll get around to Mr Vives' and Mr Hudson's phones when we can, but now you have it. It will activate a GPS ping and send an emergency signal straight to our systems.' He showed her the phone. On the lock screen was a new app. 'Press once to open the app and then put in the code to activate the alarm.'

'A code? That's not very efficient or very "panicky" is it?'

The agent shrugged. 'I suppose not, but we needed to put it in to stop newbie agents pocked dialling an air strike.'

Rachel chuckled. 'OK, what's the code, then?'

'Zero zero seven.'

She stared at him, expecting it to be a joke, but the agent just grinned. 'I'll get your security detail organised.'

He nodded respectfully to her, then moved off, speaking into a walkie talkie.

Rachel shook her head and chuckled to herself as she went back into the ward and made her way down to the bed that Dylan had been assigned to.

The boy had grown immeasurable since the first time she had met him, going from being a shy child to a confident man in only a few months. However, despite having saved several lives, he was in shock over the destruction of Headquarters and the deaths he hadn't been able to prevent and now he looked like that uncertain boy once more. It wasn't shock so much as survivor's guilt, though - she had seen it enough times to recognise it and know how best to deal with it in his case.

Many of the members had walked, hobbled or had themselves wheeled over to talk to him and Richard since they had arrived. Some had thanked them for saving their lives, others had expressed their admiration of their actions that day.

Richard had laughed them all off; he'd had an enormous amount of experience as a Displacer and now as an Elder had the calmness to go with it.

Dylan had received them, apparently cheerfully, thanking them and protesting that he had only been doing what anyone else would have done, but as soon as he was alone again his face had regained its blank aspect and he'd gone back to looking up at the ceiling. He hadn't cried, or expressed his anger at the attack, he'd just stared into space, emotionless, his eyes empty and unblinking. He wasn't injured, apart from mild smoke inhalation, a few minor burns and scorched hair, but his mind was still stuck in the moment.

Rachel stood at the end of his bed. 'Dylan.'

She spoke softly, seeing if he was going to bring himself out of his stupor, but there was no reaction so she pursed her lips and snarled. 'Mr Lloyd!'

She didn't raise her voice much, but put every ounce of command into her voice that she could muster.

His reaction was immediate, his eyes flicked to her and his body jerked involuntarily as it recognised the voice of someone who'd instructed him in martial arts for three years.

'Sit up, Mr Lloyd. Now.'

He did as he was told and she was gratified when she saw him swallow and wet his lips involuntarily.

'Are you unfit?'

'Well, my throat is a bit...'

'Are you unfit?' She raised her voice now and glared at him, holding his gaze.

In Nepal, whenever he had stopped, thinking he was too tired or too hurt to continue, she had asked him that question. It had forced him to assess himself and every single time he had realised what she had already known - that he had more to give. Just as he did now.

He looked away in shame, avoiding her eyes, and shook his head. 'No.'

'Then you are in command.'

His head shot back up and shock flared in his expression.

'Me? But...'

Rachel raised her eyebrows, daring him to complete his sentence and provoke her wrath.

'Yes, Rachel.'

She looked pointedly at her watch. 'I want you out of bed and dressed in two minutes. Report to me by the exit.'

Without waiting for his reply she turned and walked away, not looking back.

Less than two minutes later he hurried up to her.

She nodded. 'Turn, tell me what you see.'

The boy turned and gave the room a perfunctory glance. He shrugged. 'Doctors, nurses, patients...'

'Focus, Dylan. Analyse, don't just look.'

'But...'

'Do it!'

Dylan took a deep breath and looked again. He watched the medical personnel moving about the room, looked at the faces and expressions on the members, took in the security precautions and MI5 agents scattered about the room. Suddenly it just clicked.

'Everybody is safe here, the security is great, but they're still scared. The medical personnel are running around trying to keep busy so they don't have to think and most of the members are in shock.'

'Good.'

'What can we do about it?'

'*We* aren't going to do anything, *you* are. You're going to reassure them and talk to them, you're going to act like the favourite grandson that you've become to most of them, and you're going to tell them just how safe they are.'

'What about you?'

'I have a job to do. I'm going to go and help Sam protect James; the parcel was addressed to him and I'm assuming that he is the primary target and that the assassin will try again.'

Dylan's eyes widened at the thought that the nightmare hadn't quite ended and he looked at the door behind Rachel nervously as if expecting another attack.

Rachel finally softened slightly. 'You are perfectly safe here, you all are. There's nothing to worry about as long as you're in this room; it was designed to keep the Royal Family safe from a full-out attack, so I think it can protect a few old codgers and know-it-alls from a lone madman.'

Dylan almost smiled at that and she finally saw that he was going to be alright, that he was going to cope with being in charge for a while.

'Lisa will wake up at one point and I expect you to be on hand with Agent Brown to fill her in on the situation when she does.' She pointed out the agent in charge. 'If you have any doubts or requests go to him.'

She put her hand on his shoulder and pulled him around to face her again.

'Do you understand?'

He met his gaze and she saw the renewed confidence in him now that he had a job to do.

Agent Brown came over and caught her attention. 'Your detail is ready, Miss Evans, are you ready to leave?'

'Yes.' She put her hand on Dylan's shoulder. 'This is Dylan Lloyd, he will be in charge in my absence until Miss Curran is capable of taking over.'

The agent looked Dylan up and down, obviously sceptical.

Rachel smirked at him. 'Don't let his appearance fool you, Agent Brown; as you've seen, apparent age means nothing to us. Dylan is more than capable and I guarantee he'd surprise you in a fight as well.'

Dylan shifted under her hand and she felt him standing straighter, his chin coming up and his shoulders going back at her words of praise. She patted him once, then removed her hand.

'Take over, Mr Lloyd.'

'Yes, Rachel.' He nodded took a quick look around the room, then stalked off towards a group of doctors.

She looked at the agent, who was shaking his head in wonder. 'You people...' He grinned at her. 'If my agents were as capable as the youngest of your members then there's no telling what we'd be able to do.'

'Change the world, maybe?' She grinned knowingly at him and the smile instantly disappeared from his face, replaced by shock.

Worried that she might have inadvertently revealed too much she hurried on. 'My security detail?'

'Waiting outside.' He waved to one of the men by the door. 'I'll have one of my men escort you out.'

Rachel offered Agent Brown her hand. 'Take care of them, please.'

'I will, I promise.'

She grinned. 'You'd better, or you'll have me to answer to, or worse, Sam.'

He laughed. 'I get a feeling I wouldn't like that.'

'No, you really wouldn't.'

Rachel gave his hand a strong and painful squeeze, then followed the agent out.

CHAPTER 14
FLIGHT

The sun had gone down hours before and it was dark outside when Rachel came out of the hospital. One of the big black SUV's was waiting, with a black-suited MI5 beside it. He was a big, muscular man, not quite as bulky as the armed police who were still hanging around, but obviously more protection-orientated than the other agents.

He gave her a cheeky grin, which she rather liked, when he opened the passenger side door for her. 'Evening, ma'am, I'm Agent Green and I'll be your protection detail tonight.'

'You're it?' Rachel frowned, lifting an eyebrow and looking him up and down, taking in his bulging muscles and pretending that she was unimpressed.

He saw the glint of humour in her eye and laughed. 'I'm afraid so; we're spread a bit thin tonight, what with several parties on their way in from different parts of the country and your Mr Hudson wanting to stay put.'

Rachel shook her head as she got into the car. 'That's fine with me; I didn't want to have to look after any more of you boys than necessary anyway.'

The agent guffawed and closed the door after her.

She wasn't in a hurry, so Agent Green didn't use the sirens or flashing lights so as not to attract attention, but even so the trip to her flat took only slightly longer than ten minutes. Despite their banter back at the hospital they didn't talk to each other for the entire ride. As well as keeping an eye out for any threats, the agent was in constant contact with his coordinator, which required him to be speaking or listening most of the time as they guided him around traffic and gave him updates on the general situation through a wireless earpiece. Rachel wasn't really in a mood to speak anyway, preferring to maintain her own watch out of the windows while she mused about the events of the day.

When they arrived, Rachel used her remote to let them into the underground car park and the agent parked near the elevator that opened directly into it from the residences.

'Wait here, please.'

He got out of the car, closing the door softly behind him, and she watched as he pulled out his gun and a flashlight and started sweeping the area. He did so efficiently, despite the numerous cars and hiding places in the garage, first making sure that there was nobody hiding anywhere, then going to her car, a rather cute red Mini with a union jack on the roof that she had inherited from Andrew - obviously MI5 also knew what vehicles the Society members owned. He checked the locks for tampering, looked through all of the windows, then bent to inspect the wheel arches and bumpers, before finally lying down on his stomach to look underneath for any devices. Apparently he didn't find anything because he came back and opened the door for her. 'Ma'am.'

She stepped out and the SUV locked behind them as he led the way to the elevator.

She allowed him to position her to one side of the doors and he covered the lift with his gun as it opened.

There was nobody inside.

Rachel was starting to get slightly annoyed with his precautions because, as far as she was concerned, while admirable, they were completely unnecessary. It was obvious that James was the target and the delay they were causing just meant that she would get to him later than she otherwise would, giving the assassin more of an opportunity to try again.

The lift opened up on her floor seconds later and the man motioned for her to stay put while he swept the corridor and examined her door. She tapped her feet impatiently, leaning against the bank of floor numbers, her leg covering the sensor that stopped the doors closing.

Thirty seconds later the agent came back and waved her out.

'You know, I have a pretty good alarm system, the building has cameras, and there's a guard at a desk in the lobby...'

The man snorted and glanced sideways at her as if to say that such security measures weren't even worth the time. She smiled wryly and nodded. She had to agree with him, even if she didn't feel like it at that moment; she knew dozens of ways to break into the building and her own flat without tripping anything - she did it at least once a week, just to keep her hand in, after all.

She slotted the key into her door. 'I'll be five minutes. Try not to shoot my neighbours, please.'

The big agent grinned at her and shrugged. 'Can't promise anything...'

She laughed and went in. Her security system beeped at her and she hurriedly punched in the code to turn it off, then went down the corridor to the living room, where she paused to survey the huge flat that Andrew had given her. It was in just as much a mess as she remembered, with dirty plates and mugs on the coffee table and the debris from several lonely nights in front of the telly without Sam strewn everywhere.

She sighed and started across the room, heading towards the main bedroom.

Later, when she thought back, she wasn't sure if it had been instinct or whether she had seen something out of the corner of her eye, but before she was even sure what she was doing she was rolling across the floor. There was a deafening sound and a glass cabinet shattered behind her.

She snuck a quick look in the direction the shot had come from and saw the shadow lurking behind the door of the bathroom. There was another bang, but she was already desperately ducking for cover behind a heavy leather sofa.

There was another crash, different this time, and she recognised the sound of her front door banging against the wall.

The agent's shout rang through the flat. '*Miss Evans?*'

'One man in the bathroom! Large calibre pistol!'

There was nothing she could do against a proficient man armed with a gun so the best thing she could do now was to get clear, taking a worry away from the agent, and hope that he could get away when she'd gone.

She took a deep breath and waited for Agent Green to provide her with a distraction. In the meantime she thanked the training that had drummed into her the necessity to plan escape routes wherever she was staying.

There was an exchange of shots and she was immediately up and sprinting towards her bedroom. She said a quick prayer, hoping that the assassin was in fact working alone, then dived through the door.

She rolled to her feet and grabbed one of the heavy iron table lamps, ripping it from its cord and throwing it as she ran across the large room. It smashed the window - which she'd had replaced with single glazing as soon as she'd moved in, precisely for this eventuality - only moments before she leapt at it.

It was a long way to the ground and normally she would have no hope of surviving the fall, but she had planned this escape route as an absolute last resort, taking a leaf from a scene in the first *Rambo* film.

The tree was a good twenty feet below her, but it was a huge evergreen, thick and leafy, with branches that were small and snapped easily - perfect to cushion her fall. She wrapped her hands around her head and curled herself into a ball, but even so she gasped as dozens of sharp twigs ripped through her thin summer shirt and dug into her skin.

She came to a halt, hanging upside down, still some ten feet above the ground.

She groaned in pain, wasting precious seconds.

Move, damn you!

She was fairly sure it was Sam's voice in her head and it sent a surge of adrenaline through her to add to the one that had already spurred her into action and given her the courage to jump through a fourth floor window.

She twisted and turned, pushing through the branches that held her up, and dropped to the ground, rolling to break her fall. She gasped at the pain in her torn skin as she came to her feet, but it didn't stop her from sprinting away.

Above her in the flat there was a brief pause in the shooting, then three last shots in quick succession and she set her mouth in a grimace, knowing exactly what that meant.

The lights in the other flats were coming on now and she could see shadows moving around behind the curtains as her neighbours started reacting. She was sure that some of them were even now calling the police, but help would arrive far too late to do anything for her or Agent Green, all she could do now was make sure that his sacrifice hadn't been in vain and get away from the assassin.

She raced into shadowy streets that were almost empty so late at night, pulling her phone out as she ran. She pushed the panic button and tapped in the 007 code before sliding it back into her pocket.

There was a bolthole she'd scouted out half a mile away - far enough away from the flat not to be an obvious destination for a fugitive, but not so far that she wouldn't be able to get to it if she was injured. It was an old-fashioned bandstand in a nearby park, in the middle of an open space so she could see anyone approaching in time to hide or move on and, as an added bonus, there was plenty of room for a small person to squeeze under the wooden floor and hide if necessary.

She reached the bandstand after a few minutes of hard running and ducked around the side to tuck herself out of sight behind the steps to wait for help.

She glanced at her phone, but there was no sign that it was doing anything. She toyed with the idea of ringing someone, but discarded the idea because she had no idea who she would call and even if she did, it would just get them into danger as well. She decided to just trust that the panic button was working as it was supposed to.

Any doubts that she had as to whether the app had done its job were dispelled only moments later when a helicopter, a dark blue, unmarked *Dauphin*, dived over the trees a few hundred metres away and swooped to a combat landing on the grass as near to the bandstand as it could get. Four men in camouflage, carrying assault rifles immediately jumped from its open doors and spread out around it. Two of them knelt on the helicopter's far side, facing away from her to cover the surroundings, while the other two came towards her. The leader was focussed directly on her, despite her being hidden, while his partner covered him, swinging his rifle back and forth to either side.

'Stand and identify yourself!'

The leading man's shout was clearly audible over the sound of the helicopter and Rachel obeyed, not just for the command itself, but also because of the automatic weapon that was unerringly trained on her.

She stood holding her hands out to her sides. 'Rachel Evans.'

Satisfied that she wasn't a threat, the man's weapon immediately turned away from her to cover her right side while his partner faced away to cover their left quadrant. The lead man kept coming towards her, though, crabbing sideways until he got to her. He gave her a quick once over, noting her torn shirt. 'Serious injuries?'

'None.'

'Left hand on my right shoulder, crouch and follow me closely, please.'

She did as she was instructed and followed the man as he made his way back to the helicopter. The position she was in ensured that his body covered hers as much as possible and the man falling in behind them covered her from the rear.

They got to the helicopter and he bundled her in roughly. The four soldiers followed her seconds later, slamming the doors shut after them, and the helicopter took off with a roar and a gut-wrenching lurch.

One of the two flight technicians handed her a headset and waited for her to put it on before speaking. 'Miss Evans?'

'Yes?'

'Agent Brown for you.'

She gave him a thumbs up.

There was a crackle, then she heard the voice of the MI5 agent coordinating matters from the hospital.

'Miss Evans? Are you hurt? Do you need treatment?'

'Nothing serious. I'll be fine after a bath and some Savlon.'

'Good, and your escort detail?'

'Status unknown, probably dead.'

There was a brief silence before the man spoke again. 'We have men on the way to your home and the drone is already patrolling, but we haven't heard anything from him so I have to concur with you.'

'I'm sorry.'

'Thank you, Miss Evans. I'll see you in a few minutes and you can give me your report.'

'No, I need to get to Mr Hudson's house.'

'That's not advisable.'

'I don't care. I need to get to Sam and James.'

There was another silence at the other end and Rachel could almost feel the man swearing. There was nothing he could do except agree, though; she had learned that much today. 'Very well. I'll have the chopper divert to Brockwell Park and the team will escort you in from there.'

'Thank you.'

'I'll speak to you again when you are safe. You can give me your full report then.'

'Understood.'

'Good luck, Miss Evans. Over and out.'

There was a crackle and the headset went silent. Moments later the helicopter veered, changing course.

She sat back and took a deep breath, rolling her shoulders and relaxing muscles that she hadn't realised she'd been keeping in tension. She found that she was shaking gently and she snarled, wrapping her arms around herself and rubbing her shoulders against the cold, swearing at a weakness that she had thought she had banished forever in Sparta.

'Miss Evans.'

The voice sounded in the headset she was still wearing and she looked up to find the team leader sitting across from her. He was leaning forwards and, bizarrely, holding a small paper bag out to her.

'Sherbet Lemon?' He shook the bag gently up and down, making the sickly yellow contents jump around. 'The sugar will do you good.'

He shook the bag again and grinned, a grin that was echoed by the rest of his team; obviously this was an eccentricity of their leader's that they were used to.

She smiled at the man and took a sweet. 'Thank you.'

He nodded and offered the bag around to his team and the flight technicians. Everyone took at least one sweet and one of the team members took a handful with an unapologetic smile, putting one in his mouth and stuffing the rest into his pocket.

The man waited until she'd put her sweet into her mouth before speaking again.

'I'm Captain MacAlister and this is my team, Trenches, Dumbo and Soapy.'

Each of the men waved as he said their names and Rachel had to work hard not to spit out her sweet with laughter at their nicknames.

'I take it you're Regiment.'

There were more grins all round. 'Yes, ma'am! That obvious are we?'

'Let's just say I've met a few of the lads.' That, the way they moved, and the fact that their camouflage uniforms bore no insignia whatsoever, made it more than obvious for her. She grinned back at them, easily falling into the mindset of banter mixed with professionalism that she'd become accustomed to when she'd spent a few months training with the SAS before the Falklands War - one of the Displacements she'd been on before she'd met Sam.

'Oh, yes? Like who?'

Rachel could feel the smile fading slightly from her face as she remembered the friends who she'd made, many of whom had lost their lives in the Falklands and subsequent wars.

The Captain must have seen her expression change because he nodded and gave her an understanding look, although she could see some puzzlement as well, which seemed to be standard for all the men she met that day. 'Perhaps instead you could tell us why you are so important as to warrant our involvement? Is there anything you can tell us to shed a light on this evening's events? Does this have anything to do with the bomb in Grosvenor Place this afternoon?'

Rachel pursed her lips and thought quickly. She knew from past experience that soldiers didn't tend to get told a lot about why they were doing what they had been ordered to do - they were just expected to get the job done and in many cases that got more of them killed than was necessary. So, part of her wanted to tell these men everything, but the Displacer part of her knew that she couldn't.

She settled with telling them what she could.

'Yes, this is to do with the bombing. I'm a member of a group of people who work for the benefit of, well, the whole world I suppose, and we've recently made one particular enemy. He's very powerful and hired a professional assassin to kill some of us.'

'And the reason for our divert?'

'We, well, I, believe the assassin's main target is one of our leaders. He has chosen to remain in his residence and I'm going there to help protect him.'

There was a laugh from the hulking man who the captain had introduced as Dumbo, the one who had taken the handful of sweets. '*You're* going to protect him? I thought there was already a Five detail on his residence?'

Rachel looked at him and nodded. 'There is. They're not enough. I need to be there.'

The captain's eyebrows lifted and she felt his eyes flicker over her in assessment. She narrowed her eyes at him and was very happy to see him flinch back from her.

The rest of his men saw the interaction and laughed at him. After a second the captain began to laugh with them and Rachel smiled. She had missed this easy camaraderie that developed between fighting men; with Sam it was completely different. Much more intense, but different.

The captain bent down to fish around under his seat and brought up a set of camouflage clothing which he threw at her.

'Probably a good idea if you put these on; they'll keep you warm, but they'll also cover you up - you're making the boys a bit nervous.'

Rachel looked down at herself. Her shirt was torn to pieces and stained with blood and what little was left of her bra and most of her midriff could be seen through it. Unselfconsciously she pulled the shirt off and slipped the jacket on. It was a bit big for her, but she couldn't help but smile as she looked down at herself in camouflage; it had been too long since last she'd worn it.

She did the same with the trousers, pulling off her own jogging bottoms before slipping them on. She transferred her belongings, including her keys and phone, to the many pockets of the jacket before screwing up her clothes and giving them to a flight technician, who bagged them for her.

The last thing she needed to do was sort out her hair; the fall into the tree had ripped her scrunchy off and it was hanging loose and getting in her way. She looked up at the captain. 'I don't suppose you have something to hold my hair up with do you?'

He shook his head and looked around at his men, who in turn shook theirs.

It had only been an idle hope; the men all had very short hair, they wouldn't need anything to hold it back. She sighed and stuck out her hand. 'Knife please, captain.'

With a surprised look, the captain pulled out his combat knife and handed it over, handle first.

She grabbed it from him and looked at it. She smiled; it was about as far from standard issue as you could get, just what she would have expected from someone in The Regiment.

She held the knife between her knees by the handle as she reached up and gathered her hair with both hands.

A single quick swipe with the knife was all it took for her to come away with a bit over eight inches of dirty brown hair and twigs in her hands and she glanced at it wistfully for a second; Sam had expressed his love of her long hair many a time and she had really enjoyed growing it for him, but sacrifices had to be made tonight and this was likely to be the least of them.

She pulled out as much of the debris as she could as quickly as she could, then tied a knot in the hair and tucked it into a pocket of the jacket; she would give it to Sam later as an apology.

The captain held out his hand to take the knife back, but Rachel didn't hand it to him straight away, instead she spun it a few times between her fingers, twirling it expertly, dangerously, all the time looking the man in the eyes.

Those eyes widened as they watched the knife flashing in the red lights of the inside of the helicopter, the reflections looking like blood.

She finished with the very tip of the knife pinched between two fingers and offered him the handle. He took it and pulled, but she didn't let go, she kept the blade held tightly with just her index finger and thumb and laughed at the expression on his face as he realised how strong she was.

Ever since she'd been to study with Master Hamato the first time, she had continually worked on the strength in her fingers; it was one of the things that he had insisted on. After years of exercises she could now do push-ups and chin-up with single fingers.

When she judged that she'd gotten her point across she let the knife go and he almost hit himself in the stomach with the handle at the release in pressure. He put it away quickly and gave her a look of approval, but then his eyes defocused slightly as he listened to something on his headset.

He looked around at his men, all traces of playfulness instantly gone. 'Two minutes, combat drop.'

They nodded and, while they started making final preparations, the captain looked back at her.

'I want you right behind me when we get out. We're going out that door.' He pointed at the one she had used to get in. 'Take three steps then drop to your stomach and stay there until I tell you differently, understood?'

She nodded curtly, as professionally as one of his men. 'Yes, captain.'

'Good.' He looked around his team and received a nod from all of them as they finished their preparations. He said nothing more; they had no need of instructions because they had done this thousands of times in training.

The pilot's voice came over the headsets, broadcasting to all of them and not just the captain now that the objective was in sight. 'Thirty seconds.'

The soldiers and flight technicians opened the doors on either side of the helicopter and a gale blew in, making Rachel very glad for the jacket. She took her headset off and stood, joining the men in the doorways, holding onto an overhead strap for safety. Through the gaping hole she saw the house in the middle of Brockwell Park fly by in an instant, illuminated white in the middle of the dark and empty space, but then the aircraft dipped exhilaratingly as it lunged for the ground.

The helicopter hit the ground with a jolt and the first three men leapt into the darkness. Half a second later she followed the captain out, took three paces as she'd been instructed, then threw herself to the ground.

Behind them the helicopter went straight up, its nose to the sky as it clawed for altitude. In seconds it was gone, disappearing back the way it had come, and they were left with only the sound of the occasion car passing on the nearby roads.

Rachel lifted her head just enough to get her bearings. They were at the bottom of the short slope that led up towards the exit for James' house, lying in the grass that hadn't been mown for too long. The captain was in a crouch a couple of metres in front of her, alternating between looking at a map of the surrounding area - a wrinkled and well-used A to Z - and watching for threats. The other soldiers formed a perimeter around them and were scanning the area, their rifles at the ready.

She crawled forwards to join the captain. 'I know the area, let me advise you, please.' She made it sound like a request, but in fact it was more of an order; she undoubtedly knew the ground better than him and it only made sense for her to help.

A crooked smile twisted his face and he nodded without looking at her, then laid the map on the grass.

She came up to a crouch, but stayed lower than him and behind his shoulder so as to still be covered by him from the nearest houses. She pointed at the map as she spoke. 'We're here, the objective is straight ahead about four hundred metres. There are three exits to the park on this side. The first is a path between the houses ahead of us that leads directly to Tulse Hill and straight across to Athlone Road, it is narrow and perfect ambush territory. The second is to the right, half-way down the hill. It isn't as confined, but it takes us out onto the main road where we will be exposed. The third exit is about a hundred metres down the hill behind us and will take us to the bottom of Trinity Rise, but that's a bit far away from where we want to be. However, there is one more option that's not on the map. It's not as straightforward as the others, but it's the one I would recommend. It will involve scaling the fence here, but from there it will take us directly into the cover of these houses.' She pointed them out on the map. 'From there it is a short and easy path up to the old library. After we cross the road we can take back streets and foot paths through this council estate all the way to our objective. It's confined, but little known, so it should be the safest route.'

The captain looked at the map, considering the options.

'I think we'll go with that. Thank you, Miss Evans.'

'Call me Rachel; it'll be easier in a bind.'

'Very well.' He raised his voice slightly. 'Hear all that, lads?'

There was quiet confirmation from the various shadows scattered around them.

'Objective is the fence at ten o'clock. Trenches, left flank, Soapy you take the right, Dumbo you're on point. I'll bring up the rear with

Rachel in the middle.' He paused for a second to let the information sink in. 'Go.'

Instantly the three men were up and in a crouch, running towards the distant iron fence, spreading out as they went and when they were about ten metres away, Captain MacAlister motioned for her to follow them.

In the end their caution was unwarranted. Despite run-ins with first a cat, then a group of drunken students, the journey through the night-time streets was uneventful. Rachel moved with them easily as a part of their team, obeying the signals as they came and helping with the scouting whenever the captain let her. They moved slowly and carefully and half an hour later they reached the MI5 perimeter, a couple of streets from James' house, where they were met by the agent in charge of the security operation.

The agent gave the soldiers a warm smile. 'Captain, lads.'

'Evening, Agent... er, what is it this time, mate? Smith? Connery? Humperdinck?'

'It's White. We're all colours for this op.'

'Ooh, very Pulp Fiction.'

The two men grinned at each other. Obviously it was a conversation they'd had many times before, but Rachel couldn't help but wonder if the soldier knew the agent's real name and how lonely it would have to be for your friends to only knew you by an alias.

The agent gave Rachel a nod. 'Miss Evans.'

'Agent White. How is Agent Green?'

'Dead, I'm afraid.'

Rachel swore and put her hand over her eyes. It was entirely her fault that the friendly agent was dead; she had insisted on going to her flat, arrogantly believing that she could take care of herself. She took a few deep breaths, trying to calm her seething emotions, before finally looking back up at the man. 'I'm sorry. I'm so sorry...'

The agent waved away her apologies. 'There will be time enough to analyse later, for now we have a job to do, Miss Evans.'

'Right, of course.' Duty focussed her mind far better than any amount of meditation ever could and she nodded. 'Update me, please.'

'Yes, ma'am.' The agent pulled out his phone and consulted it as he spoke, getting the latest information. 'We set up a cordon around your residence as quickly as we could and even temporarily re-tasked the drone, but the assassin slipped through our noose again. We are confident that he won't be able to leave the country through conventional methods, though, and as far as we know he is now trapped in Britain.'

Rachel grimaced. 'That's not exactly comforting...'

The men around her laughed at that, a gentle huffing sound that surrounded her and gave her some well needed comfort.

'What about our members, the ones who were coming in?'

'Most have arrived and are now in the ward at the hospital. There are only two still mobile - Hamish Craig who is on the M1 in an armoured convoy en route from his residence in Edinburgh and, um, Hamish Craig... sorry that must be a mistake.'

Rachel chuckled. 'It's not, don't worry; some names are a bit of a tradition with us. You should have somewhere that they're Hamish Craig the fifth and sixth.'

The agent frowned as he flicked through something on his phone, then nodded. 'Right, got it. Mr Craig the fifth is in the convoy, they're passing the M25 as we speak, Mr Craig the sixth is en route from his base by Lynx and is due to land on the hospital roof in fifteen minutes.'

'And that's the last of them?'

'Of the ones that are in the country, yes. The four members of your American branch currently in the United States have been taken into custody by the FBI and a Mr Price, uh, Ralph Price, is in Australia. The local authorities have been notified to keep an eye on him.'

Ralph had been ordered by the council of Elders to take some time off to get used to his new status and had taken the opportunity to get as far away as possible, taking a long cruise around Australasia. Rachel almost waved away their concern for him, thinking that the arrogant man deserved everything that he got, but resisted; thoughts like that weren't worthy of the Displacers or of her. She sighed. 'Keep me in the loop on that, please.'

'Yes, ma'am.'

'OK, what about the situation here? What do you have?'

The man showed her his phone, bringing up a map of the local area. There were several flashing red dots scattered around it and he pointed them out.

'We have men concealed at each end of the street, two in the back garden of the house itself and two more in the house across the road. There is also a drone circling overhead equipped with infrared, but there's too much traffic going past, even at this hour, for it to be of much help.' He sighed. 'All we can really do is secure the immediate area around the house, but anyone can just wander up to within fifty yards and then they're only seconds away. It would be a hell of a lot easier to protect Mr Hudson if you could persuade him to join the rest of your people...'

Rachel chuckled. 'Somehow I don't think that's going to happen.'

She went over to the corner of the brick wall behind which they were standing and looked down the whole length of McKay Road towards James' home, a couple of hundred metres away at the far end of the road. It was all quiet, there was nobody around and most of the houses were dark.

She frowned. 'You know, the one thing I don't understand is why he came after me - after the explosion, as soon as he realised he'd missed he should have come straight here. He would have arrived well before you could set up and it would have been so easy to...'

She stopped speaking as a horrible thought wormed its way into her brain.

If someone was going to attack the Society then of course they would want to kill James; while not the actual leader he was who everyone turned to for advice and nothing was done without his say so. However, that reasoning was seriously flawed, because it assumed that the motive behind an attack would be to gain an advantage in the present, whereas John would be focussed firmly in the past - he wouldn't care about James because James couldn't Displace, couldn't affect the past.

No, there was only one logical target for John, one person whose death would give him *everything*.

'It's Sam. Sam Vives, he's the target.'

'But the parcel was addressed to Mr Hudson.'

'Because the bomber could safely assume that Sam would be with him and there would be no reason for Sam himself to receive a parcel.'

The agent still wasn't convinced. 'But then why did he try to kill you? Why not just attack Mr Vives?'

'Because an attack on me *is* an attack on him. Sam and I are... close. If I were to die then Sam would be distracted at best, but most likely devastated and would be easier to get to. There's also...' Rachel paused, wondering how she could explain, or even what she *should* explain, about the prophecy and her role in it as Sam's protector. 'Uh... let's just say he's free to deal with the important stuff because I have his back.' Rachel looked at the agent seriously. 'Look, I just know that I'm only important enough to target because of my relation to Sam. Hell, even James Hudson isn't as vital to our organisation as Sam is.'

'Exactly how vital are we talking about, ma'am?'

'Without Sam we are lost. And not just the Society, but the world as well.'

The agent started to laugh, but the sound died in his throat when he saw that she was deadly serious. 'How confident are you of your reasoning?'

Rachel considered. 'Eighty percent sure?'

'And the other casualties? Why not go straight for Vives? And why send a bomb in the first place? The assassin specialises in surgical strikes, not big demonstrations like this.'

'Because the man who hired him wants collateral damage. This is personal for him.'

Agent White fell silent briefly as he considered her revelations.

Rachel took the opportunity to glance around the SAS team. While they were alert and constantly scanning their surroundings they were all obviously listening with interest. She wondered what they thought about the whole situation and what they were able to understand of what was truly going on.

Eventually the MI5 agent sighed in exasperation. 'Well, assuming that what you say is correct, it changes everything. I'm going to call in for instructions.'

The agent opened a contact on his phone, but Rachel stopped him with a hand on his arm before he could make the call. 'Don't do that yet, please. Give me a little time to think how to use this to our advantage.'

He nodded and lowered the phone, waiting patiently for her orders.

Rachel looked down the road again towards James' house. Whatever they did to draw out the assassin, she didn't want the confrontation to take place there; not only would James be in danger, but there were too many neighbours. The hospital was out of the question for the same reason. Headquarters was a possibility, but it was unlikely that the assassin would return to the scene of the crime willingly. Her flat would have been perfect for an ambush, but that chance had been blown.

She idly picked at a burr on her sleeve, collected from the park, pulling it off and throwing it to one side as she considered other options.

She stopped and looked down at it.

With a smile, she turned to look at the men waiting expectantly behind her. 'I think I have a plan, a way to flush him out, but you're probably not going to like it. Do you have a large scale map of the area, Agent White?'

'Of course.' He pulled a folded sheet of paper out of his pocket and handed it to her.

She went along the wall to a street lamp and knelt down to spread it open on the floor in the pool of light. The agent and the captain followed her and crouched beside her.

'Sam and I are in the habit of training every day when we're together. When we're at Headquarters we go to Hyde Park or a nearby dojo, but when we're with James we train in Brockwell Park.'

She put her finger on the large open space of the park and ran her finger around it. 'Normally we run around the perimeter a few times before ending up in the field, near where we landed, to do some stretching and sparring.'

Her finger stopped on the field nearest to James' house where the helicopter had dropped them off.

'I suggest that Sam and I pick up our routine, maybe after a couple of days of going "stir crazy" in the house and just showing ourselves in the garden for anyone who is watching. In that time you can set up surveillance in the area surrounding the park. If we confine our activities to this field then the only clear lines of sight are from the houses to the south in Brockwell Park Gardens and the few that are outside the park fence in Cressingham Gardens. On all other sides someone would have to be well within the park and in the open in order to get to us. Unless of course our guy is a sniper as well?'

The agent shook his head. 'His kills have mostly been up close and personal, with a hand gun or knife, apart from a couple of car bombs that we believe were his handiwork and the bombing at your Headquarters. There has been nothing long-distance that we can attribute to him and, while he did have a good record of marksmanship with German special forces, he wasn't sniper-level.'

'That's a relief, but I don't feel comfortable making that assumption. Locations with clear sightlines to the house and the field where someone could set up have to be checked.'

'Of course. But I doubt it's going to be necessary; my superiors will never go for this. If Mr Vives is the main target then they are never going to sign off on deliberately putting him in danger.'

Rachel smiled slyly. 'They don't have to sign off on anything; have you forgotten that I have the final word here?'

The agent opened his mouth to speak, but ended up just closing it again with a pop when he realised she was right.

The captain could barely contain his mirth at the man's comical expressions either, but at the same time there was a hefty amount of curiosity in his eyes as he gave Rachel a sharp look. Unlike the MI5 agents she'd met that day he managed to contain himself and she gave him a wink before turning back to Agent White.

'Seriously though, I know this is risky, I know it will put Sam and I in danger, but the confrontation will be under our control and far enough away from the rest of our colleagues and members of the public for there to be no innocents in danger. I'm sure Sam will agree with me that this is the best way to go about things, unless, of course, you believe you're going to pick up the assassin before he makes another attempt on my people?'

She raised an eyebrow inquisitively at the agent and he was forced to shake his head. It was extremely unlikely that they would catch the man on their own; he was wanted the world over and still managed to slip across borders and kill people with impunity.

The two men looked at each other, then looked down at the map.

This was the captain's field of expertise and the agent waited for him to speak first.

'Soapy, did you see that church to the south of where we came out of the park?'

''Course I did, cap.'

'Think it would make a good nest?'

'Too right.'

The captain grunted and continued to scrutinise the map. 'It's far too open for my liking, but if you say this guy likes to get up close and personal then there are things we can do. My main problem is how you'll be getting to and from the field; all these alleyways are death traps.'

Rachel shook her head. 'I don't think that will be a problem; Sam and I will run to the field. We'll move quick and we'll take a different route every day. There are so many way we can get to the park that the German won't know which one we'll take. He'll be forced to meet us either at our starting point here in McKay Road, inside the cordon, or at our end point in the park. And it'll happen soon; John needs us out of the way as quickly as possible so that he can continue his plans - we've been quite the thorn in his side lately, well, Sam has anyway.'

The captain gave her a grin. 'I'm sure you're selling yourself short, Miss Evans. From what I've seen in just an hour or so you could be running the show.'

Rachel laughed. 'Thank you, captain, but if you're impressed with me, wait until you see Sam in action. He looks like a bumbling teenager and doesn't know his arse from his elbow sometimes, but when he puts his mind to a task there's no stopping him.'

Both of the men laughed with her, but she shook her head as she saw the disbelief in their eyes and smiled inwardly, wondering what their reactions would be if they ever saw Sam in a fight.

She looked back to the agent. 'Present the plan to your superiors, please, but tell them that, unless they can come up with anything I consider to be better or catch the bastard themselves, then it is the plan we will be going with, whether they like it or not.'

'Yes, ma'am!'

'Well, for now, I want to see my boyfriend and his grandfather and get to bed. It's been a long and difficult day.'

She folded the map and handed it back to the agent then stood up. 'Can I keep the clothes for now, please, captain? I'd prefer not to have to walk down the road in bloody underwear.'

'Consider them a gift, along with my respect.' He looked around his team who each gave him a barely perceptible nod. 'And that of my men.'

'Thank you.' She stepped forwards and shook the captain's hand firmly before nodding to his team.

She turned back to Agent White. 'I assume I can just walk down the road in safety?'

'All clear, ma'am.'

'Good. Well, let me know what they say up at Thames House, please, but make sure they know I won't be putting up with any funny business from them.'

'It will be a pleasure.' The agent grinned.

'Right then.' She looked around the SAS team, still on alert, still protecting her, despite their being in a secure area. 'Thanks, guys. See you around.'

There was a chorus of respectful *ma'am*'s from the men in reply and she nodded at them before striding away towards James' house.

The whole way down the pavement she couldn't help feel like she was in a crosshair and was half expecting a bullet to come out of the night at any time, but her fears were completely unwarranted and a minute later she was standing on James' doorstep in the light from the overhead lamp on the porch. She lifted her hand to tap on the door, but before she could do so it opened and she came face to face with Sam.

He pulled her into his arms, almost roughly.

'Thank god, you're safe. They wouldn't tell us anything...' His voice was full of emotion and his breath was hot on her neck as he held her and she melted into his arms, the tension flowing out of her in a rush.

They stayed like that for long minutes until Rachel realised that they were still standing in the open doorway, which wasn't exactly the most advisable thing given the circumstances. She walked Sam forwards into the hallway without releasing him and used her heel to manoeuvre the door shut.

Eventually, they realised that they were both swaying gently with tiredness and they had to let each other go before they fell over.

She took a step back and reached up to stroke Sam's face, taking in the sight of him in the weak light coming through the small windows in the door. He looked tired, haggard, and, to her shock, scared. 'How is James?'

'He's upstairs asleep. He's taking this pretty badly and Anne's death really shook him up.'

'I'm not surprised. How about you?'

'I'm OK, I suppose.' He didn't look too sure and Rachel could see that he wasn't, but she didn't push.

Sam ran his hand through Rachel's hair, noting its new length, and frowned. 'You look terrible, what happened?'

'Do you mind if I tell you tomorrow? I'm exhausted.'

'No problem, I'll take the first shift on watch, you go to bed.'

Rachel smiled at him warmly. 'You're not getting away from me that easily, boy! We have about a dozen MI5 agents, a drone and an SAS team watching us, we really don't need to keep watch. Tonight I want you in my bed.'

Sam grinned. 'Sounds good to me!' He started running his hands down her body, undoing the buttons on her camouflage jacket. 'This is a good look for you by the way...'

She slapped his hands away. 'Hey! I'm not the one who's been sitting on his arse for the last few hours, I need rest!'

'Aw...' Sam was disappointed, but he knew her well enough to see that she wasn't entirely joking and did in fact need to sleep. He smiled and held out his hand to her.

Rachel took it gratefully and let him help her up the stairs towards the spare bedroom, feeling his familiar, intense presence beside her and drawing comfort from it.

CHAPTER 15
EXPOSED

After a couple of days of training in the back garden and acting like they were bored, which they were, Sam and Rachel ventured carefully out onto the streets. They took different routes to the park each day, sometimes going up Tulse Hill, sometimes down, sometimes using the alleys of the council estate that she'd come through with the SAS team, sometimes heading in completely the wrong direction before looping back around.

Rachel sent Agent White a message every night, using codes she'd arranged with him, setting down the route that they were going to take the next morning so that security could be planned accordingly.

To carry out Rachel's plan, the security detail was increased to forty. In addition to the teams guarding the access points to James' house, there were snipers and arrest teams posted in strategic buildings around the field to which they were hoping to lure the assassin and a dozen agents covering the route to and from the park, just in case. It was a huge operation and served to highlight just how important the Displacers were.

Sam and Rachel were very glad to get out of the house, even if it was only for a couple of hours at a time, but by the seventh day there had still been no sightings of the assassin. The people at MI5 were beginning to express their doubts of Rachel's reasoning and she was starting to question herself and her assumption that the target was indeed Sam and not James or any of the other Displacers. They persisted with the plan, though, because it was the only option; MI5 hadn't come up with anything better or been able to catch the man, and the Displacers couldn't go back to their normal lives because that would just give the assassin free rein to try again.

On the eighth day, they took a particularly convoluted route to the field, keeping to the streets around the park, going most of the way down the hill to Brixton before working their way round to the other side and coming in by the Lido. They then reversed their course, going all the way back around the perimeter anti-clockwise, before ending up in their usual training spot.

They always began sparring directly from the run without pausing for breath, with one of them trying to take the other by surprise from behind to simulate an attack. It was Sam's turn to initiate things that day and he let Rachel get a few steps in front of him as they approached the sparring ring they'd paced out. He grinned, looking forward to seeing how she would react to a simple rugby tackle, and accelerated, crouching slightly to take his weight lower, but, just before he leapt, there were two shockingly loud bangs.

Rachel dropped like a puppet whose strings had been cut, leaving Sam wrong-footed and staring open-mouthed. His shock lasted only a millisecond, though, and then his training took over and he dove headlong into the long grass.

He hadn't been able to pinpoint exactly where the shots had come from because his view had been blocked by Rachel, but they had come from very close and directly in their path.

The assassin had managed to get into the park unseen and had been waiting for them.

Sam turned his head to look at the unmoving body of Rachel lying beside him and howled his grief.

The Beast wakened as emotion flooded through its host and it instantly took over, not giving him any say in the matter.

When Sam came back to himself his hands were dripping blood and he was surrounded by wide-eyed members of MI5 and the SAS, all of whom were pointing weapons at him.

There was something at his feet and he glanced down at it. It took him a moment to recognise what it was, but then he staggered back in shock and disgust; the mangled pile of bloody cloth was barely recognisable as a man anymore.

He dropped to his knees and fell forwards onto his hands, fighting back the bile that surged into his throat, chest heaving as he struggled to breathe.

Eventually he managed to force out a single word. 'Rachel.'

Hands seized him from behind and he flinched, thinking that it was the men about to restrain him, but then they slid around his sides. A warm body pressed against his and Rachel's lips brushed against the back of his neck before she breathed in his ear. 'I'm here, Sam, I'm alright.'

The tears came then and there was nothing that he could do to stop them. He curled up into a ball, still on his knees, and poured his pain out while Rachel held him.

Neither of them noticed as the men around them got to work.

The ambush had been recorded by cameras set up by MI5 in both of the sniper positions they'd established. They clearly showed how the assassin had been lying in wait in a ghillie suit in the long grass and had only taken his shot when Rachel and Sam had been a few steps away. If he had delayed any longer, Rachel would have literally fallen over him, which was why he hadn't waited until he had a clear shot at both of the Displacers.

Thankfully his two shots had been to Rachel's chest and had been absorbed by the vest that she had been wearing under her tracksuit. Even so, they had still taken her out of commission for a full minute.

The video showed that neither of snipers had been able to take a shot in retaliation because the three people in the grass had been too close together and moving too much to do so safely.

It was the ten seconds of the video after Rachel had gone down that were the most often watched by both the MI5 and SAS teams. Ten seconds that they replayed in awe, over and over.

Those ten seconds were all it had taken for Sam, for the *Beast*, to close the distance, disarm the assassin, spear stiff fingers through his eyes and into his brain, break his neck for good measure, then begin the process of pummelling his corpse into the grass with bare hands.

Most agents stopped watching there, because what came next turned even the strongest stomach; in the twenty seconds following those first ten, before any agent could get to the scene, the Beast turned a man into a sack of broken bones. It had then turned to snarl at the agents surrounding it, unwilling to give up its prey or leave the side of the woman that it loved, which was why they had turned their weapons on it in fear.

The Beast was in control for forty seconds in total before it retreated, well satisfied with its work, leaving Sam to deal with the consequences.

And the guilt.

Rachel and a shaking Sam were escorted back to the house in McKay Road half an hour later to be debriefed by James and the Deputy Director General of MI5, a Mr Firth.

Rachel had been treated for cracked ribs in the park. She'd been extremely lucky that the man had been in a hurry; normally someone of his skill would have put one shot in her heart and the other in her unprotected head.

Sam, however, was completely untouched, at least physically - his mental state was another matter.

He said nothing the entire time Rachel was being taken care of, or during the walk back to James' house and then sat silently during the debriefing in the sitting room, staring into a cooling cup of tea.

James and the MI5 bigwig had watched the videos while they were waiting, so, by the time the teams arrived, they had a good idea of what had happened in the park. There wasn't much that could be said about the fight itself; it was rather self-explanatory, which just left the matter of how the assassin could have gotten into place to make the attempt without being seen and the section chief spent most of the debriefing recriminating with Agent White and Captain MacAlister.

James didn't say anything either, he just sat in his armchair, frowning, seemingly not really listening to the conversation and never once taking his eyes off Sam. As well as having seen the video of his grandson's shocking behaviour he had heard the report from the SAS captain and had seen the way that the entire team, most of whom were now having tea in the kitchen twenty feet away, had looked at Sam and treated him. He had also seen the copious amounts of blood on Sam's face and clothing before he had washed and changed.

Sam couldn't meet his eye; for all James knew, the assassin was the first person that Sam had killed; he had lied to the Society, hiding his Displacement to Alamut from everyone except Rachel, and he knew his grandfather would be disappointed with him. And that was without saying anything about what he'd brought back with him.

The Deputy Director General wrapped up the debriefing quickly, provisionally classifying the operation as a success with the assassin taken care of, even though the man who'd hired him was still at large. He shook hands with James and Captain MacAlister and made his way from the house while Agent White collected the rest of the MI5 agents from the kitchen and dining room. They piled into the dozen or so black cars that were blocking the road outside and drove away in one long convoy through the police cordon that had been set up to close the street while the director was there.

The SAS captain and his team were the last to leave. After their rescue of Rachel they had been given permission to join the team watching the park. Their unseen presence had been a big comfort, especially to Rachel, who knew and trusted in their capabilities. Now, with their job done and nobody to tell them what to do or where to go, they enjoyed a few moments of freedom and hung around to pay their respects to the two Displacers who they had watched run and train every day.

They stayed for an hour, chatting about anything that wasn't related to the mission. They even managed to coax Sam out of his shell a bit when one of them stated that Barça weren't looking too good that year and that finally an English team was in with a chance of winning the Champions League, a statement that caused a heated argument which Sam felt he just had to join in with, even though he wasn't particularly interested in football. The sight of the four heavily-armed men in full battledress, three of them squeezed up together on a two-seat sofa in the sitting room, drinking tea from dainty cups and dunking scrounged biscuits, was amusing to say the least and even James cracked a smile every so often as he lamented years of bad fortune of his team, Millwall, in between concerned glances at Sam.

Eventually, though, it was time for them to leave as well, though, and the captain extended his hand to them both, as well as an official invitation that had come through channels from his superiors to visit Hereford whenever they wanted.

'You two are something special, we would be delighted to have you come and train with us; you have skills that we've never seen before and it would really do the lads good to go up against you.'

'Yeah, and it'll do their egos good to get their arses kicked as well!' Dumbo cut in, to the amusement and enthusiastic agreement of the rest of the team.

Rachel smiled while she shook his hand. 'Thank you, captain, we might just do that.' She didn't have the heart to tell him that she and Sam had been limiting themselves to sparring at just over half speed so as not to scare off the assassin.

'And as for you, Mr Vives, I really wish you were British so you could join us...'

Sam laughed. 'I'm half English, does that count?'

The captain chuckled. 'I don't know, but even if it doesn't, I think we would make it count for you. What do you say?'

'I appreciate the offer captain, but I already have a full time job.' Although he was flattered, Sam was more than a little disturbed that they didn't seem to be disturbed by the way he had killed a man then beaten his dead body into a pulp afterwards, an action that was deplorable at best and something that he felt should have given them pause.

'Pity.' MacAlister looked genuinely disappointed. 'But please do come down and see us some time anyway. I really want to see the look on the faces of the rest of the Regiment when they see what you can do. It's actually a damn shame we can't show them the video, but it's already been classified and taken away by Five.'

One of his men, Soapy, coughed, then glanced around the group, grinning widely. 'I grabbed a copy while those berks weren't looking, skipper.'

'Nice one, Soapy.' The captain grinned, pleased, but Sam cringed at the thought of the video making the rounds of possibly the entirety of the British Armed Forces. 'I don't know about you lads, but I need a shower. Let's go!'

The team said goodbye to Sam and Rachel, then shook James' hand one by one and thanked him for his hospitality. They trooped out into the street and piled into the black SUV which MI5 had provided for their use and took off in a squeal of tyres and gales of laughter.

Sam sighed and reached out to take Rachel's hand. They turned to go up the stairs, both desperately wanting rest and time alone together now that the danger was over.

'Oh no you don't, go and sit down, both of you. Now!'

James' harsh voice brought them back to reality and they turned to see the scowl on his face.

Chastised, they went into the sitting room and took the sofa opposite James' favourite armchair.

James sat perched on the edge of his seat, leaning forwards his elbows propped on his knees, and went back to staring at Sam.

The seconds passed slowly and both Sam and Rachel started to shift uncomfortably. It was a relief when he started talking, but the emotion was extremely short-lived.

'I read the report for that Displacement you did before you left for the summer, Sam, such as it was.' He chuckled mirthlessly, and to Sam's shock, almost cruelly. '"1100 to 1124AD. Iran. Training". It's not exactly the most thorough of reports, is it? I know you were trying to hide what you did from everyone, but I'm not stupid; I'm an Elder and I have a bit of an idea about history. I also know you and it wasn't exactly hard to work out what you were doing!'

The words came out in a rush, angrily, and the old man paused, panting for breath. When he continued there was a note of sorrow in his voice that tore into Sam's heart.

'I almost don't want to know what Hassan al-Sabbāh did to you... Bloody hell, Sam, of all the people you could have chosen to study under. What the hell did you think you could learn from him that you couldn't from anyone else?'

James shook his head and waved his hand dismissively to stop Sam when he began to reply. He set his jaw determinedly, obviously wanting to say everything that he had on his mind before giving his grandson a chance to defend himself, no matter how much it hurt both of them. 'I don't want to know, boy! But whatever it was, it was unnecessary, damn it! I can see how different you are and it's killing me. There was no need for you to put yourself through that, to make yourself into...into... whatever that *animal* was in that video. We would have found a way to beat John without you *destroying your humanity!* The old man swallowed, forcing back tears that were only partially from anger. 'And so many years, Sam... I told you what that could do to you.'

He sighed and dropped his head into his hands, but when he lifted it again after only a few seconds any grief he'd been feeling had completely gone and his face twisted with a fury that was frightening for its absolute unfamiliarity. 'But do you know what the worst thing is?'

Sam could only shake his head mutely, cowed by the force in the old man.

'The worst thing is that, knowing how important she is to you and your destiny, you didn't take Rachel with you. You didn't even consult her, did you?'

He stared a challenge at Sam, daring him to lie, but Sam found that he couldn't and he just looked down at the floor, unable to hold the old man's gaze.

'There's a reason why you two are together and your ignoring it risks everything. *Stop being so bloody selfish for once in your life, boy!*

James' roar was deafening in the small room and the power behind it was astonishing, as if somehow he'd harnessed his powers and channelled them into his voice, but, even before the brief echoes had faded, the Elder had deflated, sagging back in his armchair as the anger fled from him. He suddenly looked old and tired again, as if the effort had taken an immense toll on him. 'I don't want you *ever* doing something like that on your own again you could have ruined *everything*. And that's an order, got it?'

'Well, I did try to make him see sense the day he came back...' Rachel broke in, but instantly regretted it when James turned his attention to her.

'And as for you, young lady, you're not getting away scot-free from this! You know perfectly well how stubborn and pig-headed this damn boy can be and you can't drop the ball like you did over the summer. I don't care what he thinks is best for himself, you should have been in Barcelona those months to stop him from being so stupid.'

'I...' Rachel didn't quite know what to say, but she was saved from the necessity of searching for a way to apologise when James held up his hands and forced a smile.

'Having said all that, everything has turned out alright so far and, while I don't condone what Sam did today, especially not how far he took it, I can at least see how that kind of skill might have its use.' The old man sighed again. 'I'm sorry I lost my temper, but I'm just so terrified of losing you too, my boy. And there are other ways of doing that than just doing something stupid and getting yourself killed - I've already had two good friends leave themselves in the past, but whatever that... that... *thing* was in the video, that wasn't you. I don't know what the old man of the mountain did to you, but that wasn't the Sam Vives I know and love.'

Sam's voice was barely audible in the room when he replied. 'That's because it isn't me. It's something that I let in to do the stuff that I can't.'

James stared at Sam with his mouth open for a few seconds before shaking his head. 'I'm not even going to ask how that works.'

'Believe me, Grandad, I don't want this thing in me any more than anyone else and, trust me, I will force it out when all this is over.'

Sam hesitantly turned to look at Rachel, worried what he might find. She had seen the Beast for the first time that day, but instead of finding disgust or rejection because of what he'd done and what he'd become, she inexplicably still had love in her eye and he held her gaze as he spoke. 'I didn't tell Rachel this, but my decision to go on that Displacement wasn't a reaction to Andrew's death and it wasn't motivated by revenge or a desire to learn how to kill; I did it because it *felt* right. When I heard someone at school talking about Alamut and the assassins, something inside me just told me that was what I had to do.'

'Bloody hell, what are they teaching you at school these days?'

Sam and Rachel laughed, expecting it to be a joke, but were mildly surprised when they saw he was deadly serious.

Rachel grinned fondly at the Elder. 'It's from a video game about assassins in different moments of history. John spoke about it many times, it was one of his favourite games, don't you remember?'

James huffed and waved his hand dismissively. 'Oh, I haven't listened to a word John says in about ten years. Which I'm rather glad about now.'

They all laughed this time, the mood in the room lightening bit by bit.

'Well, I must say I'm just a bit less peed off with you now I know you felt this was what you needed to do; if there's one thing we've all learnt about you over the last year or so, it's that your instincts are usually right, even if it does always seem at the time that you're doing the stupidest thing possible.'

James and Rachel laughed again, but Sam gave them an annoyed look. 'Can we turn serious for a minute, please?'

James gave Rachel a last grin then hid his smile. 'Of course, lad.'

'There is one thing that has been bothering me through this whole thing; why didn't the Elders feel it coming? It seems you can feel everything else, so why not this? I mean it's a pretty big change that John was trying to make and destroying Headquarters isn't exactly insignificant.'

'You want to answer him or shall I?'

The way that James rolled his eyes at Rachel immediately told Sam that he was being ignorant again.

Rachel chuckled and just waved for James to go ahead.

'We can't feel the present, Sam, just the past; the present isn't history yet.'

'Oh, OK.' Sam felt pretty stupid, a feeling that wasn't eased at all when Rachel leaned over and whispered "duh" in his ear.

He pushed her away with a smile, then looked back at his grandfather. 'So what happens now? What do we do, Grandad?'

Even though this most recent nightmare was over, Sam was feeling lost and he realised that he desperately needed someone to put him back on course. For Displacer matters that person had always been Andrew, but it felt right to ask James for help.

'Despite everything that has happened over the last week or so nothing has changed, Sam. We continue as before, as we always have.'

'Without Headquarters?'

In the time that they had been confined to James' house an inspection had been carried out on the building. Unfortunately, the inspectors found far more damage to the supports of the building than had originally been documented and had condemned it. MI5 contractors would begin emptying the building as soon as Society members were free to supervise them and plans were already being drawn up to rebuild, but it would never be the same, even if they made it identical.

James huffed. 'Since when have our powers ever depended on a building? It's a blow to morale losing a part of our own history like this, but it's not going to stop us from doing our job. We'll just have to find somewhere else to meet and get drunk while repairs are done, won't we?'

He struggled to his feet, grabbed his cane and started towards the door. 'Now, I know you're both tired and need a rest, but that's going to have to wait; I think we owe it to our friends to head over to the hospital and see how they are doing. There should be a car waiting for us outside; I asked Mr Firth to leave one at our disposal. You two go and tell them I'll be right out after I've had a wee, please.'

The ride to the hospital was short, uneventful and comfortable. James sat in the front of the car with the driver in order to leave Sam and Rachel on their own and they spent the time cuddled up together as much as they could while still keeping their seatbelts on. They didn't speak, they just clung to each other for comfort, simply letting the presence of the other calm and heal them.

They hadn't been to see their friends since the day of the bombing and things had changed vastly in the hospital.

Instead of a ward, it now had more the aspect of a social club than a hospital, especially since most of the doctors and nurses were no longer needed and had disappeared back to where they'd come from. The protective screens had been recessed into the floor, making it an entirely less frightening place, the beds had been pushed closer together and there were books and newspapers scattered around, speaking to how the Displacers had made themselves comfortable. There were no members in the ward when the three arrived, though, and instead they found them in a dining room to one side, which was just as large as the one at Grosvenor Place, but even better appointed; it was meant for royalty after all.

It was just coming up to lunch time and the members were seated around two long tables, talking animatedly as they waited for their food, but silence fell immediately when the newcomers walked in.

Sam and Rachel tried to work it out afterwards, but neither of them could pinpoint who had started the applause, it had just broken out spontaneously and swelled until everybody was on their feet and crowding around. The celebration was somewhat restrained, though; none of them had forgotten that two members had lost their lives, and after the initial surge the noise died down quickly. After only a minute, the members retook their seats and silence fell as all eyes turned expectantly towards James, waiting for him to confirm what they had only heard snippets of from the MI5 personnel.

The old man stood at the end of the tables and looked around, taking in the sadness, the despair, but also the hope that was beginning to blossom in their eyes. He opened his mouth to address them, but was interrupted by a knock at the door. He chuckled and shook his head before calling out.

'Come!'

A young-looking MI5 agent, barely older than Sam and Rachel, came in. He glanced wide-eyed at the people staring at him and swallowed, almost managing to look nervous. He held a large thick envelope out to James. 'Sorry to bother you, sir, but a, uh, letter came for you.'

James raised an eyebrow and took the envelope.

The man swallowed again and almost ran from the room.

James looked down at the letter and his eyes widened. He held it up to the room and showed them the blob of red wax on it that was clearly imprinted with the Queen's seal.

After making sure that everybody had had a chance to see it, he broke it open and pulled out the contents.

It was a letter, folded in half. The paper was so thick and stiff that James actually had to put his walking stick to one side and use both hands to hold it open, but eventually he revealed a red coat of arms with the words "Buckingham Palace" underneath and a neat handwritten message.

He cleared his throat and read, his voice cracking with emotion.

'Dear friends, we have been apprised of the despicable events of the past week and their subsequent resolution and I wish to express to you my deepest condolence at your losses.

'One considers an attack on the Honourable Society of Displacers to be an attack on one's own person and, as such, be assured that all efforts will continue to be made to find and punish the perpetrators, wherever they may be.

'I was also sorry to hear of the damage to your property. There are premises of mine that may be suitable to your needs and I would like to offer them to you as a temporary measure, while repairs are being made. I fear they may not be as comfortable as your delightful Headquarters, but I would be honoured if you would accept them as a token of my gratitude.

'As always you have my wholehearted support and if there is anything that I, my government, or my security forces can do to aid you, then you need but ask it of us. Our full resources are at your disposal.

'Please tell Master Vives that my thoughts are with him, but I am confident he and Miss Evans will be able to see us through such difficult times. When the current crisis is over, they should pay a visit to us at the palace with Mr Hudson and Miss Curran; I would be delighted to have you all for afternoon tea.

'My very best wishes to you all. Elizabeth R.'

James was in tears when he finished and he held the paper at arm's length as he scrubbed his jacket sleeve across his face, making sure that he didn't drip water onto it.

Sam knew his grandfather was a staunch royalist and a letter from Her Majesty, especially a hand-written one that mentioned him by name, would obviously mean a lot to him. He gently took it from him and handed it to Rachel for safekeeping before wrapping his arms around the old man - the big, strong man who'd always been there for him as a child, but who now seemed so small and delicate.

Eventually, James pulled himself back together and extricated himself from Sam's clutches before blowing his nose on an embroidered handkerchief.

Sam smiled at him. 'I thought you said the Queen didn't know who I was?'

James glared at him, glad for an excuse to recover his gruffness. 'I didn't want you getting any more big-headed than you already are, boy.'

The Elder looked around the group, scowling at them, challenging them to make a comment about his momentary weakness. There were a few grins, but they were swiftly hidden behind hands, and he nodded in satisfaction. 'Right then! I'm starving! What's the food like in this dump?'

The food was excellent. It was even up to Richard's standards and had been for the entire time the Society had been confined in the ward. This made Rachel, Sam and James rather jealous because they had been cooking for themselves in James' tiny kitchen, unable to even order food.

Dylan was sitting on the opposite side of the table to Sam and Rachel and he leaned in towards them after the hospital staff serving the food had left. 'You were right, MI5 had clothes to match mine, had my hair cut and styled, and everything and when I spoke to my parents on Skype they had no idea anything had happened to me! Agent Brown even sorted things out so that nobody knows I've been here every day since. Neither my parents or my school know I've been here goofing off and playing video games!'

Sam laughed. 'Told you!

Rachel didn't laugh, she just lifted her chin and looked at Dylan, going into "teacher mode" as Sam called it. 'So, did anything happen that I should know about?'

The boy straightened, the gleeful grin immediately disappearing as he met Rachel's gaze with a very adult composure. 'Nothing to report, really; everything went smoothly. Well, there were a couple of mild panic attacks and a few people needed some cheering up, but nothing serious and Lisa took over after a few hours anyway.'

Dylan was making little of his involvement in the care of the group, but Sam knew that the first few hours after the trauma must have been very difficult for him, even with the work Rachel had done before leaving. It seemed he had coped admirably, though, and there was no sign of the frightened boy Rachel had described, instead there was just the confident young man he'd become in Nepal.

While Dylan filled Rachel in on what had happened over the last week or so, Sam stuffed himself and looked around the room, taking in the faces of the Society members, assessing them and feeling their mood.

They were already recovering from the ordeal of the last few days and it wouldn't take them long to get back to normal, perhaps only a matter of weeks; tragedy was a part of the life of a Displacer and death was nothing new to any of them, with the exception of Dylan.

However, Sam was sure that they wouldn't have the luxury of even a single week; Diana had already been told there would be a mission soon and John would undoubtedly strike within days, to take advantage of any weakness he might have caused in the cowardly attack.

He would find Sam ready, though, and Sam would make sure that the rest of the Displacers were too.

CHAPTER 16
CLUBBING

Diana stood outside the warehouse in South London and looked around, puzzled; this was the address she'd been sent, the one that Laura had been given too, but there didn't seem to be anything there.

From where she was standing all she could see were a few run-down, empty-looking warehouses and a garage, where a few unsavoury-looking men were lounging on a couple of decrepit sofas under a plastic awning, sheltering from the light autumn drizzle and drinking from bottles wrapped in paper bags, despite it being only eleven in the morning. The men glanced in her direction and leered, looking her up and down briefly and laughing at a comment she couldn't hear, before going back to their drinking.

It was two weeks since Quentin had sent his message to tell her to be prepared. Two weeks of absolute silence from the Master frustration at not being able to tell her friends what he was planning.

Until the day before, when a message had arrived with just a time and a place.

She read the message one more time and used Google Maps to check the GPS coordinates she'd been provided with. Give or take a few metres she was in the right spot.

Mentally shrugging, she walked towards the single entrance of the warehouse - a metal door painted black and recessed about four feet into the wall. She looked for a bell but there wasn't one. There was, however, a small camera peering down at her from above the door.

She lifted her hand to knock, but before she could make contact with the door it swung open, revealing the huge form of Tessa backlit by red lighting.

Diana smiled up into Tessa's scowling face. 'Tessa! How are you? How are the injuries?' She put her hand on the big woman's arm and squeezed gently.

Tessa's expression softened slightly and something approaching a smile twitched her thin lips. 'I'm healing well, thank you for asking.'

Her voice, as ever, was deep and rumbling, but it was softer than usual and Diana looked up at her in concern.

'What's up?'

The big woman shrugged. 'Tristan's away with the Master, I don't like being apart from him.'

'Is that all?'

Tessa nodded, but Diana could see that it wasn't; there was something in her body and her movements that Diana had never seen before, a shakiness and uncertainty. Perhaps their encounter with Sam in Paris had unsettled them more that she thought it would have.

Tessa turned and retreated through the doorway before she could press, though, motioning for her to follow.

Beyond the door was a reception room, with a desk just inside the door with a monitor connected to the camera, and several chrome coat rails along one wall. The walls were painted black and the red glow was coming from a surprisingly intricate, wrought iron chandelier with red bulbs in it. Tessa took a clipboard from the desk and ticked Diana's name off a list.

Diana sneaked a peak at the list - there were more than a dozen names on it, over half of whom were ticked off.

'Wow... Is this all of the Illuminati? Is everyone coming?'

Tessa shrugged. 'I guess.'

Diana was completely lost for words; such a gathering broke just about every rule that the Master had put in place to keep them safe from the Displacers. Either it meant that the mission they were going on was of such difficulty that it needed all of them, or they would be affecting such huge changes that secrecy and security would no longer be needed afterwards. Whatever the Master's reasoning for bringing them all together, it didn't bode well for Sam and Rachel and she smiled at Tessa and started to head towards the door on the far side of the room, intending to look for a bathroom or somewhere private so she could send a message to them. However, before she could, the big woman stuck out a huge hand to block her way.

'Phone.'

'Sorry, what?'

Tessa held out a tray, like a smaller version of those you found in airports for going through security, and Diana saw that there were dozens of them in a cupboard behind the desk that she hadn't noticed before because it was recessed into the wall.

'No phones allowed. Also no cameras, laptops, tablets, pagers, iPods or electronic cigarettes.'

'E-cigs? Really?'

Tessa shrugged. 'That last one's just for me; they're nasty things. Hate them and the posers who use them and I don't allow them in my place.'

Diana laughed at the comment, but it was to cover her dismay. She reluctantly took out her devices and placed them in the tray, giving over her only methods of contacting her friends. She watched closely as Tessa locked the cabinet, but any hope she had of sneaking back and grabbing her phone while nobody was looking disappeared when the big woman put the key into her trouser pocket - she'd only had a couple of pick-pocketing classes with Rachel and she wasn't nearly skilled enough yet to pull off a theft like that.

Unfortunately, it looked like Sam and Rachel would have to improvise yet again - it normally turned out well for them, but they wouldn't be expecting to be confronted with so many Illuminati agents and she hoped that they would be able to cope.

'Arms up, please.'

Diana did as she was requested and Tessa patted her down, but only cursorily; she obviously didn't think her friend Diana would hide anything from her. After about five seconds she grunted in satisfaction. 'Thank you. You can go in now. We've got a few more still to come, so feel free to grab yourself a drink while you wait.' The big woman jerked her head towards the screen, where a couple of people, who Diana had never seen before, were walking towards the camera.

She nodded. 'Thanks, Tessa.'

Diana went through the door on the opposite side of the room to the entrance, then along a short corridor and through another door, but then she came to an abrupt halt at the sight of the main area of the warehouse.

It wasn't a warehouse after all, it was a nightclub. A very *specialised* nightclub.

It was a BDSM dungeon.

The stark white working lights were on, which they wouldn't be when the club was open for business, and the equipment and furniture around the huge room, much of which was designed to restrain or cause pain, was brightly illuminated, not hidden in enigmatic shadows like it would normally be.

Far from shocking her, Diana looked around in interest, taking in the decor, the various stations around the walls, and the oval-shaped stainless steel bar in the middle of the room where Tessa had set out the drinks. She had played in a few clubs over the past few years, exploring her "dark side" as she called it, and she enjoyed wielding a whip just as much as the next girl, but she'd never been entirely comfortable with giving pain, no matter how much the other person wanted or needed it. Perhaps it had been her instincts as a nurse coming out, but she had never quite been able to get into the sadistic Dominatrix mentality and had since found better ways to let off steam with Sam and Rachel. Although, now that she came to think of it, she wasn't going to rule out donning her latex and leather at some point for an interesting night with her friends...

A group of men and women, who she assumed were all Illuminati agents, were huddled together at the far side of the room. There were surprisingly few of them. Granted, Tristan wasn't there, Emily Clarkwell was dead and nobody had seen hide nor hair of Tuttle since the trip to Nepal, but - she did a quick count in her head - *twelve* wasn't many if they were the entirety of the Illuminati. She wondered if perhaps there was another group Leaping from somewhere else or if there was a team in reserve, but immediately dismissed the notion; this mission had the feeling of an all or nothing gesture. It stank of desperation.

She went to the bar and fixed herself a vodka and coke at the bar, then sipped at it while she studied them. They were a very mixed bag - a few looked like they were in their late twenties or early thirties, but most were very young, a couple perhaps only fourteen or fifteen. Almost all of them, including Laura, who was the only one she recognised apart from Quentin, were standing silently and uncomfortably in a loose group, but three, predictably the youngest-looking ones, had squeezed onto a leather sofa - the only remotely normal-looking piece of furniture in the room. She saw the metal rings attached to the arms and back of the sofa and grinned; they probably didn't realise the uses that the seat had been put to if they'd voluntarily chosen to sit there.

Unsurprisingly, Quentin looked completely at home in the club. He had wandered off from the group and was inside a small roped off area around a Saint Andrew's cross, fingering the chains with one hand while waving a cat o' nine tails in his other, making it swish through the air. He had a cruel look on his face, as if he were imagining having someone bound to the cross and using the whip on them.

Diana's lip curled in distaste; if there was one person in the world who had no business being in a BDSM environment, one that was built on trust and where "safe, sane, and consensual" was the motto, it was Quentin.

'Price!'

Tessa had entered the room with a few more strangers and the big woman stalked across the room to where Quentin was standing. His cruel expression disappeared, replaced by one of alarm as he saw the big woman coming towards him.

She didn't hit him or anything, though, she just snatched the whip out of his hand, then pulled him by the arm away from the cross and out of the cordoned off area.

Price rounded on her, rubbing his arm, about to reprimand her, but instantly thought better of it when she didn't back down and just stood staring at him with her hands on her hips, refusing, for once, to be cowed by his authority.

'My club, my rules, Price, and I told you: leave the toys alone.'

'Oh, well. Then I suppose I'm just going to have to come back when the club is open, then, aren't I? I'm sure I'll have no problem persuading someone to let me play with them.' He shrugged. 'It's not really my thing, but I can see how it would be fun to make someone scream.'

'I wouldn't let a sub get anywhere near you.'

'Well, that wouldn't be your choice to make, would it?' He laughed, knowing that he was right, that it would be up to a submissive to accept him or not, then her responsibility to use a safe word if he went too far.

He grinned at Tessa for a good few seconds, letting the point sink in, then deliberately looked around the room, nodding appreciatively. 'Thank you for opening my eyes to a whole new world of possibilities.'

'I'm looking forward to punishing you after Vives defeats you again. Maybe I'll bring some of these things along and teach you exactly what those *possibilities* are.' Tessa's words were punctuated by a loud percussive noise as the thick wooden handle of the whip snapped in her hand.

Quentin flinched at the sound, expecting her to strike him, but the blow never came and he relaxed, visibly relieved. He took some time to regain his composure by straightening his clothing, pulling his Star Wars t-shirt back into place from where it had rucked up slightly while he'd been swinging the whip, then smirked and dropped his voice low to snarl at her. 'That's never going to happen again. The Master and I have a few nasty surprises in store for Vives this time. He doesn't stand a chance. We're going to destroy him *and* those fools he works with once and for all and when we get back I'm sure that the Master won't mind if I deal with you. We won't need people like you again once the Displacers are out of the picture.'

He glanced at the broken whip dangling from her huge hand, then the cross beside them and grinned evilly. 'Perhaps I'll even give you a taste of your own medicine - see how you like it.'

He laughed then turned and sidled casually over to the sofa from where the group had been watching the whole exchange. He jumped up onto a padded leather spanking bench so that he towered over the group and clapped his hands to get everyone's attention, even though he already had it.

Tessa growled at his misuse of her furniture, but he ignored her.

'Hello everyone and welcome. First of all I'd like to thank Tessa, or should I say *Mistress Tessa* for the use of her club for today's mission. She has sacrificed her one piece of privacy, the one place she kept secret from even her group leader, to give us a suitable place for what I promise will be our finest accomplishment. So, thank you, my dear, and I hope our presence in your, uh, *lovely* place, doesn't taint the wonderful *vibe* you've got going on.'

He chuckled unkindly, but nobody joined in with him.

'What's the mission, Quentin?'

Diana had seen the fury on Tessa's face at his further mockery, seen her weight shift forward slightly as she prepared to leap to the attack, and had decided she needed to diffuse the situation before something happened. However, as soon as the words were out of her mouth she realised that she should have just let Quentin keep mocking Tessa; it would have been an easy, and fun, way to stop the mission going ahead.

'The mission, Miss Birch, is secret. To prevent any leaks only I and the Master know the plan and I will only give everyone their instructions once we get to our destination.'

'You're going to take us all back? On your own? Is that even possible?'

'Of course it is, for someone with my talent.' He smiled at her condescendingly and she seethed inside, but returned his smile, refusing to let him see what she really felt about him.

Quentin looked at his watch. 'Tessa, are we connected?'

Tessa snarled as she nodded, but Quentin didn't seem to notice and just looked over his shoulder at a security camera mounted high on the wall behind him.

'Smile for the Master, boys and girls!' Quentin laughed, then jumped down from the bench. 'All right, let's do this!' He looked around the club critically. 'The bad thing about this place is that there aren't enough decent chairs to go around, so we're going to have to do this like the damn boy scouts.' He pointed to an open area next to the bar. 'Everybody get in a big circle and sit down on the floor over there.'

Nobody moved, they just stared at him, not quite sure if he was joking or not.

He clapped his hands again and shouted. 'Now, people! Come on!'

The Illuminati slowly began moving into position and Diana took note of which people obeyed without complaint, which grumbled but did as they were told and which looked like they resented taking Quentin's orders, filing the information away for later. She was also very interested to note that Tessa didn't join them, but stood at the side of the room with her arms crossed, watching them, without much apparent interest. It looked like she was just waiting for them to do their business and leave.

It took a while, but eventually everyone was sitting in a rough circle in the middle of the club and again everyone looked to Quentin for further instructions and he shook his head in exasperation. 'For god's sake! Do I really have to tell you how to do this? Join hands and let's go already!'

As she joined hands with the people on either side of her, Diana briefly met the worried gaze of Laura. She gave her a small smile and an encouraging nod before she closed her eyes and started building the energy inside her.

Two minutes later she felt the shift as they Leapt into the past.

Diana immediately opened her eyes and released the hands of the people on either side of her. She stood up, quickly followed by everyone else, and looked around, curious as to when and where they were.

They were in the garden of a house, sitting on a well-tended lawn. By the architecture, the coal-fire smog and poor air quality it was most likely London in the industrial age.

Diana took in the style of clothes she and the others were wearing and realised where Quentin had brought them.

'Victorian London *again*? They know us here, Quentin.'

'This is twenty years after we were here last, Miss Birch. It's 1899, early May if I've got my aim right. The policeman, Abberline, that the Vives boy enlisted to help him is long since retired and the memory of us has faded.

'Then what are we here for? There's nothing important happening right now, to my knowledge. Not in London anyway.'

'Miss Birch...' Quentin shook his head and tutted. 'All will become clear in good time, for now.... please just shut up.'

There were some chuckles at that and Diana coloured in anger, but she bit her tongue and said nothing more.

'Come along children, let's get settled.'

Quentin led them up the garden path towards the house. 'This is one of my family's holdings. It's empty this year because my ancestor and his family are away and have taken most of their servants with them - according to the Price family records he laid out a small fortune on a world cruise. We have the place to ourselves until the middle of next year, but our mission isn't going to take us *nearly* that long.'

CHAPTER 17
FAMILIARITY BREEDS

When Sam opened his eyes he found himself in very familiar, but subtly different, surroundings.

It was definitely the sitting room of the town house in London where they had lived while battling Quentin, but the curtains had been changed, the rugs were new, the wallpaper was older and there were a few more souvenirs on the mantelpiece over the fire.

'Where are we, Sam?' Dylan released Sam's hand and looked around interestedly, taking in the gas lamps and the lush furniture. He stroked the leather of the huge chesterfield sofa that they were all squeezed onto.

'It's London in Victorian...' Sam stopped suddenly when he realised that something was wrong. He twisted and craned his head to look around the rest of the room. 'Where's everyone else?'

Rachel flexed her hand where she had been holding onto Lisa, peering at it as if it were to blame. 'Maybe we got separated. Like you and I did when we first came here, remember? You were off having a good time with Conan-Doyle and Wilde while I was stuck here organising your dinner...'

Sam smiled at her. 'You still haven't forgiven me for that, have you? Despite the fact that we dined with them both dozens of times afterwards.'

'Never.' She grinned briefly at him, then shrugged, quickly getting back to the topic at hand. 'They'll turn up, just like you did.'

The two were all smiles, but the disappearance of the rest of their team was troubling.

The Displacers had made an effort to make as many people available as possible but, with Anne's death and the injuries from the bombing less than two weeks ago, the list of active Displacers available was lamentably short. In the end the team had amounted to just Dylan, Lisa, Julia and Hamish, but it was a bigger army than Sam was used to having. Now, though, it seemed that is was going to be just the two of them and Dylan.

Something occurred to Rachel and she sighed. 'Of course, there is another possible reason why they're not here: we had no idea when we were Displacing to, so we couldn't look to see if people were actually available to come. The others may already have a presence in the time-line.'

'Oh! Which means they wouldn't be able to come.' Sam echoed her sigh.

Dylan broke in, trying to cheer them up. 'Well, you've got me! And Laura will be around somewhere - she and Diana are on our side even if they're with the enemy.'

'I know, kid, it's just, with what the Elders have been feeling recently, I really wanted to have more people with us when we walked into the unknown.'

Sam was understandably worried. The Elders had been working around the clock since the death of the assassin, running around in a state of near panic; they were feeling a disturbance in the time-line that was bigger than anything any of them had ever experienced before and their anxiety had rubbed off onto the rest of the society. Sam and Rachel had tried not to let it affect them too much, but it had been impossible to ignore completely, especially since they'd been training with Lisa, who was more anxious than anyone else at facing her first real test as the leader of the Displacers.

Sam glanced at the sideboard near the door; when they'd last been in the house, a newspaper had been delivered every morning, and that day was no exception. He went to grab it, reading the date as he came back.

'May the 20th, 1899. That's...' he made a quick calculation. 'Eight years after we left. What are we doing back here? I mean, I love Victorian London and being the famous detective, Sir Sam Vives, but we've been here already. Why can't the Illuminati go somewhere new?'

Rachel raised an eyebrow. 'What? Like Marbella in the sixties?'

'For instance.' Sam grinned. 'Seriously, though, there's nothing that I can think of that the Illuminati could be doing here. Have either of you got anything?'

The Elders had given the Displacers going on the mission a long list of possible weak points in the time-line to memorise, along with the ways the Illuminati could attack them. There had been too much for one person to learn so they had divided it up amongst them, but they had all read the whole list at least a few times and as far as Sam could remember none of it had anything to do with London in the summer of 1899. Elsewhere in the world there were a couple of minor events taking place, like the second Boer war. However, while changing the outcome of that might have some bearing on South Africa's involvement in the Second World War, it wouldn't be nearly enough to cause the extreme feelings that the Elders were experiencing, which had been enough to give a few of them headaches.

When both Rachel and Dylan shook their heads, Sam scanned the story on the front page of the newspaper. 'The Hague Convention's going on at the moment and apparently that's a big thing. It started two days ago... I vaguely remember something about that on the list.'

He turned the newspaper round to show the article to Rachel.

She peered at it, frowning. 'Yes, it was in my part of the list, but the Elders didn't think it was very likely that...' Her eyes widened in alarm and she snatched the paper from Sam's hands. Her eyes flicked across the page as she read rapidly. 'Oh, no...'

'What?' Sam craned his neck, trying to see what she was so upset about.

She handed the paper back to him, then stabbed her finger at one of the minor stories below the fold. 'Read this.'

'Let me see.' Dylan went to stand beside Sam and together they read the column that Rachel had pointed out.

SECRET SOCIETY IN OUR MIDST!

What is the so-called "Honourable Society of Displacers"? Who are they and what is their agenda?

This reporter would like to find out, but has been refused admission to their "Headquarters" time and again.

Their strange name speaks of an unsure knowledge of English - a sure sign of foreign influence in their activities.

This publication demands to know what sinister rituals and practises go on behind the closed doors of this otherwise normal looking town house, situated right on the doorstep of our beloved Queen!

There was a picture of an all too familiar building underneath the short editorial.

Sam shared a glance with Rachel.

'What does this mean?' Dylan couldn't see the implications of the article; he had no idea what he was capable of - the subtle manipulations that were his speciality.

It was Rachel who answered him. 'It means that the very existence of the Displacers is in danger.'

Everything that James and the Elders had come up with, every single hypothesis, had been based on the assumption that the Illuminati would try to change some huge, historically important world event. They had never for one minute considered an attack on the Displacers themselves.

Dylan was confused. 'But if they destroy us, they'd destroy themselves as well, right? John was a Displacer before he created the Illuminati. If the Society is destroyed then he'll never become one of us, he'll never know half as much about history as he does now and he won't be able to make the Illuminati so strong. Maybe he'd never even find out what powers he has and wouldn't create the Illuminati at all!'

Sam couldn't help but smile as he saw Dylan trying to get his mind around the myriad of possibilities and all the likely paradoxes - he looked remarkably like Father Dougal from *Father Ted*, a comedy series that Rachel and he had binge-watched while locked in with James. Even down to the haircut.

He himself, though, was busy thanking Andrew for making him read Everett Lloyd's diaries, the ones that explored the consequences of just that type of events.

'Didn't you ever read the diaries of Everett Lloyd, your ancestor?'

'Who?'

Rachel grinned. 'I'm guessing not.'

Sam raised an eyebrow at her. 'You can talk, you've never read them either.'

'I don't need to when I've got you, do I?' She patted Sam on the arm and smirked.

Sam huffed and rolled his eyes, then turned back to Dylan. 'Everett Lloyd did a series of experiments in the 1860's and 70's which were designed to find the limits and the consequences of our abilities. I won't bore you with details - if you want those you can talk to an Elder.'

'Or if you want the *short* version you can read the books.' Rachel added with a grin.

'Yes, thank you. Anyway, the last in the series of diaries, the volume that is less well known because it doesn't normally affect us, deals with paradoxes.'

'You mean like in *Back to the Future*, where Marty saves his father from being run over, then his mother falls in love with him.'

'Um, I'm not sure...'

'Yeah! He starts to cease to exist because his mother never falls in love with his father, and nobody stops to think that if Marty didn't exist in the first place, then who pushed his father out of the way of the car.'

'Um, I guess...'

Rachel shook her head. 'I think we should kill the boy now; he's turning into John. Next he'll be quoting *The Matrix* and calling you *The One* and that's a very dark path...'

Sam gave her an evil look, but she just stuck her tongue out at him. He sighed. 'Ignore her, please, Dylan.'

The boy just laughed; he'd gotten more than used to their antics in Nepal.

'Anyway,' Sam continued. 'Everett Lloyd theorised that the time-line will act to protect itself, so that, no matter the change, things would still make sense in the present. That means that if even if the Illuminati destroy the Displacers here, everything will work out for them.'

Dylan was still sceptical. 'How?'

Sam shrugged. 'I don't know.'

'It's a mystery!' Rachel chipped in, grinning madly.

Sam laughed; she was quoting one of Violeta's favourite lines from *Shakespeare in Love*. 'Well, maybe not a mystery, but it's beyond me to explain or predict it and all this talk of paradoxes and consequences is giving me a headache. Why don't we go out and have a wander around? We can see how much London has changed since we were here last.'

Rachel clapped her hands excitedly. 'Can we take Dylan to the Savoy? I wonder if there's a Gilbert and Sullivan playing...'

'I think a meal would be good, but we don't want to scare the boy off too soon! Why don't we leave your operetta obsession for another day when we're not so tired from Displacing.'

'Aw... Alright then.' Rachel pretended to sulk, but Sam knew she was actually looking forwards to spending some more time in the Victorian era; they'd had such a wonderful time here. *After* they had defeated the Illuminati of course.

Sam offered Rachel his hand. 'My lady. Shall we promenade?'

Rachel allowed him to help her up off the sofa. 'Why thank you, good sir. We shall indeed.'

They started out of the room, arm in arm, with Dylan following closely behind.

In the hallway they were met by a young woman, a maid, about the same age as Dylan. It wasn't Mary, the woman who had been their maid before, but they all knew instinctively who she was: Mary's daughter who had taken over from her when the older woman had become the housekeeper.

'We're going out for the evening…' Sam hesitated as he struggled to dredge up the girl's name from the everyday information that they always got when they went into the past. It was something that he had problems with, but that came naturally to most Displacers. '…uh, Florence. Don't wait up for us.'

'Right you are, sir.' The maid curtseyed and gave Sam and Rachel a sweet smile. However, she gave Dylan a much more suggestive look as he passed. 'Have a good evening, Master Dylan…'

The boy blushed, grabbed his coat and hurried out of the door as quickly as he could.

Sam tactfully waited until they were outside before bursting into laughter.

London was much the same as it had been and they encountered many of the people that they had gotten to know while they had been there, all of whom greeted them as if they had never left. They were saddened to hear that Oscar Wilde had left the country a couple of years before, after being persecuted and imprisoned for his sexual orientation; they'd had so many remarkable and hilarious conversations with him that they'd been hoping to run into him again.

They dined in one of their favourite restaurants, but Sam and Rachel were tired and Dylan, who was their nephew, apparently, was almost falling asleep in his food, so they finished early then caught a cab back to the house in Pimlico, determined to get some rest and make a fresh start the next day.

They settled comfortably in their familiar bedroom, as always discarding the awful nightclothes that were set out for them, and got into bed naked.

They paused, half under the covers, and smiled as the sound of Dylan snoring carried to them from the guest room down the hallway. It had become a very familiar sound in the Himalayas and was almost comforting - signifying as it did a contented adolescent resting peacefully.

Too tired to do anything else, they curled up in each other's arms and fell directly asleep.

CHAPTER 18
RUDE AWAKENINGS

Sam and Rachel were so exhausted that the intruders were already in the hallway outside their bedroom before they became aware of them.

They rolled out of opposite sides of the bed just as the door opened and the first of them slipped in. They didn't recognise them, but they didn't have to; there was only one reason to sneak into their bedroom in the middle of the night.

They were Illuminati.

Running silently on bare feet, Sam hit top speed in two strides and leapt at the first man through the door. He thrust his foot out in front of him, striking the man in the head, breaking his neck and propelling his body into the woman who had been following close behind.

They crashed to the floor in a pile, which gave Rachel the space and the distraction she needed to leap over them and take a third intruder, another man, with a flying punch to the throat before he could even come through the door. She threw her whole weight behind it and her victim collapsed at her feet, making awful choking noises.

Three Illuminati were down in the space of less than two seconds, but there were three more waiting for them in the hallway and, by the sounds of fighting coming from Dylan's room, there was at least one more attacking him, if not more.

Sam picked himself up off of the floor and moved to Rachel's side.

It was in that moment he realised they were naked.

'Just like Sparta, eh?' He growled from the side of his mouth without taking his eyes off the enemy.

'I was a boy in Sparta, remember? In a way this is a first for me...' There was humour in her words, but she was feeling real fear for one of the first times in her life as she assessed the tactical situation and saw how untenable it was.

The Illuminati were armed and at the far end of the hallway. It would be impossible to dodge their fire in the narrow space and the only way out was past them - all they needed to do was close the distance until there was nowhere to hide.

Sam didn't see her expression and just grinned. 'Doesn't matter, they won't live to remember.'

He sank into himself as he charged, finding the Beast joyfully waiting for release. He opened the floodgates and let go, giving himself over.

The Beast surveyed its prey and snarled its disappointment. These weren't warriors; it could taste the fear pouring off of them, but the weapons, the guns they held made them deadly threats and they had to be dealt with accordingly.

The first three attackers had also had guns, but they had been overcome so quickly that they hadn't had time to even level them. The three in the hallway had more of a chance, but they wasted it in their panic as they saw death running at them.

Three badly aimed shots rang out almost simultaneously, deafening in the confined space.

Rachel rolled back into the room, her reactions were such that she had seen fingers tightening on triggers and had easily gotten out of the way.

The Beast didn't bother dodging, it just continued its charge. It felt something tug at its side, but didn't deign to acknowledge either it or the blossoming pain.

The Illuminati saw death coming for them and turned to run.

Too late.

Two steps ahead of Rachel now, the Beast took two of them down with a single leap, a hand on the back of their necks bearing its victims to the floor, where their heads cracked and blood splattered on the hard wood.

The delay let Rachel catch up and she flew past, pursuing the last one, a woman, who had reached the top of the stairs.

Seeing that she couldn't escape, the Illuminati woman turned and tried to lift the pistol with a hand that was shaking wildly.

Rachel took pity on her and slapped the pistol away while simultaneously throwing an uppercut to her jaw.

The woman's eyes crossed and she slumped to the floor.

Behind Rachel, the Beast growled, seeing its prey taken from it, but the sounds of a fight still going on nearby caught its attention and promised fresh fun. It spun and leapt through the door next to it.

Something - a whisper of cloth, or a footfall, or the breath of one of the two men who had crept into his room - woke Dylan up just as the knife started its slow descent towards his throat.

Seeing his victim waking, the man leaning over him changed tactics and immediately plunged the dagger downwards. Reactions honed in the Chelsea dojo and Nepal saved Dylan's life and he kicked out at the man, even as he tried to block the strike. He couldn't stop the knife, though, and only managed to alter its trajectory, but that was enough to keep him alive for a little longer and, instead of going into his heart, it plunged into his biceps, leaving his left arm dangling useless at his side.

Their plan to kill Dylan in his sleep thwarted, the attackers fell back on brute force and one pulled out a large truncheon and started to pummel the boy, while the other backed off to draw a pistol. Fortunately for Dylan, the foresight of the gun got caught in the fabric of the second man's pocket. Ultimately it wouldn't matter, though, because in between exhaustion from the Displacement and blood loss from his arm, Dylan couldn't do much to defend himself. He could do even less after his other arm was broken whilst blocking a blow from the truncheon that would have shattered his skull.

By the time the Beast burst in, the boy was barely conscious and his attacker was lining up a finishing blow that he wouldn't be able to avoid.

The Beast smelled the blood, saw a friend in distress and roared its rage.

It provided only a momentary distraction, but it was enough for Dylan to survive again - he threw himself sideways, away from the swing of the club, and crashed into his bedside table, screaming in pain at his injuries. He tumbled to the floor and fought against waves of blackness to roll out of harm's way against the bed where he lay, unable to move, and watched what he thought was his friend and mentor leap to the attack.

The Beast dismissed the man struggling with the gun as the lesser threat and went for the one with the truncheon. The assailant pivoted smoothly to face the incoming danger and the Beast took note of the movements, analysed them in a split second and came to the conclusion that this was perhaps a worthy opponent at last.

The Beast's charge was met and used against it and it found itself rolling across the floor to crash into the bedside table, completing the work towards its destruction that Dylan had started.

Ignoring the splinters in its back, the Beast was on its feet in an instant and it charged again, grinning wildly.

The fury and speed with which the Beast leapt back at him surprised the man and the instant's hesitation it caused was sufficient to give the Beast a far easier kill than it had anticipated. From start to finish the fight had taken four seconds and the Beast was sorely disappointed.

Thoroughly annoyed, its eyes settled on the last attacker left standing.

It was no longer in the mood for merciful death, it wanted to play.

The man with the gun had paused to watch the fight, but now that the Beast's attention was turned on him he renewed his efforts. The pocket was now ripped to shreds and the pistol was almost free. He only needed a few more seconds

A hand came down over the one fumbling with the gun and the man froze and looked up into the cold black eyes of the Beast, who grinned as it twisted the weapon to point slightly inwards and squeezed.

The Illuminati jumped as the gun went off in his hand, then started screaming.

The Beast let him fall and watched with glee as the blood slowly started spreading around his victim's hips.

It enjoyed the sight for a few seconds, but then put the man out of his misery with a stomp.

It growled, not yet satisfied; there had been no challenge to find here, but there were foes that were yet breathing in the corridor outside who might at least provide some sport.

It turned, but found the door blocked by a woman who was not quite as big or as powerful as it was, but who still exuded power. Its black eyes flashed and it growled, curling its lips in a warning - a promise of violence to whoever tried to stand in its way.

'Sam.'

It snarled in response, but the sound died in its throat as the Beast retreated, repelled by the concern and love that it saw in the face of the woman.

'Come back to me, Sam.'

The Beast fled, howling, but sensed that it would be needed again before too long and just had to bide its time until called upon again.

Sam straightened from a fighting crouch and blinked. With a single glance he took in the broken bodies, the blood splattered on every surface and the wide-eyed Dylan looking up at him from the floor and put two and two together.

Rachel's hand came down on his shoulder and he cringed back and turned away, not wanting to meet her eyes.

'Go and see if anyone needs medical attention out there, please and if you see Florence, send her to get help; we're going to need the police. Oh, and if anyone *is* left alive, tie them up and hide them in the spare room; I want to question them if I can. While you do that, I'll see to Dylan.'

She nodded and with a final concerned look at him she left the room.

He turned to Dylan, who had managed to struggle up onto his bed and was leaning against the headboard, staring at him.

Sam went to the side of the bed and Dylan's eyes flickered downwards, away from his face.

'You do know you're walking around naked, right?' The boy's voice was weak, his face was white and he was shaking. The knife had come out of his arm in the fight and blood was staining the pillow red under him.

'Best way to fight, you should try it some time.' Sam smiled encouragingly at him as he ripped a strip off a sheet and began to bind the wound; it was the most life-threatening of Dylan's injuries and he would bleed to death soon if it wasn't stopped.

Dylan looked at the broken bodies on the floor. 'Is Laura...? Was she...?'

'No.' Sam shook his head, but as soon as he'd said it, he realised that he wasn't actually sure. He just had to trust that the Beast would know who was an enemy and who wasn't.

He had a sudden image of Laura lying broken and bleeding in the hallway, savaged by the Beast, but he shoved it out of his mind and focussed on the matter at hand, quickly assessing the boy's injuries. Aside from the broken arm and the stab wound, which were bad enough, his collarbone was badly broken - the boy was very definitely out of the fight for several weeks at least.

Dylan saw his fate in Sam's expression. 'Don't send me home. Please.'

'You need to be seen to. You need blood and if you don't get that collarbone sorted you might have long-lasting problems; it's completely out of place.'

'But I want to be here for Laura...'

Sam sighed and spoke gently to him. 'I know you do, Dylan, but you can't, sorry.'

Dylan sat up, wanting to protest further, but his eyes crossed and he fell back, teeth gritted and panting against the agony. It took him quite a while to recover, but eventually he smiled weakly up at Sam. 'OK, maybe I do.'

'Do you think you can Calm yourself? Or shall I run a bath?'

'I can do it.' The boy grinned. 'Three years of extreme boredom in a Buddhist monastery has to have been good for something, right?'

'Yeah, I saw you and Laura... It looked very boring indeed.'

Dylan barked with laughter. He grimaced in pain at the sudden movement, but the smile remained. 'Not as exciting as you three being together, obviously, but we did our best.'

He settled himself back and Sam helped prop him up with the bloody pillows, getting him as comfortable as possible.

'If you see Laura, tell her I love her and I'll see her soon, please.'

'I will.'

Sam smiled at him then stepped back to watch. He was suitably impressed when the boy managed to completely obviate the pain he was in and find the necessary concentration to Calm himself. A minute later he was gone.

Rachel came running. 'Did I just feel...?'

She looked at the unused and made-up bed and Sam nodded in confirmation. 'It's just you and me now.'

'Isn't it always?' She shrugged. 'We've got two prisoners to deal with - the woman you knocked out in the bedroom and the girl I decked on the landing. They should both be out for a while yet, so they're not going anywhere. I've tied them up and stuffed them in a cupboard in the spare room.'

Sam nodded in satisfaction. 'Good, thank you.'

There was a scream from the corridor. Apparently, Florence, who lived in the servant's quarters in the basement, had finally worked up the courage to come and see what the noise was about.

Rachel rolled her eyes and turned to go, but Sam called her back. 'Rachel!'

She looked at him questioningly and he pulled the top sheet from the bed and tossed it to her.

'Try not to scare her too much.'

'You think my naked body is going to scare her more than the corpses on the landing?' Rachel put her hands on her hips and gave him a mock glare, daring him to comment.

Sam said nothing, though, he just took full advantage of the opportunity to appreciate a sight that he never got tired of.

Rachel gave him a full ten seconds to enjoy himself, then winked and wrapped the sheet around her before leaving the room.

It was only when Sam caught sight of the blood that had dripped on the bed while he'd taken off the sheet that he remembered the wound in his side. He looked at it in the mirror - there was a deep score above his ribs where a bullet had grazed past, leaving a deep trough which was bleeding profusely. The wound looked clean enough and it wasn't life threatening - he'd had much worse and survived - so he just tore a piece from the remaining sheet and used it to clean himself a bit before pressing it against his side as he wandered out into the corridor to see what else the Beast had done.

He had to count the number of bodies twice; he couldn't believe that the Illuminati had sent only eight people to attack them. They knew full well what Sam and Rachel were capable of and yet they had thought that would be sufficient.

Sam cursed when he realised why they had sent so few and that he had been stupid. Again.

They had walked into a trap, just like they had in South Africa, and it was one that they should have foreseen. *Of course* the Illuminati would have had spies outside the house to know when they arrived. *Of course* they knew there were only three Displacers to deal with; not only did John undoubtedly have a copy of the records from Headquarters from which he'd be able to work out a time when only Sam and Rachel would be available, but also the three of them had gone out, displaying themselves for the watchers. The trap should have worked and they would have died if his and Rachel's instincts hadn't woken them in time.

At least in South Africa it had been Ralph's arrogance that had almost killed them all, here he only had himself to blame. Not only had Dylan been hurt, but he had been forced to release the Beast to survive and, of course, the Beast had killed, *he* had killed. He stared down at the two dead Illuminati on the floor. They were both young men. One looked like he was in his late twenties, but the other was only a couple of years older than Sam and Rachel and was probably still living at home.

He had committed the most heinous sin that he could - that of killing a Displacer in the past. While he had no qualms anymore about killing John or Quentin, this was another matter and was just one more reason why the Master and his chief disciple had to die.

He lifted his head from the twisted bodies only when Rachel came back up the stairs some minutes later.

Their eyes met across the bodies and, now that she was no longer concerned for him or covering her emotions with humour, Sam thought he detected something in Rachel's eyes. Something he had never seen before when she looked at him.

Fear.

He looked down, ashamed, suddenly unable to meet her gaze. He swallowed and forced himself to speak. 'We should get dressed before the authorities arrive.'

He stepped over the bodies, went into their bedroom and started pulling clothes out of the wardrobe, but he stopped what he was doing when Rachel's arms went around him from behind and she leaned her head against his back.

'Thank you.'

He turned in her arms. 'For what?'

She took a step back and met his gaze unflinchingly, searching. 'You hate it, don't you? Having to become that thing.'

Sam nodded mutely.

'Then, thank you. Without you we would have died today. Thank you for making that sacrifice for us. For all of us.'

She drew him back into her arms so that she could kiss him.

Sam felt himself responding and pulled her closer, but at that moment they heard the distinctive sound of police whistles coming from outside the house.

They held on to each other for a second more, savouring the moment while they could, then let go and separated so that they could get dressed.

Sam was ready first and he picked his way carefully through the mess in the corridor and went downstairs to meet the police.

Florence was in the hallway, perched on the edge of the chair that was for people to sit in while they took off their shoes. She was bent over and weeping, her face in her hands, and there was a policeman standing on the doorstep next to her, blowing his whistle furiously into the night. He whirled in fright at the sound of Sam coming down the stairs, almost swallowing his whistle before spitting it out and fumbling at the truncheon hanging from his waist.

Sam smiled reassuringly and slowed down, holding out his hand to appear as non-threatening as possible. 'Good evening. My name is Sam Vives, thank you for coming so quickly, Constable...?'

'Uh...' The policeman stopped struggling with his truncheon and tentatively reached out to shake Sam's hand.

Belatedly, the man realised who he was talking to and drew himself up to something approaching a respectful attention position. He was young, very young in fact, not much older than Sam, and he had probably not been on the force for long. 'Constable Tompkins, sir!'

'Are you on your own, Tompkins?'

'Uh, no, sir. Me mate, sorry, I mean, Sergeant Jakes has run orf to get help, sir.'

'Very good. Well, I suppose you should carry on then, Constable.'

'Yes, sir.'

The man gave Sam a nervous nod and hesitant salute before moving away down the short path to the road and starting to blow his whistle again.

Sam grinned wryly and shook his head, then turned and knelt down in front of Florence. She shrank back from him, her eyes wide in fright.

He didn't make any effort to reach out to her in any way, he just kept his distance and smiled at her. 'I'm sorry that you had to see that.'

'Who... why...?'

'They were bad people. They tried to kill me and Lady Rachel. Don't worry about them.'

Florence nodded reluctantly, but then her eyes widened as she looked down at his shirt under the jacket that he had neglected to button in his hurry. Blood was seeping through the sheet that he had wrapped around himself as a temporary bandage and was soaking through the white material.

Sam folded his jacket closed and again tried to reassure her. 'It's nothing to worry about.' He forced a laugh. 'I've cut myself worse shaving.'

She didn't look convinced and Sam realised that he wasn't going to be able to reassure her with the scene upstairs so fresh in her mind. What she needed was a distraction.

Just as he was trying to think of something, Constable Tompkins stopped whistling, and in the sudden silence Sam heard the sounds of horses and carriages pulling up outside as more policemen finally arrived.

Sam tilted his head in the direction of the street where orders were now being shouted. 'I tell you what, why don't you go and make a big pot of tea for our rescuers, I know I could do with a cup! And make sure you have one yourself, to calm your nerves, before you come back up, alright?'

'Yes, sir.' The young girl nodded. She stood and smoothed down her skirts before hurrying away to the kitchen, looking better already now that she had something to do.

Sam watched her go, then stood with some difficulty. He wavered on his feet, his exhaustion and injury almost overcoming him for a moment, and clutched at the sideboard to keep himself from falling, gulping in deep breaths to clear his head. When the dizzy spell finally passed, he put a smile on his face and went out into the night to face the police and the awkward questions they would undoubtedly ask.

'My word! Constable Williams!'

To Sam's relief the ranking officer on the scene proved to be an old friend - Geoff Williams, who had been his driver and a big help in stopping Quentin when he'd been in Victorian London before. His red hair was thinning, driving home the fact that it had been many years since Sam had last seen him, and he had lost the freckles he'd been plagued with, but he was instantly recognisable. There was also a shrewd look in his eyes that hadn't been there before and an authority about him as he ordered the policemen around, creating a cordon in the street.

The man turned and his eyes lit up, a slow smile turning the corners of his mouth upwards.

'I asked you to call me Geoff when first we met, Sir Sam, and that hasn't changed, but my rank has; I haven't been a Constable in years! It's sub-divisional inspector now.' He tilted his body slightly to display the single diamond shaped star on his shoulder proudly. 'If me ma could see me now!'

Despite having grown up in one of the rougher areas of London the man hadn't ever lost his gentle tone and lilting Welsh accent and Sam found it strangely comforting on such an eventful night.

He grinned warmly at Sam and they shook hands vigorously; two old friends reunited.

'How is your wife, Geoff?'

'Grand, sir, grand.'

'And the kids? How many is it now?'

'Four, sir, and one more on the way. Billy, my eldest, follows your adventures in the papers, and he'll be right chuffed when I tell him you're back in town. I reckon there'll be another story for him to clip tomorrow, by the look of things.'

He jerked a thumb in the direction of a gaggle of people standing beyond the police cordon a few yards away. In amongst the inquisitive neighbours and the usual nosy people that you find wherever something out of the ordinary was happening were men in cheap suits, making notes on small pads of paper and craning their heads to see what was happening.

'Geoff!'

They turned as Rachel came out of the door and skipped up to them.

Sam shook his head in exasperation; she had come down only a few minutes after him, but, while he hadn't even had time to button his jacket, she had managed to dress, do her hair, and even put on some makeup.

Geoff nodded and gave her an even wider smile than he had Sam. 'Lady Rachel, you are looking as lovely as ever.'

Sam tutted. 'Do I have to warn you two about flirting again?'

Rachel gave him a grin, then daintily held out a hand to Geoff, who laughed before bending to kiss it.

'So good to see you again, Geoff. Inspector Geoff, no less!'

'Always just Geoff to you, ma'am.' His smile widened even more, but then he suddenly became all business as he turned to Sam. 'Perhaps you should show me the crime scene, Sir Sam?'

'Of course, Inspector.'

Sam started to lead them inside, but came to a halt when he realised that there was something that needed doing if the police were going to be traipsing around inside. 'Rachel, dear, would you go upstairs and keep an eye on our guests? Please make sure they're comfortable and not alarmed.'

Geoff raised an eyebrow. 'You have guests? Did they witness anything?'

Sam shook his head. 'I'm afraid not; my parents are staying with us and they're both rather deaf. They slept through the whole thing.'

'I'll go and check.' Rachel was fighting hard not to laugh, but failing dismally, so she clamped her lips together and all but ran back into the house.

Sam only just managed to keep a straight face himself as he turned back to Geoff. 'Shall we go inside, inspector?'

There was a small army of policemen in the road now, milling around aimlessly, and Geoff tutted when he saw them. 'Let me organise my men and I'll be right with you.' He stalked off and gave instructions to a couple of sergeants before coming back and they went up the path towards the house. In the light coming from the doorway he finally noticed that there was blood on Sam's side and he frowned. 'Doctor's on his way, sir. We can look at the scene later if you want to wait for him to patch you up first.'

Sam waved his concern away. 'It's nothing, thank you, Geoff, I can wait. Come on, in.'

They went inside, followed by one of the sergeants and a couple of constables. They found Florence coming out of the kitchen carrying a huge tray with a pot of tea, several mugs and two delicate cups.

'Ah! Tea! Excellent! Thank you, Florence. Would you like some, Geoff?'

'I wouldn't mind, sir.'

Sam glanced at the three other policemen and received eager nods from them too.

Florence started to make her way to the dining room. 'Just let me set this down, sir, and I'll...'

Sam stopped her. 'No need, Florence, I can pour.'

The maid looked mortified, but couldn't do anything except watch as Sam poured tea for himself and the Inspector in the delicate cups and mugs for the other policemen.

'Milk? Sugar?'

'Yes, please. Two.'

Sam handed Geoff his tea then gave the mugs to the others before taking his own. 'Help yourself to milk and sugar gentlemen.'

Sam sipped his tea while the policemen stepped forwards to sweeten their drinks. He found his hand was shaking slightly and he had to fight hard to stay upright as another wave of dizziness hit him; he'd had far too little rest after the Displacement and was failing fast - the Illuminati had timed their attack just right. He covered the trembling by putting both of his hands around the cup, as if warming himself.

'Do you mind if I send the rest out to your men? I'm sure they could do with a drink.'

'That would be very considerate of you, sir.'

'Florence, take care of that, please and keep it coming. Oh, and see if you can dig up some biscuits or something.'

'Yes, sir.'

As Florence hurried out the front door, Sam led the way upstairs.

All of the policemen, including Geoff, halted in shock when they saw the two bodies on the upstairs landing.

Sam grimaced, knowing that, if they reacted that way to the relatively untouched men in the hallway, they wouldn't like what the Beast had done to Dylan's attackers. 'There's two more in the guest room here and two in my bedroom down the hall. Six in total.'

Geoff stared at him for a second, then swallowed and turned to the sergeant. 'More men.' His voice croaked and he coughed to clear his throat. 'Get Sergeant Potter's men up here and see if that photographer has arrived.'

'Yes, sir.' The sergeant tore his eyes away from the broken bodies with difficulty and ran down the stairs.

Geoff took a deep breath and pulled himself back together. 'Do you have any idea who they were, Sir Sam?'

'Common thieves, I would say.'

Geoff frowned. 'Thieves don't usually come armed to the teeth like this.'

Sam shrugged. 'Perhaps some criminal I got locked up was looking for revenge and sent some of his gang. Whatever the motives, I doubt they will try again when they realise how many people they lost tonight.'

'Hmm. Well, we'll get them carted away and try to identify them, and I'll send Bert out to see if he can scare up some rumours. You remember Bert, don't you, sir?'

'Is that rascal still working for the yard?'

'Oh, yes! Got several commendations over the years and all, he has. He keeps asking about you, sir, knows how much he owes you, he does. Him and his family always say a prayer for you and Lady Rachel whenever we go over to his for dinner.'

'That's... remarkably kind of him.' Sam was surprised by the emotions welling up inside him at the thought of having made such a difference in someone's life. He just wished it was permanent and didn't only last while he was in the time-line. 'Please give him my best.'

'Will do, sir.'

There was a short silence as they waited for the sergeant to come back with the reinforcements.

Sam leaned against the wall, not trusting his legs. He was near the end of his energy and if he didn't rest soon he would likely pass out.

'Uh, can you handle this, Inspector? I should really go and check on my parents.'

'Of course, sir. No reason for you to stay up. If you'll just oblige me by coming down the station tomorrow and making a statement, then we can take care of the rest.'

'Thank you. I'll see you tomorrow.'

'I'm on duty until six in the morning, but if you come in the evening I'll be there to take it. Or you can give it to any of the other inspectors - I can tell them you'll be in.'

'No need, I'll come in the evening. Shall we say seven?'

'Seven it is, sir.' Geoff suddenly thought of something. 'Oh, and when the doctor arrives I'll make sure to send him in to see you.'

'Don't bother; it's only a scratch. Nothing a little rest won't heal.'

The big policeman looked doubtfully at Sam's side. His jacket had opened again to reveal a bloodstain a good few inches across. 'If you say so, sir.'

Sam smiled and pushed himself away from the wall. He offered his hand to Geoff. 'It really is good to see you again, *Inspector* Williams.'

'Likewise, sir. Likewise.'

They shook hands and then Sam picked his way down the hall to the spare room where Rachel had stashed the Illuminati. With a last look back and smile at Geoff, he went in and closed the door behind him.

Despite the late hour there were dozens of onlookers in the street, attracted by the commotion taking place in Sir Sam Vives' residence and Diana Birch and Kyle Adams blended in easily.

Only a short while before, they had been alone, standing in the dark across the road, where the streetlights didn't reach, but as soon as the shooting had started and the screaming maid had come running out, it seemed that the whole street had woken up and come to see what was happening.

Exactly as she had in South Africa, before the assault on the Town Hall, Diana had felt sick to her stomach as she'd been forced to stand by and watch the kill team enter the house, unable to do anything to help or warn her friends. The instructions that Quentin had relayed from the Master himself had been clear, though, she and Adams were to stay outside to witness the aftermath, then provide cover for the escape of the Illuminati. With Adams by her side there was no chance to disobey them.

Her spirits lifted slightly when the shooting died down and her team didn't come back out; if the mission had been successful they would have made their getaway within moments. Then, when the police arrived, she dared to hope, but it wasn't until she saw Sam appear, followed shortly after by Rachel, that she was finally able to let go of her fear.

However, when they started bringing the bodies out, Diana went cold.

Four of the eight who had been sent in were professional killers, hired for the night, and she didn't really care about them; they would come back to life when Sam and Rachel left, but the other four were Illuminati, men and women that she had gotten to know over the time they'd been in the past. One of the girls in particular had become quite a close friend. She was only sixteen and the thought of her dying at the hands of one of the people that she loved, even if she had been a part of an attack on them, was a conflict of emotions that she really didn't want.

'I should have been in there with them.'

Adams' growl provided a distraction, but not a particularly welcome one and Diana's eyes widened as a knife appeared in his hand, as if from nowhere. His fingers flicked opened and closed in rapid succession around its handle, then, just as quickly, the blade was gone again.

Unlike Tuttle, whose manipulation of a switchblade had just made him look laughable, or Rachel, who could do things with knives that would make a Cirque du Soleil juggler jealous, the impression she got from Adams was competence coupled with murderous intent. In the few seconds the knife had been in his hand his entire being had screamed his desire to use it on someone, his face a mask of fury, tinged with madness, and she wouldn't have been surprised to see him plunge it into one of their fellow bystanders. Even now, although the knife was gone, he was still on the balls of his feet, poised to spring forward and attack Sam and Rachel, despite the fact that there were more than a dozen policemen surrounding them.

She put her hand on his arm, receiving the full force of his glare in return. 'Quentin wanted you out here with me. He specifically gave you instructions that you weren't to go in and I'm sure there's a good reason for that.' She had to use every ounce of the control and strength she had learned over three years of meditation and training in Nepal to remain impassive in the face of so much rage, knowing that the only way to retain control over him was to gain at least a measure of his respect.

There was a flicker of something in his eyes and he shrugged off her hand, then turned away from her to look back towards the house and his prey.

'Yeah... Right... Quentin.' He relaxed lightly, chuckling evilly and sneering, the contempt he felt for the young Illuminati leader clear on his face.

It wasn't at all advisable to openly show such feelings, even when Quentin wasn't around; the one Illuminati who had questioned Quentin's authority had spent two days locked in the attic of the house with no food or water and yet the young man seemed completely unconcerned about any possible consequences of his words.

Right from the beginning of the mission she had identified the scrawny, dark-haired, sharp-nosed, thirty-something Scottish man as by far the biggest threat in the team and had done what she could to find out more about him. He was different to the other Illuminati, more independent, more unpredictable, and she had seen him at night on his own on various occasions, something that was strictly prohibited if it wasn't part of the mission.

Pretending to be suspicious of him, she had questioned Quentin and he had coldly informed her that Adams was the Illuminati's chief spy. Apparently, if the Master needed any spying done in the present then it was Adams who he called upon - for example, most of the pictures of Sam and Rachel that Diana owned, from before she got to know the two Displacers, had been taken by him. He was also one of the Master's enforcers, taking on the jobs that needed a more subtle touch than what the Twins provided.

Knowing that, she had to wonder why he had been ordered to remain outside and watch, something that Diana could have done on her own, and not joined the kill team.

There was obviously more going on than she realised, but she didn't have time to think about it at that moment; Quentin would be expecting her report soon. The thought that he wasn't going to be at all happy briefly put a smile on her face, but it was wiped away almost instantly as another couple of bodies were carried out of the house.

'Try to get closer, see if you can find out who's dead, then meet me back at base.'

Adams nodded and sidled away without a word.

Diana took one last look at her friends, her lovers, now murderers, then turned and slowly walked away.

CHAPTER 19
QUESTION TIME

Rachel was sitting on the bed in the spare room. The two Illuminati women were lying on the floor behind it, out of sight from the door.

'How are my parents?' He grinned at her.

'Please don't!' Rachel shook her head and laughed. 'How could you keep a straight face while telling Geoff that?'

'I don't know. It's a mystery.' He laughed, but then had to clutch at the wardrobe by the door to stop himself from falling over as the world around him faded.

Rachel leapt off the bed and ran to his side. She caught hold of him just as he began to topple and helped him over to the bed. 'Come on, sit down before you fall down.'

'If I sit down I'll go to sleep.'

'These two won't come around for a while yet, why don't you let me take care of that wound, then I'll watch them while you have a siesta. I'll wake you up when they do.'

While Rachel went to their bedroom to get their medical supplies, Sam sat on the bed and looked down at the two unconscious women.

They were dressed in rough grey trousers and thick brown jackets, their hair pinned up on top of their heads and hidden under flat caps, which made them look a bit like the chimney sweeps from *Mary Poppins*, just much cleaner. In a time where no woman could wear trousers without drawing attention, they had undoubtedly disguised themselves as men so they would be unimpeded by dresses for the attack - Rachel was the only woman Sam knew who could fight just as well in a confining Victorian dress as she could in a martial arts uniform. Or naked.

'Well, these two are definitely Illuminati. What about the others?'

Rachel came back over with the first aid kit, which was not much more than alcohol, a few bandages, and a needle and thread. She knelt in front of him and started cleaning his wound while she replied.

'Two of the others were as well, judging by how clean they were. The rest were probably hired toughs, but I could be wrong.'

'So we, no, *I* wiped at least two Illuminati from existence tonight.' Sam paused and swallowed, dropping his head into his hands. 'Oh god... but that's not even the worst part. The worst part is that it doesn't matter, it doesn't change anything; this won't be over until we've stopped John. No matter how many people we kill, or turn, or terrify into not working for him, he can always recruit more. None of these people have to suffer, none of them have to die. Just him.'

'You're doing what you can and what you have to.' She looked up at him from her position on the floor and smiled. 'Anyway, don't think about that now, just get some rest.'

She finished sewing his wound shut then wrapped a bandage around him. It wasn't ideal, but it was the best she could do with what they had and it was as much as any doctor in the time-line would have done.

He sighed. 'Just for a little while, then, but as soon as they even twitch, wake me up, OK?'

'OK, darling.' Rachel helped Sam to lie back on the bed.

He barely even felt her lips touch his before he was unconscious.

When Rachel shook him awake it felt like no time had passed at all, but she assured him that it had been several hours. He felt refreshed, not completely rested by any means, but far more alert, and he knew that he would be able to question the Illuminati properly now without missing anything in his tiredness.

The house was quiet. The police were long gone, taking the bodies with them and, apart from the three bullet holes in the floor and walls of the corridor outside, things were almost back to how they had been before the attack. With Dylan gone from the time-line, there had also been surprisingly little blood to clean up for a fight that had left six people dead - one of the advantages of breaking necks instead of stabbing or shooting. In fact most of the blood that was left was his.

Sam nodded in satisfaction; they were alone and now he could do what he needed to do without fear of interruption.

He looked Rachel up and down. She was unhurt, but the black rings under her eyes betrayed her exhaustion, and he felt selfish for having slept so long; even though she had come as a passenger, with him doing the actual Displacing, the energy cost for her had been almost as high.

Rachel leant over him and whispered in his ear. 'One of them's awake, she's trying to pretend she's still unconscious.'

'I know; I can feel her Preparing. Give her a jolt, would you, please?'

'With pleasure.' She gave him a kiss, then pushed away from the bed. She had dragged the two women into the middle of the room to better keep an eye on them and she gave the girl who was awake a sharp nudge in the ribs with her toe, breaking her concentration.

Sam nodded at her as he felt the energy she had been building dissipate. He swung his legs off the bed and sat up, stifling a yawn. He scrubbed his face with his hands then ran them though his hair before standing and approaching the women. Now that he had a good look at them he could see that one of them was no more than a girl, even younger than he and Rachel were, perhaps fifteen, or sixteen at the most. She was the one who had been trying to flee and she was still trying desperately to pretend to be unconscious, but her control over her fear wasn't nearly good enough.

He squatted on his haunches and leaned forwards to place a hand on the floor next to her head then bent down to whisper in her ear. 'I know you're awake, I can smell it.'

He growled, trying to emulate the sounds he knew the Beast made when it hunted. He didn't come close, but it was enough to instil fresh terror in the girl and she squealed, her eyes opening wide.

He kept his face close to hers and snarled.

She screamed and turned her face away from him, lifting her bound hands to cover her head and squeezing her eyes shut again at the blow she thought was coming.

Sam glanced at Rachel. He saw disapproval and distaste in her sour expression and felt an instant of shame, but quickly buried it; he would do what was necessary, no matter how much he disliked it. For Andrew and for Susan. For all the past Displacers and all those to come. For everyone who'd led their life serving mankind, but had it taken away from them by the greed of one man. And to prevent more people like Emily Clarkwell and this girl from being deceived and corrupted and ultimately discarded.

With one hand he grabbed her hands, immobilising her and with the other he reached out to catch her chin between his index finger and thumb and forced her head around towards him.

'Open your eyes.'

Instead of obeying, she squeezed them shut tighter and tried to turn her head away, moaning in fear.

He hardened himself to what he had to do.

In one quick motion he released her, then slapped her on the cheek. As she gasped in shock and recoiled as much as she could, he grabbed her again and pulling her back to face him. It hadn't been a hard blow, not nearly enough to do any damage, because it hadn't needed to be; it just had to be enough to shock her and convince her that he would do her more harm if she didn't obey him.

'*Open your eyes.*' He growled the words out and this time her eyes flew open to look up at him.

'Better.' He returned to his own voice. 'What's your name?'

'Bibi... Beatrice Gower.' He could barely hear her, even in the absolute silence of the early hour.

'Pleased to meet you, Bibi.' He gave her a smile that, if anything, frightened the girl more and he wasn't surprised that she screamed when he grabbed her under the armpits and pulled her up into a sitting position against the wardrobe. She only stopped when he backed off to squat in front of her, astride her legs, and he patiently waited for her to calm down a bit before continuing his questioning.

'Now, I want to know a few things and if you answer truthfully we'll let you go home.' He glanced pointedly in the direction of her unconscious companion. 'And please bear in mind that when your friend here wakes up we'll be putting the same questions to her, so you'd better hope that you both give the same answers. Do you understand?'

The girl nodded, terrified beyond belief, tears glistening in her eyes.

Sam truly felt sorry for her. It wasn't her fault that she was in this situation, like Laura and Emily Clarkwell, this girl hadn't done anything wrong, she'd just had the misfortune to be found by the Illuminati first and didn't know any better.

He leaned forwards menacingly, holding her gaze with his, keeping up the act despite the foul taste it left in his mouth.

'First question. How many of you are there?'

'Fifteen.' The girl hung her head, still reluctant to betray her colleagues, but too scared not to.

Sam shared an alarmed look with Rachel; that meant that there were almost a dozen Illuminati still unaccounted for. It was just as well the Illuminati had made a mistake and sent a too-small force; facing all fifteen of them at once, as well as the street thugs they had hired, would have been all but impossible.

'Where are the rest of you?'

'At home.'

Sam chuckled. 'And where is that exactly, Bibi?'

'In Mayfair, in Berkeley Square.'

Sam shot a look at Rachel and she nodded. She knew where that was.

He turned back and smiled at the girl, a slightly warmer, more encouraging one than before. 'Thank you, Bibi, you're doing really well.'

She sniffed miserably and looked away, closing her eyes again, refusing to accept his thanks.

'What does Quentin have planned? Apart from killing me and my friends.'

'I don't know.'

'Really?'

Sam put his finger under the girl's chin and turned her back to face him.

'Are you sure about that, Bibi?'

She flinched, jerking her head sideways away from his touch, but he was pleasantly surprised when she immediately turned on him with a glare; she wasn't as fragile as she seemed and would recover from being traumatised by him.

'I don't know!' It was half angry shout, half terrified wail. 'I swear! He split us into three teams and only told us the details of our part of the mission. He told us if we talked to someone from another team about what we were doing he would kill us!'

'So you were just on the team tasked with killing us. You don't know what the others are working on?' Sam held her gaze, searching for a sign she was lying. He found that he believed her; Quentin was perfectly capable of carrying out the threat and John was the kind of person who would give that kind of order.

'No, I don't.' She finally lost her courage completely and looked away again. Her voice when it came again was uneven and full of fear. 'I'm sorry! I'm so sorry! Please, don't kill me!'

'I'm not going to kill you.'

Sam stood up. 'Rachel, can you take her into our bedroom and keep an eye on her. I want to talk to the other one on her own.'

'OK.'

Rachel brushed past him and bent down to untie the girl's legs before helping her up and taking her out of the room. She didn't look at him once the whole time.

As soon as the door had closed, Sam flopped onto the bed and sighed unhappily as he put his head in his hands. Earlier, Rachel may have thanked him for doing what he'd had to do, but she it looked like she hadn't remotely accepted it, and now, on top of everything, she had been forced to stand by and watch him emotionally torture a young girl.

A large part of him just wanted to give up before he destroyed their relationship forever, wanted to forget about the Illuminati so that he would never have to call on the Beast again, wanted to escape from it all and live in the house up the coast from Barcelona with Rachel and Diana for the rest of their lives.

The rest of him, the part that knew what his duty was, wouldn't allow that, of course, so he straightened his back and hardened his resolve and turned his mind back to what needed to be done.

He lifted his head and looked down at the other Illuminati. She was a heavyset woman, muscular, with a hard set to her face even unconscious. She had been the one who he'd knocked down in his initial assault on the first man through the door. She looked competent and experienced which meant it wouldn't be nearly as easy to convince her to betray her friends as it had been the other woman, Bibi. That, more than anything was why she had sent Rachel out of the room with the young girl - not because he didn't want the two captives speaking, but because he didn't want Rachel seeing what he might have to do to get the woman to corroborate Bibi's answers.

He stood up and began pacing up and down the room to keep himself awake while he waited.

Rachel marched the girl into the master bedroom and closed the door behind them. She leaned her forehead against the door, ignoring her prisoner for a moment, not only because she was exhausted, but also because she needed to sort out her thoughts.

She knew that Sam was only doing what he had to do and could almost understand why he'd needed to make himself into someone who could kill to protect them and protect the time-line itself, after all, that was what she'd been doing almost her whole life, but where was the line that shouldn't be crossed? Was what Sam had done truly necessary?

The thugs who had come with the Illuminati would come back to life, none the worse for wear, as soon as they left, but the Illuminati themselves...

She saw again the look in Sam's eyes when he'd turned on her in Dylan's room. There had been a complete lack of humanity in his eyes and for an instant when she had thought he was going to attack her next. He'd blinked it away immediately, but it had been there nonetheless. She thought she'd seen the same thing when he had torn apart the bomber, but had dismissed it as her imagination. Now she was sure - there was something deeply *wrong* with Sam, something he wasn't telling her.

Back in James' sitting room, when he'd spoken about letting "something" in to do the stuff he couldn't, she'd thought he'd been talking metaphorically, about a martial arts technique he'd learnt on his Displacement by which he was able to tap directly into his instincts or something, but this went far beyond that - in the corridor he'd run at three people with guns, totally disregarding the possible consequences and ignoring a bullet wound that would have stopped most people and he'd done it laughing.

It hadn't been his laugh, though, it had been animalistic, primal.

She was beginning to see that he had been speaking quite literally - he really did become some*thing* in those moments and yes, it had saved their lives that night, but would his be destroyed forever? And next time would he be able to stop it from turning on her or their friends after it had killed its enemies?

'A-a-are you going to kill me?'

Rachel shook herself out of her dark thoughts and turned to face the girl.

She was shaking, barely able to stay on her feet, her hands still bound in front of her.

Rachel took a good look at the girl, taking in the thin wrists, the poor posture, the lack of toned musculature. She wasn't a fighter, which was why she had been in the last group, the one that had waited outside in the corridor as backup, while the others had done the dirty work.

'No, I'm not going to kill you. Nobody is going to kill you. That's not what we do.'

At the girl's sceptical look Rachel amended her statement. 'That's not what we *usually* do, anyway. Tonight has been a bit of a first.'

She stepped forwards towards the girl, holding her hands up to show that she meant no harm, then reached out slowly and undid the bindings from around her hands. She winced. She'd used torn up sheets to tie the two captives and they had bitten deep into the girl's wrists.

'Owww!' The girl groaned, clutching her hands to her as blood rushed back into them.

'Sorry! Here, sit down.'

Rachel gently manoeuvred the girl to sit on the end of the bed before going and pouring some water from the jug on her dressing table.

She handed the girl the glass and the girl cradled it, lifting it to her mouth with both hands. She was trembling so much that she spilled much of the water down her front.

'More?'

'Please.'

Rachel poured, noting that the girl's trembling was subsiding slightly.

She turned and put the jug back on the dressing table, then sat on the floor a few metres away, deliberately putting herself below the girl and in a position of weakness. She leaned back on her hands and put her legs out in front of her, crossing them at the ankles, making her body language as unthreatening as possible. She could still be on her feet and on the girl in less than a second if need be, but the girl didn't know that and Rachel wanted her to be at ease; this was the only chance she was going to get to plant the seeds of doubt that might eventually turn Bibi to their side. Although, after the night's events, that probably wouldn't be possible.

'Was that really Sam Vives?'

Rachel blinked, not quite understanding. 'Yes?'

'He's not what I expected.'

'In what way?'

'Well...' The girl paused. She obviously wasn't sure if she should be speaking to the enemy. In the end her desire to make sense of the situation she found herself in won out. 'He's not at all like I was told he would be.'

'By who? Quentin? Quentin is a jealous little fuc...'

'No, not by Quentin, by Diana. Diana Birch. You've met her, right?'

Rachel hid her smile with difficulty. 'A couple of times.'

'She described him as being gentle and kind. An enemy you could respect. But... he was... he...' The girl shuddered, thinking back to the brief, but explosive fight. 'He killed my friends.'

Rachel sighed. 'I know, and trust me, neither of us are happy about that.'

The girl snorted. 'He certainly seemed to enjoy it, and he was going to kill me too if I didn't talk!'

'He wouldn't have. Believe me, he's not like that. But he has been forced to behave that way by your lovely Master. Did you know that he killed Sam's uncle a few months ago? He stabbed him in the chest himself while on a mission and tried to erase him from history.'

The girl stared at her and shook her head. 'I don't believe you!'

Rachel shrugged. 'Frankly I don't care whether you believe it or not, but it's true.'

When the girl's expression just hardened, Rachel realised that she was being confrontational, which wasn't helping matters one bit. She took a deep breath and used the training she'd received from the Dalai Lama and his monks to sink down into the warm embrace of what, to Sam's disgust, she had once referred to as "death by a thousand kittens", trying to find the peace that had been so thoroughly shattered that night. She knew from her time in Tibet that when someone was truly in that state of inner peace they quite literally radiated calm and that was something the girl desperately needed.

It should have been harder than it was, but sixteen years of practice made it easy and soon she smiled and looked up to meet the girl's eyes.

The girl's expression slowly changed over the long minutes they sat there, just looking at each other. Even though she had no idea what Rachel was doing, her unconscious mind could feel it and her body responded. Rachel saw her breathing slow, saw colour returning to her cheeks and saw the mistrust weaken ever so slightly.

At last she broke the silence, speaking quietly. 'You know where the Displacers are based, right? That's common knowledge for the Illuminati, correct?'

'Yes.' The girl had the decency to look ashamed; Rachel had known she would have to be aware of the attack carried out on Headquarters.

'If you ever start to think that you don't belong in the Illuminati anymore just show up on the doorstep. Tell them I told you to come.'

The girl frowned, but nodded.

'You can go home now.'

The surprise and then extreme relief on the girl's face was heartrending, because it showed that she really had expected to die.

'Thank you!' The girl's voice caught in her throat and Rachel found her eyes misting. She waved away the girl's thanks and turned her head away, no longer able to meet her eyes. She didn't look back until she felt the flare and knew that the Illuminati was gone.

Rachel stood with difficulty, her body and soul heavy, and looked towards the door, but instead of going to Sam she staggered over and dropped onto the bed.

For the first time since she'd laid eyes on him, so many years ago, she didn't feel like being with him.

The woman stirred and grunted as she fought her way back to consciousness.

There was a moment of stillness and then she jolted. Her eyes flew open and she started to struggle against her bonds.

Sam had adjusted the lights for dramatic effect, knowing he would need every advantage he could get against this woman, and he stood up now and moved out of the shadows to stalk towards her.

The woman's eyes opened wide and her struggling doubled, but Sam had made sure that her bonds were tight.

He stood over her, looking down on her for a few seconds, allowing the tension to build, before crouching suddenly.

He grinned sadistically at her, then reached out to scrape a nail down the side of her face. He didn't press nearly hard enough to break her skin, but he knew that the effect would be the same. Torture wasn't often effective, but mind games almost always were - one of the many things that he had learnt on the mountain was that the promise of suffering was far more effective than the giving of pain.

She flinched back from him.

'And what would your name be?'

When she didn't answer he changed his expression slowly. The smile faded and was replaced by a hard look, a killing look.

There was a scene in *Addams Family Values* which had stuck in his mind since he'd watched the film with Violeta - Christina Ricci slowly and painfully turns her perpetual frown into a wide-eyed, beaming smile, achieving a creepy and extremely scary effect. Violeta hated when he did it to her, so he did it whenever he had an excuse to, but now he did it in reverse, having to work hard to keep the happy memories from ruining his concentration and breaking the mask he had to wear.

He saw the fear blossoming in the woman's eyes as his stare grew ever colder and all it took from him was a slight shifting in his bodyweight, full of intention that only a fellow martial artist could read, for her to start talking.

Rachel woke when she felt someone leaving the time-line and a few minutes later the bedroom door opened and the weak light from the gas lamp in the corridor spilled in. Sam's shadow briefly blocked the light before he closed the door.

She heard him moving about the room, taking his clothes off. Finally he slipped into bed.

She waited, silently, but he didn't come to her.

Somehow she knew he wouldn't; she could feel his shame, his self-loathing and knew that he wouldn't approach her until she was ready.

After so many years together, she'd thought she knew everything about him, every little foible, every mannerism, every like and dislike, every belief even, but her world had been tipped upside down that night.

'Please. Promise me that you'll never give in to that side of you again.'

There was a long pause and for a while she thought that he'd gone to sleep, but finally she felt his weight shift on the bed as he turned to face her. 'You know I can't promise that.'

'Can't or won't?'

There was another pause and then he sighed. 'I won't. Sorry.'

She reached out to her nightstand and twisted the knob on the gas lamp, feeding the flame so that light bloomed brightly in the room and she could see his face. She wanted to look into his warm brown eyes and see the Sam she knew there, not the emotionless killer that she couldn't get out of her head.

'I hate that side of you, and I know you do too, so why not? It's destroying you inside, Sam, I can feel it and it's destroying us.'

'Because I have to be ready for something like tonight. You said it yourself - we would have died if it wasn't for... it.'

'It?'

Sam shied away from her searching gaze and stared up at the canopy over the bed. 'When I told you about my Displacement to Alamut I didn't tell you everything. I *couldn't* tell you this.'

He wet his lips, still reluctant to reveal this part of himself, but their relationship was already being strained, if he continued to hide the true nature of the thing inside him from her it would ruin the most important thing in his life - their love.

'My master, Hassan al-Sabbāh, called it the "Beast".

'One of his pet projects was using hypnosis and drugs to take away any impediments his assassins had, such as squeamishness, disobedience... Free will.

'I don't know why, perhaps what we learnt in Tibet had something to do with it, or maybe my being a Displacer, but he didn't achieve the same results with me as he did in everyone else. I did what I was told, took the drugs that I was given, went through the conditioning, but instead of creating a mindless killer he turned me into something else, something instinctive and intelligent, something that I had, and still have, no real control over, but that *he* could use at will. And he used it whenever he wanted, especially during the early years. Over and over, until sometimes the Beast was all I had for days at a time.

'Sometimes I would wake up covered in blood, surrounded by bodies, exhausted and starving, aware that days had passed, but with no idea where I was. My master always sent someone to observe me, though, and they would collect me and see me safely home.' Sam laughed once, bitterly. 'I was far too valuable an asset to let wander about on my own and get lost.

'Eventually, though, my master lost control of the Beast. I don't know how or what exactly happened, I just remember going into his throne room to be sent on a mission and kneeling in front of him so that he could give the Beast its instructions. The next I knew I was chained in a cell and the ranks of assassins had been cut almost in half.

'I almost came home then, thinking that I was going to be executed, but he came to see me. He seemed to be a new man, with a new light in his eyes despite his age. He had personally taken me down, but only after he had let the Beast kill a dozen of his best men. He told me that it was the most fun he'd had in decades.'

Sam finally turned to look at Rachel and he was surprised not to find condemnation, but rather something approaching sympathy. He closed his eyes and rolled away from her to sit on the edge of the bed, not wanting that from her; he was not ready for it, or deserving.

'That was the last day that he summoned the Beast; he wouldn't risk it again. So, after then, when I went on a mission, I went as myself. I knew that the Beast was what I had been sent to that time-line to find, though, so I spent whatever time I had for myself meditating, trying to contact with it. It wasn't hard; I could feel it within me, seething at being locked away with no more blood to spill and just waiting for its chance to break out and rampage unchecked.

'Eventually I came to a kind of understanding with it,' he shrugged, 'I bribed it, really - if it remained quiet and didn't try to take over unless I let it, I would call upon it when there was more important work to be done than killing a few helpless targets and when I did it would be because there would be a threat for it to meet. You see, it doesn't just crave blood, it craves a challenge. And it only allows me some measure of control over it because I've promised to find it one.

'The Beast remained chained, silent and patient until Paris, where I set it loose on the Twins, but when it killed the bomber it did so without my permission - it saw you go down and took over without me calling upon it. That was the first time I lost control. The second was tonight. As a part of me it feels just as protective of you as I am, however, just like me it also listens to you.

'When the Beast leaves me I never know what it has done, I only get vague impressions of its feelings. Usually it's satisfied at having killed, but tonight all I felt was frustration; it didn't get the challenge it wanted and it didn't want to leave until all its enemies were dead. It did, though; something stopped it and sent it away. And that is something that has never happened before.

'Whenever I woke up after a mission, the guard sent with me would give me the full details of the results of my rampages and he delighted in telling me about the innocents that had gotten in my way and been torn apart. Tonight that didn't happen. Tonight you did something that nobody has ever been able to do, except for Hassan al-Sabbāh himself - you put yourself between the Beast and a kill and survived. You faced it down and brought me back when there was still killing to be done. You can control it when I can't, I know you can, so don't ask me to give up a weapon that we might need, instead help me to use it - help me to make sure that when I release it, it doesn't kill anyone it shouldn't.

'This isn't a decision I've taken lightly; of course I'm worried that I might lose what little command I have of the Beast, of course I'm terrified that it might change me and that it might destroy what we have, but I'm also positive this is what I have to do! So, please! Help me! Don't make me do this on my own!'

His final plea came out in a desperate rush that was almost a wail and then he fell silent, waiting for her answer, praying that she would see things his way, that he wouldn't have to leave her once more and attempt to destroy the Illuminati on his own.

She was still for a long time and he began to think he had lost her, but her answer, when it finally came, was wordless and full of love.

The bed shifted as she moved to kneel behind him and he sobbed with relief as her arms wrapped around him.

He pulled her closer as the tears fell.

CHAPTER 20
RECRIMINATIONS

Diana entered the Price house an hour after the attack and found that everybody was still awake and gathered in the sitting room, nervously waiting for her team to come back.

Quentin was reading a book in an armchair in the brightest lit corner of the room. He looked up at her when she came in and smirked. 'You're late, I hope you didn't have to pay the thugs overtime.' He laughed at his own joke then paused when he saw that she was alone. 'Where's everyone else?'

'They're gone.'

'What do you mean, gone?'

'I mean that most, if not all of the people that you sent into that house, are dead.'

She was gratified when Quentin went completely white; she dearly wanted him to pay for what he had let happen that night.

There were gasps of shock from most of the others in the room, showing that they were still somewhat innocent and hadn't quite gained the callous disregard for their fellows that people like Quentin and the late Grant Davis had. The four Illuminati who had been sent on the mission were the only ones who'd had any training, although in Bibi's case it was minimal, the rest, with the exception of Quentin, Adams and Diana herself, were mostly inexperienced and bookish and would have been worse than useless - most of them couldn't even fire a gun and their talents were better employed on other, less physical, projects. The martial arts training that Laura had received in Nepal was a secret and as far as the Illuminati were concerned she was just a hacker, so, thankfully, she hadn't been sent. She was looking particularly ill and Diana knew that she was worried about Dylan, but there was no way she could set her mind at ease, not only because she couldn't afford someone overhearing, but also because she had no idea if he had survived.

Diana ignored the other Illuminati and gave Quentin her best scowl. 'I told you not to do this, Quentin, I told you just to send hired professionals! We lost four of our members. Four! We can't afford that! Look around you, damn it! Apart from Adams this is *everyone* left in the Illuminati. At least that's what the Master told you, isn't it? What's he going to say when he finds out you got more than a quarter of his people killed?'

Even under the circumstances it was still dangerous to push Quentin, but it was the only way to undermine his authority and possibly torpedo the mission and she wasn't likely to get a better chance.

He wasn't really listening to her, though; he was lost in his own thoughts, muttering to himself. 'They should have been able to take care of them. There was only the three of them and they're exhausted from Leaping today...'

'Quentin!' Diana shouted at him, making him look at her. His head seemed to clear and the shocked expression on his face was replaced by an annoyed frown at her tone. She could tell that she had pushed him to the limit of his tolerance, but she didn't care - she was a team leader now, just like him, and even though he was leading this Leap that didn't make him her superior and his failure meant that she was well within her rights to challenge him. 'The Twins warned you about Vives. He's changed, he beat *them*, the *Twins*! Why the hell do you think they refused to come, and why the hell did you think he wouldn't beat anyone we sent against him?'

Quentin deflated again. 'I was just doing what I was told. The Master...'

'Oh, for pity's sake, can't you think for yourself for once?'

There were fresh gasps from the other Illuminati at that; the Master's word was absolute and anyone who questioned it usually received a painful visit from the Twins - a lesson they had drummed into them from the moment they joined.

She turned away from Quentin to face them now. 'Come on, you have brains, you can't tell me none of you have ever questioned him? He's just a man after all, he can make mistakes, and in this case he should have bloody known better!' She paused before hitting them with her last salvo. 'Unless of course he doesn't care if we're killed.' She gazed around the room as her words sank in, glaring at each of the men and women in turn, but they avoided her gaze. The only one who met it was Laura and she only gave her the barest of nods before looking away, feigning meekness.

Diana finally had the chance to say the things that she had been thinking for years and for once she had an audience who would take her words to heart. It didn't matter if she burned her bridges, either; this mission would resolve the conflict between the Illuminati and Displacers once and for all and, whatever the result, she was done with the Master and his greed.

She opened her mouth to continue, ready to reveal all the nasty little things she knew about Quentin and the Master in an attempt to further undermine their authority, but, before she could, Adams burst in, slightly out of breath, and interrupted her.

Quentin lifted his gaze from the carpet, where it had been throughout Diana's tirade, and turned to him, some hope in his eyes. 'Please tell me that Miss Birch has been feeding us a pack of lies.'

Adams looked at Diana questioningly, but she just waved her hand at him. 'Go ahead. Tell him what his idiocy has done.'

Adams shrugged and turned to Quentin. 'Six dead, all four of the hired help and two Illuminati. No Displacers.'

Diana closed her eyes and shuddered at the confirmation of her lovers' bloodthirstiness. 'And Bibi? Was she...?'

Adams shook his head. 'No, neither Beatrice or Margaret came out, either dead or alive. Perhaps they escaped out the back where we couldn't see them.'

'No, they would have been here by now. They didn't get away; Vives has them.' Diana gave Quentin a pointed look. 'He won't kill them, but he might get them to talk...'

Quentin looked from Diana to Adams and back again, a hunted look in his eyes. 'I...'

He put his head in his hands and sank further into the armchair. He pulled at his hair and Diana thought she heard a groan of frustration, but then he seemed to pull himself together. He straightened and when he lifted his head his eyes were once again full of the arrogance and self-confidence that had helped him win and hold his position as the Master's second. He stood and snarled at nobody in particular. 'I'm going for a walk. Pack up the house; we'll leave as soon as I get back.'

He stalked out without waiting for a reply and seconds later they heard the front door slam behind him.

Adams sauntered out of the room, whistling tunelessly under his breath, his hands in his pockets, completely unconcerned about the night's events.

As the sound of him climbing the stairs faded and the house fell silent, all eyes turned to Diana.

She shook her head and sighed, openly showing her disappointment at the behaviour of the two Illuminati, then turned to face the rest of the room. She took in the fear and uncertainty in their all too young faces at a glance and smiled encouragingly, further reinforcing their impression that she cared for them and the others didn't. 'It's alright. We'll be fine, you'll see. Now come on, you heard Quentin - go and get your things. Be back here in half an hour.'

There were usually cabs on Park Lane, a few streets away, and Quentin found one without a problem - even this late at night there was always some poor sod still at work.

He leaped into a small open buggy and snarled at the driver. 'Temple Church, Fleet Street, and step on it.'

'Step on what, sir?'

Quentin gave the man a cold look. 'Just go quickly, there's an extra shilling in it for you if we get there in less than ten minutes.' He took out a pocket watch, flipped it open and squinted down at the face in the faint light from the gas lamps.

The driver got the message and snapped his whip over the back of the horse, which immediately burst into a trot.

Quentin relaxed back into the single seat as they thundered down the lane and wrapped his coat close around him against the cool midnight air.

The horse was lathered and panting, slightly less than ten minutes later, when they stopped in Fleet Street, as close to the church as they could get, hidden as it was amongst the narrow corridors of what had once been a Templar complex.

Quentin tossed a coin at the driver as he leapt out, not caring that it was far more than he'd promised the man. He didn't stay to listen to the man's profuse thanks, but just hurried through the narrow alleys, then walked around the church towards the side entrance he'd been told would be unlocked.

The rusty hinges of the door squealed as it opened and he jumped and peered around the dark area. There wasn't the constant, never-ending sounds of cars passing in this London to cover the noise, there was only the occasional clip clop of a passing horse echoing from the stone buildings and the wail of a teething baby, but it seemed that nobody had heard. Not wanting to push his luck he squeezed through the small gap he'd already created and stepped into the chancel.

There were no signs of life in the church and it was unlit except for a dim light coming from one end, so he headed towards it, going round the outside, behind the benches, sticking as close to the wall as possible.

Half way down the room he realised that the light was coming from votive candles - it wasn't an indicator of someone waiting for him. He stopped and swore softly.

'Can I help you, my son?'

The sudden voice startled him and he spun to face the direction from which it had come, a squeal making its way from between his lips before he could clamp them shut.

A shadow detached itself from a column on the other side of the nave and came towards him, crossing through the faint shafts of moonlight streaming through the windows. It was a monk, wearing a long brown robe tied with a white rope. His hood covered his head completely and his arms were crossed in front of him, the hands tucked into the opposite sleeves.

Quentin shook his head and started to back away towards the door he had come in. 'Uh, no thank you, I was just looking for someone.'

'Looking? Found someone you have, I would say.'

'Actually, I was looking for...' Quentin stopped abruptly when he realised there was something familiar in the monk's voice and words and he squinted, trying to see him better in the weak light. He frowned as the man walked straight into the back of a bench, scattering a pile of bibles onto the floor and almost tumbling head first after them.

'Oof! Damn silly robe, you can't see a thing with this hood up! How the Jedi do it, I don't know... Well, I do, actually; they have the bloody Force, now, don't they?'

White hands appeared from with the robes and fumbled with the hood, pulling at it ineptly, swearing continuously, until they finally managed to pull it back to reveal the face of a grinning man in his late thirties or early forties with thinning hair and a scraggly beard.

'Wotcha, Quentin.'

'John? You're the Master?'

'Yup.'

Quentin blinked. This wasn't at all what he had expected; it was one thing following a genius who was a sinister disembodied voice on a computer, quite another to follow the sweaty middle-aged loser who he'd known during his brief time with the Displacers. And had he just quoted *Yoda* at him?

The man's smile vanished in the face of Quentin's obviously contemptuous inspection. 'Report, Mr Price.'

Quentin swallowed, the apprehension he'd felt at finally meeting the Master face to face returning full force as he recognised the hardness lurking inside the soft and unimpressive shell of the man in front of him as indeed being that of his leader. 'Sir, I...'

The Master's eyes narrowed as he saw Quentin's hesitance. 'I take it the attack didn't quite go as you thought it would.'

'No, sir, it didn't, and I... I'm sorry, but I did tell you...' Quentin wet his lips and hurried on. 'Why didn't you let me send Adams in, sir? He's our best fighter and the mission would most likely have succeeded with...'

He almost swallowed his tongue in his haste to stop speaking when the Master waved him to silence.

'Adams has another job to do.'

'What job, sir?'

'You don't need to know, Understood, Mr Price?'

The Master's hard glare made it clear that there was to be no more questioning of his orders and Quentin was forced to grit his teeth and nod his acceptance.

'Tell me, how many minions did we lose?'

'We lost four of the local thugs...'

'Pah! As if I care about them. How many of our own?'

'Four. Two confirmed dead and two more that we believe have been taken prisoner.' Quentin cringed, expecting to be punished and thanking his lucky stars that the Twins had refused to come.

Instead he was surprised when the Master grinned. 'Oh well, that's a *little* unfortunate, but not unexpected, and you know what they say: you can't make an omelette... '

'You're not upset?'

The Master's cruel laugh filled the large empty space, echoing disconcertingly and Quentin cringed and looked around, afraid that someone would come at the sound.

'Of course I'm not upset! Why would I be? Those two are a pain in my arse, but they're not our targets here. The attack tonight was just a distraction, a little piece of business that might send them off on a sidetrack if we're lucky.'

Quentin fumed. *If?* The Master had sent several of his best Illuminati off on a mission that he'd known was inadvisable, if not suicidal, on the *chance* that it would cause their enemies to, what? Waste some time? What kind of man was he really?

Quentin was used to the Master not being particularly concerned about his underlings, punishing them and occasionally having them killed for betraying or failing him, but he never just wasted them. People with their talents were too few and far between to waste.

He inspected the man with newly opened eyes, saw the hint of madness, the desperation, and the deep lines that weren't from age, but rather from worry, and for the first time he started questioning why he was following him, why he was obeying the orders of someone who obviously wasn't completely in control of themselves, let alone a vastly powerful empire spanning the whole world.

'Walk with me.'

Quentin followed as the Master strolled through the benches and into the central isle of the church before turning to wander slowly towards the altar.

'You know, I actually owned this church when I controlled the Templars. Hell, that's nothing; for a while I owned the whole of Cyprus! Can you imagine, how rich I'd be right now if I could have held onto that? If all those nightclubs and hotels had to pay me rent, like some big game of Monopoly?' The Master laughed in delight. 'Well, I am that rich anyway, but still, it would have been nice to have all that as well.'

By this time they had reached the altar and the Master stopped and sneered up at the crucifix hanging on the wall behind it.

'One of the first things I did, when I stopped doing everything that those idiots in the "Honourable Society" told me, was to go back to see if this guy was real, or if any of the stories about him were true.'

He glanced sideways at Quentin. 'Did you know that's one of the things they prohibit their members?' Quentin shook his head and John grinned. 'No? It's actually one of the most heinous crimes you can commit as a Displacer. They *really* don't want people going and looking up religious figures - not Jesus, not Noah, not Abraham, and certainly not Muhammad! I'm not entirely sure why - I never bothered to ask, because I didn't want to risk receiving another boring lecture - but I assume it's because the founders didn't want any of their members finding out the truth about their beliefs.'

The Master shook his head and smiled wryly as he gazed back up at the statue. After a few seconds he chuckled and picked up the golden cross from the altar table. He hefted it in his hands, grunting at its weight, and began scratching at the jewels encrusted in it as if trying to remove them.

Quentin waited for him to continue with what he was saying, but it soon became clear that he wasn't going to. 'And?' He blurted the word out before he could catch himself; for some reason he found he was desperate to know what the Master had found out.

The Master's laugh again broke the silence and peace in the church and again Quentin flinched, but this time he managed to stop himself from looking around nervously.

'I found out that it doesn't matter one iota whether these people are real or not. The only thing that matters is what you can *make* people believe. And what you can squeeze out of them for having that belief.'

The cross thunked back onto the heavy wooden altar with a thunderous crash, as if to provide punctuation to his words, his implication that the gold and jewels it was made from had been extorted from believers by lies.

The Master turned to glare at Quentin. 'You say you have two people being held captive? I hope you're already preparing to vacate your current lodgings?'

He raised an eyebrow questioningly and Quentin nodded.

'Good. Find a cheap flophouse or something for a few nights. It doesn't matter if it's comfortable or not; you won't be here much longer anyway. Oh, and by the way, I never particularly cared whether tonight's attack succeeded or failed because once we have taken care of our target in this time-line the Displacers and Sam Vives will cease to be a problem forever.'

Quentin frowned, 'But we haven't been able to find him; our attack on their Society in the press forced all of them into hiding - he's safer now than he was before.'

The Master sighed in exasperation, shaking his head as if exasperated at his minion's stupidity, but then he chuckled wryly, evilly. 'No, Mr Price, it just made him more vulnerable, and now our little Displacer friends will lead us directly to him.'

CHAPTER 21
CLANDESTINE MEETINGS

The morning after the attack, Rachel and Sam got out of bed and had a quick breakfast before leaving the house and hailing a cab to take them to the address that the Illuminati agents had given them. It was after ten when they arrived and they weren't at all surprised to find the house abandoned. They were perfectly aware that they should have made the trip as soon as they had obtained the information, but they had both been too tired - it would have been dangerous if they'd been walking into another trap, especially with almost a dozen Illuminati still in the time-line and who knew how many armed thugs on their payroll.

They searched the place from top to bottom anyway because they knew there would be something for them; they had talked about exactly this kind of situation with Diana before coming and they found her note almost immediately, tucked behind a clock in one of the bedrooms.

In her pages-long letter she confirmed that there were indeed eleven Illuminati left, including her and Laura, and gave them a breakdown of who they were and their skill sets. She went on to detail the Illuminati's plan for discrediting and bringing down the Displacers in the current time-line, but that was something they had more or less been able to work out for themselves from the article in the paper. The note also reported that Quentin would often disappear on his own for hours at a time and she suspected that there was a secret agenda that she was unaware of which was perhaps the real reason for the Illuminati being there. However, while that information was interesting, it didn't do much to help; the Illuminati always had a web of hidden agendas on every mission they went on, most of which were only revealed after careful analysis by Elders over weeks or months. Lastly, a hastily scribbled addendum told them that she had no idea where they were relocating to - Quentin was keeping that information to himself.

All in all the letter wasn't particularly useful, although one sheet of paper was taken up by a very personal and extremely explicit letter to them, which certainly brightened their morning.

Aside from the note, there was nothing else in the house that revealed anything useful about the Illuminati, beyond that none of them seemed to believe in doing the washing up or taking out the rubbish. While that was somewhat understandable, seeing as when they left all the mess would just disappear, Sam hadn't really enjoyed having to sort through who knew how many weeks' worth of filth in the kitchen in case there were any clues.

The extensive sweep took them only a couple of hours to complete and then, somewhat disappointed, they went back out and headed towards Grosvenor Place to see what the situation was at the Society.

It was a lovely spring day and their destination was only a mile away so they decided to walk, taking their time and detouring through Hyde Park, where they strolled arm in arm. It was a Sunday, so there were quite a few other people out promenading, a few of whom recognised them and stopped to chat, so it was more than an hour before they reached Grosvenor Place.

They stood on the other side of the road and looked at the building. It was almost saddening for them to see it in one piece.

In the end, Agent Black's prediction had been correct. The building had been condemned and subsequently torn down. It was currently a building site in the present, with workmen swarming all over it.

The temporary quarters that the Queen had loaned the Society were modern, extremely well-equipped and as comfortable and safe as they could desire, but they lacked the charm and charisma that the old building had. Most of the Displacers, including the two of them, had come to realise just how much they had taken it for granted over the years and everyone was looking forward to moving into the new one when it was completed.

There had been some debate in the Society as to what to do. Some of the members wanted Headquarters rebuilt exactly as it had been, others wanted something completely different, something modern and improved that was better suited to carrying out their research and better able to hold their libraries and collections, most of which had survived.

Eventually, a compromise had been agreed upon - the façade would be reconstructed exactly as it had been, as would the sitting room, but the rest of the interior would be completely redesigned. There would also be a small lift put in for the comfort of the elder Elders.

Sam and Rachel hadn't stopped on the other side of the road just to reminisce on how the building had been, though; as soon as they had come out of the park gates they had seen and heard the commotion around Headquarters - undoubtedly a result of the Illuminati's manipulative efforts - and hadn't been sure what to do.

From where they stood they had a good view of the crowd milling around on the pavement outside the Society. There were a good hundred or more people there, but only about a dozen of them were actually doing much in the way of protesting - all shifty rough-looking men holding placards with slogans, who had most probably been paid to stir things up by the Illuminati. Another man, this one with a camera, was beside the front gate and, as they watched, a postman climbed the steps and he took a photo of the man who opened the door to receive the post.

The gathering was being watched over by a couple of harassed policeman, who were standing inside the front garden at the bottom of the steps that led up to the front door, but it looked like they had no plans to move them along any time soon.

Rachel gave Sam a look. 'How about we go around to the back? I don't particularly want my photo taken, even if it'll disappear when we leave, and the members in this time-lie won't thank us for calling more attention to them.'

Sam nodded. 'Sounds good to me.'

They wandered nonchalantly away and down the side streets towards the back of Headquarters. The buildings that backed onto the house in the present weren't there; they hadn't been built until the 1930's, instead they found a tall brick wall with a locked wooden door. It was the work of a few seconds to pick the lock on the door and moments later they were making their way up the path of a small, well-cared-for garden.

'Come no further!'

They were almost at the house when the shout rang out and the man they had seen talking to the postman came through the back door, holding a huge shotgun pointed at them. They recognised him immediately as Charles Matthews, the butler they had met the last time they had been there, although older, with more grey in his dark hair. He saw who they were almost as quickly and hastily put up the gun.

'Oh! Master Vives, Miss Evans, welcome back! I'm so sorry, I didn't realise it was you.'

While nominally a servant, the man was actually the twin of one of the members and, while he didn't have the power to Displace, he had been so close to his brother that there had been no keeping the secret from him. Displacing did run in his side of the family, though, because the Illuminati hacker, Laura Matthews, was a direct descendant of his. He acted as a butler and housekeeper, as well as a kind of unofficial secretary to the Society, doing everything he could in order to free up the other members for more important work, and was treated as a full member by everyone.

The man indicated the shotgun and shrugged shamefacedly. 'We've had all sorts try to force their way in over the last few weeks...'

Sam grinned at him. 'Don't mention it, Charles. We saw the mob outside, and we know why this is happening, so your reaction to our unannounced visit is perfectly understandable.'

'You know why...' The butler's surprise was clear on his face, but he hid it quickly behind his professional mask. 'Then I suppose you'll be wanting to meet with the members.'

Sam nodded. 'Please.'

'And a cup of tea would be nice, I'm parched!' Rachel gave Sam a cheeky smile as he rolled his eyes at her.

However, instead of asking them inside as they expected, the butler sighed. 'I'm afraid none of the members are here.'

'*None* of them?' Rachel was understandably surprised; one of the rules of the Displacers was that Headquarters was never left without at least one Displacer who was ready to go into the past at a moment's notice. The measure had been vitally important when communication wasn't so instantaneous and an emergency with the time-line couldn't wait for a Displacer to be located and the rule had been repealed only recently when it had become obsolete due to the advent of the smartphone.

'Indeed. None of them, madam.'

'Oh.'

'Yes, I'm terribly sorry for you to have come on a wasted journey, but if you would like to have a cup of tea and something to eat while you're here I would be delighted to fix something for you.'

Sam and Rachel exchanged a disappointed glance and were about to refuse and leave when the butler leaned in towards them and lowered his voice. 'The members are quite aware of the seriousness of the current situation and are in hiding. I was, however, left with a way to contact them in an emergency. I will let them know you desire a meeting and that it is of the utmost importance. I take it you are in residence at your town house, Sir Sam?'

'We are.'

The butler nodded and Rachel reached out to squeeze his arm. 'Thank you.'

He gave her a smile and a short bow. 'It is nothing more than my duty, Lady Rachel.'

The man straightened up and resumed speaking in his normal tone of voice. 'Tea, sir, madam? Or would you care for something a little stronger? I do believe the sun is above the yard-arm...' He looked at them expectantly.

'If you don't think it will be too much bother, I could actually go for a cup of tea.'

'Of course not, sir, and I'll be glad for the conversation; the house has been too quiet the last couple of weeks and it has been far too long since we last had the pleasure of your company.'

Sam's stomach rumbled as he remembered the times they had visited before and he smiled. 'Oh, and if you have some of that treacle cake you used to bake...'

'I have some in the pantry, sir.' The butler grinned and stood to one side. 'Right this way, sir, madam.'

After tea they returned to their house to wait.

The butler had assured them that a response would be quick in coming and the message from the Society came that very afternoon.

It was disguised as an invitation to join a hunting party in the countryside around Windsor the next Tuesday morning, in just a couple of days.

A hunt was the perfect cover for a meeting as it was exactly the kind of thing that a gentleman in Sam's position and his wife could reasonably be expected to take part in. They had received many such invitations the previous time they'd been in Victorian London, but had never accepted them, disapproving of the "sport". They would have done the same this time if it weren't for the tiny hand-drawn hourglass in the corner of the reverse side of the invitation.

Even though they had no intention of actually joining the hunt, they nonetheless dressed in appropriate riding gear to maintain the illusion, with overcoats on top against the chill morning air.

Windsor was twenty miles from their home and it was still dark outside when they got into the carriage that Sam had arranged for the day and started to wend their way through the still empty streets, the hooves of the pair of horses clattering against the cobblestones of the slumbering city.

London was far less extensive than it was in the modern day and they left it behind surprisingly quickly, passing into beautiful lush countryside, shrouded in low mists, where in the present were only houses and endless concrete jungles.

It was a fairly long ride, but a pleasant one, and they sat close together in the back of the carriage, covered with a blanket and enjoying the scenery as it went past.

For a wonderful half an hour everything was tinged red then pink as they rode along with the sunrise at their backs, before finally the dawn fully lit the world around them and burnt off the last white wisps. With the daylight came the people, and the road, which would one day become part of the M4, became busier, but it was still far less traffic than in the city and the ride remained peaceful.

They were in no hurry, and had told the driver to take his time, so it was a full two hours before they arrived in the outskirts of Windsor and caught their first sight of the castle with its distinctive round tower. There was a flag flying from the pole, which the driver informed them meant that Her Majesty was currently in residence

The invitation had set the meeting place as the town end of "The Long Walk", a three mile-long straight path lined with trees that went out into the deer park, and that was where they were dropped off. They were there slightly earlier than the time specified on the invitation, but they didn't have to wait long before the first people started turning up, most of them leading horses and some with dogs. There were a few people among the arrivals that they knew socially from London and who greeted them warmly, but none of them were Society members.

They were starting to think that they had misunderstood the invitation and read too much into the symbol drawn on it, when a man approached them. He had a flat cap pulled low to cover his eyes and was leading a pair of horses. It wasn't until he was right up next to them that he lifted his head and they recognised him as one of the junior Society members they had met before, Joseph Halifax, the son of a minor Lord who had been part of their social circle and was even now off to one side, conversing with a group of huntsmen.

'Sir Sam, Lady Rachel. Your mounts.' He announced in a voice that was loud enough to be heard by anyone listening, then lowered it so that only they could hear. 'Stick by me. When it's safe to do so we'll separate from the hunt and I'll take you to the meeting.'

They nodded in reply and he left their horses with them and wandered off to join his father and friends.

Sam and Rachel introduced themselves to their horses and checked their tack while they were waiting.

They'd gone riding a few times last time they'd been in Victorian London and he'd done a fair bit more in South Africa, but he'd never quite felt comfortable on a horse. He was actually quite worried that he'd ruin all the efforts at subterfuge by calling undue attention to himself - he was quite capable of falling off his horse or doing something equally silly if he didn't concentrate the whole time. Rachel would have no such problem, though; she had been one of those girls who were obsessed with horses from a very young age. One of her first Displacements had been to Mongolia, around the time of the invasions, where, somewhat bizarrely to Sam's thinking, she had actually arrived a decade younger than her fourteen years, which had permitted her to learn to ride and fight from horseback like every other Mongol child.

'This is all a bit cloak and dagger, don't you think?' Sam chuckled as he painstakingly adjusted his stirrups, measuring them with the span of his hand to make sure he had them just right.

'Can you blame them? They're being attacked in the press and they have people lurking around outside their door.'

'Even so; we know how skilled some of the Displacers from this time-line are; we saw them in action at Symposium. The thugs we've come across aren't much of a threat to them.'

'Sam, you know full well that a threat doesn't have to be physical to be a danger to us. The stories in the newspapers could have far greater consequences than anything that a few angry people could do. We're a secret society for a reason and if we lose that secrecy then who knows how it would affect our work. Here there's just a few articles in the paper to worry about, but could you imagine what would happen in our present if people found out about us? The amount of conspiracy theorists and nutjobs there are, we'd never be able to work, never be able to recruit new people, never be able to have anything even resembling normal lives. We'd have to become like MI5 and we'd probably have some kind of government oversight restricting us. We'd be controlled by men with their own agendas, who would try to get us to work for the country's benefit, or their own, instead of that of the time-line. We'd probably also be so bogged down with paperwork that it would prevent us from doing *what* we needed to do, *when* we needed to do it - it would be a disaster.'

'I suppose.' Sam shrugged. It was a bleak picture that Rachel was painting, but he couldn't help but feel that the time-line would find some way to sort itself out - if the Displacers couldn't do the job then it would find someone or something else that could.

Horns sounded, announcing that the hunt was about to start, and they left their conversation behind to concentrate on the job at hand.

They mounted up with everyone else and looked around for Halifax. He was on the far side of the riders, but he had his eyes on them and gave them a nod when he saw them spot him.

At the Hunt Master's signal the riders all surged forwards, trotting down The Long Walk, a long flat strip of grass, more than two and a half miles long and about a hundred yards wide, which Sam thought looked like it had been designed for aircraft to land on, despite it being decades before they would become widely available.

Rachel and Sam fell in towards the back of the pack and gradually manoeuvred their horses until they were riding beside Halifax. The young man gradually let the rest of the party pull slightly ahead, not too far as to call attention to themselves, but just enough to let them get used to having the three of them lagging behind.

It was a simple, yet clever bit of fieldcraft for a time when military tactics usually meant walking in a straight line into gunfire and Rachel was mildly impressed despite herself. Satisfied that they were in good hands she began to enjoy the ride, looking around to take in the countryside and the peace of the early morning.

The morning mists had burned off completely now, apart from between the trees on either side where it was still clinging to the undergrowth, but the dew was still wet on the floor and the spray from underneath the horses hooves created rainbows in the air before it settled again. There were a few people out riding on their own, not part of the hunt, and others on foot, but it was still too early for there to be too many of them.

She yawned widely and shared a grin with Sam when he laughed; they hadn't gotten much sleep the two nights since the invitation had arrived.

The first evening they had gone to Scotland Yard to give their statements to Geoff and had ended up taking him and his wife to dinner and a show. It was something that they hadn't been able to do the last time because of the difference in their social standing, but now that Geoff's career was progressing he could join them without too much awkwardness and Sam and Rachel were delighted to introduce the Williams' to their friends. After describing Geoff as "the man who saved my life" Sam had assured him a warm welcome and for the rest of the night the inspector and his wife were laughing and joking with lords and ladies as if they had never lived in the slums of the East End.

Then, the day before the hunt, they had received a last minute invitation to a ball and had eagerly accepted. They loved socialising in Victorian London far too much to forgo the chance of doing so whenever they could and they weren't at all concerned about being tired for the next day's work - days on end without sleep in Sparta had given them the ability to keep going under far more extreme circumstances than missing a few hours sleep, as they had demonstrated the night they had Displaced. They had danced and laughed until past midnight, arriving home only a few hours before the carriage had arrived to convey them to Windsor.

After only a few minutes the hunt came to the end of The Long Walk and made their way up the gentle slope towards the copper statue at the top of the rise. The trees thickened beyond the hill and the horses plunged into them.

Halifax, however, came to a halt, using the statue as cover to hide them and then, when the last of the riders had disappeared into the shadows of the forest, he led them off to the left and down a different path to the one the hunt had taken, almost doubling back on themselves.

They rode for only a short time before coming out of the trees again, in sight of a village. It was a sprawling collection of large cottages and low lying buildings in small valley surrounded by trees - a "typical" English village that you would see in a movie, especially one of the "Hammer Horror" films that James liked to inflict on them, but which no longer actually existed.

'This is Old Windsor.' Halifax reined in at the top of a small rise. 'My father owns a fair amount of property here, which is why we're allowed to hunt the deer park. It also provides a nice hideaway for the members in a place that isn't remotely associated with them.'

He pointed out a building on the edge of the village next to the village pond. 'We're meeting everyone at the inn, there.'

'It's a bit early for a drink isn't it? Even for an Elder.' Sam chuckled, but stopped quickly at the look from both Rachel and Halifax. 'Jeez,

I'm only trying to lighten the mood; you two look like you're going to a funeral.'

Rachel shrugged apologetically at Halifax and spoke, completely deadpan. 'I apologise for my husband; he's foreign and he doesn't do sarcasm very well.'

Halifax gave her a delighted laugh before spurring his horse towards the inn.

Sam sighed. 'One of these days I'll get you to laugh at one of my jokes.'

She reached over to pat him on the cheek. 'Oh, Sam… It's just as well I'm not marrying you for your sense of humour.' She smirked, then geed her horse and galloped down the slope in order to catch up with Halifax.

Less than five minutes later they tied up their horses outside the inn and the young man led the way inside.

The main room of the inn, just a slightly more fancy pub really, was empty, aside from a heavy set looking barman behind the bar, cleaning glasses. He looked up at them when they came in and obviously recognised Halifax because he simply nodded and kept working.

'The members are all billeted in the village, so there was no need to have them all here waiting for you. I'll go and get them. Have a seat while you wait and if you want anything to eat or drink just speak to Christopher.' He tilted his head in the direction of the barman. 'My father owns the inn so don't worry about paying; it's on my tab.'

Halifax gave them a smile, then hurried back out.

Rachel kissed Sam and wrapped her arms around him. 'I'm pretty hungry, actually, how about you?'

'I could eat a horse!'

She pulled back from him and raised her eyebrow.

He grinned widely at her and winked exaggeratedly; he still hadn't given up on trying to get her to laugh that morning.

She chuckled, but he was pretty sure it was more out of pity than anything else.

There was already bacon sizzling in the kitchen in expectation of guests and only a few minutes later they were sitting on a bench at a table against the wall, stuffing themselves with doorstep sandwiches and drinking tea from enormous tankards. Even so, they barely had time to finish their food and wipe the grease from their mouths before the Society members started to arrive.

They drifted in in dribs and drabs until there were more than a couple of dozen of them perched on chairs that had been dragged into a rough semi-circle around Sam and Rachel.

Sir Sam Vives and Lady Rachel had a continuity in the time-line for the Displacers in the past, just as they did for civilians, so for the people there it was as if they had never left. Even though they knew rationally that the two Displacers from their future wouldn't have been there for the eleven years since the Jack the Ripper incident, the time-line made them think they had been - they had even been reading about their exploits in the newspapers. However, it was a completely different matter for Sam and Rachel; they were seeing people that they hadn't met in decades.

It was not the time to catch up on personal news, though, so when everybody had arrived, they got straight down to business.

Abraham Hudson had liaised with them before and, true to convention, the other members left it to him to lead the conversation. There was a gravitas about him, a focus that he hadn't had before, and the two Displacers immediately realised that he had gone through the Transition and become an Elder since they had last seen him. He was joined by his only child, Albert, who had only joined the ranks of the Displacers and was apparently quite inexperienced. Abraham had lost his first wife some years previously in childbirth and had taken many years to remarry, which was why there was such a large age gap between him and his son. Sam and Rachel gave the boy a warm smile when they were introduced, but it didn't seem to reassure him at all. He looked young, innocent and wide-eyed, reminding Sam of how Dylan had been when he'd first met him, but above all he looked frightened and was sitting as close to his father as he could.

Unlike most Elders, Abraham got straight to the point without any preamble - a virtue he shared with his descendant. 'Well, obviously we've seen the articles in the paper and the people hanging around outside Headquarters, but we thought it was just the usual reaction to rumours and hearsay - it's not the first time we've had to deal with some nosy journalist or over-zealous politician. We were going to wait it out; these things usually blow over on their own, but when there was no sign of things getting better we realised that there was something else going on and took precautions. Is it that Price fellow again? Or some other threat from the future?'

Rachel nodded. 'It's Price.'

Abraham grunted and the rest of the members all reacted in some way at the confirmation of their suspicions, but Rachel wasn't finished.

'But, we believe that the attack on you in the press isn't his main objective. It's just a distraction for something much larger'

'Larger? Like what?'

Both Sam and Rachel shrugged, almost in unison, before Rachel answered. 'Unfortunately we haven't been able to find out. I'm afraid we're going to have to wait for him to make his move, whatever it is, and do our best to react.'

'We're not as vulnerable as you might think.' Abraham chuckled. 'Even with your friend Price using his knowledge of our future against us we're not without our protection - we have palace guards standing by to come to our assistance at a moment's notice, which is why we're staying so close to the castle. I take it you know we're under unofficial Royal patronage?'

Sam shared a smile with Rachel before answering. 'It is something that has come up, yes.'

'But do you know why? Do you know how that came about?'

'Actually, no.' Sam looked at Rachel, wondering if she knew, but she just shook her head.

'I'm not surprised; one of the first things we did after "The Royal Event", as it's been dubbed, was to write into the hidden laws of the Society that it is to remain a secret from *all* members until they become Elders.' He motioned at the members sitting quietly and patiently, watching Sam and Rachel with almost disturbing interest. 'Most people here already know about it because it happened only a decade or so ago, but you shouldn't be told about it in your own time until you go through the transition. That is a necessary safety precaution to safeguard an event that prevented the possible dissolution of our Society, but we believe you should hear it, because it has bearing on our current situation and it is information you might need.'

He gave them a pointed look and they both nodded their understanding of his implied warning not to spread the story around.

'In February of eighty-six, there were riots in the West End because people were freezing to death and starving. Some of the more soft-hearted members were a tad imprudent...' Abraham glanced around, somewhat shamefacedly, receiving corresponding looks from some of the older men and women around him and Sam and Rachel noted with interest that they were mostly the members they had taken a shine to in their last visit - some of the least elitist of the largely aristocratic Victorian Displacers.

'Instead of simply providing food and blankets, some of our members took it upon themselves to invite some of the worst-off into our homes... and the Society itself. Unfortunately, there was an undesirable element that took advantage of our kindness and stole a couple of artefacts from us.

'We couldn't afford to lose them and obviously you weren't available to work the case, Sir Sam, so we had to turn to the police for help. The pieces in question were eventually recovered, but in the process the police realised what they were and began asking some rather awkward questions, mainly to do with why we had property that should, by all rights, have been in the possession of the crown.'

Abraham chuckled. 'We couldn't exactly tell them that we had rescued them from being lost in France by Henry the Fifth during his campaigning, so we stalled them until we had made up our minds what to do. And I must say that what we came up with was rather bold!'

He paused for effect, smiling at the pair, and they saw identical smiles on faces around them as the members recalled what they had done with not a small measure of pride.

'Lord Price, being our highest ranked member, petitioned the Queen for an audience, which was granted in due course. Lord Price, Hamish Craig, and I, were chosen to represent the Society, and only a couple of days later we were shown into Her Majesty's presence at the palace.

'Lord Price politely requested that the Queen dismiss her servants and attendants so that we could speak alone and, to our surprise and gratification, the Queen agreed readily and without question. By the light in her eyes we could all see that her curiosity and bravery had not been completely destroyed by the Prince Consort's death.'

There were mutterings of approval from the other Displacers at this observation; Queen Victoria was well loved among her subjects and none of the people who knew her and remembered what she had been like before the death of her beloved husband enjoyed seeing her in perpetual mourning.

'We explained our difficulties with the artefacts and told her that we would give her a good reason for us having those objects in our possession, but we begged permission to give her a small demonstration first. You see, one of the main reasons why the three of us had been chosen to go to the palace was that we were available to Displace - the Society had decided that, for the first time in our history that we know of, we would allow an outsider to witness what we do. Her Majesty was asked to sit and then a chair was placed in front of her from where we would, one after the other, go into the past.

'Lord Price went first and Her Majesty was suitably startled when a sheet of parchment appeared in his hand as if by magic, but she, naturally, suspected sleight of hand and wasn't entirely impressed. It was only when Lord Price started reading that she realised that something special had happened - Lord Price had come back with a previously unknown Shakespearian sonnet, commissioned by him from the man himself. It was a love poem to a young Queen Victoria, who Shakespeare had of course never met, but who Price had described in detail, paying special attention to the love she had shared with Albert.

'When Price had finished he presented the page to Her Majesty, relinquishing his place to Hamish, who immediately started Preparing. He had chosen to go to Ancient Greece and brought back a copy of some of Pythagoras' works.'

He looked pointedly at Sam and Rachel, obviously expecting some comment, and the rest of the members grinned as they did the same.

Sam glanced at Rachel, hoping that she would have some idea of what they were expected to say, but she just shrugged, and Sam was forced to give Abraham an apologetic smile. 'I'm sorry, but the classics aren't so well known or taught when we come from...'

Instead of making an unkind comment the Elder just laughed. 'No matter! Her Majesty, however, *is* a classical scholar and when she read the Greek text she immediately recognised that it was one of Pythagoras' works. Of which none survived, by the way.'

Sam and Rachel nodded, finally understanding.

Abraham laughed again when he saw that they weren't as impressed as he thought they would be and gave them a wry smile before he continued. 'That *might* have been enough to convince Her Majesty that we were something rather unusual and maybe persuade her to forgive us for our alleged misappropriation of Royal property, but we still had one card left to play, one that we believed would provide the coup de grâce, so to speak.'

Here Abraham was interrupted by a few laughs and someone called out. 'We, Abraham? It was your stroke of genius that carried the day, don't be so coy!'

There were more laughs at that and Abraham grinned and nodded gracefully as he looked around. 'Thank you my friends, although, as always, I must insist that it was Everett's influence that made me the man I am today.'

There were some downcast faces at that and Sam winced slightly. After reading Everett Lloyd's diaries he had researched the man himself, curious as to whether he'd continued his work beyond what was in them and what he'd done as an Elder, but had found out that he had been killed at a young age, shortly after writing his diaries. A promising career and brilliant mind lost to a common traffic accident.

Sam was thoroughly enjoying watching Abraham's performance. Not just because he really knew how to tell a story, but also because he had finally been completely accepted by the Society and gotten the respect he deserved. He was supremely confident and obviously loved by his colleagues - very different from how he had been in Lloyd's diaries where he had been described as young and insecure, almost an outcast because of his working class background, and many of the members had treated as a kind of servant or worse. The Elder had managed to put most of that behind him before they had met him, but there had still been some resentment towards him, evident in the behaviour of some of the "old guard", as they had been known.

It was very easy to see where James had inherited his quiet confidence and competence from.

'My "stroke of genius', as you so kindly put it, Thomas,' he bowed his head towards the Elder at the back of the group who had spoken up, 'was only possible because I had an ace up my sleeve that my colleagues didn't - I had been a bit of a devoted admirer of Her Majesty for my whole life. My Mother was a royalist through and through and made sure that I was as well, so I knew quite a bit about her. Specifically, I knew that she'd had a favourite toy when growing up: a doll from Quebec, which had been given to her by her father and that had gotten lost in the turmoil when she had assumed the throne.'

Abraham grinned widely, hugely pleased at himself. 'You can imagine how surprised Her Majesty had been when the men sitting before her suddenly had precious and rare objects in their hands, but can you imagine just how surprised she was when one of those objects turned out to be a doll that she had thought lost many years ago?

'I am not going to bore you with the details, suffice it to say that she was convinced and, during that and subsequent visits, we managed to explain exactly what we do. Her Majesty swiftly came to understand our importance and was kind enough to forgive our transgression. Furthermore, she agreed to help keep our secret and even placed us under the protection of the crown.'

'Job well done, Abraham!'

There were laughs at the gentle heckling and a few other similar comments came from the listening Displacers.

This time Abraham acknowledged them only with a smile and a wave for them to quieten down before he continued. His tone was much more serious than it had previously been, though. 'You must see why this has to be kept secret - we are not immune to having our own history changed and if an enemy in the future, like your Illuminati, found out about...'

He was cut off by a laugh from behind the bar and the Society as one spun to face the source.

'What a lovely story, I'll have to tell it to the boss sometime; I'm sure he'll enjoy it.'

Quentin was behind the bar, pouring himself a beer.

It was a melodramatic moment so typical of him that Sam would have burst out laughing if it weren't for the seriousness of the situation and the likely danger. As it was, both he and Rachel leapt to their feet and started out from behind their table, trying to get some room to fight and praying that the Illuminati hadn't brought too many friends.

Their hopes were dashed instantly as, in a scene reminiscent of the "Crazy 88" sequence from *Kill Bill*, men poured into the inn and surrounded the group of Displacers.

The remaining Illuminati, including Diana and Laura, joined Quentin behind the bar, keeping it between them and the rest of the room, as if as a safety barrier.

Sam and Rachel had stopped advancing on Quentin when the thugs started coming in and instead moved to stand next to Abraham. Sam put a hand on the Elder's shoulder and spoke in a soft voice so that only he and Rachel could hear. 'Get your people outside when you can. Leave this to me and Rachel; this is our mess.'

The reply was equally quiet. 'Some of my lads could help you out.'

'No!' Sam hissed, feeling Abraham twitch under his hand at the vehemence of his reply. 'Rachel and I will deal with this, I won't have your people put at risk.'

That brought a low chuckle from Abraham. 'They can handle these thugs...'

Sam cut him off. 'It's not the thugs I'm worried about, it's me.'

Abraham looked up sharply, but Sam just shook his head. 'Please, just make sure you get your people to safety when everything starts.'

The last of Quentin's bullies came in, closing and barring the doors behind them. In total there were about twenty men, all big, muscled and tough-looking, most of them sporting signs of having been in fights. They glared at the Displacers, cracking knuckles or rolling shoulders.

Sam glanced sideways at Rachel and they grinned at each other confidently. They were outnumbered, but that was immaterial; in the confined space their opponents wouldn't be able to attack them more than two or three at a time, and if their skills were anything like those of the men who had invaded their house, then the result was a foregone conclusion.

That changed, though, when four of the men pulled out guns.

Quentin laughed. 'Well, Vives, I'd like to see...'

Sam never heard the how Quentin finished his sentence because he had already given himself over to the Beast.

CHAPTER 22
SHOWDOWN

Sam came back to himself and screamed as his right leg painfully gave way beneath him, then almost blacked out as he tried to use a hideously broken arm to catch his fall.

He hit the ground at the same time as the battered body of the last of the thugs and just lay there, staring at the unblinking eyes of the dead man in front of him, fighting back waves of blackness which threatened to close off his mind the same way that the Beast did.

'Sam!'

Rachel's face appeared in his vision and finally broke through the haze. He pushed himself up to a sitting position using his good arm, shrugging off Rachel's hands as she tried to push him down again and looked around, not quite believing what he saw. 'What happened?'

'Um...' Rachel shrugged, momentarily lost for words. 'You did, Sam. You happened.'

They were outside, near where they had tied up their horses. The door of the inn was off its hinges and lying on the floor in two pieces, several of the windows were smashed and two broken chairs were in the flower beds along the wall. The bodies of the hired thugs were scattered everywhere, one was even hanging half out of a window.

The Society members were standing in a group, peering around the corner of the building, obviously wondering if it was safe to come back. Most of them were staring at him in shock, but a few looked genuinely afraid of him and Albert wouldn't meet his eyes. Thankfully, none of them looked seriously hurt, although quite a few were sporting cuts and bruises and Halifax was looking very white and unsteady on his feet, being held up by two of his colleagues and clutching his arm.

Sam looked away from them, saddened, and checked Rachel over. She had a few cuts and bruises, but was moving easily; as always she had proved to be, if not the better fighter, then the more intelligent of them.

His concern for Rachel satisfied, he surveyed the debris again, trying in vain to provoke memories of the fight, but then frowned when he realised there was something wrong with what he was seeing. 'I don't see any of the Illuminati. Where are they?'

Rachel looked around with a start. 'I... don't know actually, I lost sight of them in the melee. They didn't join in.'

Sam swore. 'Damn it.' He held out his hand to her. 'Help me up.'

'No, you should...'

'Help me up, Rachel, now!'

She drew back slightly at the anger in his voice, but nonetheless grabbed his hand and pulled.

He struggled up and stood, favouring his bad leg. He clenched his fists and gasped as his body involuntarily tried to curl up to protect itself from the sudden agony and his mind tried to shut down.

When he finally regained control of himself and could think again, he carefully shrugged out of his jacket, noting that the collar had been torn completely off. He winced as the movement made the bullet wound in his side pull painfully; it had opened and blood had soaked through the bandages that he still wore. He ripped the sleeves off his shirt, wadded one up, then bound it against his side with the other to stop the bleeding.

That done he started to assess his new injuries, piecing together the story that they told. The list turned out to be even longer than it had been in Sparta after his graduation fights: his left arm was broken, snapped cleanly between his wrist and elbow, so he'd probably blocked something that he shouldn't have with it; there was a huge bump on his forehead that felt like he'd head-butted at least one person... and maybe some furniture as well; blood was flowing from his nose, which was broken again, so he'd let at least one good punch through. He straightened it idly as he continued his inspection; there were cuts of various depths on his hands and forearms that told of going up against a knife wielder; he had splinters in his bloody knuckles and a broken finger on his left hand; most likely one of the attackers had tried to defend himself with a table or chair and he had punched through it anyway; lastly there was a bullet wound in his thigh. It wasn't bleeding excessively, though, so it hadn't hit an artery, and it didn't feel like it had hit the bone.

He pushed the pain of his other injuries away and sent his consciousness to the leg, testing it, knowing that if he could stand he could fight. He found that he could put weight on it, but he would be a lot slower than usual.

He finished his evaluation just in time, as the Illuminati appeared from out of the inn, led by a grinning Quentin, who kept his pistol pointed at Sam. A few of the others, including Diana, had guns as well, although they looked uncomfortable with them and didn't bring them to bear.

Sam's face hardened and he prepared to call to the Beast again, but he stopped, gaping in shock and stood motionless, thinking that the pain was making him delirious.

John had appeared from around the far corner of the inn.

He was riding a large black stallion, but instead of Victorian riding gear he was dressed in something approaching the clothes worn by Clint Eastwood in Spaghetti Westerns. He was accompanied by a couple of men who rode in the Boer style and looked like the men that the Illuminati had recruited in South Africa. There was also a thin, middle-aged man in a dark suit, which was completely unsuited to riding, who didn't look as comfortable on a horse as the others and who ignored the Displacers completely as he gazed around at the scene of destruction in appreciation.

Quentin seemed almost as surprised to see John as Sam. He hurried over as the group reined in and stood, shifting nervously from foot to foot, as his leader dismounted, then slapped his horse on the rump to make it charge off.

John watched the stallion gallop away, smiling widely, before turning to face the people watching him. 'I always wanted to do that!' He laughed, his eyes glinting.

The two impassive Boers remained on their horses, sitting almost casually, with their rifles pointing vaguely at the Displacers, but the thin man slipped from his horse and sidled over to stand near the rest of the Illuminati.

'Who the hell are you?' Diana had come up beside Quentin and was looking John up and down with a disdainful sneer on her face at his clothing.

Sam had to work hard not to smile; Diana had obviously been working on her acting skills. She of course knew who John was and that he was the Master, but John didn't know that she did and her pretended ignorance allowed her to get a lot closer to him than she probably would otherwise.

John smiled condescendingly at her. 'Why don't *you* tell her, Quentin? Our friends over there already know who I am, and I think it's about time that everybody else did too.'

Quentin spoke out of the corner of his mouth without taking his eyes off John. 'This is the Master, Diana. Be respectful for god's sake!'

A laugh almost escaped Sam as the young woman's eyes widened and she seemed to rock back on her heels before catching herself. It was a performance worthy of any West End actor, even in the nineteenth century.

'Oh! I'm so sorry, sir! I didn't...'

John waved away her apologies without even really listening to them; he had already dismissed her and his attention was now firmly fixed on the Displacers. He pulled a gun from a holster at his waist as he walked towards them, the spurs on his heels making a cheerfully incongruous tinkling noise.

He came to a halt a couple of yards away from them and smiled at Rachel.

Sam immediately shifted to put himself in front of her.

John just laughed. 'Relax, Vives, I'm just being friendly. I'm not here to kill you or your little girlie there!'

'Then why are you here?'

'I'm here for Hudson.'

'I'm here.'

John looked up as Abraham pushed his way to the front of the group of Displacers who were now standing in a huddle a few yards behind Sam and Rachel.

'No, not you. Why the hell would I want you?' John rolled his eyes and tutted. 'Where's your son, Abraham? Where's Albert?'

'What do you want with my son?'

'Well, duh! I want to kill him!'

Shocked silence greeted John's words until Abraham growled. 'Over my dead body!'

John laughed and there was a hint of insanity that neither Rachel nor Sam missed. 'Really? I can't believe that someone would actually say that in real life!' The grin disappeared instantly from his face and was replaced by a look of such hatred that Sam cringed. 'That can be arranged.'

He looked past the Elder and scanned the group. 'Come out, boy or I'll start killing people, beginning with your father here.'

Abraham laughed, brave in the face of the naked aggression on John's face. 'If you shoot us it won't matter, we'll just come back to life when you leave.'

John nodded. 'That's very true.' He moved his gun slightly to point at Sam. 'I can only really threaten these two here... Which is why my taciturn companions back there will be doing the shooting. I've been slowly working to convince various people of the devious nature of your society and one of my more inventive lies has my two friends convinced that you are agents in the employ of the Kaiser, come to betray the Boers to the British Empire. They firmly believe that you deserve to be shot on sight and the only thing keeping them from doing just that is that I've said I'm going to negotiate with you. Do you think you'd be able to come back from that? Shall I allow them to kill a few of you so we can find out?'

'No!' There was a shout from among the Displacers and Albert stepped out of the group.

Abraham tried to wave him back, but the boy ignored him and came to stand beside his father.

'If I go with you will you leave everyone alone?'

John pretended to think about the question, scratching his chin and moving his mouth from side to side. After several long seconds he grinned and swivelled the pistol to point at Albert. 'I think not.'

The young Displacer sighed. 'Well, in that case...'

The boy's hand moved so fast that even Sam could barely follow it and a shot rang out, shockingly loud in the morning quiet. Birds cried in alarm and flapped away, but then there was silence again.

John blinked, frowning and tilted his head to one side as if puzzled. 'That wasn't in the script...'

Slowly, he looked down at his chest and the brown shirt that now had a neat round hole over where his heart was, the material already turning red, he then looked back up at Albert and took in the smoking gun that had appeared as if from nowhere.

His mouth moved as if he were trying to say something more, but the words never came out as his eyes rolled back into his head and he toppled slowly to fall flat on his face. His legs rebounded once and he twitched a couple of times, but then he lay motionless.

CHAPTER 23
REVELATIONS

There was a moment of stillness that seemed to stretch on forever as everybody looked down at John in shock.

The man was obviously dead and it was unbelievable, inconceivable even, that his reign of terror could have come to such an abrupt end.

Surprisingly, it was Quentin who recovered first. He screamed something incoherent and lifted his gun to point at Sam, absolute hatred in his eyes.

'No!' Rachel's scream answered Quentin's and suddenly she was in front of Sam, blocking his vision of the man, her arms around him and her body tight against his.

There was a shot and she jerked, then stiffened and went still.

'Rachel!' He looked into her eyes, searching for signs of the pain that he knew would be there, for signs that her life was slipping away after the gunshot. He Prepared himself, ready to damn the mission and take her home to safety.

There was no pain, no sense of her life slipping away, instead there was just puzzlement as she pulled back from him and looked down at herself in surprise.

'I'm... fine. What...?'

As one they looked up at the Illuminati.

Diana was standing in front of Quentin, just as Rachel had been in front of Sam and, as they watched, her knees buckled under her and she slid gracefully to the ground.

Quentin just stood staring down at her, gun smoking and mouth open in shock.

Sam growled. He felt the beast surging within him, begging for release, but he pushed it down, snarling at it. 'No, he's mine!'

Ignoring the awful pain in his leg, he shoved Rachel roughly to one side and burst into a sprint.

Quentin saw him coming and started to bring the gun up from where Diana had dragged it down, but the avenging Displacer was on him before it was even half way.

Fuelled by memories of the man's treachery and of every time that he had hurt someone, Sam poured all of his pent up emotions and frustration into the assault along with every last ounce of fury he could summon. This time he wasn't going to let the Illuminati survive, he was well beyond the point where he had any doubt about that.

He had denied his need for vengeance for too long and was going to watch his enemy, his nemesis, *suffer* before he died.

When Sam knocked his gun away, the look of shock and surprise on the Illuminati's face mirrored the one that had been on Smithy's when he had taken the knife thrust which had been meant for his captain.

Sam followed up with several quick strikes to the chest and abdomen that drove his opponent back and left him without air. Even with only one usable arm, the attacks were too quick for Quentin to follow and he hit the man over and over, sending the Illuminati staggering and stumbling. He didn't relent, but kept up the attack, wanting Quentin to feel the same pain and helplessness that he himself had felt as his friend Francis had died in his arms after blocking the path of the bullet that would have killed Sam.

His sorrow over the death of his mother's sister, Susan, and the way that it had ruined his Uncle Andrew's life, left him without pity, and when Quentin tried to lift his arms to protect himself Sam knocked them back down, hitting pressure points to render them useless and the Illuminati defenceless.

He howled as he saw again the body of Andrew lying in a pool of his own blood and put that anguish into the kick that took the man's feet from under him and knocked him to the floor. He followed him down, thrusting a knee into his chest to hold him in place, summoning the anger he had felt at Quentin's mocking distraction, which had allowed John to carry out his betrayal, using it to push away all thoughts of mercy as he continued to punish him.

Some part of him was aware of it when the two men who had accompanied John rode away, showing the innate cowardice of the bullies that they were. He ignored them, remaining focussed on the increasingly battered man trapped and helpless beneath him, just as he ignored it when the Displacers rounded up the unresisting Illuminati, and when Rachel and Laura dragged Diana's bleeding body away.

When Quentin tried to close his eyes and turn his head Sam dragged him back by the chin, growling at him to open his eyes, and when he did, the terror in them made the Beast writhe and laugh, once more begging to be let loose to enjoy itself.

'No.' Sam told it again.

Unfortunately, playing with a helpless rag doll wasn't as satisfying as he'd thought it would be and, despite the Beast's delight and urging to continue, Sam decided that enough was enough. He wrapped his hands around his enemy's throat and started to squeeze the life out of him, his white hot rage at Diana's death leaving no room for mercy.

'Please...' The word was faint, forced out between bloody lips and broken teeth, and Sam just shook his head.

'Not this time.' He pressed harder, leaving no air for Quentin to beg anymore.

'Sam...' Rachel's voice was gentle in his ear.

Sam took no notice of her, not wanting anything to distract him from savouring the moment when the light finally faded from Quentin's eyes.

'Sam!'

'What?' He snapped.

Rachel reached out and put a hand on his arm. 'You don't have to do this.'

'Yes, I do. It will never stop if I don't - people will continue to die and lives will continue to be destroyed. I can't let that happen. He killed Susan and Diana and helped John to kill Andrew, so now I'm going to kill him.'

Sam gritted his teeth and squeezed harder.

Quentin's eyes were bulging and his face was red and Sam knew it wouldn't take much more pressure to crush the windpipe beneath his hands and end it.

'Diana isn't dead, she's hurt bad, but Laura is getting her home.'

Relief surged into Sam and involuntarily his hands relaxed slightly, but then he hardened his resolve and bore down on them again.

He shook his head. 'It doesn't matter.'

'Are you sure, Sam?'

'Yes.'

'OK, then.'

He felt her pat his arm before she walked away, leaving him alone with his prey.

Sam mentally prepared himself to take a life in cold blood, not as the Beast, but as himself.

Giving himself over to the Beast when killing needed to be done was easy and it gave him an excuse to say that it hadn't been him doing the killing. It was acceptable under normal circumstances, where survival and victory were the only thing that mattered, but this wasn't one of those times. To kill now had to be a conscious choice, made by him for the good of the time-line. For the good of the world.

He gritted his teeth and...

Froze.

He could sense something in the body beneath him, something that was causing a tingling at the back of his mind, clamouring for his attention.

Sam took some of his weight off his hands, allowing Quentin to take a gasping breath. The man wasn't going anywhere so he had time to figure out what the... feeling... was.

It was almost like Quentin was Preparing, but that was impossible; there was no way he would be able to concentrate enough in his current situation to do that.

Sam frowned as he closed his eyes and reached out, ignoring the man's weak struggling.

His eyes shot open and he smiled.

'Quentin.'

There was no response so he took one of his hands from the man's throat and slapped him none too gently.

'Quentin, look at me.'

The Illuminati focussed gradually as consciousness flooded back into him and he met Sam's gaze with eyes that were bloodshot and swollen.

'I'm not going to kill you, Quentin.'

He watched the words sink in, saw the Illuminati's brain slowly processing them.

'Why?' The voice was a barely intelligible croak.

'Because I have a better punishment for you.'

Sam reached out and touched the thing that he had sensed. He *pulled*, feeling something come free beneath him, and drew it into himself.

Quentin jerked once, as if in agony, and gasped. 'What...?'

Sam didn't answer, he just stood up and walked away.

The few remaining Illuminati had given up as soon as John had died and the Displacers, led by Rachel, had herded them together and taken their weapons. They were now standing in a group, staring in shock at the body of the man who had ruled them with an iron fist for years.

They looked up as one when Sam approached and flinched back, trying to get away from him, but they were stopped by the solid wall of Displacers surrounding them.

Sam ignored them, though, and went to where Rachel was standing with a sopping wet Laura, who had a horse blanket around her and was shivering gently.

Diana was gone. Laura had dragged her to the nearby pond and put her in, holding her there until she disappeared, just like Sam had done with Rachel in South Africa.

Rachel looked at Quentin then back at Sam. Her face screwed up in concern and she reached out to touch his face. 'You left him alive? I'm not going to say I'm upset, but I am kind of surprised; you looked so sure of yourself...'

'In the end I did something worse.'

'What's worse than killing him?'

Sam grinned at her. 'I'll tell you in a minute, but I want everyone to hear.' He looked at where Quentin had rolled over and was struggling to his knees. 'Be right back.'

He returned to Quentin and squatted down beside him, wincing at the sudden stab of pain in his leg where the bullet wound was increasingly making itself known. 'Quentin, I want you to come and join us for a nice little chat.'

'Get bent, Vives.'

'Now now, there's no need to be like that. I did you the favour of sparing your life, so you could at least be moderately polite in return. Now, do you want to make your own way over there or shall I drag you?'

Quentin swore under his breath, but nonetheless struggled to his feet. Sam hadn't beaten him so severely that he couldn't walk, but he did have darkening bruises in a ring around his neck and he was coughing and wheezing slightly.

Sam pulled him to a halt in front of his colleagues and then looked at them one by one.

According to Diana's letter, with the exception of the Twins, they were all that was left of John's defunct organisation. They were young and most of them were too frightened to meet his gaze, which gave Sam hope that they hadn't been with the Illuminati long enough for them to be so corrupted and uncaring as to be beyond saving.

'In a minute I'm going to let you all go home.'

There were obvious signs of relief among the Illuminati at that, but he brought them up short with a stern look.

'But first you have a choice to make. I'm sure by now you all know that I can track you when you come into the past and you've probably heard about the promise I made to your leaders. Well, that promise still stands - if I feel you going into the past unannounced, I will hunt you down and kill you, it is as simple as that. So, your choice is simple, either you *never* travel through time again, which would be a waste, or you can come to pay the Displacers a visit. We have some very nice Elders who will be able to tell you exactly why you should join us and what you should be doing with your lives instead of ruining the world with the Illuminati. You'll also get tea and biscuits and help with any problems you have in the present. We take care of our own and there's even medical coverage.'

He grinned and looked around. Unfortunately, though, he didn't seem to be winning them over, even with his efforts at lightening the mood; the memory of how he had ripped apart the men they had brought along was too fresh in their minds.

'Even if we believed you, what about him?' A young woman pointed accusingly at Quentin. 'If we join the Displacers how will you protect us from him? He knows who we are and he knows where our families live. We've seen what happens to people who don't do what they're told.'

The woman shrank back in fear when Sam's eyes alighted on her. She was probably cursing herself for catching his attention and he wanted to reassure her, to tell her that she was safe, that he wasn't going to hurt her, but he couldn't, not yet anyway; the young men and women had to fully understand just how much their circumstances had changed before he could do that.

They had to realise they were truly free from the grasp of the Illuminati.

Sam put his hand heavily on Quentin's shoulder, gripping it tightly. 'What do you say, Quentin? If I let you go home will you behave yourself?'

Quentin grinned, displaying ragged teeth that were covered in blood. He was obviously feeling his confident self again, sure in the knowledge that Sam wasn't going to kill him and certain that the cycle of cat and mouse that the two of them had played for years was going to continue as if nothing had happened.

'What do *you* think, Vives?'

Sam chuckled wryly and shrugged. 'That's what I thought you would say.'

He patted Quentin on the shoulder and then took a step back. 'Why don't you go home now, then? Let me talk to your friends here in private.'

Quentin laughed. 'Seriously?'

Sam nodded.

'OK. Then I guess I'll be seeing you soon.' He grinned and gave Sam a lazy salute then glared at the Illuminati. 'And I'll be seeing the rest of you a whole lot sooner.'

Quentin closed his eyes and rolled his shoulders, but after just a few seconds he frowned and opened them again.

'Is something wrong?' Sam gave him an innocent look. He motioned at the nearby pond. 'Would you like to go for a swim? Although, I don't think it would help very much...'

Realisation came over Quentin's face and he stumbled forwards and grabbed Sam by what remained of his torn and bloody shirt. He wailed with rising panic. 'What did you do to me?'

'Turns out I can't *just* feel it when you Displace, Price, I can also take that ability from you.'

Sam wasn't surprised when Quentin threw the first punch and he sidestepped it with ease, then just swayed to avoid the ones that followed.

The mad light was back in Quentin's eyes, but now it had a new intensity, as if something had finally snapped in him. He snarled and foamed at the mouth as his swings became increasingly wild, but after only a few seconds he gave up and collapsed to the ground sobbing.

Sam looked around at the Illuminati and the Displacers as they in turn looked down at the young man. There was an almost universal look of horror on their faces as the implications of what he had done sank in and he sighed. He hadn't made any friends that morning, but at that moment he didn't care; if even one of the former Illuminati showed up on their doorstep it would have been worth it and it didn't matter if they came because they were frightened of him or whether they knew it was the right thing to do; it was what was best for them and for the time-line.

To Sam's relief, the appalled silence was broken only seconds later by the rumble of hooves and a troop of household guards appeared from the direction of Windsor castle, led by someone with the unmistakable red hair of a Hamish Craig.

Sam gave Abraham a questioning glance and the old man shrugged. 'I sent for help as soon as I could. I didn't realise you wouldn't need it.'

'There's not going to be much for them to do; most of this mess will be gone as soon as Rachel and I leave.'

Sam grinned, but the smile disappeared from his face when he looked down at Quentin.

The man had curled up into a ball and was rocking gently back and forth, muttering something that sounded very much like "I'll kill you" under his breath.

Sam realised that he couldn't just leave him like that. 'Abraham, would you mind looking after Quentin?'

The Elder saw the direction of Sam's gaze and blinked in surprise. 'You want us to take care of him? After all that he's done?'

'I can't say I don't like the idea of him spending the rest of his life wandering around babbling nonsense, or forgotten in some dark hole somewhere, but he has knowledge of your future and might still be dangerous. He needs keeping a close eye on, just in case.'

The Elder nodded in understanding. 'Ah, of course. Leave him to us; there are places that we can put him - he'll be comfortable enough, but won't be a danger to anyone.'

'Thank you.' Sam watched as the guards pulled their horses to a halt and surveyed the bodies in shock. 'Can you handle them while I send the Illuminati on their way?'

'Of course.'

Abraham moved off to deal with the soldiers while Sam turned back to the remaining Illuminati.

If anything they were more nervous and frightened after his revelation about Quentin, but there was also hope in their eyes now and he hoped they were seeing the possibility of a brighter future beyond the intrigues and backstabbing of the Illuminati.

A man at the back of the group - the one who had arrived with John and the Boers - stood out from the rest, though. He was much older than the others, gaunt, with hair that was almost black and cruel eyes and Sam's heart fell as he saw the defiance in his glare. He sighed as he realised that he most likely wasn't done fighting for the day and beckoned for him to come forwards. The man did so, slinking smoothly, like a snake, through the group, his arms held loose at his sides and hands open, ready for anything, grinning in anticipation.

'What's your name?'

'Kyle Adams.'

'You arrived with John, right?'

The man nodded. 'That's right. I was the one who shadowed you here and then, while Price was ballsing things up, I went off to tell John where to find you.'

'You followed us all the way from London?'

'Of course! You didn't exactly make it hard. I'm the one John's had trailing you all around London since you got here, keeping an eye on you - I called in the goons after following you to the Savoy and back the first night you arrived, I followed you to your Headquarters, to that ball, the Savoy again with the cop... Everywhere you've been since you got here, I've been there watching you.' The man grinned proudly. 'And you didn't see me once in all that time, did you?'

'No, I didn't. You did well.' Sam smiled and shook his head, trying to look admiring. He desperately wanted to win Adams around without resorting to violence, but when the man sneered evilly, his hands twitching as if he was already imagining them around Sam's neck, he realised there was no hope of that; the man was a killer and by the looks of things he really enjoyed his work.

Sam knew exactly what was going to happen and he resigned himself to it; it was better to get it out of the way now, in the past, so as not to have someone so hateful running around in the present as a possible heir to the Illuminati cause.

Silence fell as they sized each other up and even the soldiers stopped what they were doing as they realised what was happening.

Sam stared the man in the eyes, willing him to back down, but he didn't. If anything the delay was giving the man confidence, making him think that Sam was reluctant to fight and that he had more of a chance.

Adams grinned. 'If I win will your friends let me go?'

'Of course. And if I beat you will you change your mind about the Displacers?'

The man just laughed, which saddened Sam further; he'd had enough violence and killing for a lifetime and with Quentin and the Master finally taken care of he just wanted to live in peace and put the

Beast in a cage permanently. It looked like he was going to have to have one last fight, though.

He sighed. 'OK, let's just get this over and done with then.' Sam turned and limped away, heading for an empty piece of ground nearby, using the opportunity to try to get his injured leg to loosen up - it had stiffened with the inactivity.

His senses were dulled by pain and exhaustion and if it hadn't been for Rachel's screamed warning he would have been dead immediately.

He turned to face the threat, but was slowed by the bullet wound, and gasped as the knife, which would have gone up between his ribs and into his heart, instead plunged deep into his side.

The young man laughed as he pulled the blade free, sending drops of blood arcing through the air.

Sam gasped and staggered back, clamping his broken left arm to the side of his body in an attempt to staunch the bleeding. It was deep, just below the bullet wound he'd received the first night, and blood was flowing freely. Fortunately, by the placement, he knew it would have missed his internal organs, but it would still be fatal if the fight went on for too long because this fresh blood loss, added to all that he'd previously lost, would weaken him still further.

His every instinct was screaming at him to call on the Beast, telling him that it was the only way to win, that it was precisely this kind of situation that it had been created for, but he resisted the temptation; if there was even the remotest possibility of turning Adams he had to find it and the Beast wouldn't care enough to even consider sparing the man that long, especially after blood had been drawn.

Out of the corner of his eye he saw Rachel start moving, about to intervene, and he raised his hand to stop her. 'This is my fight, my last one against another Displacer, hopefully. Let me do it my way.'

She obeyed his request and backed away, but gave him a worried and slightly puzzled look.

What she couldn't know and what he didn't understand himself, was that there was something stopping him from accepting her help. The two of them together would easily be able to overpower Adams without killing him, but once again there was some sense that this was his fight and his alone. It was the same feeling he'd had with many of the things he'd done which had somehow ended up being the *exact* thing that the time-line had needed - somehow he knew that the outcome of this fight had a relevance that went well beyond the reluctance of an Illuminati agent to capitulate.

He just hoped that didn't mean he was supposed to die at the hands of the man, but if the fight didn't finish quickly the blood he was losing would make that a very real possibility.

It didn't seem that there was much need to worry about that, though; the man seemed to be just as eager to get the fight over and done with as he was and surged forward to press his attack.

Sam was forced to twist and turn desperately to avoid the knife as it flashed in the strengthening sun, backpedalling rapidly. He watched for an opening while he retreated, but one never came; the man was too highly skilled - the fact that he hadn't heard or otherwise sensed the man's initial attack spoke to that eloquently enough, and the way he was moving, never overcommitting to a thrust, confirmed it.

However, when he saw that he wasn't getting anywhere, Adams soon stopped his attacks and instead started circling, keeping his distance.

He began to weave his knife back and forth smoothly as he sidestepped, but Sam knew better than to let himself be mesmerised by the glint of the sun off the blade and ignored it, making sure not to take his eyes from Adams'. There was a hint of annoyance in the man's expression when he saw that his opponent wasn't reacting as he'd hoped and Sam smiled inwardly; Adams' emotional response betrayed a severe lack of discipline, something that he could hope to take advantage of - if he didn't pass out first, of course.

The next distraction tactic from the man almost worked, though.

'Yoshi Hamato really hasn't done you any favours with your technique; it's unfortunate that you had to study with him when my master is obviously far superior.'

Sam frowned. 'What are you talking about?'

'You don't know?' Adams laughed, delightedly. 'Did you really think Hamato was living in the middle of the forest on his own by choice? He lacked sufficient determination to carry out the tasks that were necessary for his clan to gain power, so he was forced out by my master. I'm sorry you had to settle for second best.'

The Illuminati saw that his words were having an effect and he continued, all the while continuing to circle Sam, never letting his blade rest even for a moment.

'I'm not surprised he didn't tell you, actually. Apparently Hamato was stuck in the old ways and unwilling to change with the times, so his entire clan turned on him for their own sake. He would have been exiled peacefully if it hadn't been for your "gentle" master's treachery.

Did he tell you how he poisoned half the clan? His own family? How they died slowly, screaming in agony?'

Sam blinked, unwilling and unable to accept what the man was telling him and his muscles stiffened momentarily in shock, throwing him minutely off balance.

It was just the opening Adams had been hoping for.

The man moved so quickly that Sam barely had time to react and he blocked desperately, gasping in agony as the blade slashed across his already broken arm, cutting deeply into the muscle.

Blood flowed from yet another wound, mixing with what was already coming from him, and he staggered, forcing back the fresh agony and fighting to clear his head.

The time that he had before falling into unconsciousness was becoming ever shorter.

Overconfident and certain of victory, Adams tried again with a simple thrust, aiming to plunge his dagger into his opponent's heart and finish things, but Sam still had enough presence of mind to react and he punched out, connecting directly with Adams' throat.

It was a killing blow.

Or it would have been if Sam hadn't tried to use his injured arm. The punch lacked enough force to kill his opponent, but it did send him reeling back, choking and struggling for breath.

Bones scraped across each other and Sam screamed at the fresh agony, which sent blood rushing to his head, and with the momentary clarity it gave him he saw the chance to press his advantage, but his legs refused to move and he was forced to stand and watch, shaking gently, as Adams swiftly recovered.

The Illuminati rubbed his throat and coughed a couple of times, but then chuckled, evidently enjoying himself immensely. He obviously believed that the outcome of the fight was a foregone conclusion and once more began his circling, but this time he didn't take it as seriously - he did a little quickstep, dancing on the balls of his feet, and even jumped up into the air to do a complete turn, all the while laughing and taunting.

'Why prolong the inevitable?' The man put on an insane grin which somehow didn't quite fit his face as he continued prancing. 'I will kill you!'

It took Sam a good few seconds to realise what Adams was doing, but then he groaned inwardly; the man was actually doing an impression in the middle of a fight to the death. It wasn't a very good one, though; his rough Glaswegian accent completely spoilt it, making it sound more like a line from *Trainspotting.*

'Seriously? You're quoting *Dune* at me?'

Adams laughed. He stopped and spread his arms, giving Sam a shallow bow. 'Good catch! I'm actually quite surprised! And? What of it?'

'Well, if you're going to quote someone, maybe you shouldn't quote the guy who loses the knife fight and gets blasted into the floor.'

To Sam's satisfaction that made Adams' smile fade somewhat. 'You know what? I think I want to beat you with my bare hands.' Petulantly, he threw his knife to one side and it stuck into the earth, narrowly missing the foot of one of the female Victorian Displacers, who screamed in fear.

As all eyes went to the quivering knife and the terrified woman, Adams leapt back to the attack with a new intensity and concentration, throwing kicks and punches in a flurry, now deadly serious.

Sam hadn't been fooled by Adams' distraction tactic and wasn't taken by surprise, but he was reaching the end of his endurance, his vision blurring and reactions slowing, and the strikes began to make their way through his already compromised guard.

In desperation he reached out towards the Beast, no longer caring that it was the wrong thing to do, just wanting to survive.

There was no response.

If he hadn't known better he would have thought that the Beast was being petulant, sulking at not having been let out before.

The shock caused Sam to hesitate and he could almost hear the Beast's laughter as the blows from Adams connected more and more heavily. One particularly nasty punch struck the side of his jaw and he staggered, falling to his knees.

Sam struggled to recover, sending commands to muscles to move, but they wouldn't respond and he knelt there, vulnerable, the back of his neck open to a finishing blow.

He was on the ground for long seconds, but the end never came and slowly he turned his head to look up at Adams.

The Illuminati was standing with his arms crossed, a couple of yards away, grinning at him.

'Sorry, I was just enjoying the moment. I'll get around to killing you in a while.'

Blood was filling Sam's mouth and he had to spit it out before he could speak. 'Take your time. Please don't hurry on my account.'

As Adams laughed, Sam managed to gather enough energy to push himself to his feet. He put pressure on the wound in his side, grimacing at the pain, and took the opportunity to glance at Rachel.

Her weight was forwards, her eyes fixed on him, and he knew that he only needed to give her the tiniest of signals and she would leap to the attack. He shook his head slightly, a motion only she would catch, and she rocked back onto her heels as if he had struck her. He saw the question in her furrowed brow, saw her fear, and knew that it must look like he was committing suicide, but he also knew that she trusted him completely and, no matter how desperately she wanted to join the fight and how painful it was for her, she would stand and watch until he told her differently.

He wanted to reassure her that he knew what he was doing, but he wasn't entirely certain of that himself anymore, so he did the only thing he could and gave her a smile before turning his full attention back to Adams.

Adams had turned away and was smirking as he looked around at the audience they had gathered - the soldiers, Displacers and Illuminati were all silently watching, held at bay by Rachel and Abraham, anxiously waiting for the outcome of a battle that they sensed had a significance that was beyond their comprehension. His gaze finally fell on the still form of John, who had finally been covered by a blanket by one of the Displacers, and he chuckled again.

'I was supposed to step in and protect him. That was what I was here for. I was supposed to kill you before you could harm him.' The man laughed hysterically and turned to grin at Sam. 'Whoops! Well, I guess that boy put paid to that pretty quickly didn't he! Thank god!'

He laughed again, throwing his head back and putting his hands on his hips, a gesture that in anyone else would have been risible, but in him just seemed to add to his menace.

'You know, we went to school together, he and I. He'd already gotten his powers when I discovered what I was and he told me all about the Displacers. He was going to let the Society know about me, but I told him I didn't want him to; there was just something about what you people do that repulsed me - even as a child I knew that being a slave to time *really* wasn't the direction I wanted to go in! We stayed friends, though, and I think he liked the idea of having someone he could talk to outside of your stuffy club who understood what he was doing.'

He walked over to stand beside John's body and nudged it with his toe, as if making sure that he was really dead. 'One night he came home and went on a rant about his best friend, Andrew Berry, stealing the girl he loved. I forget what her name was, Sue or Susie or something like that... It's not important. Anyway, we got really drunk and that's when we came up with the idea of the Illuminati.'

Adams glanced sideways at Sam. 'You know, he really did love that girl. I don't know if his heart broke that day or what, but he changed; he became obsessed with destroying the Displacers and Berry in particular and that was the only thing he thought about after that.

'The plan we came up with that night was for him to slowly chip away at your Society from the inside, poisoning it and stealing recruits, while I used the information he stole to take over the world. Mostly he just wanted to play at being a Displacer still, though, having adventures and torturing himself by staying as close to the girl as he could. I let him think he was in charge and deciding what missions to send the minions on and I let him keep most of the money too, but in practice *I* was the one with the real power, it was *me* who really decided what to do and when to do it, not him. *I* was the one who sent the messages about missions and spoke to everyone on Skype, and it was *me* who made sure they all did what they were told and punished them when they didn't.

'It went well for a while, very well, and we were close to getting everything we wanted, but then the girl died and the idiot said we were going too slowly. He took over and tried to accelerate everything. For a while we made huge leaps forwards and it looked like we were going to win anyway, but then you came along and everything started going to hell. I knew that sooner or later, he'd get impatient and make a mistake, so I made sure I wasn't caught by surprise when he carried out that stupid mission to kill Berry.'

He gave Sam a shrug and what was almost an apologetic smile. 'I had nothing to do with that one, by the way, that was all him.'

Adams looked down at John's body again. He crouched and lifted the blanket to peer underneath as he spoke. 'Anyway, as you probably know, after that debacle he went on the run. These last few months it's been quite amusing to see him running around the world with his tail between his legs, although I must admit I was a bit disturbed when he sent that guy to bomb you, but still, all's fair in love and war, and I would have been the first to congratulate him if he succeeded.'

He looked up at Sam just long enough to give him a wink before turning back to the corpse. He twitched the blanket back into place, then stood up, dusting off his hands.

'Anyway, I used the distraction he was providing to put together this little mission so that I could finish things once and for all, and I must say that so far it's going pretty well!'

'Really?' Sam had been intending to let Adams talk as long as he wanted and fill in all the things they didn't know about the Illuminati while he tried to gather his strength for a last assault, but he was unable stay silent; he couldn't believe that the man thought his mission had succeeded. 'Are you forgetting your friend there? Or Quentin?'

Adams waved away Sam's words. 'Pish! Quentin is less than nothing and I was actually going to kill John myself before we went home if you didn't do it for me. I don't need him anymore, because once I've dealt with you and your boyish-looking lover over there, I'll have the boy killed and then the Hudsons will be gone forever. I'll be free to do what I want, when I want. I've always fancied being the President of America, maybe I'll give that a shot.'

He laughed, but stopped suddenly as something occurred to him. He gave John's foot a quick kick. 'Oh, and by the way, Johnny boy... "The Master"? Seriously?'

He turned his head to wink at Sam. 'The guy deserved to die for choosing a character from Doctor Who as his alias. I mean, if you guys had been a bit smarter you would have worked out straight away it was him.'

Adams laughed then rubbed his hands together. 'Anyway, that's more than enough talking for now. I'm bored! Let's get back to it, shall we?'

Without warning, the Illuminati sprinted forwards. He punched and kicked in a lightning combination that Sam withstood only with great difficulty. He twisted and turned in an attempt to parry with the uninjured parts of his body and received heavy impacts when he couldn't. He was forced away from the inn, stepping backwards almost continually to try to gain some distance, but the man pressed forwards, not allowing him space or time to recover.

Sam felt himself weakening, the scant energy he'd recovered during Adams' monologue already gone, and he wondered how long he would be able to last. Nonetheless, he gritted his teeth and kept on his feet, clinging on to consciousness however he could, determined to see the fight through to whatever end the time-line needed from him.

Unnoticed and silent, the watching crowd followed them, their interest bordering on the macabre, each spray of blood greeted with morbid fascination.

Rachel walked with them, staying in front of the group so that she would be free to leap in whenever Sam asked her to, continually having to blink away tears as she saw him hit over and over, saw his resistance declining and his chances of victory slowly disappearing.

She was dying, little by little, just as surely as he was, but something told her that she should trust him, that Sam wasn't finished, that there was something behind this incomprehensible choice of his.

She would see it through with him, no matter what the cost to them both.

Sam was fading fast as the blood loss made itself felt again, his vision narrowing and his thoughts becoming sluggish as the darkness once more threatening to overwhelm him.

However, as his brain began to shut down, something curious was happening - the less he tried to anticipate what Adams was doing and instead relied on his instincts, the less he was having to retreat or being buffeted by fists, feet or elbows.

He had no time to work out what was happening or what it meant, so he just accepted it, giving himself over completely.

He immersed himself in the peace that the Dalai Lama had helped him find and released his sense of self.

He used the horrific experience in the First World War to let go of his fear of death.

He used the single-minded purpose instilled in him in Sparta to ignore his injuries and endure.

He stopped thinking entirely and let his body move itself, placing his trust in the teachings of Master Hamato, which had been honed by countless sparring sessions with Rachel until they came automatically.

Lastly, he used the love that he had been given unconditionally by friends and family as motivation to keep fighting, to live and make his way back to them.

He became exactly what the time-line needed him to be - the sum total of everything he had learnt since he'd found himself on a ship in the Caribbean.

An interchange of blows that were far faster than the mute watchers could follow left Sam clutching his side in agony, but Adams staggered back from it with a broken nose and his left leg numb and almost useless.

Fresh adrenaline coursed through Sam, sharpening his senses and thrusting back the shadows at the corners of his eyes. New energy coursed through his body and it pressed forwards, almost of its own accord, seizing its momentary advantage with renewed determination.

Sam had been through similarly stressing situations during his training with the assassins and knew that it wouldn't last, the adrenaline would be burned away in only seconds, leaving him worse off than before, but it would be enough.

He would make it enough.

Adams was on the back foot, but he was still striking out, trying to counter the unrelenting assault and the Displacers and Illuminati scattered as he backpedalled through them, flailing wildly. The man might have been taught by Hamato's successor, might well have been one of his best students, but he didn't know Hamato's secret. He didn't know the one, most important, thing that the old ninja taught only to those students that were gifted enough to understand and implement it.

That technique is only the beginning.

The unity of mind and body, directed towards a single goal made a fighter great, but only when that was combined with a willingness to sacrifice *everything* for what they held dear did a fighter become truly *invincible*.

In that moment, when Sam found himself *truly* pushed to the limit for the first time in his life, everything became perfectly clear, and with that clarity came a realisation.

When Hassan al-Sabbāh had brainwashed his students, it had just been a way for a cruel master to get past a human being's natural instinct for self-preservation and turn them into slaves willing to do whatever he told them to, so when he had created the Beast it had been nothing more than a tool to remove Sam's free will.

Now, though, Sam was more than willing to do anything to save the people he loved and the time-line they lived in, even if it meant his own death. The Beast was no longer needed because he was finally ready to *consciously* make whatever sacrifice was asked of him.

A sigh filled Sam's head, accompanied by a chuckle, which reverberated like an echo in the mountains of Tibet before gradually fading - the Beast was gone and in its place were purpose and peace.

The instant when Adams knew he had lost resounded clearly in Sam's mind and he saw panic blossom in the other man's eyes.

The Beast would have revelled in the moment, making sure that it had its fill of carnage before taking the kill, but Sam didn't. Instead, he stunned the man with a quick combination before throwing him to the ground and pinning him in place with a knee, just as he had Quentin.

He put his one good hand on the man's neck and held him down, leaning forwards to use his whole weight to keep him there and staring his adversary in the eyes.

'Shall I do to you what I did to Price?'

Adams snarled and spit flew up into Sam's face as the man recovered from his shock at the turn in his fortunes and showed his defiance. 'I'd rather die!'

Sam reeled from the strength he saw in the man; even in defeat there was a fire in him, a certainty, a determination, and an intelligence, that neither Quentin nor John had ever possessed, and that Sam had only ever known in one man - James.

Suddenly he knew without doubt that it was to this exact moment in time that events had been leading him. Everything that he had done in the last two years and more than six decades had been preparation for one decision - a choice between life and death for one man.

Kyle Adams, an Illuminati who had previously been completely unknown to them, represented a much greater threat to the time-line than any of his companions ever had. He had the will, the knowledge and the single-mindedness to do what the vain and boastful Quentin, and the greedy, vengeance-obsessed John never could - entirely twist the world to suit his own desires and destroy everything.

He had to be dealt with, one way or the other, which meant that Sam had a difficult decision to make. He could let Adams live, take the man's powers and let him loose on this time with his martial arts skill intact, with vulnerable Displacers and a history to change. Or he could let him go home and monitor him, follow him whenever he Displaced and stop him each and every time he tried to do something, while always watching his back for the knife that would undoubtedly come.

Or...

The man's neck snapped under his hand with a crack.

Sam turned his head away until the twitches and convulsions finally subsided, not wanting to see the life fading from another human being ever again.

It had been the only way.

His every instinct, the instincts that he knew came from the time-line or whatever power had created him to protect it, had screamed at him that it was the correct and the *only* decision, no matter how much he detested it.

He sighed. It was over.

The last dregs of the energy which had sustained him through the fight drained from him and his body, that had taken so much punishment and kept going, finally gave up.

He felt soft arms wrapping around him as darkness took him in its embrace.

CHAPTER 24
RESOLUTION

It was something of a surprise for Sam to wake up. It was even more of a surprise to find that he was still in the past.

Rachel was hovering over him and when he blinked up at her, her worried look softened into a gentle smile.

'Here, drink this.'

Automatically Sam swallowed the drink that Rachel held to him and almost choked. He coughed, fighting for breath. 'What the hell is that?'

'Guinness. You need to get the iron back into your body - you lost a lot of blood and you're not going to get a transfusion out here in the middle of nowhere. Now shut up and drink some more.'

Sam forced himself to drink more of the black liquid. He wasn't a big fan of beer, preferring to drink wine when he was in the past with Rachel, but he supposed that, like tea, it was an acquired taste and he took large gulps, mostly to see her smile again.

When she finally took the glass away he was able to catch his breath and take note of his surroundings.

He was lying on a padded bench in the wreckage of the inn, hidden away in one of the quiet corners at the back, behind a kind of wooden partition. The sound of quiet conversation could be heard from the main area of the room and he thought he recognised the voices as belonging to the Displacers. His wounds had been treated and he was liberally wrapped with bandages underneath a clean shirt which looked military in nature and didn't fit him very well. Red had seeped through the bandages in various places to stain the shirt, but thankfully it wasn't fresh, so he'd probably stopped bleeding.

'I thought you would have dumped me in the pond and sent me home to heal.'

'You know I would never do that unless it was absolutely necessary; I never know when we're truly finished with a mission - you're the one who has the instinct for that.'

Sam smiled and reached up to stroke her cheek with a trembling hand. 'You don't do too badly.'

'My instincts told me to kill Diana when I first met her, remember? And look how that turned out...'

'I think we both misjudged her when we first met her.' Sam chuckled then winced at the pain the movement caused. He hadn't felt as beaten up since Sparta and he'd had a few years to gradually build up a tolerance of pain there. 'I think I'm ready to go home now, though. We're done here and I think I need an aspirin or something.'

Rachel laughed. 'I'll see if I can find you a couple!'

There were sounds of movement behind Rachel and a delegation of Displacers appeared around the screen. Abraham was accompanied by his son Albert, a couple of the other Elders and a cloaked woman, who hadn't been with the Displacers before.

Abraham looked Sam up and down with concern. 'You look like hell, son. I hope you're going to take a good long rest after what you've done today; you deserve it.'

Sam tried to nod, but just grimaced when his neck spasmed and had to settle for a smile. 'I will. The Illuminati are gone now, so I can go back to doing what I do best: being a normal, plain old Displacer.'

Abraham laughed. 'Well, I don't think you'll ever be that, but I know what you mean.' He stopped and looked nervously to the side, at the cloaked woman. 'Um, well, there's someone here who wanted to speak to you before you left.'

The woman stepped forwards and Sam looked up at her. He frowned, wondering who she was and why Abraham was suddenly acting so strangely.

His confusion was resolved as soon as she pulled back her hood to reveal a very familiar face.

She gave them both a large smile. 'Sir Sam, Lady Rachel. It has been too many years since you have graced us with your presence.'

'Your Majesty!' As Rachel bobbed a curtsy, Sam struggled to sit up. He knew he wouldn't be able to stand, let alone bow, but he was determined to face Queen Victoria with at least some dignity.

The Queen shook her head. It was a tiny gesture, but more than enough to make him stay as he was and he settled back onto the bench.

'Don't worry, Sir Sam, I won't take up much of your valuable *time.*'

They laughed at her joke and she nodded her acknowledgement.

It was one of the reasons why she was so well loved; she took an interest in her subjects and always had a personalised comment for them, no matter their rank or background.

'As you can well imagine, I am unable to fully understand the service that you have done us today, but I am assured by Mr Hudson that it has been the single most important act in the history of man. While that should seem rather like hyperbole, I know that Abraham is not often given to exaggeration, so I am inclined to believe him.'

The Queen frowned slightly as she peered down her nose at Sam and he shifted in his seat, wondering if he had done something wrong, maybe in not insisting on standing, but after a couple of seconds she just shook her head and went on with a faint smile on her face.

'From my many conversations with Abraham and his colleagues, I have come to understand that I won't remember you being here after you leave. I still can't quite see how that would be true; I remember dancing with you in London on several occasions and clearly recall your waltz as being one of the best I have ever had the pleasure of experiencing, beyond that of my own dear Albert. However, if it is true, then I insist on at least giving you a symbol of my appreciation for your actions, one which Abraham assures me will persevere.'

From within the folds of her cloak she pulled a small wooden box, about four inches per side, made of a dark wood.

'This is something my dear Albert dreamed up...' she paused and turned to Abraham and laid her hand on his arm. 'Oh, I never did thank you for naming your son after him. That was remiss of me and I do apologise.'

Abraham beamed one of the largest smiles that Sam had ever seen. 'Think nothing of it, Your Majesty, and how could I not, after you were so kind to me?'

Queen Victoria gave Abraham a smile tinged with sadness, then turned back to Sam and Rachel. She opened the lid of the box to reveal an intricate metal device held tightly in place by a red cushioned lining.

'I had Mr Brunel fabricate five of these over fifty years ago. I instructed him to make them uniquely complicated, so that they couldn't be reproduced, and he didn't disappoint. They will be given out by me and my successors when someone does something truly remarkable, and I do mean *truly* remarkable, Sir Sam. I always carry one on my person just in case, but so far I have never seen occasion to award one. Until today.'

She closed the lid of the box and stepped forwards. 'Hold out your hand.'

Sam did as he was commanded and she placed the box on it. She folded her hands around his and held his gaze with an intensity that Sam had never seen before, not even in Master Hamato or his grandfather. There was wisdom in her eyes, as well as infinite kindness and warmth, but also a deep well of sorrow which made Sam want to reach out to comfort her.

'You have our sincerest thanks, Sir Sam, as do you, Lady Rachel.' She looked from one of them to the other, meeting their eyes. 'Look after each other and, if you should ever come back, please do pay me a visit.'

She smiled, released Sam's hands, then swept away without another word.

Sam watched her go, then opened the box and inspected the object within. It seemed to be a cross between an astronomical device, a clock, and an engineering implement - all wires, cogs and elegant arcs of gold. It was chaotic and beautiful, unlike anything that he had seen before, a true work of art.

He looked up at Rachel. 'Well, now I'm *very* glad you didn't take me home!'

He handed her the box and she looked down at the small sculpture in amazement, her eyes wide. After a few seconds she looked up at him from under her eyebrows and gave him an evil grin. 'Yeah, I really should have dumped you in the pond, then I could have taken the credit for everything and this would have been mine.'

Sam laughed, but stopped abruptly as an ice-cold wave passed through him. The room spun uncontrollable and he closed his eyes until he felt that the muscles behind them were better under control.

When he opened them again everybody was looking down at him in concern.

'Wow, that wasn't nice.' He took a deep breath, then frowned as something occurred to him.

'Uh, Albert... Where on earth did you learn to shoot like that?'

The young Displacer looked down at the floor in chagrin, but Abraham nudged his son on the shoulder and laughed at the question. 'Go on, boy, tell them!'

'My first Displacement was a bit of a mistake...' Albert stopped and looked up at his father, who just gave him a nod of encouragement.

'I... I was having a bath and reading a book about the "wild west" and I guess I just closed my eyes at some point and imagined myself there. When I opened them again I was sitting behind a desk in the sheriff's office of Tombstone. That's a small town in America...'

Rachel smiled at him. 'We've heard of it; it's quite well known.'

'Really?' The boy's eyes lit up. 'And do you know about...'

Abraham stopped his son with a hand on his shoulder. 'Concise and to the point, Albert, just like you've been taught.'

'Yes, father.' The boy looked contrite, but there was a gleam in his eye as he continued. 'Well, at first I thought it was a dream, obviously...'

Rachel laughed, interrupting him. She ruffled Sam's hair, something she knew he hated, but liked doing anyway because she enjoyed teasing him. 'Looks like you've got Hudson blood in you after all, Sam! I always thought you were adopted - seems I was wrong.'

There were questioning looks from the surrounding Displacers and Sam sighed. 'My first Displacement happened the same way as Albert's; I was daydreaming about pirates and ended up on a ship, thinking it was a dream. I almost died several times before I worked out that it wasn't.'

Albert grinned and looked up at his father cheekily. He seemed happy that he wasn't the only one that something similar had happened to. 'See, father? It seems that the rule about not warning potential Displacers about their powers causes more problems than it solves. Maybe you should think about having it changed?'

Abraham laughed in reply and mirrored Rachel's gesture, ruffling his son's hair. 'If the rule is still in place for Sir Sam, then I don't think there's anything I can do to change it! Now stop trying to distract everyone and finish the story!'

Albert sighed, exactly the same way as Sam had, and Rachel burst out laughing, this time joined by Abraham.

Sam gave Albert a sympathetic smile and shook his head as if to say *what we have to put up with for love*. He pulled Rachel closer, ignoring the protests of his injuries, and wrapped his arm around her as she snuggled ever so carefully against him.

'I spent the next three years until 1881 as a deputy to the Earps, but then I got shot in a fight with a group of outlaws called the "Cowboys" led by the Clanton family. I guess I fainted from the pain or something because the next thing I knew I was back in my bath and the water was turning red from the hole in my arm.'

'The Clantons?' Rachel frowned. 'That rings a bell...'

Sam laughed incredulously. 'It should! You remember that episode of Star Trek we saw a while ago from the original series where they got stuck in the gunfight at the OK Corral?'

'That was the Clantons?'

'Among others.' Sam looked proudly at Albert with a huge grin. 'That is so cool! One of my ancestors took part in the gunfight at the OK Corral!'

Albert, grinned back. 'So you've heard of it, then?'

'Of course! It's one of the most famous gunfights in history - it's been in several films and TV shows.'

Albert blinked and frowned. 'What's "TV"?'

It was Abraham's turn to laugh again. 'Never mind, boy, that'll be a future thing that we've never heard of and will forget as soon as our friends leave.'

'Speaking of which, I think we should be going, I want to get Sam some help in a proper hospital.' Rachel gripped Sam's arm and gave him a stern look.

He chuckled briefly, but nodded, seeing the sense in her words; he was feeling worse with every second that passed.

He looked up at Abraham. 'What will you do now? Will you stay here or go back to London?'

'The rumours about the society will no doubt start to die down, now that your friends aren't around to pay people to stir up trouble. So we should be able to go back to Headquarters soon enough. Charles will let us know when the coast is clear.'

Sam couldn't help but wince when the old man mentioned Headquarters and he realised that, after visiting the building in the past, whole and familiar, he really wasn't looking forward to seeing it in its current sorry state. He met Rachel's eyes and squeezed her hand in reassurance when he saw his feelings mirrored there.

Abraham noticed the change in their mood and frowned. 'Is something wrong?'

Rachel took a deep breath before replying. 'There was a bit of an incident in our present - the Illuminati mounted an attack on us and the building on Grosvenor Place was mostly destroyed, along with much of its contents.'

To their surprise Abraham just shrugged. 'Well, if anything was lost you can always just send someone to copy it from a time when it was whole, or you can even take it if you're certain that nobody is going to use it in the intervening years. And as for Headquarters itself: it's only a building, it's replaceable. People aren't.' He frowned as he realised what he was saying. 'I hope you didn't lose any...?'

He trailed off and looked at Rachel questioningly.

She grimaced and nodded. 'We lost a couple of good men and women, yes.'

His face fell with genuine sorrow, which was echoed in the faces of his son and fellow Elders. 'Ah. I'm sorry, I really am.'

'Thank you.'

Abraham gave them a sad smile and there was an awkward silence until Sam turned to Rachel. 'Help me up, I want to say goodbye to everyone, and those Illuminati are still here, right?'

'Yes, I left them in the care of the other Displacers. They're having a cup of tea and some food.'

'You're giving them tea? Well, I hope that works better on them than it would on me...'

Rachel gave him a soft slap on the back of his head. 'You're not too beaten up to get beaten up, you know?'

He groaned and rubbed his head, then let her pull him to his feet.

He stood unsteadily, but then had to clutch at Rachel when his legs threatened to give way beneath him.

He'd been feeling strange for the last minute or so and had just thought it was just his injuries and blood loss making him nauseous, but this was something else entirely - something was dreadfully wrong with him.

A burning sensation ignited in his gut and he gasped, doubling over and fighting the urge to vomit. His heart was pounding in his ears and white sparks flashed behind his eyes, blinding him with a bright light that was strangely familiar. He sent his consciousness to the root of the pain and got confirmation of what he'd somehow already known - while the sensation deep within him felt very much like the last time he'd had one of Diana's curries, it wasn't; it was his powers flaring up. He'd taken Quentin's energy inside himself and now his whole body was alive with it. It was burning him up and he wouldn't be able to contain it much longer, but he managed to calm it temporarily with the promise of imminent release.

As his heart slowed he once more became aware of the world around him and he realised that Rachel had been calling his name.

He straightened with some difficulty and tried to give her a smile, but he was pretty sure he just ended up gurning. 'I'm alright, I just have to get home. As soon as possible.' His voice came out hoarse, almost a croak.

Rachel looked at him in alarm. 'Do you want to go now and leave me to deal with the Illuminati?'

He coughed, his throat raw. 'No. I'll be fine as long as I don't have to talk or move very much. Or do anything more than blink, although, that hurts too.'

Rachel held his glass out to him and gulped down more of the strong black liquid, which dowsed the flames somewhat.

He wiped his mouth on the back of his hand. 'Thanks.'

'No problem.'

With Rachel's help he staggered out into the main area of the inn and they stood in the middle of the room looking at the small group of Illuminati.

Before they could say anything, though, Laura stood up.

'Um, Mr Vives? We've been talking. We understand why you had to do what you've done today and we don't blame you for any of it.'

There were nervously enthusiastic nods from the rest of the young Illuminati and she paused, glancing around at them as if looking for support.

'And, um, well... we were wondering if, uh, the offer was still open for us to join you?'

Neither Rachel nor Sam could do anything except stare at her for long seconds. It was all they could do not to burst out laughing at her performance. It wasn't until she gave them a pointed stare, which her companions couldn't see, that they managed to pull themselves together.

To Sam's relief, Rachel recovered first and took charge, smiling kindly at the girl. 'What's your name?'

'Laura Matthews, ma'am.'

'Call me Rachel, Laura.' She looked around the group, meeting the eyes of the other Illuminati in turn. Some of them were still terrified, despite having been treated well. 'That goes for all of you.'

She received a couple of tentative smiles in return, but they were too anxious to relax, waiting for her answer.

Rachel nodded. 'That offer is still open and it always will be.'

There was genuine relief on their faces and not a few of them let out a breath that they had been holding.

'We'd like to take it then, please.' Laura grinned and gave them a cheeky wink.

'Then you just need to come and see us when you get back to the present. There will be someone on hand at our Headquarters to take care of you, even if it is out of commission at the moment.'

The way the worries and cares faded from the young men and women, some of them not much more than children, was almost pitiful, and again Sam cursed John, Quentin and not Adams as well, for having corrupted and misused them.

Rachel looked around the group reassuringly one last time and then nodded. 'You're free to go now. Get in contact with us as soon as you can and we will make sure you and your families are kept safe.'

Sam went cold at her words as he realised that there were still two Illuminati unaccounted for. 'And if you have any trouble with the Twins then just let me know and I'll take care of it.' His voice cracked as he spoke, but it seemed all the more forceful for it and his determined look, due more to his battle to stay conscious than anything else, just added to the effect.

The former Illuminati nodded and closed their eyes.

One by one they disappeared until only Laura was left. She stopped pretending to Prepare and glanced around to make sure that her companions were gone before giving Sam and Rachel a worried look.

'I couldn't leave without asking you: is Dylan alright? When I didn't see him with you...' She was on the point of tears, obviously fearing the worst.

Sam nodded. 'He's fine, he has a few broken bones, but nothing life-threatening. I sent him home, but before he went he told us to tell you that he loves you and will see you soon. We'll let him know that you asked after him too and that you're OK.'

'Thank you. Please tell him I love him too and I'm looking forward to not having to hide anymore!'

'Will do.'

Rachel frowned at her. 'And you make sure that Diana is taken care of, OK? Ring the number Dylan gave you as soon as you get back and MI5 will get help to you as quickly as they can.'

'Don't worry, I've got it covered.' Laura gave them both a wide smile that transformed her pale and wan features into something that was entirely more beautiful, then closed her eyes.

A minute later she was gone and it was just Sam, Rachel and the Displacers left.

Along with Quentin.

The man was sitting curled up on the floor in a corner of the room, leaning against the wall, scratching at it with a fingernail.

Hamish was guarding him, perched on one of the few bar stools that remained intact. He looked up as they approached and nodded in respect.

Sam nodded in return then took in the sight of the broken man.

Quentin was babbling incoherently, his eyes darting around without fixing on anything. It seemed that his mind, already fragile, had been destroyed by the removal of his powers - powers which had been the source of his pride, his ego, his identity, and the entire direction of his adult life.

Sam struggled to bend down so that he was close to his adversary. Close to the man he had once considered his nemesis. 'Quentin... Quentin!'

There was no noticeable response from him so Sam just stood back up.

Rachel saw his concerned look and shook her head coldly. 'He's not worth it; think of how many lives he's destroyed and how much damage he has done. He does not deserve your pity.'

'I know, but...'

'But nothing! Leave him. Put him out of your mind forever and let others worry about him from now on.'

Sam nodded reluctantly. 'OK.'

'Good. Now come on, you're going to fall over if we stay here any longer, and I don't fancy carrying you to the pond; you're a bit big for that, and besides, I don't want to get wet!'

Sam laughed, even though it hurt. 'Alright, come on then.'

He hugged Rachel to him with his good arm and together they turned to face the Displacers, who had quietly gathered around them.

'I'm sorry to have brought this trouble with me...'

'Stop talking nonsense, boy.' Sam was interrupted by Abraham, and it was he who led the charge.

Sam and Rachel were swamped by a wave of people who congratulated them and shook their hands, extremely delicately in Sam's case, telling them how proud they were of them and wishing them well for the future.

It was an uplifting end to what had been a nightmarish Displacement and when the Displacers finally backed off Sam and Rachel gave Abraham one last grateful handshake, then turned to face each other.

Sam took Rachel in his arms and leaned in to whisper in her ear. 'Marbella, 1968. Just saying.'

Rachel chuckled. 'Alright. I think you deserve it.'

Their arms still wrapped around each other, they closed their eyes and went home.

CHAPTER 25
BACK TO NORMAL

The building that the Queen had lent them as a temporary headquarters had, among other things, a dedicated medical suite with a small staff always in residence and it was there that Sam, Rachel and Dylan were rushed as soon as they came back.

Sam had fallen unconscious as soon as they arrived, so he missed the panic that the sight of so much blood over both him and Dylan had caused.

He missed Rachel instantly taking charge, despite her own wounds and exhaustion, and laying out the extent of their injuries to the two doctors who had been standing by for just such an eventuality.

He missed the shock, disappointment and shame of the other Displacers who were supposed to have accompanied them, all of which Rachel soothed as soon as she had dealt with the doctors, explaining to them where they had gone and forcing them to realise that they hadn't had any choice in the matter.

He missed Rachel's panicked phone call to Diana, which was answered by Laura. The girl was being bundled into the helicopter taking the injured woman to the hospital at the time and she'd had to hang up the phone quickly, but had promised to ring when there was any news. Sam was still unconscious when Laura called back hours later to inform them that Diana was still alive, but in critical condition and was expected to be in surgery for many more hours. She gave Rachel the details of the hospital before she was once again forced to hang up.

Most importantly, though, he missed Rachel's debriefing and the universal joy that it engendered when she informed the gathered Society of the complete and utter destruction of the Illuminati as an entity and told them to be prepared for an influx of new blood.

Sam woke up to the sound of beeping, the smell of disinfectant and a dull ache, seemingly throughout his whole body.

'Andrew?'

For a moment he was once again that frightened boy, waking up in an unfamiliar hospital room after his disastrous trip to World War One, a year and more than half a century ago.

A shadow detached itself from a chair against the wall and hobbled into the soft glow from the machines around his bed. It was only when he saw that it wasn't his uncle, but rather his grandfather, that he remembered when he was.

'How are you feeling, boy?' James reached out and carefully put his hand over Sam's wire-infested one.

'I've been better... And worse.' He craned his head looking past James, trying to see in the shadows, hoping to find someone else in the room.

'She's not here lad. She asked me to take care of you while she went to see that young woman. The one I suddenly find I owe so much to.'

'Diana? She's alive then?'

'Barely. Rachel will be able to tell us more when she comes back, but preliminary reports are not good; there was some major internal injuries and they barely got her to a hospital in time.'

Sam struggled, trying to sit up and swivel out of bed, but James' gentle hand on his chest, which he would have been able to push through without a thought under normal circumstances, held him firmly in place.

'I know you want to run off to be with them, but that's not going to happen right now. You barely survived yourself and you were running a fever when you came back that almost gave the doctors an apoplexy.' James gave Sam one of his piercing looks. 'Rachel told me what you did to Quentin and I'm assuming that had something to do with your temperature.' He held Sam's gaze for a few seconds, as if searching for something, but then he smiled suddenly. 'You've got a lot of explaining to do, lad. I hope you're ready to spend a very, *very* long time with the Council of Elders, while we try to work out what you did.'

Sam just groaned in reply and James laughed. 'Anyway, your temperature went down quickly enough, but you were in danger of some serious brain damage for a while. Not that anybody would have noticed any difference...'

Sam smiled up at the kind old man. 'Thanks, Grandad. I love you too.'

James laughed again and took his hand off of Sam's chest to pat him on the shoulder, one of the only parts of Sam that was free of bandages or bruises.

'Rachel gave her report to the Society, by the way.' James' smile disappeared and was replaced with a frown as he slipped from loving grandfather into Elder mode. 'That was some adventure you had, lad. You'll have to give your own report when you can, but is there something you'd like to talk about before then?'

Sam knew exactly what he was referring to; the killing that he had done. He looked away, turning his face to the wall and closing his eyes against the tears of shame springing to life in them. 'No. Not right now, anyway. Maybe someday.'

James sighed and patted Sam again. 'All right, Sam. That's your decision, but don't ever think that I won't be here for you, no matter what you've done. That goes for the rest of the Society as well, every one of them - you won't find any judgement, just understanding and love. We all know what you've been through and how much it has cost you to do what you had to do, for us, and we desperately want to return the favour, if you'll let us. But all in your own time, alright?'

Sam turned back to his grandfather and nodded, forcing a smile, but something wasn't quite right.

There was an insistent beeping noise coming from the monitor sitting by his bed, a rapidly accelerating and increasingly annoying sound that seemed to resonate in his head, threatening to make it explode under the mounting pressure. Numbers rose on it, quickly reaching triple digits that turned red and started blinking rapidly.

He growled as the pain intensified, overwhelming the drugs that had been pumped into him, and for some reason he found himself inexplicably angry. 'Why the hell is that machine...'

He stopped speaking, suddenly unable to remember what he was going to say, or indeed how to formulate any words at all. All he could do was stare up into a set of panicking eyes that seemed familiar, but that he couldn't quite place. Suddenly, even that was taken away from him as white sparks ignited in his vision, blinding him.

'Are you alright? Sam? SAM?'

Something made contact with his face and even that gentle touch was agony. He tried to move, to brush it off, but the effort made his entire body spasm and the pain in his head as he arched off the bed sent the blinding white flashes spearing into his brain. After what seemed like an eternity he crashed back down, the pain disappearing abruptly as his connection to his body *snapped*.

Shadows closed in, shutting off the world around him and with it all sensation, but not before a single word rang out in his head.

Rachel.

He thought it was a name, although he couldn't be sure of anything anymore, but it was a lifeline and he grabbed it and held on as tightly as he could as he was dragged down into the deep dark.

When next he opened his eyes it was to find a woman bending over him. She had a strained look on her face and dark circles under her eyes, but she smiled when she saw Sam focus on her. It was a very weak smile, though, and her eyes betrayed her exhaustion and worry.

'Rachel?' It was barely more than a grunt, but the woman laughed, a short bark that seemed to be more relief than real joy, and she threw herself at him, putting hard arms around him and squeezing, sending agony shooting through his body that he welcomed because it meant he was with her. She sobbed, wailing and crying, while simultaneously smothering him with warm kisses.

When she finally pulled back he saw the pain and worry in her eyes and panic shot through him. 'What's wrong? Is Diana...?'

Rachel cut him off with a hand to his lips and to his relief she smiled. 'She's fine, she's out of the woods and recovering well.'

'How? I thought she was in critical condition and they were still operating on her.' Sam coughed as his throat burned from the effort of talking.

Rachel took a glass of water with a straw in it from a nearby nightstand and helped him drink as she answered. 'That was fifteen days ago...You've been asleep for more than two weeks, Sam.'

'Two...?' He stared at her, trying to assimilate the information, but he couldn't. 'What happened? What's wrong with me?'

'James said your powers flared stronger than anything he'd ever felt before, by several magnitudes - we *all* felt it Sam, even a couple of the members in the States!' Her eyes lit up and she shook her head in amazement as she thought back to it, but then her face fell and she turned away from him. 'The energy just dissipated, though, and you... you *died* Sam.' She turned back to look at him and there were tears blossoming in her eyes as she reached out to cup his cheek. 'For a while they didn't think they could bring you back, but then, after a few minutes you just came back on your own somehow. But...'

She hesitated and Sam wondered what could possibly be worse than dying. He soon found out.

'But now we... Oh, Sam, I'm so sorry, but none of us can feel your powers. You might have lost them...'

'No...' Sam shook his head. It couldn't be true, there was no way that he could have lost the ability to Displace; there were so many things he had to do, so many adventures he wanted to go on with Rachel.

'I'm sorry, Sam.'

They both turned as James cleared his throat. He was standing in the open doorway and had apparently been listening for a while. He came over to the bed and frowned down at Sam. He remained that way for long seconds, but then huffed and gave then a half-smile. 'Actually, Rachel, now that he's awake I *can* feel something there, but it's nowhere near as strong as it was before. We'll have to wait to see if he recovers any more of his strength, but for now he seems, well... normal. Like one of us.'

Sam sighed in relief. He couldn't care less about being special, all he cared about was that he could continue to do his life's work as a Displacer. And, of course, have some fun running around history with Rachel. He looked up at her and smiled.

Unseen by them both, James grinned and left the room, closing the door gently behind him.

Rachel stroked his cheek. 'I love you, Sam.'

He blinked away the tears that seemed to be coming easier and easier with each passing year and covered her hand with his.

'I love you too, Rachel.'

He drew her into him, easily ignoring the pain that the movement and pressure caused, and wrapped his arms around her.

They held each other for what seemed like ages, shedding tears that were part relief and part happiness, until finally Rachel found her voice. 'Now that everything's over, how about that wedding you promised me?'

EPILOGUE

One year later.

The *Sagrada Familia* in Barcelona was always packed with tourists this late in the summer, but Violeta had wanted to go to the Basilica for her birthday, so that was what they had done. It was a strange request for a small girl on her tenth birthday, but her family had gotten used to Violeta being different from other children and had taken it in their stride.

Sam and Rachel walked hand in hand, following Violeta through the underground museum as she read each of the information posters and inspected all of the models on display as closely as she could, literally pressing her nose up against the glass. They were alone with her; Sam's parents had stayed outside and sat down on a bench in the shade, resting while they could before the arrival of a dozen children for the party they had arranged for that evening.

Rachel was heavily pregnant with their son and her feet were aching, but she had decided to come down to the museum, rather than rest with Sam's parents, wanting to stay with the birthday girl. She was as oblivious to pain and strong as she'd been in Sparta and as stubborn as ever and said that a "little discomfort" wasn't going to put her off from being with Violeta during her big day.

Violeta had been delighted to find herself with not one, but two new sisters, but it was much harder to convince Sam's parents that they had two daughters in law. They hadn't quite accepted Diana's explanation that it was a "modern thing", but had nonetheless welcomed her into their family without reserve, especially after they saw the love that the three of them had for each other.

Unfortunately, Diana hadn't been able to make it; she had recovered slowly from her gunshot wound, but still insisted in going straight to work for the Displacers. She had been kept very busy for the last year by MI5, working with Laura and Dylan, who had been inseparable since the dissolution of the Illuminati, travelling the world and recovering the Illuminati's riches from their various caches. She was arriving the next day, though, and there would be a second party for her, this time in Sam's flat and without so many children; they had found out only a couple of weeks before that she was also pregnant.

Everything was turning out just the way Sam had dreamed that it would, except that he had two wonderful women to share his adventures with instead of just the one.

He did have one regret, though, and that was that his beloved grandfather would never meet his great, great, grandchildren.

James had found an obscure document in the archives, signed by Queen Victoria herself as head of the Church of England, which granted the Displacers permission to have what she termed "unconventional weddings". The only rules set down were that the weddings were to be kept secret and registered with the reigning monarch *personally*, not the church, and they weren't to be carried out by church ministers, but rather by the head of the Council of Elders, which, being James, suited Sam, Rachel and Diana just fine. Just to be on the safe side, James took the document to Buckingham Palace with him on one of his newly-instated fortnightly visits for tea and a chat with Her Majesty. As he'd expected, she was delighted at the news of a wedding and gave her permission and blessing without reservation.

To Sam's surprise, none of the Society members so much as batted an eyelid at the arrangement. Not only did they often Displace to times and places where monogamous marriages were not the norm, but apparently it was not unheard of among the Displacers, even in the recent past. One female member in the sixties had even gone so far as to enter into a marriage arrangement with both Antony and Cleopatra after completing a mission to Egypt - a relationship that had obviously not survived her return to the present, but had apparently been quite fulfilling and, in her own words from her mission report, "a lot of fun".

The wedding took place on Christmas Eve, four months after the Illuminati had been destroyed.

James had been ill for more than a month and was getting weaker each day, but during the ceremony he had been strong and smiling, his voice reverberating around the small church that had seen so much Displacer history. He hadn't been able to dance at the reception afterwards, but he had tapped his cane in time with the music and had stood to greet the Queen when she had dropped by to congratulate the newlyweds and give them their wedding gift - an extremely expensive tea set. The following day he had been with them all for Christmas dinner at the newly rebuilt Headquarters. He'd been his old self - laughing and joking with everyone, telling stories and answering the questions put to him by the new members, as bright and alert as ever, but then, when the group retired to the sitting room for drinks, he had dozed off in front of the fire, surrounded by friends, with a glass of fifty year-old Glenfiddich at his elbow, and never woken up.

Despite the deep loss he felt for his grandfather, Sam was happier than he'd ever been in his life especially because being just a normal Displacer had taken a lot of the pressure off of him.

That didn't mean he hadn't been busy. The time-line was still "seriously messed up" as Dylan liked to say; the damage that the Illuminati had done was largely irreparable and causing a cascade effect that was making problems pop up like mushrooms. Unfortunately the only person who could solve that once and for all was the person everybody had hoped Sam was - the Changer. In the meantime, while they were waiting for that person to appear, the entire Society was scrambling to try to keep up and it looked like it was going to be a very long time before Sam would be able to start ticking adventures off his old list, although he wasn't really sure if he wanted to go on any of them anymore; he no longer wanted his damsels to be in distress - he much preferred them strong and capable.

There was still the matter of who the Changer actually was, of course, and the possibility of it being their son had come up in conversation only once - the night they had arrived in Barcelona for Violeta's birthday and the memories of Sam's early Displacements had come flooding back on entering Andrew's flat.

Sam really didn't want the kind of pressure and expectations that had been heaped on him to be placed on their child and Rachel agreed. She took his resolution to protect their child one step further, though, and promised that she would beat up anyone who tried to treat him the way they had Sam, adding that that included Sam himself.

When Sam had laughed, thinking she was joking, she had just stared at him.

He had very quickly wiped the smile from his face and found something else to talk about.

Rachel's strength, determination and stubbornness didn't mean that she was immune to having an overloaded bladder, though, and when she waddled off to the bathroom for the third time, Sam joined Violeta as she looked up at a photo of an old and white-bearded Antoni Gaudí in profile, standing in front of the bare bones of the Basilica.

'So, why isn't the church finished yet, Sammy?'

'Well, Gaudí was killed in a tram accident while he was still working on it and he didn't leave things very well organised for the people following him to carry on with his work.'

Violeta frowned and shook her head. 'That's not right. It shouldn't be like that.'

Her eyes closed and, before he knew what she was doing, she just *went*.

There was no warning, no period of Calming, no steady build-up of energy, just a single pulse of power that was so immensely strong that it threatened to make him stagger back, but at the same time was so in tune with the flow of the time-line around them that he doubted he would even have felt it if he hadn't been standing right next to her.

He stared at her in shock as she reopened her eyes and smiled up at him.

A smile that mirrored that of the girl now holding Gaudí's hand in the photo.

'That's better.'

ABOUT THE AUTHOR

Simon Brading tried his hand at many things before it occurred to him that he might have a few stories to tell. As well as the odd novel he writes screenplays and also does some acting every so often.

www.simonbrading.co.uk

For news of special offers, upcoming releases, exclusive content, competitions and events, please follow me on social media.

Instagram - @sibrading
Facebook - Simon Brading Author
Tiktok - @SimonBradingAuthor

ALSO BY SIMON BRADING

The "Displacers" series - a young adult time travel adventure series for all ages.
The Time Traveller's Nephew
The Secret of the Ancients
The Whitechapel Plot
The Price of Greed
The Time for Vengeance

The "Misfit Squadron" Series - a Steampunk series set in an alternate World War 2.
The Battle Over Britain
The Russian Resistance
A Misfit Midwinter
The Lion and the Baron
The Maltese Defence
Tales from the Second Great War
The Siege of Gibraltar
The King's Mission
The Home Front
Taking to the Skies
The Invasion of Britain

The "Twin Ambitions" series - ballet books for children ages 7 and up.
Fight to Dance
Back to Basics

The "Ni Hon - The Two Books" Series - a young adult series set in a dystopian future Japan.
The Black Book

Others
Public Enemy
Empath
The Lifeboat at the End of the Universe